FORTUNE'S FAVOURITE CHILD

When Dora Lawrence met Tim Atherton at the dawn of the new Edwardian era, she found him agreeably entertaining but she did not take him seriously. So his proposal of marriage took her by surprise—as did his hurt reaction to her refusal.

Dora thought she didn't want to marry anybody yet. Then that summer she accompanied her father Stephen on a visit to the family estate in Herefordshire. Here she would meet her cousins for the first time, sample an utterly different way of life to her own. At first repelled by fox-hunting, Dora became grimly determined to embrace rural pursuits when Ralph Challoner entered her life. Ralph, tall and commanding, overwhelmed her senses. Dora's visit lengthened into months as she fell under his spell. Even Ralph's inexplicable flashes of cruelty would not deter her from her belief that she had found love.

In later years, as war threatened, Dora would feel trapped, forever beyond the reach of happiness. But fortune had yet to smile on her . . .

Also by Margaret James

A TOUCH OF EARTH

FORTUNE'S FAVOURITE CHILD

Margaret James

Macdonald

A Macdonald Book

Copyright © Margaret James 1989

First published in Great Britain in 1989
by Futura Publications, a Division of
Macdonald & Co (Publishers) Ltd
London & Sydney

This edition published by Macdonald & Co (Publishers) Ltd
1989

Reprinted 1990

All characters in this book are fictitious and any resemblance
to real persons, living or dead, is purely coincidental.

All rights reserved

No part of this publication may be reproduced, stored in a retrieval system, or transmitted, in any form or by any means without the prior permission in writing of the publisher, nor be otherwise circulated in any form of binding or cover other than that in which it is published and without a similar condition including this condition being imposed on the subsequent purchaser.

British Library Cataloguing in Publication Data

James, Margaret
 Fortune's favourite child
 I. Title
 823'.914 [F]

ISBN 0-356-17635-5

Printed and Bound in Great Britain by
Redwood Press Limited, Melksham, Wiltshire

Macdonald & Co (Publishers) Ltd,
Orbit House
1 New Fetter Lane
London EC4A 1AR

A member of Maxwell Macmillan Pergamon Publishing
Corporation

Chapter One

'YOU'RE LOOKING A BIT GREEN, DORA. Is it the heat?'

'The heat?' Dora Lawrence glanced at the young man by her side. 'Yes,' she replied. 'Yes, I suppose it must be. It *is* very warm in here, isn't it?' Wondering why the lights in the chandelier above her head were behaving so strangely, swooping and darting and trying to hit her in the face, Dora shielded her eyes from the glare. 'I do feel odd, you know,' she added. 'Oh, Tim — I think I'm going to be sick!'

'You won't be.' Tim Atherton grinned at her. 'It's just a question of getting used to it, that's all.'

'Well, I'm *not* used to it yet.' Dora, by now quite certain that she was going to be very ill indeed, watched Tim knock back yet another glassful of champagne. 'Even if you are.'

'Me?' Tim laughed, then hiccupped. He held his glass up to the light. 'Dora, I'm not used to *this* sort of thing! Cheap college sherry — that's more in my line.' Draining its contents and holding out his glass to be refilled, he patted Dora's shoulder. 'You'll be fine,' he assured her. 'Don't worry.'

Nineteen years old only a few weeks ago, Dora Lawrence had never drunk champagne before, and she was finding the experience both exhilarating and disagreeable. She leaned against the wall of her sister's elegant drawing room with her third — or it might have been her fourth — glass unsteady in her hand. And she now observed that all the other guests at Anna's party were tilting sideways, apparently as unable to stand up straight as she was . . .

Now Tim Atherton bent his head towards her and

murmured something in her ear, causing her to shake with giggles. So he took her glass, which was messily slopping its contents all over her blue silk skirt, and put it down upon a small table nearby. 'I think that you've had enough of this stuff for the time being,' he said. 'What about a little fresh air?'

Without waiting for a reply, he grasped Dora's hand in his and led her towards an open french door. As she allowed herself to be taken outside, Dora happened to catch sight of her elder sister's face, which was set in a disapproving frown. 'Oh, bother Anna,' she thought crossly. 'She didn't *have* to ask me to her boring party. I *am* trying to enjoy myself. I *am* talking politely to the other guests. Well — guest. Tim's the only one of my own age here, after all.'

Tim and Dora walked on to the verandah, which overlooked a pleasant town garden. The lights of Edwardian London could be seen twinkling all around, for from Highgate Hill the whole city, its daytime ugliness concealed by the benign summer dusk, was laid out before them in a pattern of diamonds. Sitting down next to each other on a basketwork sofa, they both sighed with relief to be out of sight of the grown-ups.

'Very heavy going in there,' remarked Tim, stretching his long legs out in front of him and clasping his hands behind his head. 'For us non-intellectuals, that is. Whatever was Anna talking about to that bearded chap? Greek particles or something. Lord! I say, Dora — don't you find it a bit oppressive to come from such a family as yours?'

'Oppressive, Tim? What do you mean by that?'

'Well, don't you find the constant serious chat a bit overwhelming? I mean, you seem to be the only average sort of person out of the whole bunch. You're the only one who doesn't seem to be a raving genius, at any rate.'

'You think I'm as stupid as you are?'

'No, I didn't mean that at all. *I'm* not stupid! Though, if you insist that you are, I shan't argue with you. . .'

'I *don't* insist that I'm stupid! Oh, Tim, you do twist things.' Dora saw then that he was grinning at her, so she tried hard to frown at him. She failed. Realizing that she must indeed be rather tight, she tried to focus her eyes upon his. 'And anyway,' she announced portentously, 'we Lawrences are not what we seem.'

'Aren't you, eh?' Tim laughed at her. 'Whatever do you mean by that? Oh, Dora — you're drunk!'

'I'm not. Shall I prove it? Ask me to decline *dominus*, or any noun you like.'

'I don't want you to decline anything.' Tim leaned towards her. 'What did you mean about you Lawrences not being what you seem?' he enquired.

'Ah, wouldn't you like to know?'

'Yes, I would. Come on, Dora — tell.'

Dora giggled and leaned against Tim's shoulder. 'I'll tell you something amazing about my father, shall I?' she murmured.

'Something fascinating?'

'What, then?'

'Listen.' She cupped her hands and whispered into his ear.

'*What* did you say?' Tim stared at her in astonishment. 'Dora, what awful fibs! You *must* be drunk.'

'It's true.'

'Nonsense!' Tim shook his head. 'It's a pack of lies.'

'It *is* true. Go and ask Anna if you don't believe me.'

'You're joking. She'd have me thrown out of the house and rolled down Highgate Hill in a barrel.' Tim, who had himself drunk rather more than he was used to that evening, stared at his companion. 'I say, Dora,' he demanded, '*is* it true? Is your father *really* a wicked country squire? Did he honestly seduce an innocent country girl, then carry her off and lock her up in his house in Oxford?'

'Yes, that's right.' Dora nodded. 'That's it exactly.'

Tim laughed. 'Sounds like something out of a novelette.'

'Does it?'

'Goodness, yes.' Tim rolled his eyes. 'So this poor deflowered innocent became your mother, did she? And Anthony's, and Anna's? Professor Lawrence's wife is really his mistress. Is that what you're saying? Oh, Dora — you're having me on. Well, aren't you?'

'No, I'm not having you on.' Dora bent towards her companion and muttered something which caused him to laugh out loud.

3

'Now that's preposterous!' he cried. 'I can't believe *that*.'

'Please yourself, Tim Atherton. It's true.'

'Rubbish.' Tim grinned at her. 'Oh, Dora, what d'you take me for, eh?'

Dora was now so close to Tim that he could smell the scent of her hair and the warm natural fragrance of her skin. More than that, a loose strand of hair had detached itself from her over-elaborate coiffure and was tickling the side of his face. He caught the lock in his fingers and pulled it taut; then he let go, allowing the natural curl to spring back into shape. He tried to tuck it into the chignon at the back of her head and he found, very naturally, that his face was now near to hers. So he kissed her.

'Tim!' Dora blushed crimson. 'You mustn't do that.'

'Why ever not?'

'It's not decent.'

'*I* think it's extraordinarily decent. Jolly nice as well. Don't you like it?'

'Like it?' Dora considered, then decided that, on the whole, she did. Yes, it was quite pleasant. 'You mustn't do it,' she admonished, severely. 'Someone might come out here.'

'And if they were to find you in the passionate embrace of an ardent young man they'd drop dead of horror on the spot. Oh, very well — I'll behave myself.' Tim moved away from Dora and lay across the sofa, swinging his legs over the arm. 'Tell me a few more of those fibs about your evil old papa,' he said.

Dora felt a fresh burst of giggles bubbling up inside her, along with the champagne, and she tried to clamp her lips together in order that neither the giggles nor the gas should escape. She failed, and she attempted, without much success, to turn the results into a coughing fit. 'You really do think I was lying, don't you?' she demanded, red in the face. 'Well, except for the wicked bit, and the part about locking my mother up, it's all perfectly true.' She hiccupped, loudly. 'My father isn't the least bit wicked, you know,' she added.

'Oh, but he *must* be!' Tim grinned at her again. Now he began to twirl an imaginary moustache; he contorted his pleasant, good-humoured features into a malevolent leer.

Adopting a melodramatic posture and frowning majestically at her, he grabbed Dora by the wrist. 'Come here, my pretty peasant,' he growled. 'I must have my evil way with you!'

'Your *what?*' giggled Dora.

'My evil way, of course.' Tim laughed. 'Is that how it was, d'you suppose? And what about the village beauty, eh?'

'What about her?' Dora looked at the tall, blond young man sitting next to her who bore no resemblance whatsoever to her small, dark-haired mother. 'That's not a part *you* could play!'

'Isn't it?' Tim sniffed. 'Miss Lawrence, I'll have you know that in my time *I* have trodden the boards as Ophelia. *And* as Desdemona. So there. Now let me see.'

Tim pushed his jacket back from his shoulders and stared wide-eyed at Dora. 'No, no, Sir Roger!' he lisped. 'No, indeed, I cannot go with you! Upon my honour, I shall *never* submit to your base desires!'

He flopped backwards on to the sofa and covered his face with his hands. 'Oh, Sir Roger, you overpower me!' he squeaked. 'Let me go! Pray, Sir, unhand me this instant — I haven't milked my cows. Sir Roger, I shall scream! Oh! Ah! Oh!' Overcome by his own wit, Tim giggled. 'You see, Dora?'

'Brilliant.' Dora shook her head at him. 'You ought to consider a career on the stage.'

'Haven't finished yet. Do you know,' he murmured, in a mincing falsetto, 'it's really rather nice, after all . . .'

He was enjoying himself so much that Dora couldn't help laughing at him. His imitation of her father was — at least as far as accent and intonation went — quite convincing. Obviously Tim had, while up at Oxford, studied his tutor rather more intently than he had his books. He mimicked Dora's mother rather well, too.

But to hear him making fun of her parents wasn't really very amusing — and Dora now wished that she hadn't told him anything. She bent towards him and touched his arm. 'You won't tell anyone what I said, will you?' she asked.

He looked fiercely at her, trying to make his own finely arched eyebrows knit as angrily as Stephen Lawrence's heavy ones did. 'Perish the thought, damn it all!' He was still wicked Sir Roger.

'Because I made it all up!' she went on, desperately.

Tim looked at Dora's hand, which was lying upon his sleeve and covered it with his own. 'I know that,' he replied, laughing. 'Dora, you do have the most remarkable imagination, you know. The very idea of *your* gloomy old father getting up to that sort of lark; well, it stretches credulity, and that's putting it mildly.' He raised her hand to his lips and kissed it. 'What about a dance, Dora?' he asked. 'Are you capable?'

'I think so. We'd better go in, anyway. Anna will be angry with us if we don't mingle with the crowd . . .'

Tim pulled a face. 'Heaven protect me from the wrath of Mrs Harley,' he muttered, widening his eyes at Dora. He helped her to her feet, pulled her into his embrace and held her close to him. In her fuddled state Dora was glad of his chest to lean against, and grateful for the support of his arms around her as they danced. She stumbled around the drawing room now feeling distinctly ill, and afraid that she was going to be violently sick, after all.

* * *

She had not, of course, made it all up. As Dora unpinned her hair and took off her jewellery, she stared hard at herself in her dressing table mirror, observing that her large brown eyes were most unattractively bloodshot, and wondered what on earth had possessed her to tell Tim Atherton all about her parents' unhallowed union.

To betray her whole family to a comparative stranger, to expose her father to the possible ridicule of one of his ex-students, was unforgivable. Alone in her bedroom, away from the noise, heat and excitement of the party, Dora understood that only too well. She replaced her bracelets in their boxes, and grimaced at her reflection.

It wasn't as if she even knew Tim very well. He'd presumably been invited to Anna's party — given to celebrate the fact that Anna's husband, John, was now permanently settled in England as a director of a large firm of wine-shippers, and to show off Anna's brand new town house — to keep Dora company.

Everyone else there that evening had been at least ten years older than Tim and Dora. But John Harley had been at college with Tim's elder brother, and Tim had graduated that summer, so presumably it had been decided that he was a suitable person to keep Dora amused . . .

'He didn't believe me,' she told her reflection. 'No one knows about our family, and if he said anything to his friends, they'd just laugh at him.'

All the same, Dora would have given a great deal to have had that evening's conversation deleted from the recording angel's ledgers. She could imagine the terrific family row which would explode over her guilty head if the details of her father's past became common knowledge among his undergraduates. She trembled at the idea of being known to be the source of such information.

Even though she was grown up, and even though he'd never struck her in her life, Dora still had a very healthy respect for her father and his temper. And, apart from that, she loved both her parents dearly — she wouldn't willingly have upset either of them. 'Oh God,' she muttered. She pulled her nightgown over her head, buttoning it right up to her throat, as if to protect her body from some indefinable threat.

'He *didn't* believe me,' she told herself, for the hundredth time, as she climbed into bed. 'No one would ever take Mama for a kept woman. And Papa's nobody's idea of a philanderer. Well, he's *not* a philanderer!' And, repeating all this over and over to herself as a kind of litany, Dora attempted to go to sleep.

* * *

The sun was trying to hit her between her aching eyes as it flickered through the gap in the white summer curtains. Dora, finding that she felt sick lying down, endeavoured to sit up, but then discovered that, during the course of the night, her head had been mysteriously altered in size and shape and was now too heavy to lift. In addition to this, her eyes had obviously been removed, boiled in vinegar and re-inserted in their sockets, together with a teaspoonful of grit.

She turned over and burrowed down into the bedclothes, having decided that she definitely couldn't face Anna over the breakfast table. Her brother-in-law, John, who could usually be relied upon to take her part, would have gone to the City by now. And Anna was always so severe and waspish when her husband wasn't there.

'Go away!' Dora pulled the bedclothes over her head, determined to ignore whoever was now tapping upon her bedroom door.

But Dora's visitor was not to be denied. Creaking excruciatingly, the door opened. 'Well, Dora?' Her elder sister's crisp, businesslike voice cut into Dora's brain like a buzz-saw. 'How do you feel?'

'Absolutely terrible. Don't draw back the curtains, Anna — please!'

Anna smiled grimly and flung them back. A hot, white dart struck Dora across her face. She turned away from the light, and moaned.

'Come along, Dora, sit up.' Anna perched on her sister's bed and shook her shoulder. 'You'll be much better after some coffee and toast.'

'I couldn't eat anything.'

'Yes, you could.' Anna beckoned towards the open door and a maid came in with a laden breakfast tray, which she placed upon the bedside table. 'Miss Dora not well, Madam?' she enquired.

'Miss Dora is perfectly well thank you, Addison,' replied Anna, firmly. 'Close the door after you, please. You may as well open your eyes,' she added, sharply.

Dora knew better than to argue with her sister. She sighed and rolled over on to her back. Letting her eyelids open slightly, she peered narrowly at Anna and saw that her sister was as immaculately dressed and neatly coiffured as usual. Wincing, Dora allowed her tormentor to plump up her pillows and to help her into a sitting position.

'Well?' asked Anna. 'May one know when the wedding is to be?'

'Wedding?' Dora gaped at her. 'What wedding?'

'Yours, of course. I assume that you and Tim Atherton are engaged?'

Dora dropped her piece of toast, butter side down, on the sheet. 'God forbid,' she muttered.

'I hope He will.' Anna leaned towards her sister and tapped

her wrist. 'You were not behaving very well last night, Dora,' she added, severely. 'It's just not done, you know, to hug and kiss as you and Tim were doing unless, of course, one is engaged to be married. I'm quite sure that you must have given Tim the idea that you'd welcome a proposal . . .'

'Oh, good Lord — I hope not!' Dora gulped down some black coffee and grimaced, both at the bitter taste of the drink and at the idea of marrying Tim.

Anna pursued what she considered to be her advantage. 'You're far too young to think of getting involved with men, you know,' she continued. 'And even if you were old enough to be contemplating marriage, Tim's not suitable at all.'

'Isn't he? Why?'

'Oh, Dora — you know why.' Exasperated, Anna sighed. 'He chases anything in a dress. He's already acquired a reputation as a rake. *And* he's stupid. He barely scraped through his finals last month; he must have been one of the most thick-headed students my poor father ever had the misfortune to teach.'

Dora bit her lower lip. 'Have you anything else to say in his favour?' she enquired.

'Don't be so flippant, Dora.' Anna folded her arms and looked hard at her younger sister. 'He couldn't afford a wife,' she continued. 'His brother will inherit all Sir Michael's money. That whole estate is entailed upon the eldest son, so don't encourage Tim to think he would make you an ideal husband.'

'He's very good company, though.' Dora bit into another slice of toast and, feeling a little stronger now that she had some food inside her, she met Anna's critical stare with a defiant one of her own. 'And he's handsome. Even you must admit that he's very nice-looking.'

'Oh, for goodness sake, Dora — what's that got to do with anything?' Anna helped herself to a cup of coffee. 'You could do very much better for yourself, you know, than to marry Tim,' she said. 'Oh, can't you see? He isn't the sort of man who will *do* anything with his life.'

'Does he have to *do* anything?'

'Well, a man ought to have some ambition, some career in mind. Oh, yes, I admit that he's agreeable. And, yes, he's presentable enough, if you like those bland, mousy looks. But he's feckless, he's spoiled, and he's lazy. Goodness only knows what he'll do now that he's come down from Oxford. Loaf around other people's houses, I expect. He'll become a professional cadger, an upper-class layabout, the eternal spare man. You know the type.'

'There's no need to make him out to be such a total wastrel.' Dora scowled at Anna. 'Anyway, you can stop fretting. I'm not going to marry Tim Atherton. The thought hadn't even crossed my mind.'

Anna sniffed. 'Well, let's hope it hasn't crossed his. What *were* you two laughing and whispering about together last night then, if it wasn't your future together?'

Dora felt her face redden and was aware that such a degree of blushing would hardly allay Anna's suspicions. 'We were just chatting,' she muttered.

'About what?'

'Really, Anna, you've no right to cross-examine me like this. We were having a private conversation.' Dora scowled at her sister. 'Good heavens,' she continued, angrily, '*you* don't like it if anyone so much as asks you the time.'

'Oh, very well — have your little secrets.' Anna shrugged. 'But just remember, Dora, that you're only nineteen. You're still a child. And,' she continued impressively, 'you should also consider your position in life before you ever think of marriage. If our parents were an ordinary married couple, if we —'

'I know, Anna, I *know*.' Dora, driven to the limits of her self control, dared to interrupt her sister. 'Don't go on so. I'm not going to marry anyone. Oh, why can't you just go away? I'd really prefer to die in peace.'

A sudden eruption of howls, shrieks and yells, apparently coming from the garden, made Anna dart over to the window. From it, she could see her eldest son Marcus, a large, fine-looking boy of nine, pushing his younger brother far too high on a swing. She tapped on the window and mimed her displeasure.

Dora replaced her coffee cup on the tray and lay down on her stomach. 'I'm going back to sleep,' she mumbled. 'Do tell Marcus and Robert to shut up. Why do they have to make so much noise?' She closed her eyes, hoping that when she woke up again the feeling of having had a small dead animal in her mouth overnight would have disappeared and that she would feel more able to face Anna. After all, she was staying with her for the rest of the week before going home to Oxford.

She had to see Tim Atherton again, soon. Perhaps last night he'd been as inebriated as she had. And she dared to hope that he would have forgotten everything she'd told him.

Chapter Two

SINCE LEAVING SCHOOL AT THE age of sixteen, and having declined the offer of a place at one of the women's colleges — for she had had enough of studying, she felt, to last any reasonable person a lifetime — Dora had found herself with nothing much to do.

Girls like her were, as far as their parents were concerned, something of a nuisance. Out of the schoolroom and not yet into the bridal bed, of a social class which did not expect its young women to work for their living, and having no ambitions anyway, Dora had spent the succeeding three years in hectic idleness. Usually she was in the company of Annie Vesey, the Dean's daughter, or in that of Miriam Gordon, the only child of another university lecturer, and Dora's best friend.

There had seemed no reason why this happy state of affairs, this constant round of shopping, walking, paying calls, performing the odd, undemanding act of genteel charity, should not continue indefinitely . . .

But then Miriam had taken it upon herself to spoil everything. Dora's elder brother Anthony, newly graduated from Cambridge and about to take up a research lectureship at King's College there, had one evening casually remarked that he was going to marry Miriam.

Dora had looked up from her copy of a fashion magazine and given him a sarcastic sisterly smile. 'Does Miriam know that?' she'd enquired sweetly.

'Not yet.' Anthony grinned back at her. 'But I'm going to suggest it to her tomorrow. It won't come as a total surprise to her, I'm certain of that.'

He looked at his father, who was studying a column of figures in the financial pages of *The Times*. 'I have your blessing, I hope, Papa?' he asked. 'And yours, Mama?' he added, as something of an afterthought.

His mother, who was sitting beside him on the sofa, merely smiled at her son. 'Of course you have, dear,' she replied, continuing placidly with her sewing. 'Stephen? Did you hear what Anthony said?'

'Mmm?' Anthony's father finished the page he was reading, then shook out his newspaper. He stretched his legs out before him, stifled a yawn, then looked critically at his son.

'I doubt if the withholding of *my* blessing would make any difference to your plans,' he remarked, heavily. He consulted his watch, rose to his feet and walked over to where Anthony sat, touching him lightly upon the shoulder. 'I don't know about Gordon's blessing, though,' he added. And, hands in his pockets, he walked out of the room. They heard the street door slam behind him.

'He mentioned something about a wine committee meeting at seven,' remarked Dorcas. 'He'll be back for dinner.' Rummaging in her workbasket for a skein of thread, Anthony's mother sighed. 'So you're going to be next, are you dear?' she asked. 'Ah, well. I suppose it's time.'

* * *

Anthony had expected the result of his announcement to be absolute consternation; he had anticipated a volley of exclamations and a barrage of questions. He now saw that he was going to be disappointed of all that. He might just as well, he thought sourly, have been telling his family that he intended to have his hair cut, to order a new suit, to go up to London for the day . . .

He edged closer to his mother and took the embroidery out of her hands. 'You're fond of Miriam, aren't you, Mama?' he asked, anxiously.

'Very fond. You know that, dear.'

'Fond enough to welcome her as your daughter-in-law? You won't mind that she's not English? Or Christian? It doesn't bother you that her family is Jewish?'

Dorcas, whose affection for her only son was such that she would have given her blessing to a proposed union with a Red Indian, an Ethiopian or a Geisha girl — provided, of course, that the woman in question seemed likely to make Anthony happy — stroked his heavy black hair back from his forehead and smiled at him again. 'If you wish to marry her, and she likes you enough to want to become your wife, then I'm very happy for you both,' she said.

'I did wonder about you two,' she added, almost to herself. 'Last term, you *were* home rather more often than you needed to be — and you *did* seem to be spending a great deal of time with the Gordons.' She laughed. 'You told us you were playing chess with Dr Gordon. Anthony — you *are* a sly thing!'

'Well, *I* think it's all quite preposterous.' Dora, annoyed and aggrieved to find that she was evidently the only member of the family to whom Anthony's bombshell had come as a complete surprise, was beside herself. 'I've never heard of anything so ludicrous!' she cried. 'If a girl like Miriam wants to spend the rest of her life with *him*, she ought to see a doctor! She must have gone mad — she should be locked away.'

'Really?' Anthony grinned. 'That's your diagnosis, is it?'

'Yes, it is.' Dora glared at her brother. 'Of course, Miriam won't want to marry you,' she said, scathingly. 'Why should a beautiful woman like Miriam want to tie herself to an ugly little goblin like you? Mark my words — if you ask her any such thing, she'll just laugh in your face.'

* * *

But Dora was to be proved wrong. Anthony might not have made any formal declaration to her, but he and Miriam had seen enough of each other over the previous two or three years to have arrived at an understanding.

On the morning following his announcement to his family, Anthony had eaten his breakfast quite placidly, had chatted to his mother, had discussed the political situation with his father and had completely ignored his little sister's scowls. At eleven o'clock he took himself off to the Gordons' flat, which was on the top floor of a large Victorian house in Norham Gardens.

As he walked up the stairs, he wondered if he ought to have brought Miriam some flowers. Should he, perhaps, have a ring in his pocket, all ready to push on to her finger when — if — she agreed to become his wife? He shrugged. It was too late for any of that foolery now. He knocked upon the appropriate door.

'Hello, Anthony.' Miriam opened the door and stood on the threshold, smiling at him. 'I saw you coming up the road,' she added.

'Did you?' Anthony returned her smile, taking in her dark, willowy beauty. He observed that today she was looking very pretty in a pink cotton print which, the bodice being tight, became her very well. 'May I come in for ten minutes?' he asked.

'Yes, do. You didn't want to see Papa, did you?'

'Er — no, not particularly. Is he in college?'

'Yes.' Miriam led the way into the sitting room. 'And Mama's in the kitchen,' she continued. 'She and Hannah are doing something quite revolting with a dead chicken.'

'Both out of the way. Good.' Anthony sat down on the sitting room sofa and held out his hand to Miriam who, after a moment's hesitation, took it, and flopped down beside him. 'Well?' he enquired. 'And how are you?'

'I'm very well.' Miriam blushed. She glanced at her white hand, its fingers imprisoned inside Anthony's fist. 'Shall I fetch us some coffee?' she asked.

'No. I had some before I came out.' Anthony looked at the girl beside him. 'Miriam?' he asked. 'Will you give me a kiss? No one will know if you do,' he added, persuasively. 'If your mother's up to her elbows in chicken feathers, she won't come in.'

Miriam considered this. Her mother was certainly busy, but that didn't mean she wouldn't suddenly come dashing into the sitting room on some pretext or other. She was about to refuse Anthony's request.

But then, allowing inclination to override propriety, Miriam changed her mind. She leaned across the sofa and kissed Dora's brother full on the mouth, allowing him to take her in his arms, to stroke her hair, even allowing him to pull her so far forwards that the swell of her bosom was resting against his arm.

'Ah, that's lovely!' Now, Anthony had found the small

hollow beneath Miriam's jawline, he had rediscovered his favourite part of her; the place where the delicious perfume of her hair mingled with the scent of her skin. He kissed her ear. 'Oh, Miriam,' he murmured, contentedly. 'You *are* beautiful. So exactly right!'

'Am I?' Suddenly embarrassed, Miriam took his arms from around her waist. 'Oh, you must let me get up,' she said. She smoothed her dress. 'I'd better go and make us some coffee now.'

But still Anthony held her. 'Miriam?'

'Yes?'

'Before you go — I want to ask you something.'

'What's that?'

'Can't you guess?'

'No.' She looked at him candidly. 'So ask away.'

'Will you marry me?'

'*Marry* you?'

'Yes.' Anthony looked at her earnestly. 'Miriam, I don't think you're really surprised, are you? You must have been expecting this?'

Miriam was too honest to flirt or to dissemble. But she was, nevertheless, somewhat startled by the directness of Anthony's proposal. 'Well,' she began. 'We've been friends for some time —'

'More than friends, Miriam. Much more than friends.' Anthony took her hands in his and looked into her eyes, willing her to accept him. 'Do you remember the first time I kissed you?' he asked. 'It was one day last April — here in this very room.'

'Yes, I remember. But, Anthony — friends may kiss, you know, and mean nothing more than friendship.'

'I don't kiss my friends in the way I kiss you!' Now Anthony held her hands so tightly that her fingers were crushed together. 'Miriam,' he continued, urgently, 'I shall be going back to Cambridge in October. Papa's bought me a house there. I want a wife — and I want my wife to be a tall, dark-haired, beautiful girl. Miriam, I want her to be you.'

'Do you now?' Miriam shrugged. 'The world's full of tall, dark women, you know.'

'But I want *you*!' He took her by the shoulders and shook her. 'I love you. And that, of course, is the deciding factor in all this. I love you. I love you!'

'Do you? Well, Anthony, I —'

She got no further. Anthony pulled her into his embrace and began to kiss her, repeatedly; he covered her face with kisses. 'Miriam,' he pleaded, 'say you'll be my wife.'

'I'll have to think about it. I'll —'

'What is there to think about? Oh, I'd forgotten —' Suddenly, Anthony felt a cold tremor of anxiety dart along the length of his spine. 'Miriam, does it matter to you that I'm not Jewish?' he demanded, almost feverishly. 'Or that — well, you know about my parents, don't you?'

'None of that makes any difference to me. But, all the same —'

'Do you love me?' Anthony's fingers gripped Miriam's shoulders very hard now, making her wince. His fierce dark eyes bored into her face. 'Miriam, *do* you?'

'I —'

'Miriam, *do you*?'

Helplessly, Miriam stared back at him. 'I think you know I do,' she replied.

'Then you'll marry me.' Sighing with relief, Anthony let her go. He rose to his feet and beamed at her. 'Shall we go and tell your mother?'

'No! No, not yet.' Miriam caught his hand in hers and pulled him down beside her again. 'Talk to your father first,' she said. She shook her head at him, smiled the sad, patient smile which had first so endeared her to him. 'After all, your parents may object to your marrying a Jewish girl.'

'They won't.' Euphoric with delight now, Anthony kissed her again. 'They won't mind in the least. Why should they?'

* * *

'Miriam's accepted me, Papa.' An hour after he'd proposed to her, Anthony was facing his father across the litter of books and papers which lay upon Stephen's desk. 'So I'd like to get married as soon as possible — certainly before the beginning of next term. Can we arrange it?'

'Have you spoken to her father?'

'To Dr Gordon? Oh, not yet.' Anthony sat down. 'We — Miriam and I, that is — we thought it might be better to discuss it with you first.'

'I see.' Stephen rose to his feet and walked across to the window. 'What do you intend to do about the — ah — religious side of things?' he asked. 'Do you mean to convert, for instance?'

'Convert?' Anthony shook his head vehemently. 'No, of course not. Why should I do that?'

'Why, indeed.' Stephen, anxious not to upset his son, shrugged. 'But in that case you may find that although Miriam's happy to take you, you'll be unacceptable to Gordon and his wife. Had you considered that?'

'Yes.' Anthony looked steadily at Stephen. 'But I may take it that I have *your* consent, at any rate?'

'You may.' Stephen's habitually solemn features broke into a rueful grin. 'Yes, indeed you may. She's a most delightful girl,' he added, complacently. 'Much too good for you!'

Anthony nodded. 'I know that.'

'Do you?' Stephen actually smiled. 'Well, I wish you the best of luck with Gordon,' he said. 'Don't harangue the poor man, and do try to remember that, if he agrees to all this, it's his daughter who will be honouring you — not the other way around!'

* * *

Anthony wasted no time in asking, or rather demanding, the consent of Miriam's father. For, as far as Anthony was concerned, the fact that Miriam was Jewish was irrelevant. Entirely godless himself, he was prepared to argue away any objections which Miriam's parents might raise to their only child marrying an atheist . . .

As it turned out, however, there was to be nothing more than a token opposition on the part of Miriam's mother and father. If Sonia Gordon had daydreamed that one day her handsome, dark-haired daughter would perhaps stand under the wedding canopy with a Rothschild, she kept this fantasy to herself.

'Well, whoever you marry, your children will be Jewish,' she told her daughter, firmly. 'My grandchildren will receive instruction in our religion. Miriam, you will make sure of that, won't you? You'll never allow them to baptize your sons and daughters?'

Miriam nodded, smiling tolerantly at her mother. 'There'll be no baptisms,' she replied. 'Papa likes Anthony,' she added. 'Don't you, Papa?'

She laid her hand upon her father's arm and turned her bewitching smile upon him. 'There'll be more games of chess now, won't there?' she enquired, cunningly. 'And some pleasant arguments over the interpretation of this and that? You can dismember Homer together.'

Isaac Gordon shrugged. 'All the same —' he began.

Miriam looked into his eyes, her own dark ones full of eloquent pleading. 'Papa, I love Anthony!' she cried. 'He may not be the son-in-law you'd have expected, but he's a good man; you know that. And he and his family have been our friends; they were kind to us when there was no need for them to help us at all.'

'That's true.' Isaac shrugged. 'So you're marrying this man out of gratitude?'

'No! I'm marrying him because I love him. And because I can't imagine being happy ever again — that is, unless I become his wife.' Miriam looked beseechingly at her father. 'You just asked me if I was marrying Anthony out of gratitude. Does that mean you've given your consent?'

'He loves you?'

'I'm sure of it.'

'And you love him?'

'Yes!' Miriam shook his arm. 'Yes, yes, yes!'

Isaac Gordon nodded his head. 'Then there's nothing more to be said, is there?' he asked, calmly. 'Sonia, have I time to take a walk before dinner?'

* * *

Dora, hurt and angry that Miriam had not seen fit to confide her partiality for Anthony, was irritable and snappish with them both. She felt that Miriam had deceived her, and it never crossed her mind that her friend, while feeling some affection for Dora's brother, might have been too diffident to hope that such affection might be returned by clever, sharp-tongued, aggressive Anthony Lawrence. Dora sulked for days — and found that she was left to herself and her ill-humour while preparations for the wedding went ahead.

'Won't you congratulate me just once, Dolly?' asked Anthony, on finding his sister alone in the drawing room one morning.

'Congratulate you?' Dora threw the magazine she'd been reading on to the floor. 'For what? For turning my friend into an old matron at the age of nineteen? She'll be a mother by the time she's twenty. What a waste!' Dora sniffed, and began to twist a skein of her hair around her fingers, tugging at it crossly.

'Oh, little sister — don't be so sour!' Anthony sat down and looked earnestly at Dora who was glaring at him from across the room. 'I love Miriam. She loves me — or at least, I think she does. Don't begrudge me my happiness.'

'Your happiness? You just want a housekeeper — that's all it is!' Dora went over to the sofa where Anthony was lolling, and pinched his arm. 'You just took one look at that house in Pearson Street, which Papa was silly enough to buy for you, and you decided that it needed a woman to keep it clean and polished. Admit it! After all, you've shown no interest in girls before now.'

'Haven't I?' Anthony grinned at his sister. 'I might have been the terror of Girton, for all you know.'

'You?' Dora laughed. 'You spent *your* three years as an undergraduate getting drunk and falling out of punts,' she cried. 'But now you've got yourself that lectureship, haven't you? And now you fancy yourself as a great scholar, don't you? A grand old man of letters surrounded by a family of clever children, with a doting wife to look after the whole ménage. But Anthony, why on earth you had to pick on my friend for this honour, or why she seems to regard it as such, is a total mystery to me.'

'You don't like me taking your friend away — is that all it is?' Anthony shook his head at her. 'Oh, Doll — you've plenty of other friends. There's Annie Vesey —'

'Annie!' At the mention of the Dean's daughter, Dora grimaced. 'Annie's so taken up with her rights for women nonsense that she's an absolute bore these days. Oh, damn you,

Anthony! Why did you have to steal Miriam?'

'Dolly, my poor little Dolly.' Anthony put his arms around his sister and pulled her into a bear-hug of an embrace. 'It's not like that at all,' he murmured, into her hair. 'Just you wait until you fall in love.'

Dora jerked away from him. 'You're so sure of yourself, aren't you, you grinning hobgoblin?' she demanded. 'You know, you're *exactly* like Papa. You look just as he must have done at the same age, and you behave in the same sledge-hammer fashion. Oh, you're impossible! Why are you in such a hurry to get married? To get it all out of the way before next term starts, I suppose. Did you give poor Miriam a chance to consider your proposal? Or did you simply say, "Will you marry me, yes or no?" and demand an answer straight away?'

'Ah.' Looking at his sister's angry face, Anthony giggled. 'Wouldn't you like to know? Well, Dora — perhaps I went down on my knees and crawled across the carpet to where she stood, proud and haughty, spurning me with her shoe. Perhaps I kissed the hem of her gown and grovelled at her feet, told her I wasn't worthy to touch the ground upon which she trod. And then, perhaps, I asked her if she might one day consider me as a suitor — told her that she could, of course, take all the time she wanted to make up her mind . . .'

'And perhaps you didn't.'

'If you want to know that badly, Doll, why don't you ask your friend?'

'She wouldn't tell me.' Dora sniffed. 'She'd regard it as a betrayal of your confidence in her, the poor, deluded girl. She's altered out of all recognition since you bewitched her with your flashing smile.'

'Has she? Really?' Anthony laughed. 'Oh, come on, Dora!' he cried, 'don't be so bitter. It's not such a terrible fate for a girl, is it, to be marrying a man she's fond of? Surely?'

'Miriam will be bored stupid, locked up in that poky little house with half a dozen screaming infants.'

'Will she? Well, Doll — what do *you* want out of life? Don't you see yourself as a wife and mother some day?' Anthony looked at Dora. 'What's your ambition?'

Dora glowered back at him. 'My ambition? Well, it's to be

something more than a mere bedwarmer to a conceited Cambridge don.'

'Oh, I *see*. A truly modern woman.' Anthony rolled his eyes. 'So what can we expect of you?' he demanded. 'Going to climb a few mountains, are you? Explore the upper reaches of the Nile?'

'Oh, *do* shut up!' Then, suddenly, Dora grinned. In spite of her annoyance, a smile twitched her lips. 'Has it occurred to you,' she enquired, 'that your own true love is at least two inches taller than you are? You'll look ridiculous, walking down the aisle together!'

'Down the aisle?' That finished Anthony. He clutched his sides and cried with laughter. 'You're jealous, Dolly!' he gasped, when he could speak. 'Oh, poor Doll — you're jealous!'

'I'm not.'

'You are. Yes, you are!'

'I'm *not*. Anthony, as if I'd be jealous of you —'

'But you are, all the same!' Suddenly, before she could escape, Anthony grabbed his sister and pulled her into his arms. Lying back he hauled her on top of him and hugged her so tightly that she could hardly breathe. 'Doesn't anyone love you, my poor little maid?' he asked, rocking her backwards and forwards so violently that her hairpins began to work loose. 'Dear little Dora, I may love Miriam, but I still love you. I always shall. And I'll always give you a cuddle!'

'Let go!' Dora glared down at him. She took a fistful of his hair in each of her hands, and tugged it hard. 'Let go, you stupid great oaf!'

'Give me a kiss.'

'I'd rather kiss a snake. Let go, Anthony, damn you!' And, since he still held her, Dora finally jammed both her elbows into her brother's chest, completely winding him.

'Oh, God, Dolly — you're an Amazon. Fisticuffs, body blows and swear words as well!' Anthony rolled on to the floor and lay on the hearthrug, groaning and laughing at the same time. 'Dora, you've half killed me.'

'Good. But before you die, listen to me for a moment. For your information, I'm not jealous. Marry Miriam — see if I care. An idiot and a fool, that's what you two are. You'll be very well suited.'

And, with that, Dora flounced out of the room and slammed the door behind her.

※ ※ ※

The wedding was arranged. After a short civil ceremony attended only by the immediate families of the couple concerned, Anthony and Miriam took the train to Cambridge and set up home in the little red brick house in Pearson Street, to live — as Dora sarcastically put it — happily ever after.

So Dora had been happy enough to accept Anna's invitation to spend a few weeks in London. After all, she had nothing else to do.

Chapter Three

Anna's house, a newly built red brick villa situated in a quiet, tree-lined road in North London, was Dora's idea of a perfect home. Comfortable, warm, its furniture a pleasing mixture of pale woods and soft, deep upholstery, it had large, high-ceilinged rooms which all smelled delightfully of lavender polish, fresh paint and new carpets.

But these were not its main attractions because, best of all, it contained an absolutely luxurious bathroom. Tiled in pink and pale green, this was a splendid apartment in which Dora spent hours and hours, either soaking herself in hot, scented water, or examining her face in the mirrors and daydreaming while she listened to the noise of the cable trams which rumbled up Highgate Hill.

Downstairs the house was very versatile. Folding doors dividing the large drawing room from the smaller dining room could be pushed back to create a space the size of a small ballroom. And in Anna's own private parlour, in the family sitting room on the first floor, and in the bedrooms, white paintwork and beige carpets, elegant furniture and unfashionably pale wallpapers gave the place something of a Regency air, which Dora found most appealing.

Heavy mahogany doors complete with stained glass panels separated the inside world from the outside. Anna had always wanted a large garden, and here she possessed one. A small terrace at the back of the house gave on to a wide flower bed, beyond which was a tennis lawn, itself encircled by rockeries and rhododendron bushes. These last, very recently planted, were still small, but they were varieties which would become enormous with the passage of time.

'Pinks and purples — all sorts of mauves and violets,' Anna had declared when selecting her plants. 'No yellows — I loathe yellows.' Of course, no one had argued with her . . .

* * *

As Dora lay in her bath that morning, she found herself wishing, for the umpteenth time, that her sister wasn't *quite* so dictatorial. But at any rate, she reflected, as she reached for another bar of Anna's deliciously perfumed French soap, at any rate the house was welcoming. Dora was perfectly content to be there. In the next week or so she intended to explore London. She had already decided that Tim Atherton would be a suitable companion with whom to do this. When she felt better, she'd write him a note. He'd said he'd be in town for the next few days.

With a great slurp, Dora rose from the now rather cool and somewhat scummy water. She wrapped herself in a large, white bath towel, then brushed her teeth three times. She decided that she felt a little better.

Back in her own bedroom, she shrugged on a dressing gown and glanced at the bell-pull on the wall, wondering if she dared ask Anna's personal maid to come and pin up her hair.

She decided that she wouldn't. Addison was certainly competent enough, but she did tend to tug as she brushed, and Dora's head still felt as if only a little force would be enough to detach it from her neck . . .

So she brushed her waist-length brown hair herself. Then, very very gingerly, she scooped the whole lot up and jammed in a couple of hairpins, hoping that it would stay in a sort of bundle at the back of her head. She dressed, and went downstairs.

'Hello, Dora.' Her nephew Marcus was slumped in an easy chair, reading the sporting pages of a newspaper. 'Mum said you have a fearful headache!'

'I have. So don't speak too loudly.' Allowing herself to sink into the chair next to his, Dora looked at Marcus. 'Where are your horrible little brothers?' she asked.

'Out with Nanny, being walked.' Marcus grinned. '*I'm*

considered too old to be walked any more,' he added. '*I'm* allowed to exercise myself.' He stood up and went over to the window where the sun caught the lights in his blond hair and outlined his fine profile. Dora reflected, not for the first time, that he was going to be something of a liability when he was older, provided, of course, that adolescence did not ravage his somewhat startling beauty.

'Could you walk *me* round the garden, do you think?' Dora felt in need of some fresh air, but was not at all confident that she would manage to put one foot in front of the other without tripping herself up . . .

Marcus favoured her with an enchanting smile. 'Certainly,' he replied, graciously. 'Poor Dora — you ought to lay off the fizz. You know that, don't you?'

'You cheeky little horror!' Dora attempted to glare at him but found that her frown had somehow turned into a grimace of pain. She held out her hand to him and, obligingly, Marcus helped her up.

Nearly as tall as she was, and very well-made, he was strong enough to support her as she tottered out into the sunshine. 'You're absolutely right, though,' she told him, as they made their way down to the lawn. 'I'll never touch champagne again — for as long as I live.'

* * *

'So, little sister — what do you intend to do with yourself this summer?' John Harley looked quizzically at his sister-in-law. 'Do you intend to start earning your own living? It's quite possible, you know — and a modern young lady like you needs an interest, something to stimulate her brain. I could find you a clerk's job at our accounting house in Shoreditch, if you like.' He laughed at Dora's disgusted frown and held out a decanter. 'You really ought to try a little of this St Estèphe,' he added. 'It's excellent.'

'No, thank you very much.' Dora covered her glass with her hand. 'It was your excellent Bollinger last night which made me feel like a revived corpse this morning.'

'Don't force her, John.' Anna looked severely at her sister. 'After all, she can't take it. She can have some soda water instead.'

'Can't take it?' John shook his head. 'Well, she must learn to do so. A fine red Bordeaux like this is one of life's essential pleasures. Come along, Dora, hold out your glass. You can always adulterate your wine with a little water, if you must.'

Obediently, Dora held out her glass.

It always amazed Dora that her sister's husband not only contradicted Anna, but that he flatly disobeyed her as a matter of course, and was still alive and healthy; was still, in fact, the sun around which his wife's existence revolved.

Anna was always so absolute with everyone else in her household that none would have dreamed of arguing with her, for she was sharp-tongued, short-tempered and extremely sarcastic. And because she was so clever, everyone was in awe of her . . .

A.M. Lawrence was a well-regarded classical scholar. Her name was as familiar to the current generation of students as those of Liddell or Scott. Anna wrote and published a steady stream of articles and books, seeing no reason why the fact that she was a wife, a mother and, most potentially damaging of all, a woman, should prevent her from continuing the work begun under her father's guidance when she had been little more than a child.

These days, Anna's reputation was at its height. She corresponded with a wide circle of academics throughout the world, addressed otherwise exclusively male assemblies and wrote prefaces for other people's books.

Most terrible of all, however, she was an incisive and savage reviewer. Her style disdained the polite evasions of some forms of literary criticism, and could be dismally direct about the shortcomings of any books upon which she'd been asked to give her opinion. The editor of *The Times* had lost count of the occasions when he'd been asked, humbly, 'What did Mrs Harley think of it?' For Anna made and ruined reputations.

Dora, who had been delighted to leave Greek and Latin behind her when she left school, couldn't honestly see why on earth Anna bothered.

As he poured the wine into Dora's glass, John caught his wife's eye and she smiled at him. Dora looked away.

It was such an intimate kind of smile that it was almost a

secret code between them. John returned it, and, reddening, Dora bent her head over her meal, wishing she was not with them. For it was almost as if both of them had suddenly thrown off all their clothes and were embracing passionately across the laden dining table.

Dora reflected that her own parents were just as doting. But, being such antiques, they were easier to live with. Now, feeling the sexual current emanating from her sister and her brother-in-law, seeing John caress Anna's hand with his own, Dora excused herself and went up to her room.

* * *

'He's downstairs, miss. In the hall.' The housemaid looked interrogatively at Dora. 'Shall I show him into the drawing room?'

'He's very early.' Dora was still at her dressing table, putting up her hair. 'Yes, please, Mary — do that. Oh, Addison — *could* you help me with the back of my hair? I can't quite get it right without your expertise.'

'Certainly, miss.' Anna's maid, who had looked in just at that moment to see if Dora needed her assistance, smiled at the girl's reflection. She liked Miss Lawrence. Used to Anna's snappishness and hyper-critical severity, it was a pleasure to wait on Mrs Harley's younger sister who was always so polite.

It seemed that Anna had perhaps been right to have been suspicious of Tim Atherton's intentions. Dora had not needed to write to him, or flatter him into acting as her escort while she saw the sights of the capital. For Tim had called every day since the party. He had taken it upon himself to show London to Dora — and Dora to London, too.

He knew so many people and had so many friends that Dora's week had passed in a blur of excursions and new faces, seen, introduced to her and forgotten.

She was, she supposed, enjoying herself. Tim was a pleasant, if exhausting, companion. 'No,' she'd said, the day before yesterday. 'No, I really couldn't climb the Monument. Oh, Tim — my legs ache. And I haven't a head for heights.'

'Oh, but you *must* come.' Tim and another young man, one of his dozens of intimate friends, had both grinned encouragingly at her. 'We'll help you up, won't we, Harry?'

'Rather.' Harry whatever his name was had given Dora a reassuring wink. 'We won't let you fall, you know.'

So Dora had allowed herself to be persuaded. And when coming back down the narrow stairs, she had tripped over her long skirt, tumbling into Tim Atherton's arms — and he had held her rather more firmly than he'd needed to for the rest of the way down.

'We'd better take her somewhere for a spot of tea.' Harry, a small, dark-haired Irishman, offered Dora his arm. 'Poor thing, now will you look at her?' he demanded, intensifying his brogue and grinning at her. 'If it isn't exhausted she is!'

'I really think I ought to go home.' Dora looked pleadingly at Tim. 'Will you find me a cab?'

'Oh, you can't go home yet. Look — come and have a cup of tea, a few cakes — and then you'll be fine. I told Michael and Fred — you remember them, don't you? — that we'd meet them in the Strand at six. There's a new farce on at Drury Lane.' He grinned at her. 'Buck up now, Dora. Never say die, eh?'

So Dora had bucked up. She'd eaten her cakes, drunk her tea and carried on gamely.

'Good morning, Dora!' As she walked into the drawing room, Tim had turned from the window to smile at her. 'You look rather fetching today,' he added, coming forward and giving her a light kiss on the cheek, as he evidently felt entitled to do. 'That pink really suits you.'

Dora smiled back at him. She turned this way and that, inviting him to admire her. She held out her hand to him, then snatched it away again and twirled round, flicking his ankles with her skirt.

'I thought we might go to an art gallery this morning,' Tim continued. 'Then have a bit of lunch somewhere — by ourselves, today.'

'That sounds splendid.' Dora looked through the window. 'Tim, do I need a coat?'

'No, just a jacket. The velvet one, I think, with all the braiding on the revers.'

She nodded. 'I'll wear it just for you.'

* * *

Dora surreptitiously eased her shoes off and flexed her aching toes. She handed Tim the menu. 'You choose,' she told him. 'I like everything. Goodness, I thought we were going to have an easy time of it today, but I'm already exhausted. All that culture — it's made me ravenous.'

'Think of the good it's done your soul. Now you know a Goya from a Fragonard, which you certainly didn't yesterday.'

'I'm not sure how long the knowledge will stick.' She smiled at Tim. 'How do you know so much?' she asked. 'You spoke to that man with such authority — he was amazed at your erudition.'

'Don't be sarcastic, Dora.' Tim blushed. 'Oh, I just like pictures,' he muttered, as if confessing to a particularly shameful vice. 'If I had any money of my own, they are what I'd spend it on.'

They ordered and the waiter went away. 'I've been summoned to the old ancestral seat next week,' began Tim, letting his hand sidle slowly towards Dora's, gain its objective and tap, with the tips of his fingers, upon her fingernails. 'The old man talks of sending me out to India.'

'India?'

'Afraid so. The good old outposts of Empire, don't you know, where all younger sons find their paths lead them in the end. Apparently the old fellow has an interest in some tea garden out in Assam.'

'Ah, Assam.' Dora had never heard of it. 'So you're going to become a planter, are you?'

'I damn well hope not.' Tim grimaced. 'Oh, I said I'd go out there for a few years. How d'you fancy India, Dora?'

'Not at all. Flies, heat and blacks. Ugh.'

'Temples, jewels and maharajahs? The sun setting against the foothills of the Himalayas, the scent of spices on the warm air, the white marble palaces on islands set in deep blue lakes?'

'I don't think so, Tim.' Dora leaned towards him. 'Surely you don't *have* to go?' she demanded. 'I'd miss you terribly if you did. We've had such fun together this past week.'

'I really don't see how I can get out of it.' Tim's hand edged over Dora's, covering it completely. 'That is, unless I get married or something.'

'You wouldn't want to do that, would you?' Dora slid her hand from beneath his and laughed. '*I* don't intend to get married for at least ten years,' she added. 'I just can't imagine myself tied to a house and surrounded by children.'

'Haven't you ever met anyone to whom you'd like to be married?'

'Good Lord, no!' Dora giggled. 'Have you?'

'Well, perhaps.' Just then, their soup arrived and both fell to eating as voraciously as if they had had no food for a week.

It was dusk when Tim finally hailed a cab and gave the driver Anna's address. Tired, now, her feet so sore that she could not have hobbled another step, and her head aching — for Tim had taken her to an afternoon concert and the music had been rather too loud for her taste — Dora collapsed gratefully into her seat and lay back, happily anticipating a peaceful twenty minutes or more.

A couple of days had passed since she had decided that being kissed by Tim Atherton was certainly a pleasurable experience — that it was something to be enjoyed and an appropriately relaxing conclusion to a long, demanding day.

This evening, Tim had wasted no time. As soon as he and Dora were safely inside the cab, he had put both his arms around her and drawn her on to the comfortable pillow of his chest. Now he was letting his lips work their way down her face from temple to jawline, printing a row of soft, dry kisses along their path.

'That's nice, Tim.' Dora sighed contentedly and closed her eyes. 'Very nice.' In a matter of moments she would, she was sure, be fast asleep.

For she felt safe with Tim Atherton. There was nothing dangerous about him, nor anything very exciting, either. Dora could quite happily allow him to kiss her for hours without feeling anything of that almost electrical charge which she could practically hear crackle whenever her parents brushed past each other, let their hands touch, gave one another the most perfunctory kiss of greeting or farewell.

She couldn't imagine herself standing behind Tim's chair and wrapping her arms around his neck, pulling him gently back against the softness of her bosom — just as her mother habitually did with her father, the sensation of his head lying against her breasts quite obviously being delightful for them both . . .

The cab rolled into Canterbury Gardens. Tim released Dora, who yawned violently, shook herself and tried to wake up. Having paid the cabman, Tim raked his fingers through his hair and took Dora's hand in his. 'May I come in for half an hour?' he asked.

Roused by the cool evening air on her face, Dora came out of her reverie. 'Yes, of course you may,' she replied. 'Do come in. You could have a drink with John.'

'Mr and Mrs Harley have gone out for the evening, miss,' said Addison. 'There's a cold supper laid out in the little sitting room. Do you wish me to fetch something hot for you and Mr Atherton?'

Dora shook her head. 'You can go to bed, Addison,' she replied. 'I'll only be up for ten minutes or so.'

The maid bobbed. She bade Tim and his companion goodnight and she left the room.

Dora wasn't at all prepared for the suddenness of Tim's subsequent action. He darted across the room, closed the door firmly behind Addison, then walked quickly back to where Dora stood. He caught her round the waist and pulled her close to him; he covered her mouth with his and began to kiss her with a fervour which he'd never displayed before. 'Oh, Dora,' he murmured. 'Darling Dora, aren't you lovely?' Or at least, that was what she thought he'd said . . .

Eventually, however, he was obliged to pause for breath. Drawing away from him slightly, Dora saw that his eyes were feverishly bright, their pupils dilated. He was breathing heavily, and two bright spots of colour had appeared on his cheeks. Then he began to kiss her again, enfolding her in a passionate embrace. He lifted her off her feet and then, laughing, he began to swing her round and round the room in a kind of demented polka.

Not knowing how to cope with such behaviour or, as it happened, feeling any particular panic or responsive desire herself, Dora had allowed herself to be swept into his arms and whirled about the room. Accustomed to Tim's energetic showing off, she assumed that in due course he would calm down a little and eat his supper. But two or three minutes passed, and still he held her . . .

'Put me down, Tim,' she said, evenly. 'You're making me giddy.'

'Giddy?' He grinned at her and kissed her again. 'Oh, darling, you are enchanting!' But he did put her down. He pulled her across the room to a small sofa and flopped on to it, dragging Dora down beside him. 'You will marry me, won't you?' he asked. 'Dora, you will?'

He was still flushed from exertion and grinning happily. There was no sign of apprehension or doubt, either in his facial expression or in his voice. He was evidently certain that she would say yes.

Dora looked closely at him, at his nice, open, very Anglo-Saxon face, at his fair complexion which was somewhat inclined to redness on the cheekbones. His wide grey eyes were large and candid, his mouth firm and well set; fair hair was brushed straight back over a high, smooth forehead. And she saw that he was just a child. He might have been twenty years old, but he was little more than a schoolboy, a fresh-faced innocent playing at being grown up. This was just the latest of his silly games.

'Oh, Tim,' Dora giggled. 'It's very nice of you to ask me that. Do you know, I've never had a marriage proposal before. But I couldn't marry you. Really, I couldn't.'

He grinned at her. 'Of course you can.' he said.

'I *couldn't*!' Dora was growing tired of this charade, and wanted to go to bed. 'Honesty, Tim — I really couldn't do that.'

'Couldn't you? Why not?' Tim frowned, his self-confidence now beginning to ebb away. 'Don't you like me? Oh, darling Dora — I love you.'

'Of course I like you.' Dora shook her head at him. 'But not enough to marry you. Good heavens, Tim — I hardly know you!'

'Nonsense.' His frown deepened, creasing his forehead into the lines which would not appear there for another ten years or more. 'That's utter nonsense. You've known me for ages.

This week, you've come to know me well enough to let me take you out all day, every day — and to kiss you, too. Have you forgotten that I've spent at least an hour of every day kissing you? I must have kissed you in half the cabs in London, now I think about it! Of course you know me.'

He attempted a smile, but his anxiety turned it into a grimace. 'You can't pretend that you feel nothing for me, can you?' he demanded. 'Not after everything that's happened?'

'Oh, I *like* you, Tim. I like you very much indeed. But really, you're being very silly tonight. Goodness, I might have let you kiss me once or twice, but I haven't given you any reason to suppose I'd want to marry you.'

'Haven't you?'

'No, I don't think so.' Dora leaned across him and patted his shoulder, shook him gently. 'Don't look so sulky, Tim,' she said. She waved her hand in the direction of the table. 'Shall we have something to eat?'

'I'm not hungry.' Tim looked into Dora's face. 'Listen, Dora,' he began. 'If you don't think you've given me any reason to suppose you'd want to marry me, you must be very stupid.'

'Tim!' Dora stared at him. 'That's rather unfair.'

'Is it?' He continued to look into her eyes, and then scowled. 'You're not stupid, though, are you?' he went on. 'You're a flirt. Do you realize that, Dora? You're a flirt and a tease. There are names for the kind of woman you are. And you deserve to be called all of them.'

'What?' Offended, her colour and temper rising, Dora glared back at him. 'Well, honestly, Tim,' she cried, 'how can you be so horrible? How dare you suggest — as if I would have dreamed — would you want me to lie to you, then? To say I love you, when I don't?'

She folded her arms and looked down at the floor. 'I really think you ought to go now.'

'I think so, too.' Tim stood up and straightened his tie. Dora glanced up at him and saw that he was biting his lower lip and looked near to tears. She pitied him then and was sorry to have been so sharp. She hadn't meant to hurt him — and, after all, he'd brought it all on himself. But even so . . .

She touched his sleeve, but he shook her off and walked over to the door. 'Goodbye, Dora,' he said, quietly. 'I don't suppose I'll see you again for a few years. I wish you well — in spite of everything . . .'

'Oh, Tim, don't be so melodramatic!' Dora, now only too well aware that he'd meant what he'd said, and annoyed with herself for having handled everything so badly, willed him to smile at her, to say it had all been a joke. She looked pleadingly up at him. 'Don't be so angry with me.'

'Angry?' His face, which had been flushed with mortification, now became ashen. 'I'm not angry with you. God in heaven — you *are* stupid, after all. Ignorant, childish and *stupid*!'

He jerked open the door and went out, leaving Dora alone in the sitting room. As she heard him go down the stairs, she wondered why she suddenly felt so close to tears herself.

Chapter Four

THE SUMMER WENT ON QUIETLY. In Oxford, the undergraduates had gone down and Dora's father talked of going to Hereford soon, to pay his annual visit to Ashton Cross. He liked to get that over with early in the summer break, for the countryside bored him — and although he took his obligations as a landlord seriously, they bored him even more. In addition to that, Dorcas would never go with him; and when he was away from her, he missed her very much indeed.

'What are you doing with yourself these days, Dora?' he enquired one morning, as he was about to leave the house in Summertown to walk into college.

'Doing with myself?' Dora considered. 'I paint a little,' she replied. 'Last week I did some rather good watercolour sketches; and I've drawn some of the specimen plants in the botanical gardens . . .'

'What about this week?'

'Oh, I've been walking. I've done some sewing, I've visited friends. I've been very busy these past few days, helping Mama with her charity work. And I —'

'You always look bored to me.' Stephen frowned at her. 'At your age,' he added, 'Anna was always busy. But you don't seem to have any direction in your life. Are you quite certain that you don't want to take up that place at Lady Margaret Hall?'

'Papa, I'm not a scholar. You know that.' Dora grimaced at him. '*I* don't feel called upon to translate the *Illiad*,' she cried. '*I* don't want to hob-nob with the Master of Balliol.'

'I dare say you don't.' Stephen's features relaxed as he smiled at his small, pretty daughter, reflecting that if she was empty-headed, she was nevertheless very pleasant to look upon. 'I'm going to Hereford soon,' he told her. 'Why don't you come with me?'

Dora stared at him. 'To Hereford, Papa? Well, would I be welcome there? I mean, at Ashton Cross, you —'

'Of course you would be welcome. In *my* house, among *my* family, as *my* daughter — why shouldn't you be? I don't doubt that your cousins would be very pleased to see you. And Dora —'

'Yes?'

'If you do come, perhaps you could persuade your mother to accompany us? I've been trying to do that for years, but she might listen to you.'

At that precise moment Dorcas crossed the hall, and, hearing herself mentioned, she stopped. She looked from father to daughter. 'Were you talking about me?' she asked.

'Papa was asking me if I'd like to go to Ashton Cross. And he wondered if you —'

'I can't come, Stephen — you know I can't.' Dorcas smiled at him, shaking her head. 'Anna's coming here next week, and she'll be here for at least a month. She's going to be starting that series of articles with Dr Lawler; had you forgotten? So I shall have my hands full with the boys.'

Dorcas looked placidly at Stephen. Patting his arm as if to soothe him, she made him relax his habitual frown. 'I'm needed here, you see,' she said, reasonably. 'Otherwise, of course —'

'Yes, of course.' Stephen shrugged, then straightened his lapels. He walked out of the house and into the sunshine of the Banbury Road, letting the front door slam behind him.

Dora smiled at her mother, who shook her head again and smiled back. She wasn't at all disconcerted by Stephen's obvious annoyance. Such displays of irritation were, after all, quite commonplace with him.

Dora agreed to go to Herefordshire for a week. She fully expected to be bored stiff while she was there, but she was nevertheless curious to see the place where her parents had grown up, living within a couple of miles of each other, although in very different circumstances.

* * *

The pleasant journey through the green heart of England was made, as Stephen usually made it, by train. Arriving in the small market town of Hereford, Dora found the medieval city somewhat too provincial for her sophisticated taste. But she decided that the Herefordshire countryside was charming. Its pastoral beauty immediately took her fancy.

And she was enchanted by the manor house. She had not expected it to be so big — had not anticipated this great, square, red-brick Georgian castle. It was, in effect, a child's idea of what a house should look like; a doll's house enlarged to more than human proportions, its inmates brought to life.

Its huge rooms had high, white, plastered ceilings and wide Rumford fireplaces; and in these, even at midsummer, fires always burned. Full of sunshine, the rooms were lit by large sash windows, none of which appeared to have been sacrificed to the depredations of the Window Tax. And, in the centre of the house, there was a beautiful wide staircase down which a princess, clad in a priceless ballgown, might have been happy to glide. Outside there were courtyards and endless outbuildings, for stables, offices and laundries, all of which adjoined the main house.

A very noisy place, the manor house's many rooms were always full to overflowing, for the family was large, and was even further augmented by servants and various hangers-on in the shape of impoverished cousins and children's friends. Indeed, the estate seemed, in effect, to be a little kingdom sufficient in itself. And it soon became obvious to any visitor that it was ruled over by Dora's uncle, Henry Lawrence, a large, grey-haired man, deep-voiced and heavily made, who looked exactly like the patriarch he was.

Accustomed to the quiet, studious atmosphere of her home in Oxford, Dora found the air of cheerful, busy disorder which greeted her on her arrival somewhat disconcerting, but delightful all the same.

'So you are Dora!' Mrs Henry Lawrence, a mother of nine children who would have quite happily gone on to produce nineteen if Nature had not called a halt to her fecundity, looked complacently at the newcomer. 'I'm so glad to meet you. Did you have a pleasant journey?'

'Thank you, Aunt Katherine, I did.' Dora, aware of a sea of faces, all of which looked very much alike, leaned forward and kissed her aunt. Then, glancing nervously around her, she observed that the Lawrences' dark looks, so evident in Anthony and Anna, were very dominant here.

Without exception, all her aunt's children were black-haired, sturdy individuals, dark-eyed and well made; unlike Stephen's two slim, small-boned daughters, these country-bred children lacked all pretension to delicacy of face or figure. Dora felt that she was surrounded by trolls. 'I'm very pleased to have been invited here,' she added, hesitantly. 'It's lovely to meet you all . . .'

'And we're delighted to see you.' Mrs Lawrence turned to a young man of about twenty who was standing beside her. 'This is James,' she said. 'And here's Michael. Katherine? Oh, there you are. Now, you three, look after Dora. Show her the house. It's *such* a rabbit warren of a place!' she added, smiling apologetically at her niece. 'It's bound to take you a few days to get your bearings.'

With James and Katherine on either side of her and Michael bringing up the rear, Dora was taken on a tour of the manor house. She decided that her aunt was right. It was a rabbit warren — in more ways than one.

'How many of you are there?' asked Dora. 'Altogether, I mean?'

'Nine.' Katherine, a tall, black-haired girl of about Dora'a own age, led her cousin back down the main staircase and into the long drawing room which ran along the width of the house. 'But my three elder brothers are all out in the world; George and Alec are in the City, and Edmund's an engineer.'

She grinned at the brothers by her side. 'James is at Cambridge, Michael's still at Marlborough,' she continued. 'And then there are the three brats; they're still in the nursery. You won't have to suffer *them*.'

Dora smiled. 'And what about you, Katherine?' she asked. 'What do you do?'

'She doesn't do anything.' Michael nudged his sister. 'She's bone idle, aren't you, Kath?' He turned to James. 'Come on,' he added. 'We're due at the Westons at five.' And with that, the two young men took their leave of their cousin and departed, leaving Katherine and Dora alone.

'Michael's more or less right,' said Katherine. 'I don't do much. In season, of course, I hunt. But the summer's always a bit dull here, I'm afraid.'

She flicked her hair, which flowed loose down her back, away from her face. 'I'd like to help Dad with the running of the estate,' she added. 'But, since I'm a girl, he won't let me interfere, as he puts it.' Katherine sniffed. 'You'll find that your uncle has a very low opinion of women's capabilities.'

'Has he?'

'Oh, yes. I've never been to school, you know. Mama did suggest it, but Dad said no. So she taught me to read and write herself.' Katherine shrugged again. 'I'm quite unlettered, you understand. So you won't be able to show off your erudition to me — I shan't know what you're talking about.'

'*My* erudition?' Dora giggled. 'Anna and Anthony inherited all the brains,' she said. 'There weren't any left for me.'

'Oh.' Katherine looked hard at Dora, but then she grinned. 'I was so afraid you'd turn out to be a skinny, nervous bluestocking,' she said. 'I had an idea that I'd be spending the whole summer lumbered with a moaning, bespectacled misery who'd be sure to suffer from asthma.'

Dora laughed. 'I don't get asthma,' she said.

'Don't you? Splendid! Well, let's go outside. I'll show you the stables.'

Brought up with no expectations of inheritance, fully aware that they would have to make their own way in life — for the Ashton Cross estate was the property of their uncle, their own father being merely his elder brother Stephen's agent — Henry Lawrence's children were a rough, noisy, independent rabble who preferred to be out on their ponies than indoors with their books.

'You say you don't ride?' That first morning, James had stared at Dora across the breakfast table, gaping at her with as much astonishment as he might have done if she'd revealed that she could not fasten her own buttons.

Everyone else had left the table. Only James and Dora were still in their seats, and now the two of them faced each other across an array of broken eggshells, dirty plates and empty tea and coffee pots. 'Do you never go anywhere on horseback?' he demanded.

'No, I don't.' Dora laughed at her cousin's incredulity. 'There's never been any need to learn,' she explained. 'You see, James, we go in carriages in civilized parts of the country.'

'Well, you'll have to learn now.' James grinned at his companion. 'Your father's an excellent horseman,' he told her. 'So, if one can inherit such talents, you should soon pick it up. Come on, I'll see about a pony for you.'

'What — now?'

'Yes, why not?'

'Dressed like this?'

'Well —' James looked at Dora's light muslin dress and shook his head. 'First of all, you'd better go and find Katherine,' he said. 'Ask her to lend you some breeches and a shirt. You'll learn to ride astride, won't you? You won't insist on being a lady and going side-saddle?'

'Side-saddle?' Dora grinned. 'No, I don't think so,' she replied. 'It looks so very uncomfortable.'

* * *

Over the next few weeks, her cousins taught Dora to ride. They were much entertained by her efforts to control the whims and fancies of the gentlest horse in the stables, an old bay pony, a docile creature who nonetheless realized that he was carrying a rider whose self-confidence was non-existent.

The three brats, a trio of little girls who virtually lived in their smart new-fangled jodhpurs, enjoyed sitting in a row on the paddock fence watching Dora trying to coax the bay pony into doing as she wished. They were full of useful advice.

'Don't jerk his head like that,' called Edith, throwing her apple core on to the grass for the pony to gobble up. Which of course he did, so that Dora, unprepared, lunged forward and almost fell off.

'*Do* try to sit up straight. Tuck your elbows in.' Jane demonstrated the correct posture. 'Like this.'

'And why aren't you wearing your hat?' Louise, very

safety-conscious, slid off the fence and went to fetch it. 'Here,' she said, severely. 'Put it on.'

'You're hopeless.' Jane, who had about as much tact as most eight-year-olds, frowned at her cousin. 'You'll never learn.' And her sisters nodded their heads in agreement.

But despite the gloomy forecasts of the three brats, Dora gradually mastered the old bay pony. She progressed to Sorrel, a good-natured, pretty little chestnut mare, whom Katherine had recently abandoned for a larger, stronger, more high-spirited hunter.

After a fortnight at Ashton Cross, Dora was taking a morning ride with either James or Katherine every day. 'By the autumn you'll be able to hunt,' remarked Michael. 'You'll be able to help us chase and murder little foxes,' he continued, mischievously, for Dora had, a few days ago, held forth on the barbarity of foxhunting, and denounced the bloodthirsty hooligans who indulged in such a disgusting pastime.

'Your father's a splendid huntsman,' added James. 'Truly, Dora, he is — you should see him on the field. Your own dear Papa slaughters little creatures with the best of them — and he loves it.'

Dora had observed that her own dear Papa, her solemn, scholarly father, was indeed a different person while at Ashton Cross. He even looked different. His black suits exchanged for tweed jackets and flannel or moleskin trousers, he talked to his brother of crop yields, of new machinery, or of which spread of arable land ought now to be converted to dairying. Even his voice seemed to alter, his precise Oxford enunciation softened to an almost rustic drawl, and he slurred his vowels and consonants together into the lilting, semi-Welsh accent of rural Herefordshire.

But, after a few days, she realized that he was playing a part. The bluff, down to earth country farmer he was imitating wasn't *him*. Whereas his brother Henry's eyes were animated as he laid out schemes for the following year, describing the virtues of a new breed of sheep or enthusing about the virility of a particular Hereford bull, Stephen merely listened with polite attention, adding no comments of his own.

Dora supposed that he would soon go back to Oxford. As

the days went by she noticed that more often than not his eyes were glazed with boredom. Wanting to be by himself for a while, away from the constant racket in the manor house, he would take one of the horses out for a gallop and bring the poor animal back half dead, dripping with sweat, eyes rolling, mouth a-slaver with foam. He was serving his sentence, that was plain. Gritting his teeth, he was putting up with all this until he should be released back to real life, to Dora's mother, to his work in Oxford . . .

'Would you like to stay with us a little longer, Dora?' Her aunt's pleasant voice cut into Dora's thoughts as she sat at the dinner table on Stephen's last evening at Ashton Cross.

Dora, surprised and pleased to have received such a proof of affection and regard, considered this. She smiled at her aunt. 'Yes,' she replied. 'Yes, I think I would. Thank you, Aunt Katherine.' She looked across the table. 'That is,' she added, 'if Papa agrees.'

Stephen shrugged. 'It's entirely up to you, Dora,' he said, absently. 'Do as you wish.'

Dora could see that he was, in spirit, already back in Oxford. She shook her head, and smiled at him.

* * *

'Do you like my father?' she asked James one day, as they sat on a stile in the summer sunshine, watching their horses crop the long, sweet grass.

James, who had proved to be a splendid substitute for the perfidious Anthony by looking and behaving very much as Dora's brother did, grinned. 'What a question!' he replied. 'Why do you ask?'

'Because I wish to know, of course.'

'Ah, well — yes, I like him. Now, that is. When I was younger, I was rather in awe of him.'

'Really?'

'Oh, yes. We all were.' James shrugged. 'Just imagine it, Dora — he used to descend on us for two or three weeks every summer, frequently during the harvest, when everyone was busiest anyway. And then everything had to be in order — the house cleaned from cellars to attics, the grounds immaculate, the outbuildings newly whitewashed. The maids would be in tears and my mother would be frantic.'

James looked at his cousin. 'From what I've seen of him, I don't imagine that your father would have noticed if the place had been *inches* deep in dust.'

'He wouldn't have.' Dora giggled. 'You ought to see his study in Oxford — it's a rubbish dump. The maids aren't allowed inside in case they touch his papers, and he flies into a terrible rage if anything gets moved. He hates anyone handling his books.'

James laughed. 'He used to send us books,' he said, 'hundreds of them, delivered in wooden crates — history books, story books, all the new publications. We used to share them out. I'll show you my collection, if you like.'

'He loves buying books.' Dora chewed her lip for a second or two, then touched her cousin's sleeve. 'James, did you know about us?' she asked. 'About our mother and her children, I mean?'

'We gradually became aware that my uncle had a family in Oxford, that he had some children there.' James looked at Dora. 'We never thought about it — at least, I didn't. After all, we'd never met any of you, and your father never mentioned you when he was with us.

'I remember that one year he didn't come — your mother was very ill, and he was afraid she might die. My mother wanted to go to Oxford and offer her help, but my father wouldn't let her, although he didn't give any reason why.'

'You don't think too badly of him?' Dora frowned. 'I mean, I expect people around here make remarks.'

'Oh, God, no!' James shook his head. 'It's all in the distant past as far as they're concerned. And anyway, there's a farmer on the other side of Ledbury who lives with both wife *and* mistress, two women and a dozen or more children in the same house. We're not exactly ignorant of the ways of the world here.'

James leaned over and looked into Dora's eyes. 'You'd be surprised at what goes on in the country,' he added. 'Out here in the middle of nowhere, you know, the squires do as they please — and sometimes *their* pleasures are fairly outrageous. I say, Dora —'

'Yes?'

'Don't worry about something you can't help. Whatever your father did or does, *you're* not to blame, are you? His behaviour isn't that unusual, anyway. So if no one makes remarks about him, why should they insult you?'

'I'd like to meet the man who'd *dare* to insult Papa. But James, I'm not so able to ignore other people's opinions as he is. When I first found out about it all, I cried myself to sleep for a week.'

'Well, take my advice and don't think about it any more. Now, we'd better get back. There'll be black looks from Dad if we're late for dinner, and it's quite an entertainment when he loses his temper. Provided you're not the cause of his anger, that is. So come on!'

* * *

By the middle of August Dora had explored most of her father's estate, had ridden round its perimeters and was beginning to have some vague idea of the huge responsibilities so many green acres entailed. Henry Lawrence was the employer, either directly or indirectly, of a couple of hundred people, from tenant farmers down to landless labourers whose very existence depended upon the goodwill of the Squire.

The Challoner family's fields abutted the northern boundary of the Ashton Cross domain. And, even to Dora's inexperienced eyes, it was obvious where the Lawrences' land ended and the Challoners' began.

'Is Mr Challoner a bad landlord, James?' asked Dora one day, observing a tussocky plain on her left, which was spread with docks and thistles — good arable land gone to waste.

'I wouldn't say he's *bad*. But over the past few years he's made some disastrously wrong decisions and lost a great deal of money. He swims against the tide. For instance, he's determined to grow grains when he'd do better to go in for hops and dairy cattle. And he doesn't diversify; all his income is bound up in his land.'

'Isn't ours?'

'Oh, good Lord, no! Listen, Dora, if the Ashton Cross estate was suddenly obliterated from the face of the earth, the Lawrences would be able to survive. Your father and mine have other sources of income — investments of various kind, stocks and shares. We wouldn't be destitute.

'But the Challoners, you see, have everything tied up in their land. And Mr Challoner wastes money; he spends thousands upon game preservation, for example. He employs a dozen gamekeepers, several watchers, he buys in birds which cost a fortune to raise and yet *he* doesn't even shoot.'

'Then why —'

'Oh, it's the principle of the thing. Game belongs to the gentry, you see, so it's the mark of a gentleman to maintain acres of coverts and to fill his woods with gin traps. Andrew Challoner's a fossil, Dora. He's stuck fast in the mud of the nineteenth century, half asleep.'

'*Quite* unlike the go-ahead, wide-awake, twentieth-century Lawrence family,' Dora teased.

'Exactly.' James nodded gravely. 'That's precisely it.'

Dora looked across the farmland to a stand of beech trees on the horizon. 'Your father works so hard,' she murmured. 'James, does he do so willingly? Does he mind spending his life managing a place which doesn't even belong to him and never will?'

'No, of course he doesn't.' James shook his head. 'Oh, Dora, you must have noticed by now that Dad's a born farmer. He loves this land. Now, if your father had stayed here, mine would have had to go into trade or something, which he'd have hated.'

'He doesn't resent the fact that he's doing all he does for someone else's children?'

'Oh, here we go again. Dora, you are boring!' James grinned at her. 'Look, I'll race you to that clump of trees at the top of the rise. You have thirty seconds start. Well, off you go then. Move!'

Chapter Five

FEELING, NOW, THAT SHE WAS getting on well with her riding, Dora hoped to be fairly proficient by the time the hunting season began. She was curious to see this ritualistic slaughter taking place, for she couldn't imagine her cousins, noisy and energetic though they undoubtedly were, deliberately taking the life of a small, furry creature.

'I shan't hunt myself,' she'd informed them, firmly. 'It doesn't seem right,' she added. 'It's cruel, and it's not — well, it's not British.'

'Not British?' Michael grinned at her. 'Of course it is.'

'Foxes are vermin, Dora. They must be controlled.' This from James, in response to Dora's request for a sensible comment upon the subject.

Michael leaned forward. 'Shall we catch a fox cub for you, Dora?' he asked. 'You can keep it as a pet. Mind you, it'll stink your bedroom out — a dozen stale chamber pots would be nothing to it!'

'They often get away, you know.' Katherine, seeing Dora looking tearful, patted her hand. 'They're clever little beasts. It's the hounds who get their hearts broken. You ought to see the look of baffled misery on a thwarted foxhound's face.'

'And it's such good fun.' Michael rose to his feet. 'You really ought to try it before you condemn us as a bunch of barbarous lunatics.'

Outnumbered, and having to accept that she didn't really know what she was talking about, Dora conceded defeat — for the time being. She continued to ride every day and practised low jumps in the paddock, little realizing that she was actually training herself to follow a hunt . . .

* * *

'Can I go out by myself today?' she asked James one bright, dewy morning. She'd found him busy in the estate office, closeted with his father and the land agent.

'I don't think you should. Not yet.' James marked the place in his ledger and looked up at Dora. 'Take Katherine or Michael with you.'

'They've gone into Hereford. Oh, please, James! I'll be very careful.'

Dora's uncle looked up from a stock book and grinned at his pretty niece. 'Oh, you can manage little Sorrel, can't you?' he asked. He glanced at James. 'She'll be all right,' he averred.

James shrugged, unconvinced. 'I suppose she will,' he said, doubtfully. 'But look, Dora, before you leave, you must get one of the grooms to see that she's properly tacked up. And keep out in the open. Don't let her take you into any of the spinneys.'

'I won't.' Dora smiled. 'Thank you, James. I'll see you at lunchtime, I expect.'

'Yes.' Already, James was busy with the accounts book again. 'Take care,' he murmured, as he jotted something down.

Out on the broad expanse of common, Dora let the little mare have her head. Exhilarated, her exuberance undiminished by the light burden on her back, Sorrel cantered across a stretch of rough grass towards a stand of beech trees at the far end of the common.

Dora was enjoying herself. The sun was warm on her back; released from its net, her hair was blowing loose in the wind. She felt that life had nothing better to offer than a canter on a lively little pony.

The trees were now a couple of hundred yards away from them. Remembering James's advice about keeping in the open, Dora tried to slow Sorrel down, but the mare was enjoying herself far too much to do that. Kicking up her heels and charging on, evidently determined to do exactly as she pleased, she took no notice whatsoever of her rider.

'Slow down, Sorrel!' Panicking now, and forgetting the appropriate form of words which the mare might have understood, Dora shouted a stream of orders into the pony's ears, each command more desperate than the last. 'Slow down, idiot!' she begged. 'Damn you, Sorrel — slow *down*. Oh, God — *stop!*'

Sorrel ignored her completely. And eventually, her mouth too dry to shout any more, Dora could do nothing but hold on tightly. Instinctively, she grabbed Sorrel's mane. The reins, which she had not been holding correctly, fell from her hands. She hoped that when the mare reached the trees she would *have* to slow down.

But as they entered the outskirts of the little copse, Sorrel was still going at full tilt. There being no undergrowth among the beeches, she galloped on unhindered while Dora lay flat against her neck, clasping her despairingly, terrified that she would be knocked off or brained by an overhanging branch. Sick with fear, she closed her eyes and prayed. A hard knock to her elbow just then gave her a stomach-churning jolt.

On reaching the other side of the copse, however, Sorrel tired of galloping at last. She slackened her speed and cantering gave way to a desultory trot. She stopped and, nonchalantly, began to crop grass. Still shaking, Dora sat hunched in the saddle, listening to the thudding of her own racing heartbeat.

She hadn't seen the man on the beautiful grey hunter, although he had watched her whole performance from his vantage point on a rise of land to the left of the copse. Now he came trotting towards her and stopped within a few feet of where Dora sat. She was still breathing heavily and cursing Sorrel for a mean-minded nag.

'Whatever did you think you were doing, letting her go through the trees at that speed?' he asked, eyeing Dora with undisguised scorn. 'Why didn't you slow her down? Or turn her head and go on across the common?'

'Because I bloody well *couldn't!*' Dora, her face still red from terror and breathlessness, muttered this to herself as she stared down at the mare's sweating neck. 'I haven't been riding long,' she replied, stiffly. 'I'm not very good at it yet and so —'

'*Good* at it!' The man let out a snort of sarcastic laughter. 'You're absolutely terrible. I've seen children on seaside donkeys who've had more graceful seats than yours.'

He dismounted and walked over to her, then looked up into her face. 'You're James Lawrence's cousin, aren't you?' he asked.

'Yes.' Dora looked at him sideways. 'Dora Lawrence. How do you do, Mr — er —'

'Challoner. Ralph Challoner. I'm very well, I thank you, Miss Lawrence.' He held out his hand, which Dora felt obliged to take. Holding it firmly in his, he grinned at her. 'I'm surprised at Lawrence,' he added, shaking his head. 'He must be out of his mind, letting a novice like you go out on her own. Well, I'd better ride back with you.'

'There's no need. Really.'

'I am a far better judge of that than you are.' Ralph Challoner looked enquiringly at Dora. 'Do you feel well enough to go now?'

'Yes, I think so. Thank you, Mr Challoner.'

'Ralph. Please.'

Dora looked at him properly then. The sun was shining on his upturned face and Dora observed that the man was young, that his pale blue eyes were mocking her and that there was something about his expression which disturbed her even more than her recent experience with Sorrel had done . . .

※　※　※

'Are you hurt, Dora?' Katherine came forward anxiously, meaning to help her cousin down from the mare.

Ralph Challoner explained to James what had happened. He made the point, Dora could not help noticing, that only a complete fool such as James would have dreamed of letting another complete fool like Dora go out by herself.

'I've only banged my elbow, for heaven's sake!' Her face reddening, Dora was embarrassed to be the centre of so much fuss. 'I'm not badly hurt.'

'Thank you so much for bringing her home, Ralph.' Katherine looked boldly at Dora's preserver, giving him a saucy smile which he did not return. 'I'm sure we're all extremely obliged to you.

'A veritable knight on a white charger, isn't he, Dora?' she added, cheekily. 'Did he race after you and grab Sorrel's bridle, thus averting —' Katherine rolled her eyes, 'a dreadful tragedy?' She stroked the long white mane of Ralph's horse with a covetous hand.

Ralph Challoner turned the grey's head and walked the animal past Dora who, still seated upon Sorrel, was the only one who heard him say, 'I'll see you again soon, Dora. Goodbye for now.'

Katherine helped Dora to dismount. 'So how do you like him, then?' she enquired. 'What do you think of the handsome heir to the Challoner millions?'

Dora nursed her injured arm. '*Is* he?' she asked.

'The heir, yes. To millions, no.' Katherine grimaced. 'Your gallant rescuer was, as I don't doubt you already know, the great Ralph Challoner, only son of our revered neighbour. He has, as you will have gathered, a great sense of his own importance — far more so than befits anyone whose father is letting his land go to ruin and who treats his tenants like animals. You look a bit shaky still, Dora. Lean on me.'

Dora did so. Together she and Katherine walked into the manor house. 'Come and have a hot bath,' continued Katherine. 'You'll feel much better then. I say, those breeches of mine are far too big for you. Hadn't you better go into Hereford and get some riding clothes made to measure?'

Dora hadn't intended to dream of Ralph Challoner that night. She woke up the following morning faintly annoyed with herself, cross that his face had appeared in her mind just as she was drifting off to sleep and that it had apparently stayed there all night. In fact, it had still not disappeared from her imaginings by the morning.

As she dressed, Dora found that she was singing to herself. She was letting her mind play over Ralph's features, itemizing his finely modelled oval face, his pale skin, his straight nose, his piercing blue eyes. And she remembered, too, his excellent figure, for he was very well made, tall and broad — six feet at least. Indeed, he was a very proper man.

She did not see him again for more than a week. There was no reason why she should have done, for the Lawrences did not visit the Challoners. But then, one Wednesday morning, Dora went into Hereford with her aunt and, on the way back to the shop where she had agreed to meet Mrs Lawrence, she almost fell over Ralph as he stepped out of a saddler's shop in Eign Gate.

'Hello, Dora.' He laid a steadying hand on her arm. 'I told you I'd see you again.'

Dora stared at him, annoyed to find she was completely tongue-tied. A hideous scarlet blush was, she knew, staining her cheeks and neck. 'Well, how are you?' she heard him ask, as if from far away.

She looked hard at the point in front of her, which happened to be the silver-gilt pin in Ralph's tie. 'I'm quite well, thank you,' she managed to squeak, at last.

'Your elbow is better?'

'Oh yes.' Her voice sounded more normal now — to herself, at any rate. 'It was only skinned and bruised,' she added, with a nonchalance she certainly did not feel.

'What are you doing in town?'

Dora scuffed the pavement with her shoe. 'I've just been measured for some riding clothes,' she replied.

'Ah.'

She detected sarcasm in that monosyllable and looked up at him defiantly. 'You find that funny?' she demanded.

'Not at all. I was just thinking that whatever you've ordered will have to be an improvement on those awful things you were wearing last week.'

'Oh, *they* were old. The breeches were some of Katherine's, you know.'

'I thought perhaps they were.' Ralph met Dora's eyes and then let his gaze slide down the length of her body. He laughed. 'Dear Katherine,' he murmured. 'She's a splended girl, but she *is* rather broad across the — ah — no, that's cruel. Shall I say, she hasn't your pretty figure.'

He shook his head. While he was still grinning at her, Dora noticed that his teeth were very sharp and white; that one eyetooth was slightly crooked, giving his face something of a wolfish look. 'I'm sure you'll look very fetching in your new clothes,' he said. 'As, indeed, you look today.'

Dora blushed crimson, both with embarrassment and gratification. 'I told my aunt I'd meet her in Stallard's at three,' she began.

'Then you'd better keep your word, hadn't you?' Ralph stood aside to let her go by. 'Dora,' he added, quietly, as she passed him, 'I'll meet you near Dawson's Copse tomorrow; we'll go for a ride together. Come about half past two.'

Dora did not reply. She walked on down the road, wanting to look back, but not daring to do so. As she went on down Eign Gate, she was aware of his gaze upon her and could have sworn that his eyes were burning holes in the back of her dress.

* * *

'Mr Challoner said he'd take me riding today,' announced Dora that morning. 'So if you're busy, James —'

Katherine looked up, regarding Dora with interest. 'When did you see the dashing Ralph?' she asked.

'I met him yesterday, in Hereford. He offered to take me out riding this afternoon.'

'*Did* he indeed?' Katherine made no attempt to conceal her fascination. 'Dora, dear,' she murmured, 'you're as red as a pillar-box. Can it be that the debonair Mr Challoner has stolen your heart away?'

'Don't be ridiculous, Katherine!' Dora glared at her cousin. 'He was merely being neighbourly, I assume.'

'I'm sure you're right. Well, my father says that you're not to go riding by yourself any more, so I'll come with you to your point of assignation and hand you over to your noble escort myself. That would be the best thing, wouldn't it, James?'

'What?' James, who was busy reading a stock report was obviously not listening to his sister. 'Oh, yes — certainly.'

Dora made herself meet Katherine's eyes. 'Come with us, why don't you?' she asked, as casually as she could. 'You know Ralph much better than I do, after all.'

'Precisely — I do.' Katherine smiled an enigmatic smile. 'I know him very well indeed. Oh, I won't come with you, thank you. I have better things to do with a sunny afternoon than chaperone you and *that* fellow.'

* * *

Dora and Ralph watched Katherine canter away, her long black hair streaming out behind her. Ralph touched Sorrel's bridle. 'Well, Dora,' he said. 'I thought we'd go up to the ridgeway, and then I can show you the Malvern Hills. They look very fine on a day like this.'

'That sounds nice. But I have to be back at the manor house by six. Uncle Henry said —'

'I shall deliver you to Ashton Cross by half past five. Shall we go?'

For some time they rode along in silence. Ralph led Dora along a narrow bridleway on either side of which the summer vegetation was waist high, or higher. In the soporific haze of the hot afternoon the sound of buzzing insects was loud and the stands of beech and oak, with which the countryside was dotted, seemed to float against the deep blue sky. As unreal as a painted backdrop, the Malvern Hills loomed on the far horizon, their lower slopes green and wooded, their tops naked, baked brown by the summer sun.

But Dora wasn't interested in the scenery. She was looking fixedly at Ralph, and now that she could gaze at him unhindered, she realized that he was even better in the flesh than he'd appeared in her imagination.

She wondered how old he was. Twenty-two? No more than twenty-five, certainly. His brown hair was, she noticed, slightly too long; it curled over his collar and round his ears. There was a dark patch of sweat between his shoulder-blades now, for the sun was very hot. Dora could feel her own clothes sticking to her.

He looked round suddenly, making her start. 'Don't grab at the reins like that,' he rapped. 'You'll hurt her mouth. Try to relax a little.'

Dora looked at him. 'What?'

'I said, try to relax.' He grinned at her. 'Let your shoulders lie back,' he continued. 'You're all hunched up; you'll have terrible backache if you insist on crouching like that. When are you going back to Oxford, Dora?'

Dora, trying to take in and obey his instructions, frowned. 'Oxford? Oh, I don't know. I have an open invitation to stay here as long as I please — or at any rate, I assume I have.'

'Have you, now? Well, that's excellent news. You'll be here for the opening of the hunting season.'

'When is that?'

'We begin about the first of November. Look, it's a bit

difficult along this next stretch, so I suggest we get off and walk them through these trees. The path's kept clear, but there are overhanging branches. You know all about those, don't you?'

Dora nodded ruefully. She dismounted and followed Ralph along the dappled path, grateful for the shade.

The hot, blue August afternoon was still full of the increasingly drowsy sounds of summer. Dora heard, or imagined she heard, water splashing on rocks. Then the path widened, and she saw the stream beyond the trees.

'Bring Sorrel down here — there's some grass by the water's edge.' Although he was barely three yards ahead of her, Ralph's voice sounded very far away, and Dora, pushing her way along the path, was glad to find him standing at the water's edge, hands in his pockets and kicking pebbles into the stream. 'What's the matter?' he asked, seeing her grimace.

'Gnats.' Dora snatched off her hat and swatted the cloud which was circling above her head. But this failed to deter them and now a fresh swarm descended and buzzed around her face. She could feel them biting her upper arms, and wondered how they'd managed to find their way under the fine cambric sleeves of her blouse. She waved her hat around wildly trying to drive her tormentors away.

'Don't do that. It's pointless — they only come down again.' Very lightly, Ralph touched Dora's arm and directed her attention to a place where the trees gave way to a grassy clearing. 'Come along — come away from the river. The horses will be quite all right for five minutes.' He took her hand in his and led her back up the bridleway.

Dora wasn't unprepared for what happened next. She'd been aware of the mounting tension between her and Ralph, had noticed how he'd been looking at her, and had been willing him to touch her for half an hour or more.

But she had had very little experience of embraces. Tim Atherton had been her only previous admirer, so Dora was therefore somewhat startled when Ralph suddenly grabbed her by the shoulders and pushed her up against a tree. Without any preamble of exploratory touches or kisses, he jerked her head back and stared fiercely down at her, holding her chin so firmly that she had no choice but to look up into his face.

He kissed her very hard, full on the mouth. He bit her lips until they bled, and by pinching her jaws, he forced her to open her mouth, obliging her to let her teeth part and admit his probing tongue against her own.

Surprise and a great, sudden surge of excitement stopped Dora from resisting him. Now she was aware of streams of perspiration trickling down her back and between her breasts. She was bathed in sweat — the palms of her hands were sticky with it. Dora, normally so calm, so placid, so unmoved, was suddenly shaking with desire. Her heart was thudding and her breathing was irregular and harsh.

When at last he stood back and looked at her, he saw how aroused she was and grinned, the same wolfish grin which she remembered from that meeting in Hereford. 'Well,' he said, quietly, 'what a revelation. I expected you to slap my face, at least. But instead —'

He reached out and allowed his hands to rest lightly upon her breasts; he traced the outlines of them, his fingers like burning brands on the light material of her blouse. He felt her nipples harden under his passing touch and smiled again, slightly more pleasantly this time.

'No stays,' he remarked. 'Your figure is your own. There's no artifice about you, is there, Dora? There's no deception. What I feel, what I see, is really you. You're incapable of dissimulation, aren't you?'

Dora didn't reply, couldn't have spoken. She stood motionless in a patch of sunlight, staring at Ralph. Her hands, hanging by her sides, felt like lead weights. Her heart, still thumping, threatened to burst. Breathing through her mouth, she wondered if she might faint, but she knew, deep inside her, that she wouldn't.

Ralph shook his head. 'Not today, Dora,' he said. 'Yes, I know there's nothing you'd like better but really, it's much too soon.' He kissed her again and pushed her hair back from her forehead, cooling her hot face with his cold hands.

'You *are* beautiful,' he observed, in a calm, detached voice. 'Flesh that melteth at a touch to blood — here, and here.' He touched her cheek, then he let his hand travel down her neck. He laid his other hand upon her bare forearm, applying pressure with his fingertips and causing a red mark to appear on her white skin.

Then he let her go. Brushing past her, he walked off down the path. 'We'd better get back,' he called. 'It's after four; the Malverns will have to wait for another day.'

With a start, Dora came out of her reverie. She went running down the path after him, caught his hand and smiled up at him, her face a study of perfect bliss. And Ralph, obligingly, let her cling to him.

They were within sight of the manor house by the time Dora felt anything like her usual composure returning. 'I won't come into the stable yard with you,' said her companion. 'I don't want to create a precedent, after all.'

Dora coughed, cleared her throat. 'Whatever do you mean?' she cried. 'Don't you ever visit my cousins?'

'Hardly ever, and then only on business.' He sighed. 'I'm not especially welcome here — hadn't you realized that? Well, Dora, thank you very much indeed for your most delightful company. It's been a very pleasant afternoon.'

'But when shall I see you again? When will you —' Dora heard the panic in her voice and thought she might choke if she tried to say any more. So she caught at Ralph's sleeve and held him, preventing him from riding away.

He shrugged, then met her eyes. 'I dare say our paths will cross,' he replied, offhandedly. 'I'm often out riding, you know. I attend to some of the business of the estate these days. My father isn't well, and various things need my attention.'

'I know that!' Near to desperation now, Dora clung to him still more tightly. 'Oh, Ralph, I never meant that you have all the time in the world, I don't expect you to idle away your days with me, but —'

'They don't like you to go riding by yourself, do they?' Ralph sighed again. 'So I can't ask you over to the Grange to visit me — much as I should like to.'

'I can walk!' Dora's face was within inches of Ralph's and her anxiety was a complete contrast to his absolute passivity. 'I can walk to wherever you will be. Tell me where to come, when to come and I shall. Believe me, I shall.'

He took her hand from his sleeve and placed it firmly upon

Sorrel's neck, winding the reins through her fingers in the correct fashion. 'I'll see you near the stand of beeches where I first met you, some time during the course of Monday afternoon,' he told her.

And then, without even saying goodbye to her, he turned his horse's head and rode away.

Chapter Six

'STILL NO NEWS FROM DORA?' Stephen, who had been back in Oxford for almost a month now, sorted through the pile of envelopes next to his plate and grimaced. He was evidently disappointed that there was nothing from Ashton Cross.

'There's a postcard. Look.'

Dorcas passed it across the breakfast table. Stephen took it, skimmed through it and shrugged. 'Not exactly verbose, is she?' he grumbled. 'Two sentences, conveying nothing.' He looked up at Dorcas and scowled. 'What's she doing with herself?' he demanded.

'Oh, Stephen, what do you think? She's probably going out riding, and she'll be exploring the countryside. She has plenty of young people to talk to and I expect they organize tennis matches, picnics — all that sort of thing.'

Dorcas leaned across the table and patted Stephen's hand. 'Don't fret about her, dear,' she added, soothingly. 'I can't imagine that she'll be missing a pair of dull old things like us. We might as well leave her at Ashton until she wants to come home.'

'If she ever *does*.' Sulkily, Stephen paddled his coffee spoon in the dregs of his cup. 'I shouldn't have left her there,' he muttered. 'Oh, damn it, Dorcas — she's a silly little thing, but the house seems so empty without her.'

Dorcas rose to her feet and went round to where Stephen sat. Standing behind his chair, she wrapped her arms around his shoulders. 'Shall we have a few days away from Oxford?'

she asked him. 'Before the beginning of term? We could go somewhere by ourselves — take a little holiday. Stephen, when was the last time you had a proper rest?'

'Where did you want to go?'

'Devon. I'd like to see the moors, and I rather wanted to visit Exeter.'

'Exeter?' Stephen twisted round and looked up at her. 'Whatever d'you want to go there for?'

'Oh, no special reason. But I was reading a novel set in that part of the country and I took a fancy to see it.' She smiled disarmingly at him. 'Very frivolous of me, I know.'

'If you wish to go to Exeter, dear, then we shall.' Stephen took her hand in his. 'You won't mind a train journey?' he asked.

'No, I don't think so. Oh, I know I used to complain about going away, but that was in the days when we used to have all that luggage, *and* the children, *and* the nursemaid — there was so much to worry about. And it's time I stopped fretting about the possibility of a crash; if one *were* to happen, the world can well spare an old woman like me.'

'*I* couldn't spare you.' Stephen tightened his grip on her hand. 'And you're not old yet. Unlike me, you carry the weight of your years well.'

Dorcas pushed a strand of Stephen's grey hair back from his forehead. '*You* look distinguished in your old age,' she said. 'You improve with keeping. And you never were handsome, were you?' she added, wickedly.

'I know that. I remember you telling me that I was ugly more than thirty years ago. It's just as well, isn't it, that the children take after you?'

'I do love you.' Dorcas leaned over and kissed him. 'Stephen, I *do* love you.'

'Silly woman.' He let go of her hand. 'You arrange this holiday, then,' he told her. 'I can be away from Oxford during the last week of September, so find us somewhere to stay for four or five days, perhaps.' He reached across the table and gathered his letters together. 'Do you know, Dorcas?' he asked.

'What?'

'You have some grey hair. There's a streak of it in your

crown. So don't flatter yourself that you're immortal, will you?' He stood up and grinned at her. 'Soon you'll be as grizzled as I am!'

'Oh, go away. Go to your boring old faculty meeting; go and torment your underlings. Go and lay down the law about next year's work!'

They hugged each other, kissed and Stephen went off to college in an unusually good humour, pleased to be settled back in his regular routine.

* * *

August turned to September, then October. Dora wrote to her parents at last, telling them that she intended to return to Oxford around the middle of November. She wanted, she said, to stay until the start of the hunting season, as she hoped by then to be a proficient enough rider to follow the chase, and she was curious to see what it was all about.

James returned to Cambridge, Michael to his last year at Marlborough. Katherine and the three brats were the only cousins left at the manor house, and Katherine's mornings now seemed to be taken up with teaching her younger sisters to read and write. Not that her pupils were grateful for her efforts...

'Oh, I can't work this morning, Kath!' Louise, who had come downstairs clad in her riding clothes, looked pleadingly at her teacher. 'Darrow told me that they're starting cubbing over at Leigh today and I *did* so want to go and join in.'

'Did Darrow offer to take you?' Katherine, who knew how partial the head groom was to her little sister, opened Louise's copy book. 'Or did you pester him until he agreed to let you tag along?'

'He offered.' Louise grinned at her two fellow pupils. 'But it was only me he meant. Not *them*, as well.'

'Don't want to go anyway.' Edith opened her reader and bent her head over her book. 'I hope you fall off,' she added, uncharitably. 'Into a ditch. One with plenty of dirty water in it.'

'Jealous!' Louise giggled. 'Ede, you're jealous!'

'I'm not!' Edith glared at her sister. 'If you think I'd *want* to spend a whole day riding up and down the side of a field along with that smelly old man and all those stupid peasants from Leigh, you must be crazy.'

'Darrow's not a smelly old man.'

'He is!'

'Just because he —'

'Oh, shut up, the pair of you.' Katherine, seeing that if Louise were forced to stay at home she would poison the atmosphere for everyone, got up and opened the door. 'Off you go, Lou,' she said, graciously. She glanced out of the window. 'It's going to rain,' she added. 'You'll be soaked.'

'Don't care.' Louise, grinning, went off to the stables. And Katherine, together with Jane and Edith, sat down to start work.

She wondered if there was any point in having another talk with her father about the education of the three brats. Louise was clever, and the other two were at least moderately bright. There were three or four good boarding schools in the city.

She sighed to herself. She could just hear him saying, 'School, Kath? And for what? They'll grow up, get married, have children. Why do they need Latin and French, when they'll probably be farmers' wives? Eh?'

Preoccupied with her sisters' education though she was, Katherine missed nothing where Dora was concerned. Already knowing the answer to her question, she put it with no little degree of malice in her dark eyes. 'Where do you go, Dora?' she enquired sweetly, one October evening. 'Where do you go every afternoon, all by yourself?'

'What?' Dora blushed, and frowned at her cousin; she glanced anxiously across the drawing room to see if her aunt were listening.

Katherine grinned at her. 'Mama's fast asleep,' she murmured. She rose from her chair and went to sit beside Dora on the sofa. 'Dear cousin,' she continued, silkily, 'you heard what I said. Where do you go?'

'I don't go out by myself *every* afternoon.'

'Well, most afternoons, then. I've been wanting to go into Hereford with you for more than a week now but every day there's been some excuse. So what has been keeping you so busy, eh?'

'I just go for walks, that's all.'

'Ah, that's all.' Katherine looked down at her fingernails. 'I see.'

Dora scowled at her cousin and then she grasped the nettle. 'Why do you hate Ralph Challoner?' she asked.

'I don't hate him.'

'But you're not *friends*.' Dora looked reproachfully at Katherine. 'None of you are his friends,' she continued. 'And he must be lonely. He must have *been* lonely — as an only child he must have envied all of you having each other when he had no one at all. Didn't he ever have anything to do with your brothers? Why do he and James glare at each other so?'

'Oh, he and James *certainly* dislike each other.' Katherine grimaced. 'There's no doubt about that.'

'Buy why?'

'James was Challoner's fag at school,' replied Katherine. 'I believe that Ralph has hard hands.'

'But they're grown up now. Surely childish grievances should be forgotten?'

'Maybe.' Katherine glanced across the room at her mother, listened for a second or two, then satisfied that she was fast asleep, took a deep breath and continued. 'I imagine Ralph must have given James a difficult time of it,' she said. 'I remember one Christmas holiday in particular when James came home with his shirt literally stuck to his back. Nanny had to sponge it off him with salt water. *Didn't* he flinch!'

'Flinch?'

'Oh, yes. You see, Dora, Ralph had given him an especially bloody Christmas present. We couldn't imagine what James could have done to deserve such a thrashing — and James certainly wouldn't tell.' Katherine looked anxiously at Dora. 'Do let me put you on your guard, Dolly,' she whispered, urgently. 'You must have noticed by now that Challoner's not — well, he's not a very gentle sort of person, and I'd hate it if you —'

'Did your father speak to Ralph's father?' interrupted Dora.

'About what?'

'About Ralph's hurting James, of course.'

'Oh, no.' Katherine grinned. 'That wouldn't have been the thing at all. But two of my older brothers — George and Alec,

I think — were home at the time. They happened to meet Ralph in one of the coppices during the course of the holiday and they explained to him that he'd been rather mean to James.' Katherine laughed then, showing sharp, white teeth. 'They must have been very convincing, Dora. Ralph was much more careful with James after that.'

'Oh, well then — it was just a boys' quarrel.'

Katherine nodded. 'Of course it was.'

'And all boys thump each other, don't they?'

'They do indeed.'

Dora looked enquiringly at Katherine. 'So why are you telling me all this?' she asked.

Katherine shrugged. 'You have a brother, haven't you?'

'Yes — Anthony. Why?'

'Didn't he ever talk to you about his school?'

'Not really.' Dora spread her hands. 'I think he liked school, as it happens. And he certainly never came home with *his* shirt stuck to his back.'

'Oh.' Katherine rubbed her face and yawned. 'You *are* a little innocent, aren't you, Dora?' she asked. She leaned forward. 'Listen to me,' she muttered. 'At some boarding schools, it's not unknown for the older boys to take — ah — fancies to the younger ones. Do you know what I mean?'

Dora sniffed. She had no idea at all what Katherine was talking about. 'I think so,' she replied, doubtfully.

'Well then — Ralph was one of the seniors when James was in the lower house, and James was rather a pretty child. And I imagine that Ralph thought he could put his fag to whatever use he wished. But you see, Dora, James didn't choose to be Challoner's tart, so — ' Katherine's whisper rose hoarsely 'so Challoner used to thrash him. Do you understand now?'

'Yes.' Dora nodded. 'Yes, I do. And I think you're making a mountain out of a tiny, insignificant bump in the ground.'

'You do, do you?' Katherine grimaced. 'I could tell you a few other interesting stories about Challoner, you know.'

Dora rose to her feet. 'I don't want to hear them,' she said. 'I don't want to listen to tales, gossip and innuendo. If you have anything specific to accuse Ralph of, then do so now. Otherwise, Katherine, shut up.'

At the sound of Dora's raised voice, her aunt stirred. She opened her eyes. 'Ah, Katherine,' she murmured, sleepily. 'Dora, my dear. Could you ring for some tea? I expect Henry will be in soon.' She smiled at her daughter and her niece. 'Have you had a pleasant chat?' she asked.

* * *

Dora met Ralph regularly. Almost every day she would walk along the road towards the boundary of the Ashton Cross estate, past the neat grass verges and white-painted metal palings, until she reached the public highway into Hereford.

There Ralph would meet her — on neutral territory, as he chose to describe it — and would walk with her for an hour or so. 'They don't mind you coming out with me?' he asked her one day. 'They know where you are and whom you're with?'

'Oh, yes.' Dora smiled at him. 'Well, Katherine does. I don't imagine anyone else minds much what I do.'

'Ah.' Ralph pushed his hands into his pockets and walked along the road, silent.

'And it's not as if I'm doing anything wrong, after all.' Practically running to keep up with his long strides, Dora caught at Ralph's wrist, obliging him to slow down a little. 'It's not as if we're misbehaving in any way.'

'No.' Stopping, Ralph turned to look at her, his six foot frame towering over Dora's scant five foot two. 'No, I suppose we're not.' Sighing gloomily, he began to walk on, more slowly this time. 'Although the reasons for anything I do are likely to be misinterpreted by that lot,' he muttered, sourly.

He must have known that all the time she was with him, Dora was longing and longing to be kissed, hugged and embraced, but he hardly ever laid a hand upon her. When, however, he did touch her, he would do so without any warning. Suddenly, by the roadside, in full view of anyone who might pass by, he would pinion her against a convenient wall, grinding her shoulder-blades against the rough stonework of a barn or stable while he kissed her greedily, bruising her mouth, making her lips bleed.

He seemed to like the taste of her blood; he would bite her quite deliberately, gnaw at the inside of her lower lip until it bled. But then, apparently satisfied, he would kiss her more gently, more lovingly.

Dora would have found it hard to decide which was more exciting, which made her head spin the more — being chewed, or being caressed. And it never once occurred to her that perhaps a lover ought not to enjoy causing pain...

He would stop kissing her as abruptly as he had begun. Breaking off in mid-caress, snatching his hand from her temple or shoulder as if she had suddenly become red-hot, Ralph would stride off down the road, without seeming to care if she followed him or not.

'Wait for me, Ralph!'

He'd give her no answer, but walk on unheeding, as if he were deaf.

'Wait for me!' Panting, Dora would come up behind him, grasp his cold, dry hand in her warm one, hoping he might kiss her again.

Innocent that she was, it was easy for Dora to assume that she was in love. She could not, after all, explain her feverish state in any other way.

She had long since decided that Ralph Challoner was the most high-minded of men. He'd never, she thought, been careless of her. He never pulled at her clothing, or offered anything but a kiss, or the lightest, most reverent touch on her shoulder or bosom. It hardly crossed her mind that he well understood how to wind her up into a state of almost unbearable excitement, and that he did so deliberately in order to walk away from her, leaving her wanting him. If she still held him, he pushed her away almost angrily, leaving Dora to reflect that it was a good thing that at least one of them had some self-control.

'I was thinking of getting married some time soon,' he told her, one dull, grey October afternoon. 'What do you think of that?'

She stared at him, stricken and knotting her fingers together inside her mittens, 'To whom, Ralph?' she asked. Her voice was, she hoped, almost normal.

'To you, of course. Stupid girl!' He grinned at her, his wolf's smile. 'Well, Dora? Would it be a good idea? What do you think?'

He let her kiss him that day. He let her hold him in her arms, hug him around the waist while he gazed across the water meadows, towards her father's land.

In her more rational moments, which were extremely rare at that time, Dora understood that she was obsessed. There was no other word for her state of mind except, perhaps, possessed.

But she welcomed the sensation of it, luxuriated in it. He loved her — of that she had convinced herself. He was so careful of her, so sensible. 'He could have taken me at any time, on that first day out, even,' she thought. 'I'd have given myself to him — welcomed him. But he's never so much as thought of forcing me. He's behaved like a gentleman throughout and treated me as a lady.'

She looked forward to making a present of herself, unreservedly and absolutely, to such a man.

Chapter Seven

Dora wrote to her parents straight away. In a short but informative letter which was bubbling over with happiness, she asked earnestly for their consent (which she did not for a moment doubt would be forthcoming) and their good wishes.

While waiting for a reply, she walked about the countryside in a daze of bliss. At night she lay in her bed dreaming of Ralph, and while she was actually with him, she skipped along the country roads like an over-excited March hare, making him laugh at her. 'Why do you think I'm funny?' she asked him, one day. 'Why do you grin at me like that?'

'I wonder why you're so happy, that's all.'

'Don't you know?' Dora threw her arms around him and hugged him. 'It's because I'm with you, of course. Oh, darling — you have such a low opinion of yourself, haven't you?'

'Have I?'

'Oh yes!' Dora beamed up at him. 'But you really mustn't be so self-effacing, you know. Ralph, you do make me happy. I feel positively alive when I'm with you!'

'Mmm.' Ralph took Dora's arms from around his waist and pushed his own hands into his pockets. 'I'd better get back now,' he murmured. 'I have to see the land agent at four.'

'Shall I meet you tomorrow?'

'No, I ought to go into town and talk to my father's lawyer.' Ralph scuffed a tussock of grass with his foot. 'One of the tenant farmers is being difficult about his rent, and we're going to have to get him out.'

'Oh.'

'I'll see you on Friday, though, shall I?' Ralph looked enquiringly at her. 'I'll meet you up at Langton's Copse, if you like.'

'Yes.' Dora nodded enthusiastically. 'Yes, I'd like that.' Langton's Copse, a dreary plantation of pine trees on a cold, north-facing hillside, was hardly the most romantic of trysting places, but Dora did not care. She went back to the manor house for her tea, already counting the hours until Friday afternoon.

There was a letter, which had come by the afternoon post, waiting for her. In it her father ordered her to go back to Oxford for a week or two; he would expect her home by Thursday afternoon. He did not congratulate her. He merely referred in passing to 'this projected engagement' and wrote that he wished to talk to her about it, which sounded very ominous indeed.

A short letter from her mother, enclosed with his, was only slightly more gratifying. While Dorcas was, she wrote, pleased that her daughter had met such a charming young man, she wondered if Dora were certain of her feelings? Did she not wish to spend a little more time single before tying herself down to being a wife and a mother? And Ashton Cross was so remote — was Dora sure she'd be content there?

'After all,' concluded Dorcas, 'you're so very fond of society, and entertainment. . .'

Dora crumpled these two missives into balls, flung them into a waste paper basket and went upstairs to pack a suitcase. Walking down the landing she met her aunt. In a voice in which the irritation was only too evident, she informed Mrs Lawrence that she was obliged to go back to Oxford for a few days. 'May I come back next week,' asked Dora, pleadingly, 'for the hunting, as we planned?'

'Of course you may, my dear.' Dora's Aunt Katherine looked anxiously at her niece. 'Is everyone well in Oxford?' she asked.

'Oh yes.' Dora sniffed. 'My parents are perfectly well. Papa just wants me to go home for a few days; that's all.'

'I see. Well, Dora, come back to Ashton Cross whenever you wish. You're welcome here at any time.'

Katherine, the only member of the household as yet in on the secret of Dora's engagement, came up to her cousin's bedroom and sat on a stool, watching Dora throw a heap of underclothing into a carpet bag.

'Would you meet Ralph on Friday, at two?' asked Dora. 'Could you ride over to Langton's Copse and tell him I've had to go home for a few days?'

'Langton's Copse?' Katherine stared. 'That's nearly four miles from here! Dora, you're not telling me that he asked you to *walk* all that way, just to have the dubious pleasure of half an hour of his society?'

'*Would* you go and tell him?' Angrily, Dora fastened her bag. 'If it's too much trouble,' she added, 'I could write him a note. I expect one of the stable boys could deliver it.'

'Oh, there's no need to involve the servants in your intrigues. I'll go.' Katherine sighed. 'I'm glad you're going away for a few days,' she observed.

'I didn't think my company was that objectionable.'

'It isn't.' Katherine touched Dora's arm. 'What I mean, as I'm sure you understand, is that I'm glad you'll have a little time to yourself. To think rationally about Challoner.'

'What do you mean, Katherine? Think rationally, indeed — by that I suppose you expect me to decide not to marry him, after all?'

'I really do feel you're being a little hasty. You don't know him very well. You're rather rushing into things, aren't you?'

Dora sat back on her heels. 'Look, Katherine,' she began. 'I know you dislike him. I know you think I'm out of my mind. But I love him! And he — well, he seems to love me. And that's all I *need* to know about him.'

Dora picked up a pile of coat hangers. 'It seems to me that none of you have ever given him a fair chance,' she went on. 'None of your brothers and sisters are willing to talk to him. And you only open your mouth to be cheeky.'

'So you feel you ought to make amends for our rudeness, do you? Katherine grimaced. 'Well, aren't you overdoing it somewhat? *You* can talk nicely to him, if you want to. *You* can go riding with him. But, for God's sake, Dora, you don't have to marry the man. That's taking self-sacrifice too far!'

'You don't understand, Katherine.' Dora pushed a collection of bottles and jars into a case. 'If you've never been in love, you don't know how I feel.'

Katherine leaned across the dressing-table and caught her cousin by the wrist. 'Listen to me, Dora,' she said. 'Since you came here, I've become very fond of you. We all have. And I think you're making a terrible mistake in accepting Ralph Challoner. So would everyone else in this house, if they knew what you'd done. Why won't you listen to me? Why won't you *think*?'

'Because all you have to say about him is that you don't like him, that he's not a — what was it you said? — a very gentle sort of person. That's so vague as to be meaningless. The only crime he's ever committed against any of you is that he hit James years ago and your brothers punished him for that. You go on and on about him being disagreeable, but what can you expect when you're hardly cordial towards *him*?'

Dora put on her coat and found her gloves. 'You're only interfering in all this because you have nothing else to occupy your mind. You're entertaining yourself by trying to make trouble between Ralph and me.'

'Nonsense!' Katherine exclaimed. 'There's plenty I could be doing. At the moment, I ought to be with the children; they're incapable of working properly unless I'm actually with them.'

Dora's cousin looked out of the window and sighed. 'Dad sees to it that his *tenants'* children go to school,' she continued, bitterly, 'but he seems to imagine that his own daughters will learn to read and write by some process of absorption. Oh, Dora, it's all so frustrating! Look at me — stuck indoors half the day, when I could be out helping him with the running of this place. I could be useful to Dad, if only he'd give me the chance.'

'But he won't do that, will he?'

'No.' Katherine scowled. 'Because I'm a girl. Because I'm part of the inferior half of creation, a female creature fit only to breed.'

'You ought to think about finding yourself a husband, then.'

Dora nodded meaningfully at her cousin. 'That's what women are for, after all. To be wives and mothers.'

'Really?' Katherine laughed. 'Oh, I see. So, in marrying Ralph Challoner, Dora Lawrence is fulfilling her destiny, is that it? This marriage is all part of the great scheme of things?'

'I'm going to marry Ralph.' Dora jammed her hat on to her head and skewered it with a pin. 'Are you still coming with me to the railway station?' she asked. 'Or would you rather not?'

'I'll come with you.' Katherine rose to her feet. 'I'll take you in the pony trap. Come on.'

As they drove along the bleak, autumnal roads, Katherine made a last effort to make Dora see sense. 'You notice those houses over there?' she asked, pointing with her whip. 'Those little hovels near the spinney?'

'Yes.'

'They belong to the Challoners. My father wouldn't keep animals in such conditions, let alone people.'

Dora shrugged, but said nothing.

'They're very hard on their tenants,' continued Katherine. 'Andrew Challoner thinks nothing of evicting them, whatever the circumstances. This woodland on our left belongs to him. It's full of gin-traps and gamekeepers and, as you already know, old Challoner sees to it that the poaching laws are rigorously enforced. He's had his keepers beat little children found in his woods. Ralph himself —'

'Oh, I don't want to know!' Dora put her hands over her ears. 'I don't care if he's had a dozen poachers flogged to death.'

* * *

Dora spent the long train journey to Oxford in a state of the fidgets, repeating over and over to herself, I love him, I love him, that's all that matters, that's all that matters. The rhythm of the train seemed to agree with her.

She repeated these same sentiments to her parents. She dismissed their misgivings and reaffirmed her determination to have Ralph. She told them again and again how much she loved him, and demanded their consent to her marriage. After a day or two she had made herself so thoroughly tiresome that her father was wishing her back at Ashton Cross.

Dora, on the other hand, found that her spirits were now very much higher, for she assumed that Stephen's silence meant he was coming round to the idea.

'I shall have to visit Challoner,' he said gloomily, having spent the previous half hour of a dull Friday evening being harangued by his daughter. 'Dora, before we go any further I must have a few things sorted out.'

'Things?' Dora looked hard at him. 'What things?'

'If you're as determined as you say you are to become this fellow's wife, we shall need to discuss a marriage settlement. And before I enter into any agreement with him which concerns you, I shall need to know what Challoner's current financial situation is.'

'Agreement? Concerning me?' Dora stared. 'Papa,' she cried, 'I'm not a medieval princess! I don't need a dowry! You're not proposing to descend on Ralph's father in his own house, are you? You're not going to demand that he shows you his accounts and ask him how much he expects you to give me?'

'Precisely that, Dora. Not a pleasant prospect for me.'

'But you're being ridiculous. You didn't make a fuss like this when Anthony got married. You didn't make any fuss at all.' Dora looked reproachfully from her father to her mother. 'Ralph doesn't want Papa's money,' she told them. 'He only wants me.'

'Andrew Challoner's not a fool, even if his son is.' Stephen stared moodily at the fire. He kicked a piece of coal and flames shot up the chimney. 'The Challoners won't take you for nothing, Dora,' he muttered. 'And don't imagine that the prospect of becoming related to *me* will fill their hearts with joy.'

He rose to his feet and took an envelope out of his pocket. 'I was given some tickets for a concert on Sunday night,' he said, firmly changing the subject. 'I hope you will come with us, Dora. It's to be Mozart and Vivaldi — tuneful stuff.'

Dora studied her fingernails. 'That would have been very nice, Papa,' she replied, sulkily, 'but I have arranged to go back to Hereford on Saturday, so I shan't be able to accompany you.'

※　※　※

'She seems very attached to that young man, don't you think?' Dorcas was sitting on the sofa, her feet on a footstool. She was sewing, as usual, for someone else's baby.

She was not at all perturbed when she received only a grunt from Stephen by way of a reply. 'I think our children choose their marriage partners well,' she went on, placidly. 'Anna and John — well, they're perfectly suited, aren't they? And as for Miriam and Anthony, they seem very happy in that dear little house in Cambridge.'

She shook out the folds of the dress she was embroidering. 'So I shall expect Dora to be just as contented with her Ralph.'

'Don't talk such nonsense, Dorcas!' Stephen looked up from his newspaper and glowered at her. 'You know as well as I do that one doesn't *choose*. It's not like going into a shop and picking out the item one likes best. Marriage is a lottery — everyone knows that.'

Stephen turned a page. 'And anyway,' he growled, 'neither you nor I is in a position to talk of choosing well. *We* could hardly be cited as arguments in favour of holy matrimony.'

'That's beside the point,' said Dorcas, firmly. 'I can't imagine that a sensible girl like Dora would have fallen in love with a man who didn't deserve her.'

'Wouldn't she?' Stephen dropped his newspaper on to the floor and went to sit beside Dorcas. 'Listen to me, dear,' he said. 'The fact is, I don't want my daughter to marry a Challoner. This boy might be tall, handsome, charming *and* all the rest of it, but I'm quite sure he'll be no good for Dora.'

'Why, Stephen? What have you got against him?'

'Nothing against him personally — I've never even met him. But I know the rest of the Challoners, and I don't like them at all.'

Stephen leaned back and sighed heavily. 'I remember that when I first inherited, my mother disagreed with the way in which I was managing the estate, so she wrote to Arthur Challoner — that's this young fellow's grandfather — to ask him to remonstrate with me.' Stephen frowned. 'To show me the error of my headstrong ways.'

'What happened?'

'The old man came riding over to my house, stamping

around as if he owned it. He stood in my drawing room, in front of my fire — I can see him now, Dorcas, six foot five, as red as only a three bottle a day man can be — and he thundered away about my duty towards my dead father, my responsibilities towards my living mother, my obligations as a landlord and a magistrate.

'What he meant to impress upon me was that my tenants should be lodged as squalidly and my labourers paid as little as possible. That it was not my province to see that the children on my estate received some education. And, most important of all, I should ensure that any transgressions of the Game Laws were punished with the utmost severity. I've no reason to believe that Andrew Challoner is any different from his father. I don't doubt that he will have passed on his pernicious values to his son.'

'Well, if he has, Dora can show Ralph the error of his ways.' Dorcas finished a row of stitching and broke the thread.

'I doubt if Dora has very highly-developed powers of persuasion.' Still scowling, Stephen rose to his feet and paced about the room. 'I shall write to Henry,' he muttered. 'I shall go over to Ashton at the end of term.'

'Don't look so mournful, Stephen.' Dorcas smiled at him. 'Don't underestimate what the love of a good woman might achieve,' she added, teasingly.

He took her hand and held it firmly in his. 'I've never underestimated that, I hope,' he said. 'Shall we go up now? It's been a very devil of a day, and I'm sick and tired of everything.'

* * *

'He's invited me to dinner with his parents,' announced Dora over breakfast one morning. She grinned at Katherine. 'Prepare me,' she added. 'What are they like?'

Katherine chewed her toast thoughtfully, pushing a strand of her black hair out of her eyes. 'Actually, Dora,' she replied gravely, 'they're a pair of vampires. They have sharp yellow teeth and long fingernails. They sleep in their coffins all through the day, and wake as soon as the sun has gone down.'

She frowned at Dora. 'Take some garlic with you,' she whispered urgently. 'And remember that they fear the sign of the cross.'

Dora gave up. Since she had returned to Ashton Cross, Katherine had been very cool towards her, and when she did speak to Dora, it was only to be facetious. Dora found herself wondering if her cousin might perhaps have some affection for Ralph herself — for if Katherine had been slighted by him in the past, it might explain her almost constant waspishness.

Dora rose from her chair and looked at her watch. It was still very early; there was time to put her hair up in a net and pin it firmly before she set off. For that day, Dora was going to try to follow the hunt.

It was still dark as she and Katherine walked across to the stable yard. As they saw to their horses, Katherine chatted to the groom and, by degrees, she seemed to recover her good humour. 'Stay close beside me,' she told Dora. 'I won't take any of the higher jumps, and I'll make sure that Sorrel can keep up with Nimrod. If we lose the others, we lose them.'

'Thank you, Katherine.' Dora smiled to show her gratitude. 'But I don't want to spoil things for you,' she added. 'Don't feel that you have to lag behind just for my sake.'

'I must look after you, stupid!' Katherine grinned. 'You don't want to break your neck on your first day, do you?'

'I suppose not.'

'Well, then. And don't worry. We'll be in at the end, whatever happens. I shall see to that!'

*   *   *

Dora had imagined that a hunt would be a grander occasion than this one had turned out to be. She'd assumed that the picture outside the manor house on that chilly November morning would resemble the prints she'd seen of the *Meet on Boxing Day*. She'd expected dashingly turned out riders on splendid mounts.

But the collection of people clustered together in the cold half-light looked less than impressive: a couple of tenant farmers on stocky, winter-shaggy ponies, the local clergyman on a mare who seemed as nervous as he was impassive, and two ladies from a neighbouring estate who, red-faced and leather-gaitered, might have passed for men as they sat astride their horses and talked to each other in high-pitched, carrying voices. As a group of huntsmen, this scruffy gaggle was far from Dora's romantic ideal.

There was not a single pink coat to be seen; in fact, the huntsmen looked downright shabby. Gloomy but excited, they had the expectant, fidgety air of men about to go into battle. Already muddy, the dogs nosed around, sniffing and jostling, jumping on each other, and were cursed and sworn at by the whipper-in.

'There's Ralph.' Katherine pointed him out as he came towards them.

Unlike the other riders, he was very smartly turned out. Clad in black, his clothes fitted him perfectly and he was a splendid sight on his large white horse. When he saw Dora he touched the big grey's reins and stopped beside her. 'You'll still be coming to visit us on Thursday?' he asked, ignoring Katherine completely.

'Yes, of course.' Dora, who was already very cold and was wishing herself back indoors, tried to smile. 'I'm looking forward to it very much.'

'So am I.'

The Master called to him. 'Be careful, Dora,' he murmured, before answering the man. 'I don't want you to come to any harm today.' And he left her.

A little while later, they all moved off. The hunt was under way...

By mid-morning, Dora was tired, half-frozen, bruised and thoroughly bored. She and Katherine were by themselves now. There was a heavy drizzle and she was soaked through to the skin. Mentally and physically exhausted, all she wanted to do was to get home and lie in a hot bath in front of her bedroom fire.

Katherine, on the other hand, was still brimming with energy and enthusiasm. She had walked Nimrod up to the brow of a hill and was standing up in her stirrups, looking all around her and listening hard. 'There they go!' Her face lit up with pleasure. 'They've got him now, Dora!'

'What?' Dora, who had heard nothing at all, wearily pushed her damp hair out of her eyes and yawned. 'What do you mean?'

'Over by Cobben's Spinney. I thought they must have lost

him, but that call means they've got him after all. Come on!' She kicked Nimrod into a canter and rode past Dora. 'Oh, do get a move on!' she yelled back over her shoulder. 'We'll be in at the end if we get going now.'

The two of them urged their horses on. As they rode towards the spinney, the sounds of the hunt grew closer, echoing across the bleak meadowland. Just as Katherine had predicted almost two hours ago, it hadn't mattered that they'd lost the others. The fox, a young dog, had foolishly doubled back and was now running in the direction of the two girls, hotly pursued by the rest of the riders and a pack of deliriously excited hounds in full cry.

Flashing across the meadow towards Dora came a copper streak, tongue lolling, black socks caked with mud. She saw the fox's face; she saw that he was exhausted to the point where his heart must break, and that his eyes were glazed with despair.

Poor, inexperienced novice that he was, outmanoeuvred and outrun, he met his bloody end in the open field. A few feet away from where Dora sat the hounds fell upon him. Before the huntsmen could get to them, they were biting and tearing, had disembowelled and mutilated their quarry before anyone could stop them.

Ralph dismounted and pushed his way through the excited mêlée of wagging tails and red, grinning, canine faces. 'Leave it! Get away! Leave it!' Striking the seething mass of bodies with his whip, Ralph lunged forward into the midst of the hounds. He snatched up what remained of the fox, and bore it away from the dogs.

Brushless now, its head a crimson, spongy mess, what he held in his hand was hardly recognisable as the beautiful animal it had been only minutes since. Ralph did not need his knife to remove one of the creature's legs, for the front two were hanging merely by tendons, and it required only a sharp tug to detach one of them completely.

Throwing the rest of the carcase back among the dogs and holding his gory trophy, Ralph walked across to Dora. 'Here,' he said, holding it out to her.

She stared at him, a blood-stained, mud-spattered huntsman. Already in tears of anger and disgust, she sat immobile. What was she supposed to do? Take the horrible thing from him? Then what should she do with it?

'Bend forward, Dora. Nearer!' With his free hand, upon which the fox's blood was now drying stickily, Ralph caught her behind the neck. He jerked her head forward and then, when her face was within a foot of his own, he began to smear her cheeks with the blood dripping from the fox's paw.

Dora felt the warm liquid, salty and sharp, trickle into the corners of her mouth. She gagged and tried to twist away, but Ralph held her firmly and would not let her go.

'Keep still,' he whispered fiercely, looking into her eyes. 'Take it like a man!'

'That's enough, Ralph!' Katherine reached over and snatched the paw from his hand. 'You're supposed merely to touch her with it, if you really must, not to wipe it all over her.'

'Shut up, you interfering bitch.' Ralph's pale blue eyes narrowed. And then, in full view of everyone, he pulled Dora yet closer. Before the fascinated stares of the other riders he began to kiss the fox's blood, and Dora's own tears, from her face.

Katherine felt a surge of triumph. He'd gone too far now. This revolting exhibition would open Dora's eyes to what Ralph Challoner was really like. It wasn't too late to save her, after all.

Chapter Eight

'YOU'RE NOT STILL GOING?' Incredulous, Katherine stared at her cousin. 'You're not going to dinner with him, are you?' she demanded. 'You *can't* want to see him — not after what he did to you!'

'Of course I'm going.' Dora dabbed scent inside the crook of her elbow, then turned from her dressing-table and smiled complacently at Katherine. 'It's traditional, isn't it?' she asked. 'Being blooded, I mean. Ralph was only following the custom; I know that now. I looked it up in a book, you see.'

'*Did* you?'

'Oh, yes.' Dora giggled. 'I did make a fuss, didn't I? Weeping and complaining about a little bit of blood.'

Katherine saw that her cousin was beyond human assistance. She opened the door of Dora's bedroom and walked back along the landing, wondering what, if anything, she could do now.

In her totally bewitched state, it had not occurred to Dora to wonder why Ralph had never invited her to the Grange. As his fiancée, she might have reflected, she ought to have met his parents months ago. And, eventually, this thought crossed Ralph's mind.

'You must come and visit me at home,' he told her, as they walked through a dripping conifer wood, their feet soaked and their clothes stuck about with pine needles. 'Would you like to do that?'

Dora, who would have visited Ralph in a leper colony, a fever hospital or a prison hulk, nodded. 'I'd like to see where you live,' she replied.

'I'll take you there,' promised Ralph. 'You can meet my parents. I tell you what — come over for dinner next Friday. Is James back from Cambridge yet?'

'Yes, he arrived yesterday.'

'Then he can bring you over and I'll take you home.' Ralph looked at his watch. 'It'll be dark soon,' he added. 'Hadn't you better start back?'

Dora giggled. 'Oh, I brought Sorrel today,' she said. 'I left her by the sheep-pens further down the valley. So I can stay with you a bit longer, can't I?'

'Mmm.' Ralph shrugged. 'Get back all the same, I should. It looks like rain.'

* * *

The manor house in which the Lawrences lived was an extremely fine Georgian building. Dora had thought so the minute she first laid eyes upon it; its plain, classical lines had appealed to her visual sense, and its air of obvious comfort and convenience had attracted the sybarite in her.

But, although the manor house was a comfortable home, the Grange was in another realm altogether. As architectural achievements, there was no comparison between Stephen Lawrence's unpretentious, gentleman farmer's house, and Andrew Challoner's splendid mansion. The Grange was, quite simply, a masterpiece.

A drive of fine, immaculately swept gravel, bordered by huge chestnut trees, led up to the house. A long, low, two-storeyed building, surrounded by trimmed lawns and some magnificent cedar trees, it was built of grey stone and roofed with tiles upon which the lichen grew in a thousand fantastic patterns.

All the windows at the front were large and well-proportioned. With white-painted sills and surrounds, which contrasted elegantly with the grey stonework beside them, they were obviously the result of some neo-classical improving.

But to the sides, and around the other areas of the house, this plain, eighteenth-century beauty gave way to details characteristic of other times. Begun some time during the Middle Ages, the house was now a mixture of a whole range of styles. There was a half-timbered wing on the west front, and a thatched stable block behind that. High, Tudor chimneys rose from the roof, and Jacobean gables decorated the upper storey.

All this confusion of taste and style, all these modifications of a dozen or more generations, could have resulted in an architectural mess. But, somehow, every one of these heterogeneous elements fused and blended. The result, as Dora saw it, was a building which was timelessly beautiful and which was, of course, unique.

If Dora had not been besottedly in love with Ralph before, the moment she saw his house she was quite beyond help. The idea of being the mistress of such a marvellous place, of ordering its affairs, of having children who would inherit it, enchanted her.

She was late back from her dinner party with her prospective in-laws. Coming into the drawing room just as the family was about to go up to bed, Dora was flushed and somewhat breathless as she plumped herself down beside Katherine. Her eyes were sparkling and her hair was starting to come down.

'So how did you get on?' Dora's aunt smiled at her niece who, she thought, looked extremely pretty that evening. 'How did you like Mr and Mrs Challoner?' she asked.

'Very much indeed, Aunt.' Dora returned her aunt's smile. 'I didn't expect Ralph's parents to be so sweet to me, but really, they couldn't have been kinder.'

Katherine yawned, stretched and stood up. 'I don't doubt that you found them absolutely charming,' she remarked nastily. 'All the Challoners have perfect manners, if nothing else.'

Dora was too happy to be disconcerted by Katherine's snide remarks. 'Mr Challoner told me he was delighted that Ralph and I are engaged,' she said. 'And Mrs Challoner is going to have her pearls altered for me. She says that when I'm married I'm to have the rest of her jewels.'

'How very generous of her.' Katherine sniggered. 'Have you seen this valuable collection?' she enquired. 'It probably consists of three pairs of earrings and a ghastly old necklace or two.'

Dora ignored her cousin. 'He — Mr Challoner, that is — was saying how well he and my father always got on as boys,' she continued. 'And he doesn't doubt that in the end everything will be arranged to the satisfaction of us all.' Dora got up and walked about the room. 'Oh, Aunt!' she cried. 'I'm so happy!'

Katherine watched her. 'Well, that's all right then,' she muttered, brushing some crumbs from her creased skirt. 'I dare say, though, that it will come as quite a surprise to my uncle when he hears that old Challoner considers them to be friends.'

'What was that, Katherine?'

'Nothing.' Katherine walked over to the drawing room door. 'Good night.'

Dora's good humour was indestructible. She sat by the fire, watching it burn low, seeing in it pictures of her own bright future.

☆   ☆   ☆

Stephen spent a weekend at Ashton Cross, paid a call on his 'dear friend' Andrew Challoner, and returned to the manor house looking as black as the dismal winter afternoon. Dora, who had been testily informed by him that, whether she liked it or not, she was spending Christmas in Oxford, was inclined to be just as sour.

She sat opposite her father on the train, refusing even to look at him until they were rattling on through the Cotswolds. She answered his remarks in monosyllables and glared at him when he told her that Anthony and Miriam had promised to spend the holiday at the Summertown house.

'I had assumed that you would wish to see your brother and your best friend,' said Stephen, heavily. 'But it seems that I was mistaken.'

'No, indeed, Papa.' Dora looked out of the window at the bleak December countryside. 'You weren't mistaken. There's nothing I'd like better than to be surrounded by happy couples,' she muttered, just loudly enough for him to hear.

Stephen opened his case and took out a sheaf of papers upon which he began to scribble. He ignored his daughter the rest of the way to Oxford.

☆   ☆   ☆

'There's absolutely no point in trying to talk me out of it,

Mama.' Dora picked at the fringe of the tablecloth and glowered at her mother. 'You haven't even *seen* Ralph.'

'But Dora, your father thinks —'

'He's jealous, that's all it is. He doesn't like the idea of anyone marrying his daughters. Don't you remember what he was like when Anna and John were here together that first time? He shut himself up in his study, and he sulked for a fortnight.'

'Dora, he knows the Challoners and he doesn't consider this young man to be a suitable match for you.' Dorcas looked earnestly at her daughter. 'Why don't you invite Ralph here?' she asked. 'Then I could meet him, we could see —'

'Oh, Papa wouldn't allow that.' Dora bit her lower lip. 'He spent two minutes alone with Ralph, you know — they were together in the drawing room at Ashton Cross for a whole two minutes. Then Papa came out scowling and muttering to himself, and he wouldn't speak to anybody for the rest of the afternoon. Ralph was quite upset.'

'Why was that?'

'Oh, Ralph wouldn't say. Well, you know what Papa can be like. I expect he spoke to Ralph as if he were a first year undergraduate who'd been caught climbing into Somerville or something. So, you'll have to come to Hereford if you want to look Ralph over.'

'Oh, well, I'm not sure that I could do that —'

'Mama, you'll have to come for my wedding.' Dora grabbed at her mother's hand. 'You won't miss my wedding, will you?'

'There *is* going to be a wedding?'

'Of course there is!' Dora rose to her feet and walked about the drawing room. 'I'm going to ask my aunt if I can be married from Ashton Cross. I want everyone to come.'

'I see.'

Dora heard her father's footsteps in the hall. 'Can't you persuade him, Mama?' she asked, beseechingly. 'He's being so unreasonable.'

At that moment Stephen came into the drawing room. Dora gave him a bright smile and began to talk of something else. She was living for January the seventh, when she was due to return to Herefordshire.

On the evening before she was to go back to Ashton Cross, Stephen invited Dora into his study. He sat her down in an easy chair and took one opposite her himself.

Dora looked into the fire. She wasn't going to be lectured any more, she decided. He could talk to himself.

'Dora?'

'Yes, Papa?' She stared at the flames.

'Tell me honestly, child — what are your real feelings for Ralph Challoner?'

'I love him.' Still Dora looked into the fire. 'I've told you a thousand times. I love him.'

'You're certain that you do? He loves you?'

Dora looked up. 'I have every reason to think so.'

'What would you say if I told you that I consider this to be an unsuitable match, and I forbade you to think of Ralph Challoner any more?'

'I'm sure you wouldn't be so cruel, Papa.' Dora looked at him anxiously now, her resolution to be cold with him quite forgotten. 'And you'd be so very, very wrong!' she cried. 'I can't imagine that I shall ever meet anyone who will suit me as much as Ralph does.'

'I see. Dora, imagine yourself married to him. Now, you do realize how much damage you will do to yourself, and to others, if you *don't* love this fellow?'

Dora, hardly beginning to understand what Stephen meant, nodded. 'I know what you mean,' she replied. '*You* love my mother,' she added, hitting him well below the belt. 'And *I* love Ralph.'

'You do, do you?' Stephen reached across for her hand and began to chafe it in his. 'Dora, I must tell you this,' he said. 'I married a woman whom I hardly knew, and whom I certainly didn't love. It was a dreadful mistake, and it caused me — and many other people — a great deal of unhappiness. Do you feel that you know Ralph Challoner, do you know him through and through? Do you really understand him, do you know his nature? Dora, does he know *you*?'

'Of course he does!' Dora sighed. 'Oh, Papa, do we have to go through it all again? I love him. He loves me. Isn't that enough?'

'Perhaps it is.' Stephen rose to his feet. 'I suppose it will have to be. Well, I shall see Andrew Challoner again. We'll come to some arrangement.'

Dora could hardly contain her delight. 'Oh, *thank* you!' she cried. 'Oh, thank you, thank you, my dearest, darling Papa!' She threw her arms around his neck and kissed him, beaming with delight. 'You don't know Ralph very well yet,' she told him. 'When you understand him better, you'll like him. I know you will!'

'Perhaps I shall.' Stephen frowned. 'Well, Dora — we shall see, shan't we? We shall see.'

* * *

Invited, as seemed only polite, to dine at Ashton Cross, Ralph behaved with a degree of self-effacing courtesy which agreeably surprised the Lawrences assembled round the dining table. He fended off Katherine's sniping comments with polite good humour. He was civil to Dora's uncle, discussing fatstock breeding programmes with him for a good five minutes. And he was attentive and respectful towards Dora's aunt.

'He seems to have grown up into a nice enough lad,' remarked Henry Lawrence when Ralph had departed. 'Always was a bit shy, if I remember rightly.' He picked up his newspaper and began to read the agricultural news.

Katherine snorted. 'He's a two-faced hypocrite, Dad!' she cried. 'He's bewitched poor little Dora and now he's trying to get into your good books. He thinks he can get round anyone if he grins enough and agrees with every word that's said about black-faced sheep!'

Puzzled by this outburst of vehemence, Katherine's mother glanced up from her sewing. 'He seems to be very fond of Dora,' she observed. 'I think we should assume that he is as attached to her as he appears to be. Don't you agree, Henry?'

Henry Lawrence looked up from his farming gazetteer. 'Hey? Oh, young Challoner. He's sound enough at bottom, I imagine.' He grinned at his daughter. 'He was a bit of a tearaway as a boy,' he conceded. 'I'll grant you that. But we all have to grow up.'

Dora returned to the drawing room looking flushed and very happy, two spots of colour bright on her cheeks and her lips very red. 'Shall I send for some tea, Aunt?' she asked.

'No, dear, Katherine's already seen to that. We were just saying —'

'— how charming dear Ralph has suddenly become,' interrupted Katherine. 'He'll be going shooting with James next. He'll be riding with George and Alec. We'll just be one great big happy family!'

Dora shot Katherine a withering glance. 'I was hoping, Aunt, that I could be married from here,' she began diffidently.

'Well, of course you may, dear child!' Her aunt leaned across to where Dora sat and patted her hand. 'Of course you shall. It's hardly necessary to ask *my* permission. Oh, my dear girl, I'm so happy for you! So very happy!' She dabbed her eyes. 'You'll be the making of young Ralph,' she added. 'I'm quite sure of that.'

Katherine opened her mouth to speak, thought better of it and went off to bed, in disgust.

* * *

Mrs Challoner, a feeble, mouse-like woman, a chronic hypochondriac dominated by her husband and habitually ignored by her son, ventured to remark that she'd been favourably impressed by her daughter-in-law to be. 'I liked her,' she murmured, her once pretty face almost animated. 'She seemed so anxious to please, didn't she? And she's obviously very fond of dear Ralph.'

'Hmm.' Andrew Challoner nodded. 'She's an obliging little thing,' he agreed. 'Hardly the girl I'd have chosen, but there it is; the boy seems set on having her. She'll bring a bit of money with her, of course. Not as much as I'd have liked, though.'

He sighed. 'I can't expect Stephen to settle as much on his by-blows as he might have given to a legitimate child. But I'll get as much out of him as I can.'

'They do say that Stephen is devoted to Dora's mother.' Mrs Challoner nodded significantly at her husband. 'I think he must be, don't you? After all, it must be twenty years or more now since he — well, you know —'

Andrew Challoner drained a tumbler of brandy and filled his glass again. 'I imagine we can count on a few thousand for Miss Dora,' he said. 'And, if I keep my nerve when I talk to

Stephen next time, a good deal more besides.'

* * *

Although Dora was now considered a proficient enough rider to go out on Sorrel by herself, she and Ralph still took long walks together, retracing their steps over the same few miles of countryside, wandering up and down the same lanes, through the same woods.

One afternoon they sat on a stile looking across the frosty January meadows, talking. Or rather, Ralph talked and Dora listened.

'My father wants to leave the Grange,' Ralph told her. 'He has a small house in Cheltenham and the present tenant has, as it happens, just given notice. So it will be refurbished and made ready for them.' Ralph grinned at Dora. 'We shall have the old barn all to ourselves.'

'That will be lovely, Ralph.' Dora hugged his arm and kissed his cheek, rubbing her face against his. 'Oh, Ralph, I can't wait to be married! Can you?'

'I expect I shall manage to contain my impatience.' He pulled away from her. 'Don't cling to me like that,' he added, petulantly. 'It's rather annoying.'

'Sorry, Ralph.' Dora let him go. 'Shall we go for a walk?'

'Yes.' He slid off the stile. 'Come on — run!'

He streaked off ahead of her, stopping and turning round when he reached a boundary oak against which he leaned and waited for her. She came up to him panting, smiling her habitual beaming smile. She flopped against his chest. 'Oh,' she cried, breathless, 'you go far too fast for me!'

'You're so very slow.' He looked down at her feet. 'And you wear such silly shoes. I'm surprised that you can even walk in them, let alone run.'

'They're very pretty shoes!'

'Are they?'

Dora considered. 'Yes,' she replied, decidedly. 'Yes, they are.'

'I think they're hideous.' Stooping down suddenly, Ralph unfastened the buckles. 'Take them off,' he said. 'Now.'

'What?'

'Take them off. And your stockings!'

Dora giggled; the sight of Ralph kneeling at her feet had sent a sudden surge of the most deliciously erotic excitement coursing through her veins. She laid her hands upon his shoulders. 'You do it,' she murmured, into his hair. 'You take them off for me.'

So he did. He jerked off her shoes and pulled off her stockings; his hands warm on her bare legs, he grinned up at her. 'You look like the little match girl now,' he told her, as he stood up. 'Barefoot and shivering in the snow. I used to like that story.'

Dora hopped up and down on the frosty ground. 'Will you kiss me, Ralph?' she asked. 'Will you? Please?'

'If I do, will you walk home again without anything on your feet?'

She looked at him, her eyes wide, their pupils dilated with desire. 'I'd do anything for you,' she replied. 'Anything at all — you know that. Only please, will you kiss me?'

'Yes.' He took her in his arms and kissed her hard, crushing her against him. Then he picked up her shoes and flung them, one after the other, deep into a spinney.

He walked away. And Dora, laughing, ran after him.

* * *

The agricultural depression of the 1880s had hit Andrew Challoner hard. Mistaking the mood of the times, consistently taking the wrong decisions, he had ploughed up pasture and leys to turn the land over to arable crops, while the Lawrences had done the opposite, building up their dairy herds, making their stock of Hereford bulls the finest in the western shires.

Time had seen the estate at Ashton Cross show a steady increase in profit, while the Challoners did less well with each succeeding year.

The Challoners' estate was considerably larger than that of Ashton Cross. The land itself was better — the fields were well-drained and the soil fertile. But since the turn of the century, and well before that, England had been increasing her imports of food. Now, England's own farmers produced barely a third of the population's requirements. And Andrew Challoner, if he knew this, failed to benefit from the knowledge.

He still grew wheat, which he was unable to sell for a decent price. Saying that *he* was a gentleman, not a stock breeder, he could not be bothered to raise the cattle which would have done so well upon his land. And, most foolishly of all, he wasted money on game preservation, protecting pheasants which he did not shoot, looking after hares and rabbits at which, had they been served at *his* table, his fine gentleman's palate would have revolted. He bought horses he could not afford, and he bred them for the love of it, not for profit.

Finally, heavily in debt and faced with the prospect of selling off some of his best land, Andrew Challoner had approached Henry Lawrence and suggested the possibility of a deal. Henry, with his elder brother's consent, had advanced a loan of ten thousand pounds, the security being a wide tract of the best of the Challoners' pasture, which abutted the western perimeter of the Ashton Cross estate.

The years went by and Andrew Challoner fell further and further behind with his repayments. 'Damn them,' he told his wife. 'Let them wait for their money. I'm a neighbour, after all — a friend, even.'

But, in his heart, Andrew Challoner knew that he had to repay the debt; neighbour or not, Henry Lawrence would hold him to it and expect to be repaid, in one way or another, in the end.

The Challoners, therefore, needed to be wary about disobliging the Lawrences, who could now foreclose on the loan at any time. Over the past few years the Challoners had found it hard to lay their hands on the interest due, let alone make any repayments upon the capital sum. And Ralph Challoner was only too aware of this great black cloud which hung over his inheritance and which, if he married Dora Lawrence, might vanish as if it had never been.

So Dora was, in effect, to be the basis of a business transaction. She herself was not to find out about this for five or six years. Stephen, unwilling to exert what he had decided would be unfair pressure on his daughter, had told himself that it would be pointless to suggest to her that perhaps the Challoners were so desirous of this alliance because they hoped that, if Dora married Ralph, the debt might be cancelled. There was, after all, the possibility that Ralph Challoner really loved his pretty daughter. There seemed little doubt that Dora, always candid and ingenuous, loved *him* . . .

※　　※　　※

'We'll go into the estate office, I think.' Stephen and Henry, two stocky, grey-haired farmers, were well aware that beside *them* Andrew Challoner, tall, gentlemanly and for all his sixty years, still a very handsome man, looked like a true aristocrat flanked by a pair of lowering Welsh peasants. They led their visitor across the stable yard.

Spread out across the table were the ledgers and all the various documents connected with the loan. Andrew Challoner sat down and stared at the great mass of paper, then he laughed. 'You'd better explain to me what you have in mind,' he said, lightly, 'and then I'll tell you what I propose.'

Stephen, never one to prevaricate, sat down opposite his neighbour and clasped his hands together. 'Ralph wishes to marry Dora,' he said. 'You're happy that this wedding should take place?'

'Ah.' Andrew Challoner grinned. 'Your daughter is a charming girl, Stephen,' he replied. 'Quite charming. My wife and I are delighted with her. But there are, regrettably, certain — shall I say — impediments to be overcome. My dear fellow, I don't need to be brutal, do I? You know what I mean. The circumstances of Dora's birth —'

'You owe us a considerable amount of money.' Stephen looked levelly at Andrew Challoner. 'And so, although you are too well-bred to be frank with me, I shall be direct with you. Is there any possibility that the loan we advanced to you will ever be repaid?'

Andrew Challoner shrugged, let his eyelids droop as if he were in pain, or as if he had detected a particularly unpleasant smell. 'Well, Stephen,' he began, languidly. 'Things have not been easy for me this year. The price of corn —'

'Quite.' Stephen picked up a pen. 'It's as I thought. This, then, is what we suggest.'

Two hours and much haggling later, it was finally agreed that the repayments on the capital of Andrew Challoner's debt should be indefinitely deferred. That the interest due should be offset against Dora's marriage portion, which was to be five thousand pounds from her father over the course of the next ten years.

Stephen comforted himself with the thought that his grandchildren would one day own Andrew Challoner's estate.

Andrew Challoner congratulated himself on having, in effect, wiped out a debt simply because a providential fate had decreed that Stephen Lawrence's bastard daughter wouldn't be able to contain her desire to be tumbled by his handsome son.

* * *

'We've done it! We've got them just where we want them!' Andrew Challoner had arrived back at the Grange in a high good humour. He looked hard at his son. 'You won't touch the woman until you're married,' he rapped. 'Do you hear me, boy?'

Ralph shrugged, then almost imperceptibly, he nodded. 'Yes, I heard you.'

'Good.' His father grinned. 'Haven't had her already, have you?' he asked. 'God knows, you've had plenty of opportunity. And knowing the sort of stock she comes from, it wouldn't surprise me if —'

'I hope you don't seriously imagine I'd have done any such thing.' Ralph allowed a faint sneer to distort his fine features. 'I'm not like her father, you know,' he said, coldly. 'I *can* control myself.'

'I hope you can.' Andrew Challoner sat down and drew a sheaf of papers from his pocket. 'If we can get on with it now,' he murmured. 'If we can get the bloody Lawrences off our backs, there's a hope that you'll be able to make this place pay again. So don't spoil the whole show by rolling pretty Miss Dora in the hay and giving that tribe of usurers and debauchees any cause to back out of it now.'

Ralph lit a cigarette and blew smoke into the air. 'I've already told you,' he said, 'that there's no chance of my doing anything of the kind. So don't worry. I won't compound your stupidity with any of my own.'

* * *

Given formal approval for her plans and told that she might go ahead and arrange her wedding, Dora threw herself into a breathless round of preparations. She was so wrapped up in her own schemes and daydreams that she failed to notice that her prospective husband was hardly as enthusiastic about their future together as she was. Dora was in a world of her own.

Chapter Nine

THE DAY OF THE WEDDING dawned hot and cloudless, a perfect July morning apparently made to order for the happiest day of Dora's life — for so she intended this day to be.

'Katherine!' Dora, who had been awake since four o'clock, knocked upon her cousin's bedroom door. 'Katherine? Are you up?' Opening the door, she went in and found Katherine in bed. She was still, apparently, fast asleep. Dora pushed her cousin's shoulder. 'Katherine! Oh, *do* wake up.'

'What time is it?' Pushing a strand of hair out of her eyes, Katherine raised herself on one elbow. 'Five o'clock? Six?'

'Seven.' Dora drew back the curtains. 'Look! It's a beautiful day.'

Katherine blinked. 'So it is. Just what you ordered, eh?'

Later that morning Katherine smoothed the satin of the wedding dress, then adjusted Dora's veil. Pinning on a small spray of orange blossom and arranging the delicate white flowers so that they lay neatly against Dora's temples, Katherine stood back to admire her handiwork. 'Lovely,' she said, at last. 'Beautiful. Much too good for him,' she added, just loudly enough for Dora to hear.

'Katherine!' Dora shook her head at her cousin. 'Now, don't spoil everything for me. Wish me happiness, can't you?'

'Mmm. Dolly, I wish you — the best.' Katherine bit her lower lip. 'Yes, that's it. I wish you the best.'

'Thank you.' Dora looked at her cousin. 'Katherine, is there anything I ought to know?' she asked lightly. 'About Ralph, I mean. Over the past few months you've dropped so many hints, you've muttered to yourself about him, you've made some very nasty remarks to me. Is there anything —'

'No, Dolly.' Katherine turned away from Dora and looked into the mirror. 'No, there's nothing. Really, there's nothing at all.' She turned round again, took Dora's hands in hers, then kissed her. 'And I don't see how any man, looking at you, could do anything but love you . . .'

* * *

Dora's family was large; the Henry Lawrences alone almost filled the bride's side of the church. Resplendent in their best clothes, their dark good looks offset by their wedding finery, they smiled and nodded to each other, commented on the weather and remarked what a splendid day it was.

The Challoners, on the other hand, barely filled one pew. Ralph's immediate family, and half a dozen of his sporting companions, together with their wives, accounted for the bridegroom's side.

Stephen handed his daughter to Ralph Challoner with a reluctance which was almost tangible, but Dora was too happy to notice how gloomy her father was. She almost sang her responses. 'Oh, I do!' she'd wanted to cry. 'Yes, yes, I do!' She beamed at the clergyman, smiled ecstatically at Ralph and when he kissed her, she dropped her flowers and flung her arms around him, hugging him in real earnest. As she came out of the little church and into the sunshine, she knew that she would never be so happy again.

As the only one of her parents' three illegitimate children to marry from the ancestral home and to have a traditional church wedding, Dora meant to enjoy the rest of the day as much as she possibly could, and to see that her guests did as well.

The wedding breakfast, laid out in the elegant drawing room of the manor house, was splendid, and her uncle's family made a tremendous effort to ensure that every one of the guests had a good time. So Dora was somewhat distressed to observe that her mother was obviously ill at ease, to notice that her father's mouth was still set in a tight, hard line, and to see that her brother and sister looked almost as sour as Stephen did.

John Harley, however, made a little more effort to be

convivial. He chatted to Ralph for a few minutes, then came through the assembled throng to give Dora his congratulations, detaching her from her mother-in-law and leading her away to a quiet corner of the room. 'I wish you every happiness, my dear little sister,' he said. He kissed her. 'I'm sure you *will* be happy,' he added. 'Challoner seems a pleasant sort of fellow.'

'Thank you, John. I'm glad *you* think so.' Dora glanced across to where her parents stood in grim isolation with her brother and sister. 'Mama says she intends to go back to Oxford on the six o'clock train,' Dora told her brother-in-law. 'Aunt Katherine's prepared a room for her, but she won't even consider staying the night. And she and Papa barely arrived in time for the service as it was.'

'Well, Dora —'

'John, just look at them! You'd think they were at a funeral, not a wedding. I wish they'd at least make a pretence of enjoying themselves. It's not much to ask, is it, that they should speak to my husband and his parents, should mix a little with the other guests? Do you know, Papa refused point blank to make a speech. He said it wasn't necessary. And you know how much he likes the sound of his own voice.'

John patted Dora's hand. 'I'll go and make Anna circulate,' he said. 'I'm not sure I can do anything with the others. Your father is in one of his moods; he's daring one of these bumpkin squireens here to go up and say something insulting to your mother, although any fool could see it would take a braver man than any in this room to do that! And your mother's terrified, poor thing. Look how white she is; look at the way she's clutching Anthony's arm.'

Dora looked, and saw how tense and pale her mother was. 'I'll introduce her to Aunt Katherine,' she said. 'No one could be afraid of Aunt Katherine. If I go and detach her from Ralph's mother, will you bring Mama over to meet her?'

'Certainly. In fact, I'll do better than that.' John walked across to his wife and in-laws. 'Come and talk to your sister's new family,' he said to Anna, holding out his arm to her. 'They are all very anxious to make your acquaintance.'

'Are they?' Anna frowned at him. But she took his arm all the same, and permitted her husband to direct her towards the

Challoners. 'I can't think why,' she muttered. 'I can't think they'd have anything to say to *me*.'

'You'll be surprised. Ah, Dorcas — here comes Dora's aunt.'

Dorcas, safe between Stephen and Anthony, allowed herself to be introduced to Henry Lawrence's wife. 'I must congratulate you upon having such a sweet daughter,' said Mrs Lawrence. 'Dora's a charming girl. We've all become so fond of her.'

Dorcas allowed herself a faint smile of acknowledgement. But her grip on Stephen's arm tightened, and it was obvious to Katherine Lawrence that Stephen's mistress — such a pretty, nicely-dressed and reserved little woman, not at all what she'd expected — was wishing herself anywhere but at Ashton Cross.

Dora led her brother away to another part of the room. 'I do wish you'd cheer up,' she said. 'You look almost as gloomy as Papa. And why are you all in black? You and he look just like a pair of undertaker's mutes!'

Anthony laughed, revealing white teeth in his dark face. 'I'm sorry, Dolly,' he replied. 'But I hate all this kind of thing. I only came to please you. It is my *best* black,' he added humbly. 'You know I never was a peacock — not like your handsome husband.'

'He *is* handsome, isn't he? Oh, Anthony — I do hope you like him.'

'I've only said two words to him. He seems — well, he seems a well-set-up sort of fellow. And he knows it.'

'What's that supposed to mean?'

'He seems very sure of himself, very much aware of his own beauty and cleverness.'

'He's really quite shy. If he seems a little overbearing, that's because he's nervous.'

'Ah, I see. Then I make allowances. Dora, will we see you both in Cambridge soon? Miriam's dying to show off the baby.'

'I'm dying to see him. Why didn't she come today?'

'It's a long journey there and back in a day. And it *is* only a month since she had Jonathan.'

'You could have stayed here, you know. They'd have been glad to have you.'

'Yes, Uncle Henry's family seem a pleasant crowd.' Anthony shrugged apologetically. 'Well, it can't be helped now. I shall go back to Oxford with the parents.'

Dora shook her head at him. 'Shall I be Jonathan's godmother?' she asked.

'Oh, no.' Anthony laughed. 'Nothing like that.'

'Of course, I forgot you're a pair of heathens. Well, I shall send him a present anyway. Not a Bible. Oh, Anthony — I'm so happy!'

'Good for you, Doll. I hope he deserves you.'

'I don't deserve *him*. Oh, look! My mother is smiling. Whatever can Aunt Katherine have said?'

'And look at Papa. He's smiling too. Well — almost.'

'Wonders will never cease. And here comes Ralph.' Dora looked from her brother to her husband, at the two men in the world most dear to her, and she willed them to be friends. 'Did Anthony tell you he's living in Cambridge?' she asked Ralph, hoping that her brother might begin a conversation.

'No, he didn't.' Ralph eyed Anthony as unenthusiastically as he might have looked at a particularly mangy foxhound which its owner was entreating him to buy. 'What's he doing there?'

'I'm a lecturer,' replied Anthony. 'At King's.'

'Really.' Ralph yawned. 'So now there's a veritable dynasty of schoolmasters in your family. Dora, look — I must go and speak to my father.'

'Must you?'

'I must.' Ralph detached Dora's arm from his sleeve and looked Anthony up and down. 'What's that on your jacket?' he asked. 'That white smudge? Chalk?' And Dora's husband strolled away.

Embarrassed, Dora looked after him. 'Just his joke,' she murmured, anxiously. She touched her brother's arm. 'Anthony, don't look so cross.'

Anthony grinned. 'I'm not cross.' He looked at his hands. 'I've ink on my fingers, too,' he added, wryly. 'Oh dear! Dora, I've let you down badly, haven't I?'

* * *

Thinking about it afterwards, Dora reflected that wedding

nights are probably an embarrassment for most couples, so she tried to be philosophical about the fact that hers had been a bitter disappointment to her.

She'd felt such a complete failure. She, of course, had been ignorant. Ralph, whom she had assumed would be careful with her, had been clumsy and rough.

He'd appeared to be in such a hurry. Once started, he went on relentlessly, seemingly oblivious of her evident pain. He'd pushed and forced his way inside her, causing her almost unbearable agony. Then at last, when he'd seemed satisfied with himself, he'd rolled back on to his pillows, breathing heavily and smiling contentedly.

A few moments later, he sat up. Noticing the blood on the sheets, he reached across and touched it, as if to confirm that it was really there. He licked his fingers, then grinned at his wife. 'Did I hurt you?' he asked.

'Only a little.' Dora assumed that he had not meant to cause her distress and would be sorry if he knew just how much he'd upset her.

'Liar.' Ralph's grin became broader. 'Your teeth were clenched and your face was white.'

'It *did* hurt.' Dora looked away from him. 'But only a little,' she repeated.

'You're stoical, my dear wife. You'll be the mother of heroes, I can see.' Ralph touched Dora's shoulder and pulled her round to face him. He looked at her, surveying the marks his teeth had made on her neck and the red blotches on her arms and chest which would, tomorrow, be purple bruises. He nodded with satisfaction. 'We'll try again, shall we?' he asked. 'You might as well get used to it, after all.'

That second time, it was not quite so bad.

* * *

Dora knew, as soon as she saw him, that her husband's valet would be her enemy. Alfred Crawley hated her on sight. He had welcomed her to the Grange politely enough, but she could feel his dislike lapping over her in a nauseous tide.

He was a hideous little man — ape-like and wizened, of indeterminate age. A few wisps of gingerish hair still adhered to his almost bald skull, but much more of it grew from his nostrils, protruded from his ears and escaped from the immaculate white cuffs at his bony wrists. Bow-legged and stooping, he was crab-like in his movements and as silent and creeping as a spider.

Dora made up her mind that he would have to go; he made her uncomfortable and spoiled the otherwise perfect bliss of her married life. She decided that she would speak to Ralph about him.

So Crawley was the cause of their first quarrel. 'I won't dismiss him,' said Ralph, firmly. 'He's not only my valet — he runs the household, and damned efficiently, too.'

'I'd prefer to have a female housekeeper, Ralph.' Dora snuggled up against her husband. 'Look, I'm not asking you to throw him out of the house just like that. He must be near the age when he'd want to think about retiring, anyway. How old *is* he?'

'About fifty-five, I think. But he's always looked as he does now — sort of dessicated. He'll look the same when he's eighty.' Ralph, who was sitting next to Dora on the drawing room sofa, pulled her into his arms and, jerking her head back, kissed her on the mouth. 'What don't you like about old Crawley, then?' he asked a minute later.

Dora, feeling the familiar excitement beginning to tremble inside her, wrapped her arms around her husband. 'He stares at me,' she murmured. 'And he doesn't like me.'

'That's nonsense.' Ralph grinned at his wife. 'He probably likes you too much. Poor Crawley — he's devoted to me, you know; always has been, ever since I was a child. I expect he's jealous of you. And he's jealous of me, being married to such a lovely creature.'

Assuming that Ralph was softening now, Dora giggled and allowed him to bite the lobe of her ear. She stroked his hair. 'Please, dear Ralph,' she whispered. 'Please, won't you give him notice?'

'No, I shan't.'

'But why? I've told you he annoys me. Please, darling,' she wheedled. 'Tell him he must go. Just to please me?'

Suddenly, Ralph stopped caressing her. He sat up straight and looked Dora full in the face. 'Don't you *dare* talk to me like that,' he snapped. He caught her chin and pushed her head right back, hurting her. 'Don't think you can get round me by purring like a cat, by rubbing yourself up against me like a whore. Listen to me, Dora. I am the master in this house. I hire my servants. I take no account of whether or not you happen to find their personalities pleasing. Do you understand?'

Dora, surprised and upset, pushed his hand away and rubbed her bruised face. Tears stood in her eyes now but then anger came to her rescue, bubbling to the surface like a boiling spring. She stood up. '*I* am the mistress here!' she cried. 'The running of this household is my responsibility now, not yours or Crawley's. If you won't allow me to manage my servants as I think fit, I shall walk out of this house now. I shall not come back.'

'Go, then.'

'What?'

'You heard me.' Ralph looked up at the ceiling. 'Go, if you wish. I shan't stop you.'

Her bluff called, Dora was now in a quandary. Pride would not allow her to admit defeat, but she could hardly leave the Grange and walk through the night to — where? To Ashton Cross? To explain herself how? She knew she was beaten. 'I'm going to bed,' she said sulkily. 'In the morning I shall tell Crawley that he must leave.'

Ralph was at the door before she reached it. He caught her arm and twisted it behind her. 'You will do no such thing,' he said, softly. 'Will you, Dora?'

'I shall!'

He pushed her elbow into the small of her back. 'No, you won't,' he told her. 'You will promise me that you won't. Otherwise, I may be obliged to break your arm.' And he wrenched it again, making Dora wince.

But then she rallied. She trod sharply on his foot. Digging her high heel into his flesh, she scraped it backwards up his shin, causing him to cry out in astonishment and pain.

'Little bitch!' Momentarily, he let her go, then pulled her round to face him; but, with her good arm, she elbowed him in the stomach, winding him. She jerked open the door and ran upstairs.

To her surprise, he did not follow her. He slept that night in one of the spare rooms. At breakfast the next morning he behaved as if nothing unpleasant had happened, and kissed Dora affectionately before he went out to meet his land agent.

And Crawley stayed.

Dora meant to make a success of her marriage — she was determined to work at it. She decided to forget the quarrel. Crawley was, after all, only a servant — he could not harm her. And she imagined how annoyed *she* would have been had Ralph demanded that Dora dismiss her own maid, Mrs Johnson, simply because he did not like her face.

She decided that the best thing to do would be to make Crawley's life so difficult for him that he might be glad to give notice soon. 'And any other domestics,' she decided, 'I shall hire myself.'

But however much work she piled upon Crawley's sloping shoulders, however unreasonable her demands, however rude she was to him, the valet bore his cross without murmuring. He was, as Ralph had said, devoted to his master, whom he considered to be a perfect man. His soft, brown, spaniel eyes melted when he looked at Ralph, and his sugary pink mouth — such a nasty, effeminate kind of a mouth on a man — would hang open. Dora almost expected his tongue to come lolling out.

Dora and Crawley settled down to a long war of attrition. Neither willing to concede defeat, they both dug in, and waited.

* * *

Firmly convinced that she could change her husband for the better, six months of marriage having opened her eyes to the fact that Ralph did indeed have some faults, Dora tried hard to understand him, and in understanding him, to improve him.

But here she was at the mercy of her own ingenuous, candid nature. She mistook her husband's innate viciousness for awkwardness, shyness, insecurity — for almost anything but what it was. And she was for a long time optimistic about her chances of success.

She had, after all, first-hand evidence in her own family that a loving partner could ameliorate the most unbending temper. She had observed the soothing effect John Harley had upon

Anna's habitual sharpness. 'And Mama can manage my father; she can even cajole him out of his worst rages,' she said to herself. 'Ralph is nothing like as surly, irritable and unreasonable as Papa can be.'

Summer became autumn, which turned to winter. 'You're not going out today, are you?' asked Dora sleepily, looking out at a freezing morning which was blowing a tempest and threatening sleet. 'Why don't you come back to bed for an hour or two?'

But Ralph was already up and getting into his riding clothes. 'Of course I'm going out,' he replied. 'There's a vixen up in Denton's Copse who's been doing God knows how much damage to the coverts there, and today I'm going to see that Madam gets it. You ought to come too,' he added, grinning at Dora's drowsy face. 'You could blow the cobwebs out of your hair.'

'I'd more likely catch double pneumonia. I can't think why you don't.' And, turning over, Dora went back to sleep.

Ralph lived for hunting. Two or three times a week now he was up before five, dressed, breakfasted and ready to go. Dora, whose distaste for hunting had been ineradicably fixed by her first experience of it, would not see him until he returned late in the afternoon. He would come striding into the house, soaked with sweat, splattered from head to foot with mud, sometimes bloodstained, usually exhilarated. On the other hand, if anything had gone wrong, he would be in the foulest of foul tempers...

So, when he broke his right leg, shattering the femur, this was a tragedy for him. He cursed his own stupidity for taking an impossible jump, cursed the tree for being in the wrong place, cursed his horse for letting him urge it on to attempt something as hopeless as that high hedge on the boundary of a waterlogged field. His pride was almost as badly damaged as his shocked, bruised, broken body.

He was determined to be riding again within six months. His courage impressed Dora. White with pain, he would nonetheless rest his weight on his injured leg and force himself to walk around the house, up and down stairs, for hours at a time. Later he made himself get on horseback, levering himself into the saddle, his face a mask of agony. Then he would jump around the paddock, his teeth gritted and his face ashen as each jolt sent a fresh spurt of pain through his body.

He got through the summer and looked forward to hunting again in the autumn. 'Of course I shall,' he had replied when Dora asked him if he really meant to hunt that year. 'There's nothing at all wrong with me now. Don't make such a fuss.'

But, in the end, he had to give up hunting for the season. Coming home at the end of each meet looking like a revived corpse, his face blanched and strained, he was at last obliged to admit that he was perhaps not quite fit enough to withstand the rigours of the field — just yet . . .

The fact that one day he had fainted while out on a hunt was so wounding to his pride that he spoke to no one for a week. 'You must rest for the remainder of the winter.' Ralph's doctor, a large, red-faced Scotsman, who was a foxhunting man himself, was absolutely firm. 'If you don't, you'll end up a cripple. Do you hear me, Challoner?'

'I heard you.' Ralph glared at his medical adviser. 'Look, MacAndrew, there's no need to rub it in.'

'You'll do as I tell you?'

'Haven't much bloody choice, have I? Not with you in the North Ashton as well.' He scowled. 'Get us both a whisky, will you?'

For a while it was a charm and a novelty to have her own establishment. Dora played house quite happily for a year or two, making life as comfortable for herself as she could. She failed to dislodge Crawley, which annoyed her. She made his life a misery but he paid her back in kind, by arranging for there to be no hot water when she wanted a bath, by telling callers that she was out when she was, in fact, at home, by accidentally emptying a potful of scalding coffee over a favourite rug . . .

In the end, all this became quite an enjoyable little game for them both. Crawley was gratified to observe the displeasure on his mistress's face when he removed the lid from a serving dish to offer her the chicken she had *not* ordered. She, in turn, was entertained to see his glower if she authorized a holiday for a housemaid without first advising him.

'Sarah is missing, Madam,' he informed Dora one morning, pursing his horrible pink mouth in irritation. 'I can't think where she can have got to.'

'Oh, Crawley — I forgot to tell you.' Dora turned from her writing desk and favoured the valet with a brilliant smile. 'Sarah's sister is getting married on Saturday,' she continued. 'So I told her that she could go over to Ledbury for the wedding. She's coming back on Sunday evening.'

'Sunday!' Crawley's face became thunderous. 'Madam, she can't be spared until Sunday.'

'She can.' Dora stood up. 'Oh, don't make such a fuss,' she added, sweeping from the room, as good as brushing Crawley aside as she went through the door.

Crawley glared after her. Seeing that the drawer of Dora's writing desk was still open, and that the key was in the lock, he removed the key and slipped it into his pocket. He'd take an impression of it later. Access to Mrs Challoner's private papers might be useful to him some day.

Dora failed to appreciate that she was thus gradually turning a passive rival into a determined enemy. Crawley had a vindictive, spiteful nature which Dora did not fathom and for which she made no allowances. He stored up his hatred for her, letting it ferment into a rich, green brew which he would pour out, hot and steaming, into Ralph Challoner's ear when the time came.

Crawley already had a store of useful information. Having lived in Herefordshire all his life, and been in the Challoners' service for forty years or more, he knew all about Dora's mother.

When all that business had blown up, he'd read the newspapers. He knew that Mrs Hitchman — as she should properly be called — had been married to the murderer. And he had reason to believe that his master, while fully aware of his father-in-law's background, knew nothing of his mother-in-law's past life in Hereford. Young Ralph had been away at school when all that scandal had been splashed over the local press. The information he could give his master on the subject might be very acceptable one day.

*   *   *

Dora visited Ashton Cross regularly, giving no one there any reason to suspect that she was at all dissatisfied with her married life. A certain desperate gaiety about her made Katherine suspicious but no one else seemed to imagine that she was anything other than content.

'You get bonnier as you grow older, my dear,' her aunt had remarked as she and Dora sat in the drawing room at Ashton Cross one afternoon drinking tea together. She sighed comfortably. 'You were quite right to marry Ralph, you know,' she added. 'You've been the salvation of that young man; he's so polite these days, so charming and considerate. And he was so wild once. Dora, my dear, is there any sign of a baby yet?'

'I'm afraid not, Aunt. But I'm sure there will be one of these days.'

'I hope so, Dora. It's time you thought about a family. Now, I really must speak to you about Christmas. Are you going over to Cheltenham this year? Or will the two of you come over to us at the manor house? We'd love to have you, you know.'

'I — I'm not sure what Ralph has in mind.' Dora found these occasions of family togetherness, when she and Ralph were under the relentless scrutiny of all the Lawrences, particularly trying. 'I'll speak to Ralph,' she promised. 'I'll let you know.'

Dora could not help but observe that Ralph Challoner's methods of estate management differed from her uncle's, and she was determined to give him the benefit of her good advice. 'My father gave up game preservation when he inherited,' she remarked one day. 'Why do you employ so many keepers? I think it would be a good idea if you gave up keeping those coverts, all stocked with pheasants which nobody shoots. It's a terrible waste of money. And why do you always insist on a prosecution if a tenant takes a rabbit or a bird? It's not as if you take a gun out yourself these days.'

This, had Dora bothered to consider it, was hardly the most tactful way in which to approach a man who had curtailed his shooting as reluctantly and, he hoped, as temporarily as his riding. 'It's no concern of yours whether I employ one keeper or fifty,' he replied. 'What has your uncle been saying to you?'

'Nothing. But James did once remark that those traps you use are illegal. You could be prosecuted yourself if a man was caught in one, you know.' Ignoring the glare which now darkened Ralph's features, Dora looked at him earnestly. 'Why don't you consider giving up game altogether, and buy some dairy cattle instead?' she asked. 'They'd be far more profitable, after all. My uncle would be glad to advise you, I'm sure of it.'

'I don't doubt it.' Ralph scowled at his wife. 'Nothing would give Henry Lawrence more pleasure than to come and lay down the law to me.' He took Dora's hand and shook it, pinching her fingers and making her wince.

'Listen to me, you little simpleton,' he muttered. 'I am a gentleman. My family has owned this land for eight hundred years. There were Challoners here when the Lawrences were nothing but a pack of Welsh hill farmers scratching a living from a few barren mountains over in the west. I don't see things in terms of profit and loss. I'm not a money-grubbing farmer with straw in his hair and dirt under his fingernails. I live as my ancestors did, on the rents of my lands, and I shall continue to do so.'

'Then you're a fool.' retorted Dora, wrenching her hand from his grasp and flexing her crushed fingers. 'My uncle said you'd be bankrupt in a few years unless you woke up to the fact that we're now in the twentieth century, not the Middle Ages.'

'Did he now? What does he know about it, the interfering old idiot?'

'Don't be so rude! Listen, Ralph — if you'd only profit from his advice, you'd be a far more successful farmer than you are now. Don't you care about your tenants? Don't you feel that it's your responsibility to see that your labourers are in work and your land made to produce as much as it can?'

'All that is my land agent's concern, not mine.' Ralph leaned across the sofa and laid his hand upon Dora's shoulder, gripping through to the bone. 'Are you coming to bed?' he asked, his eyes bright.

Dora looked at him. Such a question would, only a matter of months ago, have produced an unequivocal affirmative; the very idea of being in bed with her husband had then been sufficient to make her heart thump and her mouth water. He might have hurt her but he'd also excited her and made her whole body melt with desire for him. His very smile, that wolf's grin, had been enough to make her shudder with delight.

But now, seeing him grin at her, feeling his hard fingers biting into her flesh, she didn't want him at all. She didn't know why, but there it was. Perhaps being scratched, bruised and bitten didn't appeal to her any more. 'No, not just yet,' she replied. 'I think I'll stay down here for a while longer and read a book. Could you let go of my shoulder, Ralph?' she added, crossly. 'It hurts when you pinch me like that.'

Things between Ralph and Dora came to a head when she heard that Ralph's land agent, a sour-faced individual whose favourite pastime seemed to be nailing live squirrels and moles to fences, as examples to their kind, had served notice to quit on an indigent tenant family who were behind with their rent.

'You can't just evict them.' Dora, whose personal maid had told her all about the family concerned, glared at Ralph. 'Mrs Morris is ill. And it's the middle of winter — you can't just turn them out into the cold.'

'I can do as I please.' Ralph grinned at Dora. 'They withhold their rent, so I shall evict them from my property. It's quite simple.'

Dora stared and was about to retort, but then she realized that there was no point in wasting her breath. The following morning she had her pony brought round and rode the three miles to the Morris's cottage, where she spoke to the tenants.

'I told Mr Morris that he can stay in his cottage for the time being,' she told Ralph when he and she met for dinner that evening.

'You did *what*?' Dropping his napkin, he stared at her. 'What did you say?'

'Are you going deaf, Ralph?' Calmly, Dora laid her napkin on her lap. 'I went to see Mr and Mrs Morris. I told them that they could stay in their cottage until spring.' Dora began to butter a roll. 'The poor man told me that he has had no work for seven weeks now,' she continued. 'So I've instructed Kirkman to find him something to do in the stables on Monday. And I've sent some food over to keep them going until the man gets his first wages.'

Ralph's face turned from white to scarlet, then became ashen again. Dora felt her legs growing weak. She shrank against the back of her chair, wondering if it might be a good idea to escape now.

'So you see yourself as the virtuous lady of the manor, do you?' asked Ralph nastily. 'While I, no doubt, am cast as the wicked squire, who turns the peasants out into the snow?'

Dora tore up her bread. 'The woman has consumption, Ralph,' she replied. 'She'll be dead by next summer. There are seven children in that cottage — if you can call it a cottage. It's a hovel with a dirt floor.'

She leaned towards him and met his eyes. 'My uncle would never let his property get into such a state,' she said, angry now. 'I'm almost ashamed to be the wife of a landlord who can treat his tenants so shabbily, who can disregard human suffering so callously, who seems to have no compassion at all. My uncle —'

'Oh, yes, your uncle!' Ralph's face twisted into a sneer. 'Your precious uncle — and his whoremongering brother — they're bright examples of model bloody landlords, aren't they? They've never evicted anyone in their lives, have they? If a blackguard won't pay his rent, your marvellous uncle says, "Never mind, old chap — pay when you can. This is the Garden of Eden, after all!" Huh!'

'My uncle gives his labourers decent wages so they can afford to pay their rent. He makes sure they have work throughout the winter so they're never unemployed and starving.'

'Oh, shut up, Dora.' Ralph narrowed his eyes at his wife. 'You don't know the first thing about estate management. And you've sentimental ideas about the peasants. They're just a parcel of idle, drunken, shiftless layabouts. They like living in squalor.'

'Rubbish, Ralph! That's absolute nonsense. On my father's estate —'

'Oh, for God's sake, Dora! My uncle this, my father that. I don't give a damn what your sainted relations do at bloody Ashton Cross. *I* am the landlord here, not you. And my agent will do as I tell him.'

Ralph pushed his soup plate aside. 'Now that you've told the malingering Morrises they can stay, we'll leave them there,' he muttered. 'But Dora —'

'Yes?'

'If you interfere once more in the running of this estate, I'll make you sorry for it. I warn you — I won't tolerate any further charity work by you at my expense.'

Dora was about to retort when the door opened and Crawley entered, bearing a tray. He set out an array of dishes and retired noiselessly, a smirk on his face. Dora and Ralph finished their meal in silence.

Later, as she and Ralph sat in the drawing room, Dora watched her husband from behind the book she was pretending to read. He lay back on the sofa, smoking, obviously thinking about something.

'I think we'll have them out, after all,' he announced, suddenly. 'She's tubercular, you say. Well, she can go to the workhouse infirmary then, and the brats can go with her. I dare say the man can take himself off somewhere and not bother me.'

Dora stared at him, hardly able to believe her ears. 'You mean that?' she demanded, incredulous.

Ralph grinned. 'Certainly I do. It's the best thing to be done, after all.'

Seeing him grin like that, Dora's self-control gave way completely. 'God in Heaven,' she cried, 'you're horrible!' She glared at him, furious now and red in the face — all sense of personal preservation was lost in her anger. 'You're stupid, you're cruel and you're vindictive,' she continued. 'It's just as James says — your labourers are paid starvation wages and go in fear of the workhouse. Your tenants live in daily terror of eviction. It's no wonder if they're idle. To whom do they owe any loyalty? Why should they work hard for *you*?'

Ralph, momentarily stunned by such an outburst, stared at his wife. Then, slowly, deliberately, he stubbed out his cigarette. 'Shut up, Dora,' he muttered. 'Shut up! I give you fair warning.' He rose to his feet and walked over to where she sat. Taking her by the shoulders, he pulled her out of her chair and shook her. 'I won't have you talking to me like this,' he muttered, through clenched teeth. 'Do you hear me?'

'Let me go.' Dora, trembling with anger, tried to wriggle free. 'Let me go, Ralph!' She kicked his ankle, and trod on his foot. 'Let me go!'

'Bitch.' Ralph looked into her eyes. 'I should thrash you,' he said, icily. 'I should give you a hiding. I should teach you a little respect for your husband.'

'You wouldn't dare.' Dora kicked him again. 'You great coward, if you so much as lay a finger on me, I'll tell my cousins. They'll half kill you if you hurt me.'

'Your cousins!' Ralph laughed. 'They're not here now, are they? They can't protect you when they're three or four miles away.' He shook her again. 'Shall I show you who's the master here, Dora?' he asked, softly. 'Shall I show you what happens to upstarts who don't know how to conduct themselves towards their betters?'

'My betters!' Dora spat into his face. 'Ralph, you're a wretch. Nothing but a wretch.'

Ralph stared at her. He saw the absolute contempt in her eyes and, suddenly, all the bravado drained from his own expression. He pushed her away from him with such violence that she fell heavily and lay in a sprawling heap in the corner of the drawing room.

Crawley, bringing in the coffee, was knocked flying as Ralph tore off down the hallway and out of the house.

Chapter Ten

DORA INFORMED RALPH THAT IT was high time she visited Anthony in Cambridge and she asked him if he would like to go with her. 'I mean to go anyway,' she said, 'but I'm sure they'd be pleased to see us both.'

'Why should I wish to go to Cambridge?' Ralph had not even looked up from his newspaper. 'Your schoolmaster brother and his Hebrew bride have no attraction for me.'

'Then I shall go by myself.'

'Do as you wish.' Ralph gave a great yawn and threw the paper on to the floor. 'I shall have some people over for a shoot.'

'Then you'll be filling all the larders with rotting carcases. I'm glad I shall be away.'

Ralph laughed. 'And I'll be glad you're not here. You don't take to Fred Garret, do you?'

'No, I don't.' Dora thought of Ralph's favourite sporting crony, a big, red-faced, bachelor landowner who lived in utter squalor in a crumbling country house a few miles from Ashton Cross. Fred Garret was a dirty, uncouth individual who always seemed to smell of blood. In his filthy jackets and stained breeches he looked more like an impoverished eighteenth-century squire than a modern farmer.

'What don't you like about him?' enquired Ralph.

Dora grimaced. 'I can't bear him, that's all,' she replied, folding her letter to Miriam. 'He stares at me so.'

'Ah, that's because he lusts after you.' Ralph grinned. 'He'd like to ravish you. His idea of paradise would be Dora

Challoner gone to earth in a haystack, her clothes ripped to ribbons, her hair —'

'Don't be so disgusting, Ralph.' Dora stood up and walked past Ralph's chair. 'How do *you* know, anyway?'

'He told me. The last time we were drunk together, he couldn't talk of anything but you.' Ralph rolled his eyes. 'Do you know, Dora, it's an exciting idea. Perhaps we could organize something — for old Fred's birthday, maybe. I dare say we could find a way of obliging you to co-operate.'

'Oh, shut up.' Dora walked out of the room and slammed the door behind her.

* * *

Dora arrived in Cambridge alone. She made excuses for Ralph, telling Anthony that her husband was too busy to visit just then, but that he sent his good wishes. 'Ralph says,' she added, 'that he hopes you are all well and that the children are thriving.'

'How very civil of him,' observed Anthony, grinning at his sister. 'His manners must have improved beyond recognition if he really said that.'

Miriam's little boy Jonathan, a bright, engaging child as dark as his parents, delighted his aunt. Looking at him, Dora felt a pang of regret, a longing for a baby of her own. But then she imagined Ralph's fury unleashed on a small child and wondered if her failure to conceive was providential after all.

Anthony had become a complete replica of his father, both in face and figure. By adopting Stephen's ferocious scowl he could send Jonathan into fits of giggles. Frequently, Anthony's son lay on the floor of the drawing room absolutely helpless with laughter. 'Be Grandpa, Daddy!' he would cry. 'Be Grandpa again! Growl at me!'

So Anthony would. And then Jonathan himself would stand up and give a creditable imitation of his grandfather's baleful glare. 'Where are my spectacles?' he would mutter, hands behind his back as he stared around him. 'Dorcas, have you seen my dictionary?'

'You shouldn't encourage him to make fun of Papa.' Finding her brother and her nephew at this game yet again, Dora looked reproachfully at Anthony who frowned at her.

'What was that Dora?' he demanded gruffly. 'Go down on your knees when you address the Regius Professor!' He blinked at her, peering shortsightedly just as his father did. 'What did you say?'

'I said, don't sneer at your father. It's not funny.'

'Oh, don't be so stuffy.' Anthony swept his son into his arms and tickled him. 'Papa wouldn't care,' he added, in a tone of voice which suggested that Anthony wouldn't be at all bothered if Stephen *did* object to such mockery.

Dora frowned at him. She wondered why Anthony was so set on distancing himself from his father. Why did he insist on living in Cambridge, why did he stay at King's, when almost any of the Oxford colleges would have been happy to welcome him? When living in Oxford might have added another twenty years to his life?

For Anthony was not strong. In addition to suffering from debilitating headaches which made him physically sick, he was miserably ill with colds and bronchitis for most of the winter. The climate of the Fens was too damp for anyone as susceptible to chest infections as he was.

But he resisted the lures held out by Oxford. He intended to remain in Cambridge for life, he said, however long that might be. The possibility of being regarded as a pale shadow of his father apparently frightened him more than the prospect of an early, avoidable demise.

'Surely you would be just as happy in Oxford?' Dora had asked Miriam, as she heard her brother hacking and wheezing in his study next to the sitting room one autumn morning. She moved a draught for Jonathan, who delightedly jumped three of her pieces.

Miriam frowned. 'Dora must crown you now, Jonathan,' she said. 'Take one of your men back and make a double piece, like that. No, Rachel,' she added, picking up the toddler who was intent on spoiling the game, and sitting the little girl upon her lap. 'What did you say, Dolly?'

'Are you happy here, Miriam? Why do you stay in Cambridge when it's so bad for Anthony's health?'

'You think I can control Anthony, Dora? You think that if I say, "We must move to another place," he will do so? Oh,

Dora — Anthony pleases himself.'

'So you're *not* happy.'

'Yes, I am. I'd be happy anywhere with Anthony.'

'How very sentimental of you, Miriam. You can't really mean that.'

'I do.' Miriam folded her hands across her bulging stomach and smiled, like a Madonna. 'Why do you think I'm lying?'

Miriam's voice, still accented despite her many years in England, was low and soothing, the most beautiful voice Dora had ever heard. Redolent with soft Russian consonants, there was also a faint lisp which Dora — and presumably Anthony, too — found enchanting. Dora looked up and shook her head. 'I don't think you're lying,' she replied, 'but you're misguided, maybe.'

Anthony came in at that moment, hatted and gloved against the November cold. He leaned across his wife to kiss her; fleetingly, he stroked her pregnancy. Dora saw his hand rest momentarily upon Miriam's bosom, and she looked away.

What maulers men were. Forgetting that once there had been a period in her life when she had actively welcomed mauling, Dora shuddered. Miriam, sitting there enlarged and swollen beyond her usual neat slimness, might have been a prize cow being assessed for the butcher.

Dora coughed to remind her brother of her presence. 'Will you still be here tonight?' he asked, crouching down upon the carpet between his sister and his son.

'No.' Dora smiled at him. 'I'm going to get the train to Oxford; I said I'd call on the parents before I go back to Hereford. I've asked and asked them to visit us at the Grange,' she added. 'But they won't come. There's always some excuse.'

'I wonder why that could be?'

'Mama dislikes trains, but she's afraid to admit it in case we laugh at her.' Dora looked at her brother, daring him to contradict her. 'That's why.'

'I dare say you're right.' Anthony patted his sister's shoulder, then got up from the floor and went out of the room. Hunched in his overcoat, his hands pushed deeply into his pockets, he looked more like Stephen than ever.

'Daddy!' Jonathan, outraged that his father should have

apparently forgotten him, rushed out of the sitting room and into the hallway, closely followed by his little sister. The two children caught at Anthony's coat tail. 'Kiss, Daddy! Kiss!'

Anthony picked them up, whispered something to Jonathan which made him snicker and then, pressing a sixpence into his hand, returned him to his aunt. 'Look after yourself, Dolly,' he said, kissing his sister. 'If you ever need to get away — you know what I mean — you're always welcome here.'

Anthony was such a kind man. Perhaps, Dora reflected, that was why Miriam was so fond of him, and put up with all the mauling and the horrible stuff which went with it. It was, after all, such a mean trick that nature played upon women — causing them to fall in love with men, who would then simply use them for the gratification of their beastly desires. Dora thought of Ralph and Fred Garret sniggering together, and grimaced.

'What are you thinking about, Dora?' Miriam's voice broke into Dora's idle thoughts, bringing her back to reality with a start.

'Nothing, really.' Dora offered Jonathan a biscuit. 'Miriam, do you love Anthony?' she asked. 'Do you really love him? Everything about him? Do you know what I mean?'

Miriam laughed. 'I don't love *everything* about him,' she replied. 'I wish he wouldn't smoke those disgusting French cigarettes. I wish he wouldn't drop ash all over the house. I wish he would wear some dressing on his hair, so that he wouldn't always look so wild and untidy. I wish he wouldn't tease the children so much, because they don't always understand his jokes. But otherwise — yes, I love everything about him.'

'Everything else?'

'Yes, certainly. He's my lover, my friend, the brother I never had. You love him too, don't you, Dolly?'

'Yes.' Dora sighed. Miriam obviously didn't understand.

* * *

Dora arrived in Oxford late in the afternoon. She walked into the town and through Cornmarket, then on up to St Giles and along the Banbury Road. The red-brick houses which lined it looked so dowdy and ugly compared with the manor house at

Ashton Cross and with the Grange, that Dora wondered how her father could bear to live in a suburban villa, like a bank manager.

She would send for her luggage later, she decided. Her mother always put her own wardrobe and personal belongings at her daughter's disposal, and Dora kept a few of her own clothes in her old bedroom at the Oxford house.

'Where's Papa?' she asked, as she met her mother in the hall. 'It's after five; shouldn't he be home by now?'

'Oh, he'll be in college until at least half past six.' Dorcas helped her daughter off with her coat, then hugged her, pleased to see Dora looking so well. 'He works too hard,' she added ruefully. 'I really don't see why he shouldn't retire but, of course, he won't hear of it.'

'What would he do if he stopped teaching?'

'Ah, now that's the thing, isn't it? He doesn't actually *do* much teaching these days, though. He creams off the brighter students for his tutorials, of course, but his main interest is the running of the department. He can interfere as much as he pleases now he's in charge, and —' Dorcas giggled disloyally, 'you can imagine how much he enjoys *that!*'

Dora nodded. 'I can just picture it,' she agreed. 'The day he stops laying down the law will be the day he dies.'

'Quite. Oh, don't stand here in the cold, Dora. Come and have some tea — it's all ready. Now, how is Anthony, and what's little Jon up to these days? Did he do his impression of your father for you? *So* funny! That child should be on the stage.'

Dora went into the small sitting room which her mother used during the daytime, sat down and sighed contentedly, happy to be home, for this *was* home. Architecturally undistinguished though it might be, it was the place where she was comfortable, made welcome and loved . . .

'I saw Annie Vesey a day or two ago,' remarked Dorcas, pouring tea. 'I told her you were expected home. She left a note for you — a scrappy little thing — I wouldn't dignify it with the name of letter. Now, where did I put it?' Dorcas leafed through a pile of papers on the mantelshelf. 'Ah, here.' She handed her daughter a sheet from a drawing pad, which was covered with Annie's hectic scrawl.

'She asks me to meet her for tea.' Dora smiled. 'She says she's very busy these days, but not too busy to make time for me.' Dora looked up at her mother. 'What's she doing?'

Dorcas shrugged and passed a plate of sandwiches. 'She's involved with those WSPU people, I believe,' she replied. 'The Dean is *frantic*.'

Annie Vesey, the Dean's daughter and only child, was a former schoolfriend. She waited impatiently for Dora, looking out of the window of the cafe in Cornmarket while she half-heartedly scanned a pamphlet and fiddled nervously with her newly-bobbed hair.

Dora arrived a few minutes late for her meeting with this uneasily modern young woman, and plumped her old-fashioned self down beside her friend. 'Hello, Annie. How are you?' she asked.

Having been a slight, bony child, Annie Vesey had grown up into a small, thin, pretty woman, a light and fragile blonde of the type to whom men are either irresistibly drawn ("She's ethereal — she's like a flower, a water sprite"), or by whom they are absolutely repelled ("I can't bear those scraggy, anaemic women, no bosom, no backside — give me something with a bit of meat on her bones!"). Not that either attitude would have interested Annie. She despised the male sex completely and often said as much, loudly, to anyone who would listen to her. She put down her pamphlet and greeted Dora.

'What's all that about?' Dora indicated the reading matter spread out on the table.

'The Women's Social and Political Union,' replied Annie crisply. 'You've heard of us, Dora? We've begun the fight, at last, and now we shall see *real* progress towards the emancipation of women.'

'Indeed,' Dora caught the waitress's attention and ordered tea. 'Soon?'

'Of course!' Annie grinned at Dora. 'We're organized, we're strong and we're united. I am an area representative,' she added, with some degree of pride. 'Look!' She showed Dora the green, white and purple flash upon her lapel. 'I wear this with pride,' she continued. 'Do you know, I was spat at yesterday — in Queen Street.'

'Goodness.' Dora ate a sandwich. 'What does your father think of your activities?'

'Oh, he's totally opposed, of course.' Annie waved her hand dismissively. 'But then, he would be. He thinks I'm an abandoned hoyden, and tells me that no decent man will ever wish to marry me now. He even quoted the scriptures at me.' Adopting the somewhat lugubrious gravity of her father's countenance, Annie cleared her throat impressively. 'Who can find a virtuous woman?' she intoned. 'For *her* price is above rubies.'

'Who is this Ruby?' Dora giggled. 'I thought you were opposed to matrimony as an institution, anyway. You used to say you'd never, ever tie yourself to a man.'

'Quite. Nor will I. They're all the same — oppressors, enslavers, brutes. I don't want anything to do with any of them.' Her voice had taken on its rhetorical, platform timbre now and people turned to stare at her.

'It's all right, Annie.' Soothingly, Dora smiled at her friend. 'I accept your right to voice your own opinions, and *I'm* not going to spit at you. But I don't know about that elderly gentleman over there — he's gone quite purple!'

Annie turned to stare at the said gentleman and, to Dora's surprise, he dropped his gaze. Obviously discomfited by Annie's gimlet glare, he looked the other way and went on meekly with his tea.

Dora herself was feeling somewhat uncomfortable by now. Something about the glint in Annie's pale blue eyes reminded her of Ralph at his most disagreeable. 'Why do I attract such people?' she wondered to herself. Then she thought of Anthony — of her own father. 'Not all men are oppressors, you know,' she said, evenly.

'Aren't they?' Annie stared. 'Well, Dora, I'm surprised you can say that. But then, you're married to a country squire, aren't you? To a fellow who forms part of the backbone of this great country of ours, who is doubtless a staunch member of the Conservative Party and who is also a splendid example of male absolutism at its most arbitrary, I shouldn't wonder.'

'Don't, Annie.' To hide her embarrassment, Dora laughed. She poured out tea for them both. 'I won't have you spouting your platform jargon at me,' she added. 'If you despise men, why do you want to be like them? Do you want a political career? Are you set on entering Parliament?'

Annie folded her arms. 'We don't want the vote so that we can be *like* men,' she replied. 'We want it as a tool, to do women's work, which men have left undone, or are unsuccessfully trying to do.'

Dora grinned. 'Whom are you quoting now?' she asked. 'I've certainly heard *that* somewhere before.'

'You'll hear it again — and again until our cause is won. I say, Dora, will you join us?'

'I don't know about that. I don't care for your methods, you know — I don't feel that smashing windows and attacking Mr Lloyd George will advance your cause. I don't even know if I want the vote.'

'It's not just the vote. It's a whole range of things. If women and men *together* control the destiny of the nation, this will pave the way for a true communion of friendship between the sexes. Men and women will meet each other as equals. And this awful sexual dependence which is so prevalent at present will completely disappear.'

'I'm not sure about that.'

'It will, it will!' Annie's eyes glittered. 'It must! Once women can take the reins of government into their own hands, male tyranny will be overthrown for ever. That's what the men are afraid of, of course. That's why they revile and persecute us. And women like you, Dora, women who sit on the sidelines, mocking or indifferent, *you* are traitors to your sex.'

'Then to the barricades!' Dora snickered into her teacup, amused — not by the content of her friend's diatribe, but by Annie's awful, bombastic method of delivering her message.

Annie frowned. 'You may laugh,' she muttered, sourly. 'You may sneer. But it's high time things were changed, that men's attitudes towards the female sex altered completely. Do you know, Dora, it's been estimated that on marriage seventy five per cent of men are diseased? And,' she continued, in the same sepulchral tone, 'that this disease is then passed on to their wives, who in turn give birth to sickly or deformed babies. Or to no babies at all. Soon, if responsible women do nothing about it, the human race will be so debilitated that it will die out of its own accord. You haven't any children, have you, Dora?' she enquired, almost as an afterthought.

'No, I haven't.'

'Why is that, I wonder?'

Dora reddened. 'None have come,' she replied. 'I don't know why.'

'Ah!' Annie looked at her friend in triumph, as if to say, "My lord, I rest my case". The true fanatic's cruelty was now apparent in her pale eyes, and she rose to her feet. 'Go back to your husband, Dora,' she said. 'Go home. But remember what we have discussed today. I must leave you now — there are things to be done.'

Dora, feeling that she had had enough of Annie Vesey to last her for the next fifty years, walked out of the cafe with her friend. Annie, she decided, was definitely unhinged. But as Dora sat in the cab rolling back down St Giles, she wondered if she *was* a traitor to her sex. Did she owe it to herself, and to women in general, to take this matter further?

* * *

Katherine Lawrence came over to the Grange a few days after Dora had returned to Herefordshire. Now a well-developed woman in her mid-twenties, she had a magnificent Edwardian figure, a mane of shining black hair and flashing dark eyes; she was a splendid sight riding astride her huge black hunter.

'Hallo, Doll.' She sat down in an armchair and looked complacently round Dora's pretty sitting room. 'Had a good time in the seats of learning?'

'I enjoyed my little holiday.' Dora smiled. 'It's always pleasant to see my family again.'

'I expect it was pleasant to get away from the brute, as well.' well.'

'Katherine, really!' Dora shook her head. 'Actually, I was wondering what had become of Ralph. I suppose he's gone shooting, but I haven't seen him since he got up this morning.'

Katherine grinned. 'I don't suppose that breaks your heart.'

'No.' Dora attempted a light, social laugh and poured out

the coffee which Sarah had just brought in. Far from breaking her heart, Ralph's absence was positively welcome to her that morning. In fact, she rather wished he'd put a bullet into his horrible self.

On her return from Oxford he had greeted her with indifference, but he'd later come into her bedroom and exacted the marital dues to which he presumably felt he was entitled. He had forced himself upon her with his usual brutality, and left her feeling cold and assaulted, almost hating him.

At that moment, the door opened and Ralph walked into the room. Perfectly well and looking very handsome, his pale face flushed with exercise and the gobbets of mud from his boots dropping all over the carpet, he smiled at his wife. He walked with a slight limp still but this added to, rather than detracted from, the dignity of his bearing.

He leaned over Dora and kissed her with the same hard, violent cruelty which had once thrilled her but which now merely annoyed her and hurt her neck. He *would* jerk her head back so . . .

After kissing Dora for a minute or so and stroking her neck as if he and she were alone in the room, he turned to Katherine. 'Ah, Miss Lawrence!' he said, grinning. 'What an honour.'

'Good morning, Ralph.' Katherine looked out of the window, determined not to be provoked.

'I didn't see you when I came in.' Ralph flopped down on the sofa beside his wife. 'Otherwise, of course, I'd have —'

'You must be going blind then,' interrupted Katherine testily. 'Lord knows I'm big enough!'

'Yes, indeed you are!' Ralph's mouth twisted into a sneer of amusement. 'I was thinking as much only a day or two ago. Your hips in particular are becoming quite enormous. It's all that riding astride which does it, you know. Why don't you learn to ride like a lady? Dora has managed it at long last, so it ought not to be beyond *you*.'

Katherine scowled at him but she did not reply.

'I heard something about you in Hereford a day or two ago,' continued Ralph, who was now caressing Dora's breast in a proprietorial manner and observing that his behaviour disconcerted Katherine, who had reddened and was now staring down at the floor. 'Something quite sensational.'

'Really?' Katherine looked up at him. 'What was that?'

Ralph stroked Dora's hair. 'I was told that you and your fellow lesbians were holding a meeting about votes for women,' he replied. 'That there'd be a rally in High Town with flags and banners.'

'The WSPU is holding an open forum on Wednesday evening,' Katherine agreed. 'Perhaps you and Dora should come along.'

Ralph snorted in derision. 'I don't think so,' he replied. He stood up and stretched; then, having effectively poisoned the atmosphere in it, he walked out of the room.

'You're involved with Mrs Pankhurst's ladies too then, Katherine?' asked Dora.

'Yes. Why? Are you, Dolly?'

'Me?' Dora shook her head. 'No. But I was talking to a friend in Oxford about it all. Annie's very much the moving spirit of her local branch.'

'Is she now? Well, I hope she persuaded you of the virtues and merits of our cause.' Katherine scowled. 'With a husband like Ralph Challoner, one would have to be a halfwit not to see that progress is possible, after all.'

'Oh, Katherine! Don't talk like that.'

'Sorry. I keep forgetting that you must still be in love with the brute.'

Dora walked across the room and opened the door. 'It's a lovely day,' she said firmly. 'And I don't suppose anyone's taken my little mare out while I've been away. Shall we go out on to the common for an hour?'

Katherine, slightly abashed, nodded. 'All right,' she replied. 'Come on.'

* * *

Dora, to Ralph's utter amazement and total disgust, attended Katherine's meeting. She had dressed and had the car brought round in spite of his prediction that she would certainly kill herself driving along country lanes in the dark.

'You drive me, then.' Dora smiled sweetly at her husband. 'And then you can come to the meeting.'

'I damn well won't do *that*!' He scowled at her and slopped a measure of whisky into the glass by his side. I can't think why you want to go,' he grumbled. 'Why d'you want to sit and listen to a lot of bloody Sapphists squawking on about getting the vote?' He drank down his whisky and grinned. 'The only kind of women who get involved with that sort of organization are ones like Katherine,' he added.

'Katherine?'

'Yes. Great ugly cows who never get a man between their legs. And that's not you, is it, Dora? Not my beautiful Dora?'

'I'm going anyway.' Dora pulled on her gloves. 'Don't wait up for me, I'm spending the night at Ashton Cross.'

She became involved, she supposed, because she was bored, and because it was so nice to make friends with a group of well-educated, intelligent, interesting women. The frustrated spinsters, the rabid lesbians of Ralph's fevered imagination were hardly represented among the ranks of the WSPU and its milder cousin, the absolutely non-militant National Union.

Hereford is a small town so the number of women brave enough to commit themselves to such a cause was necessarily small as well. Dora felt welcomed and needed at a time in her life when she was otherwise lonely, disillusioned and miserable.

'I don't say anything to Ralph,' she replied when Katherine asked her what Ralph thought of her involvement with the women's suffrage movement. 'He thinks we're all mad, or worse.'

'He would.'

'He can't help his nature.' Dora looked reproachfully at Katherine. 'He's as much a victim of his upbringing as anyone.'

'Oh, of course he is.' Katherine sniffed. 'I'd wondered if you might have changed him a little — civilized him a bit.'

'You can't change people. You can bring out the best in them, maybe — that's all.'

'Very philosophical, Dolly.' Katherine patted her cousin's shoulder. 'You're not happy with him, are you?' she asked.

'I'm perfectly happy.' Dora looked levelly at her cousin. '*Perfectly* happy,' she repeated, the emphasis daring Katherine to take the matter any further.

Ralph was indeed, Dora had long since decided, a victim of his upbringing and of his sex. Beneath the brutality and aggression, she could now see a lonely, undirected man who was not at all fitted to be a modern country landowner. Ralph, she decided, would have made a splendid medieval brigand. He was a mass of nervous energy which was misapplied and fast going to waste in a stagnant backwater of rural England.

But even Ralph wasn't unpleasant all the time. For long periods he was placid, even likeable. Dora hoped that he might soften as he reached middle age. 'And there might be a child,' she told herself. 'Children, even.'

She learned to ignore her husband's sarcasm. When his company became too burdensome, she took herself off to Oxford, Cambridge or London. Life jogged on, comfortably enough. She was surprised when she realized that she'd been married seven years. Or could it be even more than that?

Chapter Eleven

CAROLINE ANDERSON FINISHED HER LETTER, blotted it and folded the paper. She pushed it inside an envelope and, instead of leaving it on the hall table for one of the servants to take to the post, she went out and slipped it into a letter box herself.

'There.' She walked home, exhilarated but now also in a state of considerable trepidation. 'Oh, he won't come,' she thought. 'Why should he? He's bound to be busy, he won't want to come and have lunch with me.' But, all the same, there was, surely, an outside possibility that he would?

Caroline let her mind conjure up a picture of Marcus Harley; she let herself look at the face which was in her constant daydreams and of which she knew every single detail. Marcus, the eldest son of John and Anna Harley, her parents' bridge partners and near neighbours; Marcus, who spent his summer holidays fooling around with her brother Stuart at OTC camps and on boring fishing trips . . .

But all this wasn't a mere schoolgirl infatuation or passing fancy for her brother's friend. Nor did Caroline think that Marcus's startling beauty had very much to do with it. Indeed, if he *hadn't* been so handsome, if he were just an ordinary boy with a wobbly voice and a few spots on his face, things might have been easier . . .

'But I *want* him!' she thought, despairingly. 'I want him so much. Oh, God — people do die of love, they must do. It's killing me, wanting him.' For want him she did; she'd thought of nothing else for weeks and weeks and weeks . . .

* * *

'Where are you off to this week?' Ralph walked through Dora's dressing room, smacking a riding whip against his thigh. He smiled at his pretty wife, his expression for once indulgent enough.

Dora smiled back. For several months now he had been relatively pleasant to her; they'd found no reason to argue or fight. Perhaps the hoped-for mellowing was beginning to take place.

Dora stuck her last hairpin into position. 'I'm going up to London,' she replied. 'Why don't you come with me? Ralph, I'm sure the Harleys would love to see you, and you know you get on well with John.'

'He's a decent enough chap — for a tradesman. No, I won't come. You go by yourself. Buy a few new dresses, eh?'

'I may do.' Dora caught her husband's hand. 'Will you drive me to the station?' she asked. 'For the ten o'clock tomorrow morning?'

Ralph nodded. 'Very well,' he agreed.

Dora jumped up and kissed him. 'Thank you,' she said. 'Thank you very much — darling,' she added, as an afterthought.

Crawley, who happened to be walking down the landing and chanced to hear this matrimonial exchange, grimaced. Mr and Mrs Challoner were getting on very well together these days. Too well, in fact. Thinking hard, Crawley sidled off down the servants' stairs, rubbing his face with his bony hands.

The following day, as she leaned out of the window of her first class compartment and patted her hat, Dora looked hard at Ralph. 'Change your mind,' she said. 'Change your mind and come.'

He grinned. 'No, Dora, I won't do that. A week with your sister would drive me insane.'

The guard blew his whistle. Ralph pulled Dora's head towards him and kissed her, then he drew back and watched the train steam out of the station.

Dora had taken Ralph's point. Indeed, there had been a time when only an hour or so of Anna's company had been enough to give her younger sister a headache. But this was no longer the case. Anna had become nicer as she moved towards middle age. She was no longer so sharp and contradictory and this gave Dora increased hope that Ralph, too, might become more reasonable as time went on.

Not that Anna had anything to be unreasonable about. She was married to a man who obviously adored her, she had three clever sons, she still pursued her brilliant career as a classics scholar; soon, she would have published as much as her father had.

Three clever sons. Of these, Marcus was still Dora's — and everyone else's — special favourite. Still ravishingly attractive, he had fulfilled the promise of his childhood and gone through adolescence apparently immune to the physical and emotional difficulties which beset most boys. He was very tall now, taller than his two brothers, who were unmistakeably Lawrences. Dark and heavily built, Robert and Neil were two satyrs on either side of a beautiful blond god.

'Do you worry about Marcus?' asked Dora one day, looking at Anna quizzically over her cup of afternoon tea.

'Worry about him? What is there to worry about?'

'If I had a son who looked like Marcus, I'd lock him up.'

Anna laughed. 'Away from the temptations of the flesh?'

'Well, something like that.'

'Mmm. Well, Dora, I'm used to the way he looks. I don't even notice it any more. And I'm resigned to the fact that for the rest of his life women — and some men — are going to be throwing themselves at his feet. He's accustomed to adoration, though — I don't think it's spoiled him.'

Anna laughed again. 'Dora, do you remember how Papa used to pick him up and carry him about the house in Oxford, talking to him while Marcus dribbled into his hair? Papa, who never usually notices children at all?'

'Yes, I remember. But Marcus was such a charmer, you must admit.'

'I know. He still is. Anyway, Dora, he'll be beyond my jurisdiction soon. He'll be off to Cambridge in the autumn, then it will be too much wine, far too many women, and he'll be ruined.'

The entry into the drawing room of the paragon himself put an abrupt end to the discussion.

'Been talking about me, Mum?' Marcus leaned across the little tea table and picked up a sandwich and a couple of cakes, swallowing each one whole and scattering crumbs upon the carpet.

'Where have you *been?*' Anna frowned at her son, or tried to. 'You were supposed to drive Dora to Regent Street this afternoon. She had to take a cab.'

'Got held up. Sorry, Mum. Sorry, Dora.' Marcus flopped down on to the sofa beside his aunt, and smiled delightfully at the two women. 'Any tea?' he enquired. 'I'm parched.'

'Here.' Anna poured him a cup and handed it to him. 'Well, now you're back, you can —'

'Afraid I have to go out again.' Marcus swallowed his tea in great, slurping gulps. 'Got to see a chap about some books.'

'Books?'

'Yes. This fellow was sent down last year, so I said I'd have his Greek texts. I dare say he hasn't even opened them. It'll save a few bob, Mum. Look, I may be a bit late for dinner.'

He stood up and grabbed a handful of sandwiches, then was through the door and gone before Anna could argue with him.

'He's been drinking.' Anna sniffed disapprovingly. 'And he's been with some woman. When he leaned across me I could smell scent — and his waistcoat buttons were mismatched.' Anna sighed. 'I just hope it wasn't some awful creature from Covent Garden.'

Dora shook her head. 'You don't imagine that someone who looks like Marcus would need to go to a brothel, do you?' she asked, laughing. 'I'm sure that any girl with eyes in her head would pay *him*. Anyway,' she added, 'I could smell it too. It wasn't some cheap cologne — it was one of those heavenly French flower oils. Goodness, she must have been drenched in it for so much to have stuck to him. You'll have to ask him who she is.'

'As if he'd tell *me*.'

* * *

Marcus walked down the Embankment almost singing; he wanted to throw his hat into the air and kick it along the pavement. He'd felt obliged to go back to the house on Highgate Hill for tea, to make some excuse to Dora and apologize for not turning up to take her shopping as he'd promised. But now he was practically running along the river's edge, anxious to get back to Caroline.

He reached the tall Georgian town house, the merchant's home which was now converted into five small apartments. He ran up the stairs and tapped on the door of the first floor flat. Finding it open, he went inside.

Caroline was sitting on the sofa, her fair hair neatly pinned into a coil at the nape of her neck. She turned to look at him and, as she did so, a radiant smile spread across her face, making her look perfectly beautiful.

'Hello.' Marcus closed the door, letting down the catch on the lock. 'Wasn't long, was I?'

'No. Did you take a cab all the way?'

'I went on the train.' He plumped himself down beside her. 'Missed me?' he asked.

'Mmm. I did. But —'

'You didn't think I'd come back.'

'Well —' Caroline blushed. 'I thought that perhaps you'd have had to stay and talk to your aunt.'

'Oh, I can talk to Dora any time. Caroline?'

'What?' Caroline now saw that he was blushing too, and she smiled at him again. 'What is it?'

'Can we — shall we go back to bed?'

'You really mean that? You want to — you'd like us to —'

'I want to!' Marcus leaned across Caroline and took her by the shoulders. Contorting his handsome face into a gargoyle of grotesque cupidity, he leered so horribly that, in spite of herself, she laughed at him. 'I'd like to eat you alive,' he muttered, talking out of the side of his mouth. 'That's what I want. Do you know,' he added, 'there wasn't any tea to speak of at home, and I'm starving.'

He relaxed his features then, and touched Caroline's collar bone. 'Caro?' he asked, his voice quite normal now. 'I'd like to make love to you again. Will you let me?'

Caroline wrapped her arms around his neck. 'Yes,' she said. 'Yes, of course I will. There's nothing I'd like better, as I'm sure you must know perfectly well.'

Everything went marvellously that second time. Less nervous and far less anxious now, Caroline kissed Marcus slowly and carefully, making each individual caress tell. Innocent and unpractised as she had been until that afternoon, she had nevertheless learned very quickly. And now, feeling that she understood what would please her partner, she held nothing back.

Neither did Marcus. Soon, Caroline was in such a state of bliss that she found she was laughing out loud with delight. He wanted her, he wanted her — she couldn't believe it, but it seemed to be true.

He was in less of a hurry this time. Understanding himself better now, Marcus waited until both he and his mistress were ready, and when he took her it was at the right moment for them both.

Afterwards, Marcus stretched, pushed his blond hair out of his eyes and positively beamed at the naked girl beside him. 'You're splendid, Caroline,' he murmured, kissing her ear. 'A lovely girl. A wonderful girl.'

He yawned. 'God, I'm tired,' he sighed. 'Isn't this sort of thing exhausting?'

'You have a rest then.' Caroline smiled back at him. 'Minnie won't be home for hours. No one will disturb us.'

'That's good.' Marcus lay down beside her and closed his eyes. In a matter of seconds he was breathing regularly, fast asleep.

It had taken considerable nerve and courage for Caroline Anderson to invite Marcus Harley to her parents' small Chelsea flat for lunch. All the same, it was with a vague but wholly conscious intention of subsequently enticing him into her parents' comfortable double bed that she had laid her plans and then acted upon them.

She'd been astonished at her own audacity. Nice single girls, who'd been well brought up, did not go to bed with young men —especially not with young men whose parents knew hers, whose friends included her elder brother.

But wanting Marcus was killing her. She could think of nothing else but him. A childhood affection for a nice boy who had never pulled her hair or teased her had somehow grown into a violent adolescent attraction, which then became a longing which Caroline felt was burning her alive.

Marcus had accepted the invitation to lunch and had not seemed at all surprised when Caroline herself opened the door to him.

'Minnie's gone out,' she told him diffidently, explaining the housemaid's absence. 'She's gone to visit her sister,' she added, glibly. 'Mama told her she could, and I didn't have the heart to cancel her afternoon off.'

'Ah.' Marcus smiled. With exaggerated gallantry, he presented Caroline with the bunch of summer flowers he had bought from a street vendor just outside the house. 'We're alone then?' he asked.

'Yes.' Caroline reddened. 'Well, you've known me for such a long time that it doesn't seem to matter — I mean, it's not improper, that we're here by ourselves. Without a chaperone, that is.'

'No, it's not improper at all.' Marcus looked round the small sitting room. 'How long have your parents had this place?'

'A year or two. Daddy uses it when he's working on a case, and they come here after the theatre sometimes.'

The meal was a cold one, salad and some chicken which Caroline had, somewhat inexpertly, prepared herself. She watched Marcus chew his way through a rather large lump of cucumber and hoped he wouldn't get indigestion. She bent her own head over her plate.

Caroline was now wishing desperately that she'd never asked him to come. He must surely think she was very peculiar, asking him to lunch like this. She was very surprised that he'd turned up.

He must have been at a loose end, she decided. She imagined him and Stuart laughing together about it later, Marcus giggling as he described the horrible meal she'd given him, and she blushed even redder.

She dropped a piece of tomato on to her lap and, blinking back the tears of mortification which had now gathered in her eyes, she scooped it up with her fork. She bit her lower lip. Fancying herself as a seductress was quite absurd. She was no Lola Montez — she could see that now.

Just then, Marcus looked up and smiled at her. She was a

nice girl — he'd always thought so. Not spiteful, not a giggler, not sharp. And she didn't gawk at him in the embarrassing way so many people did.

'Very decent salad,' he said courteously, spearing another wedge of cucumber.

'Thank you.'

'Did you do all this yourself?'

'Yes.'

'It's very — er — nice.' Marcus sighed inwardly. This was heavy going. Caroline might be nice, but she was such a boring girl. No, that was unfair. She was a little dull, perhaps. She never had much to say for herself. But she was Stuart's little sister, and since she had asked him to lunch, it would have been unkind and rude not to have accepted her invitation. She was a pretty girl, he decided, looking at her now.

A girl with a face like a Dresden shepherdess, and a small, neat body which was a little awkward, though certainly not clumsy. She could properly be described as coltish — that particular word fitted her exactly. Coltish. Or fawnish. Was there such a word? If there wasn't, he decided, there ought to be.

Caroline, aware that she would be uneasy in the role of hostess, had raided her father's wine cellar for a few bottles of red burgundy and a couple more of claret. An hour or two before Marcus had arrived she had opened two bottles of Mr Anderson's Médoc and now she offered some to Marcus. 'Wine?' she enquired, rather too brightly.

'If you have some too.'

Caroline poured two glassfuls.

She drank hers down very quickly, then felt the colour flood into her already hot cheeks. Recklessly, she refilled her goblet, awkwardly clinking the neck of the bottle against the rim of her glass.

Marcus looked at her. 'Steady on,' he said kindly. 'This stuff has quite a kick to it, you know.' He took the bottle out of her hand and replenished his own glass. 'You've gone quite pink,' he observed. 'You're obviously not used to this, are you?'

He was laughing at her. He must think she was a complete idiot. 'I *am* used to it,' she lied haughtily. She blinked at him, now finding that the daylight hurt her eyes, for the sun was reflecting off the river and filling the little flat with bright afternoon light. 'I think I've had enough to eat,' she added. She rose unsteadily to her feet and went to sit on the sofa.

Marcus came and sat beside her. To Caroline's surprise, he laid his arm across the back of the cushions and then, leaning over, he kissed her.

'Marcus!' Guiltily, she jumped. She rubbed her face with her knuckles. 'Oh, Marcus!'

'Oh Marcus what?' Marcus, who had brought his glass with him, took a gulp of claret. 'Did I do something unacceptable?'

'No! Oh, no! But you don't have to, you know —'

'I don't have to what?'

'Er — kiss me.' Caroline turned away from him and bit her lower lip.

'Oh, that's all right.' Marcus smiled genially, the very personification of *noblesse oblige*. 'I don't mind. I like to kiss you,' he added, rather more chivalrously. 'In fact, I'd like to kiss you again.'

Marcus wasn't unused to wine, but he'd seldom had a whole bottle of vintage claret all to himself, and never during the middle of a hot, summer's day. Caroline hardly drank alcohol at all; and now, after two glasses of heavy red wine, she was feeling distinctly tipsy.

Marcus looked at her. Yes, she was really rather attractive. Small, maybe — lacking the fine contours of the beauties whom the old King had always seemed to fancy, but all the same, Caroline was a nice, pretty, scented woman. She did smell quite delicious. And her eyes were so attractive, a deep shade of navy which was flecked with a lighter blue. 'You don't mind if I kiss you?' he asked her, ten minutes after he'd first begun to do so.

'No.' Caroline blushed. 'I like you to.'

'Good. Then you won't mind if I hug you, too.'

Marcus slipped his hand inside her blouse and touched her shoulder. She made no resistance, so he moved his hand downwards. Finding, to his surprise, that Caroline appeared to be wearing very little under her silk blouse, he continued his exploration and, a quarter of an hour later, he had made a very thorough investigation of her upper chest.

Marcus had kissed girls before, but he had never previously encountered such compliance — such evident desire. Shaking his head to clear it a little, he kissed her again, much more adventurously this time. He opened her mouth with his and explored its interior with his tongue. To his surprise, she didn't object. She kissed him back.

He reached for a second bottle of wine and sloshed some of it into his glass, gulping it all down in one mouthful. He hiccupped. His head swimming, he looked at the blurred vision before him. He'd never before seen a girl so lovely, so beautiful, so absolutely desirable. He began to unfasten the buttons on her blouse.

Caroline now had Marcus in the precise situation in which she'd long dreamed of having him. As he undid the last of the four buttons on her blouse, pushed back the thin material and bent his head to kiss her throat, she felt she might well faint. She wondered if she'd taken leave of her senses. But, even as her head swam, even as her conscience reproached her, she realized that she'd be a fool to stop him now. 'If I pass this chance up, I'll regret it,' she told herself. 'I'll be sorry — I'll be sorry until the end of my days.'

She stood up, supporting herself against the side of the sofa, and smoothed her hair back from her forehead. Standing before him, a blonde, Anglo-Saxon version of the most desirable of houris, she looked levelly at Marcus. 'Do you want to go to bed with me?' she asked him, astonishing herself even as she spoke.

'You're not old enough to go to bed with men.'

'I'm eighteen!' Caroline, who had never for a moment imagined that her *age* would have been a disqualification for going to bed with Marcus, stared at him, stricken. 'How old are *you*?'

'Nineteen.' Marcus grinned at her. 'Nineteen and a bit.' He stood up and took her hand, but then suddenly wrapped his arms around her waist. He picked her up and held her so that her eyes were on a level with his. 'Yes,' he murmured. 'Yes, let's go to bed.'

They went into Mr and Mrs Anderson's bedroom and sat

down on the wide double bed. Caroline helped Marcus to take off her clothes, undoing some of the more complicated fastenings, feeling all the while that she was no better than a Piccadilly whore, but not caring if this was the case or not.

Marcus threw off his own clothes and took her in his arms. He kissed her then, all at once, he pushed her on to her back, leaned over her and pinned her down on the counterpane. 'Oh, God!' she heard him mutter as he lay on top of her, his hands gripping her shoulders, his whole body shuddering. 'Oh, God, Caroline — wait for me!'

And then, in one violent spasm which convulsed them both, it was over. Marcus rolled away from her, turned on to his stomach and buried his face in the pillow.

'Sorry,' he mumbled at last. 'I'm sorry, Caroline. But I couldn't help it; I just couldn't help it.' He raised himself on one elbow and looked at her. 'Oh, Caro – you really shouldn't have let me do that.'

Caroline, who only a few moments before had been happier than she'd ever been in her life, was now mortified. She pulled the counterpane around herself and buried her face in her hands. 'I'm sorry, too,' she whispered. 'Oh, Marcus, I didn't intend to make such a mess of things. I did try to get it right. I know I'm clumsy and ignorant, I know I'm not —'

'Whatever do you mean?' Marcus gaped at her. *'You're* not to be sorry,' he said. 'Look, what I really meant was, I shouldn't have behaved as I did. Not with you. And you — well, you were wrong to let me.'

'You like — you prefer more experienced women, I suppose?'

'What?' Marcus stared. 'Good God, no — I didn't mean that at all! I meant — well, since I've never been to bed with a girl before, I shouldn't have practised on you.'

Caroline stared back at him. 'You've never done this before?' she whispered.

'No.'

'Never?'

'No, never.' Just a little calmer now, Marcus took Caroline's hands in his, looked into her eyes. 'And neither have you.'

'No.' Caroline looked down at the bedclothes, fixing her eyes on a piece of the pattern on the counterpane. 'No, of course I haven't.'

'I've never — you've never.' Suddenly, Marcus giggled. Now he had recovered his composure completely. He sat up, stretched and looked at the girl by his side. 'But that doesn't mean that I don't want to do it again,' he murmured, grinning at her.

'Oh.' Caroline bit her lip. 'But not with me, I imagine. I mean, I'm not pretty, I don't know how —'

'Don't be so bloody silly!' Marcus kissed her neck, took a lock of her long, fair hair between his fingers. 'Caroline, you're lovely. Your skin's beautiful. You're a gorgeous woman.'

'Am I?'

'Yes!' Marcus kissed her, parting her lips with his. 'Yes, you are. Well, *I* think so.'

'But *you're* drunk.' Wanly, Caroline smiled at him. 'You don't know what you're saying.'

'I do!' He shook her arm and glared at her. 'And I'm not drunk! Or at any rate, no more than you are!'

*   *   *

As he walked quickly along the dirty London pavement and began the climb up Highgate Hill, Marcus was aware of a feeling of absolute euphoria. He shook his head. 'I *am* drunk,' he thought. 'Drunk as a costermonger on a Saturday night.'

But then he thought of Caroline, of her smooth honey-coloured skin, of the way her back curved in such a beautiful, fluid line from her neck to her waist, and he didn't care if he was totally inebriated. For he was experiencing a delicious sensation — a feeling that he'd arrived in a situation where he'd always longed to be.

He couldn't remember ever feeling so happy or comfortable before — an odd experience, seeing that Marcus Harley had hardly known a moment's *dis*comfort in the course of his whole life.

The following day he met Caroline in Regent's Park. As they walked about in the sunshine, he wondered why he'd never noticed before how pretty she was.

By the end of the week, Marcus had decided that, if he was not actually in love, then he was certainly in a state very closely bordering upon it.

*   *   *

Dora thoroughly enjoyed her stay in London. Marcus, although obviously preoccupied with some secret scheme of his own, made the time to take his aunt about a little. In spite of the calls on his day made by his supposed *affaire*, he escorted Dora to art galleries, to the large department stores of the West End, to parks and gardens. They went out in the evenings, and Dora found it undeniably pleasant to be taken to the theatre by such an agreeable young man.

She returned to the Grange to find her husband in a very sour temper, in a mood very far removed from the light-hearted humour in which he had sent her off to London only a couple of weeks before. 'Is there anything wrong, Ralph?' she asked, as she stood in the hallway taking off her hat and looking around her at the familiar surroundings of her home. 'You don't look very happy to see me.'

'I'm going out.' Ralph picked up his riding whip and walked over to the door. 'I shan't be back for dinner.'

Dora shrugged. 'Suit yourself,' she replied, to his departing back. She would, she decided, spend her own evening at Ashton Cross, where the welcome was always warm.

Ralph came home at midnight, went to his wife's bedroom and got into her bed. After he had taken her as roughly and inconsiderately as he always did, he sat up and scowled at her. Reaching for the whisky bottle which he had brought with him, he splashed some of the liquid into a tooth mug and glared at his wife. 'You didn't ever tell me that the whore was married to a murderer,' he remarked.

'What *are* you talking about?' Dora rubbed her face, which was sore where he had grazed it. She looked at him, puzzled.

'You know what I mean, you dissembling little bitch.' He took another gulp of whisky. 'You never informed *me* that although you're old Lawrence's bastard, you're also the legal child of a convicted, executed murderer. You are, aren't you, Dora? I didn't know that. It seems that the rest of the bloody county does. Why wasn't *I* let in on the secret?'

'I never thought to tell you.' Dora herself had only learned about her mother's marriage to Daniel Hitchman, the Hereford grocer who had been convicted of the murder of a governess a good fifteen years ago, when she herself was almost grown up.

Anna had explained the whole affair to her, saying how, for the first ten years of her own life, she had believed herself to be Daniel Hitchman's child.

Dora, sickened and unwilling to believe such a horrible story, unwilling to imagine her own sweet-natured, lovable and loving mother married to such a man, had tried to block it from her mind. She wished that Anna had never told her such a dreadful tale, and said so. 'You ought to know,' Anna had replied quietly. 'It's part of our past, whether you like it or not. Don't worry, I shan't mention it again. It gives me no pleasure to remember such things.' And Dora, wishing she had never asked that casual question about Anna's early childhood, had done her best to forget the whole disgusting business.

'How do you know about it now, Ralph?' she asked.

'What's that to you, whore's child? I *do* know.' He glared. 'You tried to deceive me. You'll be sorry.'

Over the previous couple of years, Ralph had been drinking a great deal. He did not get drunk, but neither was he often completely sober. Dora supposed he took spirits to dull the pain he obviously still felt from the leg he'd broken so badly a few years back — for now he rode and hunted as much as he ever had, coming home some days so blanched and in such obvious distress that he reached straight for the whisky bottle. Now he sat glaring at Dora, his eyes dull with malice, his breath sickly with alcohol. 'Why did you keep it from me?' he asked, shaking her.

'It wasn't a question of keeping anything from you.' Dora shrugged, trying to twist out of his grasp. 'I never thought to tell you. It's hardly relevant.'

'Isn't it? I think it's very relevant.'

'Who told you, Ralph? Was it Crawley? He must know — he's lived here all his life. He has the sort of prying, nasty mind which would ferret out and remember such things . . .'

'You don't deny that it's all true?'

'No, I don't deny it.'

'That's just as well.' Ralph poured himself some more whisky, this time filling the glass to the brim. 'What a pedigree,' he muttered. 'God, what a bloodline! The product of an illicit union between a fornicating farmer and a tradesman's runaway wife. So, my pretty Dora, my virtuous little bride, tell me about your Mama's husband. What was he like? Did she have half a dozen other children by him? Have you a brood of indigent half brothers and sisters somewhere? Or did Hitchman carve them all up to sell as sausages and pies?'

'Oh, shut up, Ralph. Don't be so disgusting.'

'Answer my question, Dora. Did she have other children, did she breed, that harlot of a mother of yours? Can I expect that one day my house will be overrun with your poverty-stricken relations? With a set of beggars from the workhouse in Hereford, perhaps?'

'My mother has three children: Anna, Anthony and me. You know that.'

'Three little bastards. One, two, three.' Ralph lolled tipsily against his pillows. 'Or, to put it another way, the grocer had three pretty children, all got upon his wife by the rutting squire of Ashton Cross.'

'Don't!' Dora glared at Ralph. 'You foul-mouthed wretch, you wouldn't dare say such things in front of my father. So don't say them to me.' She snatched the glass from his hand and furiously threw the contents into his eyes.

'Oh, your father! Your precious bloody father!' Ralph dashed the whisky from his face and caught Dora by the hair. He wrenched her neck back. 'I'd dare say anything I please to that obscene old lecher,' he hissed.

'Let me go!' Dora squirmed. 'I don't want to listen to you any more. Let me go!'

'Why did I ever marry you?' Ralph gave her a vicious shake. 'What was the point? Oh, you're pretty enough, I'll allow that. But you're also a harlot's daughter, and that's a disgrace.' He scowled at her. 'A disgrace, isn't it, Dora? Or is it a blessing, perhaps? Well, it would be, if you'd picked up a few tricks from Mama. Do admit, Dora, that your Mama must be very artful to have kept *your* father interested in her for all these years. With such antecedents I can't understand why you're so bloody hopeless in bed.'

'What?'

'You heard me.' Ralph grinned. He pulled Dora's face close to his and looked into her eyes. 'Come on, whore's daughter,' he murmured, sneering at her. 'Behave like your mother for a change. Do something exciting, can't you? Use your imagination and entertain me.'

'What do you want me to do? I don't know what —'

'No, you don't, do you? Oh, just do something. Anything! God, you're useless! You just lie there like a bag of bloody washing. You're about as erotic as a sack of turnips!'

'Ralph, you know you hate it if I kiss you, if I take the initiative in any way —'

'I don't!'

'You do! I used to kiss you but you'd always push me away —'

He pursed his lips and studied her. 'I know what I'd really like,' he muttered. 'Later, perhaps, I'll have it. Yes, you and your damned lesbian friends, you and your bloody votes for bloody women, it's what you all deserve . . .'

Dora felt her blood freeze; the hairs on her neck rose. She was afraid — of what she didn't know — but something in Ralph's look scared her. 'You're drunk,' she snapped. 'You don't know what you're talking about. I'm going to sleep in another room.'

'Come back here!' He lunged at her, missed and Dora raced off down the landing, into a spare room where the bed was kept made up for Fred Garret. She slammed the door and, breathing heavily, turned the key.

Nothing happened. At about three in the morning Dora woke, cold and shivering, still alone. She went on to the landing, heard nothing, so she went back into the spare room, piled more blankets on the bed, and fell asleep. As dawn was breaking, Ralph came to find her.

He came into the room, took off his dressing gown and got into bed beside her. 'Lie with your back to me,' he murmured. 'On your side. That's right.'

Half asleep, assuming that he wanted a little more room, Dora did as he requested. Then she felt his arms around her, holding her tightly — too tightly.

'Don't, Ralph. That hurts.' Dozily, she tried to push him away, but he still held her — and now he began to kiss her, biting at the back of her neck with sharp, painful kisses. She protested again but then she felt him relax slightly, so she relaxed too. And still her eyes were closed.

She didn't know why she suddenly felt afraid, what made her open her eyes and try to get out of the bed. But it was too late to escape. All at once his arms were tight around her again, squeezing the breath from her body, hurting her. 'Let me go, Ralph,' she said. 'Don't do that. I can hardly breathe when you hold me so tightly. Oh, damn you — let me go!'

'Stop struggling, Dora,' he muttered. He pulled up her nightgown. 'Behave like a grown woman, not a snivelling little boy. Don't be like your whining cousin James always was. This will be a new experience for you. You'll enjoy it, if you let yourself . . .

He laughed then, which terrified her, for at last she understood what he intended to do. 'You're hurting me,' she cried, desperately trying to get away from him. 'Oh, God, Ralph — don't do that to me! You mustn't do that — you can't!'

But he could, easily. He now had her arms pinioned behind her back. Helpless, Dora felt as if she were being crucified. She could breathe only with difficulty, and if she turned her head from the pillow into which he'd pushed her face, the pain in her shoulders was unbearable.

He was excited now, out of control, deaf to any appeal she might still have the strength to make. He held her down. Far stronger than she was, Ralph held his wife in his arms and did just as he wished with her. And at last, half suffocated and almost out of her mind with the pain he was causing her, Dora lost consciousness.

She woke up in the bright morning sunshine to find Ralph lying across her body. Blood patterned the sheets, blood from cuts and scratches both on his body and hers. Ralph was fast asleep. A seraphic smile on his face, he slept as soundly as a little child, as deeply as one perfectly at peace.

'Damn him!' thought Dora. 'Damn him, damn him!' Hatred gathered in her, a white hot conflagration which seared through her body and exploded in her mind, filling her with a new strength. 'Damn him,' she repeated. 'I'll kill him, the devil. I'll kill him — I *will*!'

Chapter Twelve

During the course of the summer, Marcus had improved his acquaintance with Caroline Anderson. More than improved his acquaintance. Now as irremovably fixed in Marcus Harley's heart as the polar ice cap is upon the roof of the world, Caroline had learned to please him, delight him and bewitch him. He adored her whole-heartedly and, although his mistress might not have expected such total fidelity, he had no desire to try out his own new-found amatory skills on anyone but her.

'You can come to see me,' he said. 'When you come to see Stuart, you must visit me as well. No one will think that's odd. Oh, Caro, don't look so sad. Cambridge is only an hour's train ride away.'

'We won't be able to go to bed together there.' Caroline sniffed.

'No. Well, perhaps not so easily as we do now. But perhaps I can smuggle you into college now and then.' Marcus giggled. 'You could be rolled up in a carpet and delivered, like Cleopatra!'

Caroline did not laugh. 'I don't want to get you sent down,' she said, miserably. 'I don't want to be responsible for ruining your career.'

'No, I know you don't.' Marcus patted her shoulder. 'We'll have to be very careful.'

'And there'll be other women now,' added Caroline, in the same dismal tone of voice. 'You'll meet other girls — you'll fall in love, maybe.'

'I doubt that.'

'Do you?' Caroline looked at her lover. 'Oh, Marcus — don't think I don't realize what a favour you're doing me by going to bed with me like this. I know perfectly well that when you see what else life has to offer, that you — well, you won't want *me* any more.'

'Don't be silly.'

'I'm not being silly.' Caroline sighed. 'I'm just a harlot, after all — an easy whore. The sort of woman that men despise.'

'Is that what you really think?'

'I —'

'You what?'

She looked at him. 'I wanted to sleep with you,' she said. 'I wanted to go to bed with you. I wanted to be able to say to myself, Marcus Harley is the most desirable man in England, and for a while — for a very little while — he was mine.' Caroline studied her fingernails. 'Now you know I'm a stupid harlot,' she muttered. 'As if you were ever *mine*!'

Marcus took her hand in his and kissed it. 'You do talk the most absolute rubbish sometimes,' he said. 'I'm not the most desirable man in England, I haven't any money for a start. Caroline, you're always going on about how I can't possibly want you, but has it ever occurred to you that *I* need affection? That I've wondered, perhaps, if you might even love me?'

'I *do* love you!' Caroline stared. 'I love you more than my life!'

'Well, then.' Marcus grinned. 'Nothing can alter what's passed,' he continued. 'And there's no reason, is there, why we can't always be as happy together as we are now? *I* love *you*. I think that very probably I always shall.' He kissed her again and sat up. 'Now, Caroline, give me a smile.'

She tried to smile but couldn't. And then Marcus himself felt a faint twinge of anxiety. Deliberately he smothered it. 'We'd better get dressed,' he told her. 'Come on, Caro — find your clothes.'

* * *

'What will you do later, Marcus?' asked Caroline, as the two of them sat on the edge of the Serpentine, watching the children sailing their boats. 'After Cambridge, I mean. Will you go into the firm with your father?'

'I expect so.' Marcus lobbed a pebble into the water. 'Dad was saying something about sending me off to France for a couple of years, then — well, we'll see.'

Caroline grimaced, thinking of the pretty French women who were even more of a potential threat than the Cambridge undergraduates.

'My parents are thinking of giving up that flat,' she said. 'It's expensive to run, and they don't use it much. But I was wondering about getting a job and living there myself. What do you think?'

'Splendid idea!' Marcus turned to her and grinned. 'Caro, that would be marvellous.'

'You approve of working girls?' she asked, deliberately misunderstanding him, trying not to smile at his apparent enthusiasm for, she assumed, their continuing friendship. 'You think women ought to earn their own livings?'

'Oh, definitely!' He nodded. 'My mother's always worked, after all. She always has some project or other on the go.'

'I suppose she has.' Caroline smiled at her lover. 'I'll speak to Dad,' she promised. 'He's more or less agreed that I can take a stenographer's course, and so —'

'You hold him to it.' Marcus covered Caroline's hand with his. 'You insist, if it's what you really want to do. Caro, is Minnie visiting her sister again this afternoon?'

'I told her she could go out for an hour or two.'

'Excellent.' Marcus stood up. 'Well, shall we go and see if she's dusted the furniture properly? Can't have housemaids taking advantage, can we?'

* * *

Caroline watched him walk along the road, his hands in his pockets, the summer sun shining on his fair hair. A few yards away from the house, he stopped, bought a bunch of roses from a flower seller and the woman beamed at him, as all women did.

Caroline told herself that the flowers were certain to be for his mother. Marcus had told her that he was expected home at three, and it was now well after five. The roses were a peace-offering.

She still couldn't believe that he loved her. Liked her,

perhaps — she was a convenient enough tart, maybe. But Cambridge, a paradise full of attractive girls, would certainly change him. 'I'll lose him,' she thought, sadly. 'But he liked me once. And that can't be taken away from me.'

* * *

Cambridge *was* paradise. Marcus thought so at once. He was enchanted by the charm of the university buildings, which were, on the whole, so elegant and attractive, so much more carefully laid out and readily accessible than those of the Oxford colleges. There they always seemed turned in on themselves, huddled behind grey protecting walls.

He was especially delighted by the beauty of King's. He felt that if he managed to get a First and a fellowship, he'd be quite happy to spend the rest of his life there.

There was, however, a serpent in this Eden. Marcus met him on his second day in college. This particular viper lurked on his staircase, in the form of a third-year medical student.

Gilbert Addams was a middle-sized, very dark young man who reminded Marcus of his grandfather, but his scowl and habitually truculent expression did nothing to invite confidence or friendship.

Marcus had nodded to him once or twice as he ran up to his rooms, but Addams held aloof, ignoring the freshman, pushing past him rudely and appearing not to see him as they passed each other on the stairs.

'Blow him, then,' thought Marcus, who by the end of his first fortnight was well on the way to making a dozen or more other friends.

Trouble between the medic and the freshman blew up on the day that Marcus asked Addams' bedder if he would mind getting some food and drink in for him. Marcus intended to have some people round to his rooms for an informal party. When Marcus passed him on the stairs, he mentioned as much to the medical student.

'What?' Gilbert Addams glowered at Marcus. 'Look here, Harley,' he rapped. 'Curtis is *my* bedder. And if you think you can smarm *your* oily way into his good graces, you can bloody well think again.'

Marcus, whose own bedder was a decrepit elderly man who

didn't look capable of lugging cases of bottles upstairs, had not realized that bedders were their particular masters' exclusive property. He had, in any case, tipped Curtis very generously, and the servant himself had not objected to doing as he was asked. 'Now just *you* look here,' he began. 'Curtis doesn't mind getting in a bit of stuff for me, so I don't honestly see why you should.'

'Don't you, indeed? That's a pity.' Gilbert Addams evidently did not wish to discuss the matter any more. 'Leave Curtis alone in future,' he barked. 'Is that clear?' And, attempting to push past Marcus, he made to walk down the stairs.

But Marcus stood his ground. 'I didn't realize,' he began, trying again. 'Addams, I'm sorry if I kept Curtis from seeing to things he ought to have done for you. But I didn't —'

'Get out of my way, will you?'

'Listen, Addams —'

But Gilbert Addams, who was already late for a physiology lecture, didn't want to listen. He pushed Marcus up against the wall of the landing and held him there, glaring at the startled freshman. 'When I tell you to move,' he muttered, 'you will move.' He gave Marcus's lapel a shake. 'Do you understand?'

'Let me go.' Marcus tried to wriggle free, smiling what he hoped was a conciliatory smile. 'Come on, Addams,' he said reasonably. 'Let me go.'

'Oh, that's a lovely smile!' Gilbert Addams looked into Marcus's eyes. 'Go on, pretty boy,' he jeered. 'Smile nicely at Mr Curtis; grin at him like that and he'll desert me completely. He'll attend to your every need — those you already have and maybe those of which you're not yet aware.'

'What did you say?' Marcus felt his face redden. 'Now just listen to me, Addams —'

'Yes?' The medical student grinned. 'You do look particularly fetching when you blush,' he added. 'Has anyone ever said so? Has any nice man ever told you that a bit of colour in your cheeks does wonders for your pretty face? And that —'

'Shut up!' Gilbert Addams had now gone too far. Angered by the implied insult, Marcus drew back his fist and punched the medic hard, knocking him against the opposite wall.

Slipping on the step, Gilbert grabbed at the air and caught Marcus's cuff, dragging his aggressor half way down the staircase.

Over and over they fell, coming to rest on the landing below in a tangled knot of writhing limbs, Marcus firmly pinned underneath the other man.

Gilbert, who was shorter than Marcus but just as heavy, was obviously the more practised fighter. Soon he had Marcus on his back, was astride him and had his wrists pinned to the floor. 'Give me a kiss,' he said, grinning at Marcus's helplessness. 'Come on, Danny boy. Let's see if you're as sensual as you look!'

Things could have become very unpleasant then. Marcus, despite having spent years being pestered and drooled over by both amorous boys and lecherous schoolmasters, had nothing against homosexuals, but he resented the assumption that he might be one himself. He glared at Addams. Freeing his hands, he grabbed him by the collar and was about to punch his ugly face.

But then, suddenly, he saw the funny side of it. Marcus began to laugh. Looking up at his tormentor, he giggled helplessly. 'Get up, you stupid sod,' he said. 'Oh, for Christ's sake, move!'

'Who're you calling a sod?' Just as heterosexual as Marcus was, Addams glared. 'Who the hell are you calling a bloody sod?'

'You, you great hairy gargoyle.' Grinning, Marcus pushed Gilbert's chest. 'You, you black ape!'

And then, Gilbert Addams laughed too. He got up, brushed his trousers and grinned at Marcus. 'Thanks to you,' he said, 'I've missed the start of my bloody lecture. Well, there's no point in going now. Why don't you come and have a sherry? College stuff, perfectly vile, but it makes you drunk if you have enough.'

Marcus rubbed a bruise on his arm. 'All right,' he agreed. 'Why not?'

* * *

'Jenny,' said Gilbert, a few days later. 'Jenny, meet Marcus. Isn't he lovely?'

Jenny Westbrook, a small, dark-haired girl whose father was a professor of classics at the university, smiled up at her fiancé's handsome friend. 'Hello, Marcus,' she said, easily, holding out her hand. She grimaced at Gilbert. 'Isn't *he* a pain?'

'He is indeed.' Marcus smiled back at her. 'How do you put up with him?'

'He's the cross I've been put on this earth to bear.' She giggled and pushed her hand into Gilbert's. 'Now, you revolting creature — are we going on the river today, or tomorrow?' She turned to Marcus. 'You'll come, won't you?' she asked. 'Do come with us! Please.'

So Marcus did.

Marcus's first couple of years at Cambridge passed by very pleasantly. He found the work — as much of it as he was prepared to do — undemanding. And, naturally, he was himself much in demand, as an ornament, as an accessory, as a love object. Making dozens of acquaintances, Gilbert Addams and Caroline's brother Stuart remained his only real friends.

Surrounded by women — and men — whose intentions towards him were only too obviously dishonourable, he had, on several occasions, been tempted. Once, he succumbed.

Stephanie Garside, a statuesque brunette undergraduate, made no secret her determination to have Marcus Harley for her own. Eventually, she did manage to inflame and cajole him into a half-hearted affair, but he felt so guilty about smuggling her into his rooms, so uneasy in bed with her, that there was no pleasure in it for either of them.

For it was always Caroline who was in his mind. Even as he kissed Stephanie Garside's beautiful mouth, even as he caressed Stephanie Garside's white shoulders, he thought of Caroline's sweet little face, of her solemn blue eyes, of her small, neat body curled up in his embrace. 'It's no use,' he told Stephanie, as he walked back with her through the dark streets to her lodgings. 'We've tried, but it doesn't work. I can't see you any more.'

She had protested, asked for reasons. But Marcus would not elaborate, and the next time he saw her he was unnecessarily curt with her.

Gilbert Addams laughed at him. 'God, you're daft,' he said.

'Stupid, that's what you are. Throwing a goddess over for that little brown mouse. Now, if Stephanie Garside had propositioned *me* —'

'You'd have had nothing to do with her. Jenny would murder you if you so much as looked at another woman.' Marcus opened a book. 'Now, can you shut up and go away?' he asked. 'I've an essay to write.'

※ ※ ※

Dora was delighted and flattered when, during the summer of 1912, her favourite nephew came all the way from London to visit her.

Marcus Harley was, in Dora's opinion, the best-looking young man in England. His face and figure seemed to combine the best of the Lawrence family traits, which together with the fair good looks of his father, had produced a young man of almost god-like beauty. Dora could stare at him for hours, admiring his perfect face and tall, upright figure.

One morning she watched him stroll across the lawn behind her house. As graceful as a young Apollo, he resembled an engraving she'd seen in one of her father's books. Except that Marcus was better looking. His face bore none of the condescending haughtiness of the god's. Marcus was *nice*.

He saw her standing on the terrace, and waved to her. 'Come on, Dora,' he called. 'Let's go and see if the otters are on the river bank. I've never seen an otter.'

He held out his hand to her, and she went running to him, smiling. 'Otters!' She slipped her arms around his waist and looked up into his face. 'Marcus, you're *so* beautiful!' she cried, beaming up at him. 'I've been watching you from the house and I was thinking that I might have you for breakfast.'

'I'd be a bit stringy. Stick to kippers, I should.' He grimaced. 'Dora, you do say embarrassing things,' he said. 'You're such a tease.'

'I'm not a tease. And, anyway — you are beautiful. You know you are.'

'Oh, yes, I do know.' Marcus sighed. 'My schooldays were a misery. You've just no idea how tiresome it is when people are always falling in love with you. I've had to thrash quite a few chaps, just to keep myself pure.' He smirked affectedly.

'And it's exactly the same at Cambridge. Except that now there are women trying to seduce me, too. Do you know, Dora, my tutor — well, it's a strain, I can tell you.'

'Conceited devil.' Dora hugged him, liking the feel of him through his thin cotton shirt. 'Would you consent to be seen walking down King's Parade with your ancient aunt?' she asked him. 'I shall be coming to Cambridge soon. I shall look you up and embarrass you.'

'My dear little aunt, nothing would give me greater pleasure than to see you there. By the way, where's Ralph got to? He said he'd come riding with me this morning.'

At the mention of her husband, Dora shuddered. 'He got up at four o'clock,' she replied. 'I expect he's lurking in the woods, killing things. He'll be back for breakfast with corpses in his pockets and blood on his hands. He enjoys murdering animals,' she added sourly.

'He'll get the chance to kill people some day soon, I expect.' Marcus grimaced. 'This year, next year — the war with Germany won't be delayed for much longer.'

'There won't be a war.' Dora frowned at Marcus. 'Nobody wants a war.'

'The Kaiser does. He can't wait to try out all his new bombs and guns and other toys. He's dying for a fight.'

'But not with us.' He can't possibly want to fight us. He likes the British, and he's Queen Victoria's grandson, after all.'

Marcus threw back his head and laughed. 'He's Queen Victoria's grandson! Oh, Dora, you are comical sometimes. Look here, Wilhelm, old chap — you can't pick any fights with us. The old lady wouldn't have liked it!' Marcus hugged his aunt. 'Dolly, don't be so naive.'

'Don't you be so cheeky. Remember that I used to spoon bread and milk into your horrible little mouth not so very long ago.'

'Ah, sorry, Aunt Dora.' Marcus smiled charmingly at the little woman at his side. 'Oh, look — here comes the hunter. Ralph can come and see the otters too.'

Dora had been surprised to observe that even Ralph wasn't proof against Marcus's extraordinary charm. While her nephew was at the Grange, Ralph had behaved as well as any wife could have wished and was a perfect host to his admittedly undemanding guest. The illusion that she and Ralph were a united, happy couple almost deceived Dora herself, and it was a shock to her when, after Marcus had left, she was brought thudding back to reality.

For she was now afraid of her husband — of his temper, his cold, determined cruelty; and, more than that, she was ill with dread that he might attack her again, might hurt her in that awful, humiliating fashion . . .

He never did anything of the sort. In fact, since he'd upset her so badly, he had been gentle with her, had come to her bed and been careful — even kind. It was now more than a year since that horrible night. But there was always the fear that he might, and Dora lived with the knowledge that she would not be able to prevent him.

'Just a short holiday, Ralph,' she said defensively, holding out the postcard for him to read. 'Miriam's about to have another baby, so she'd be glad if I was there to help with the other children while she is laid up. And didn't you want to go over to Martley, to stay with the Carradines for the shooting?'

'You'll come back?' Ralph narrowed his cold blue eyes at her. 'Dora, you must promise me that you'll come back.'

'Of course I'll come back. Why do you think I won't?'

'I think you dislike me. Over the past couple of years you've altered; you're not my sweet, loving Dora any more.' He sighed bitterly. 'Sometimes I think you hate me.'

Dora stared at him. She'd meant to keep both her fear and her hatred a secret, the better to extract any revenge should the chance to do so ever arise. 'You're mistaken,' she said coldly. 'I just want to see my best friend, that's all. Really it is.'

'All right, Dora.' Ralph leaned over her and kissed her cheek, lightly, even affectionately. He stood by her for a moment, his hand resting on her shoulder. 'You may go,' he said. 'Dora, you mustn't hate me. I can't help myself sometimes; you must know that.'

He walked out of the room and she heard his footsteps clatter down the stone-flagged passage to the gun room. Hate him? How could she help but hate him?

Chapter Thirteen

CAMBRIDGE WAS, AS ALWAYS IN the summer, a pleasant dream. Dora visited Marcus, who was loafing around in his rooms for part of the long vacation, and was gratified when he introduced her to his friends. She had imagined that he'd want to hide her away, his ancient aunt. Being well over thirty years old, she was, after all, a veritable antique.

'Dora, this is Caroline Anderson. Stuart's her brother — we're at the same college.' Marcus smiled at his aunt. 'Will you come on the river with us this afternoon?'

'I'd love to. But you won't want me to row or anything, will you?'

'Row?' Stuart grinned. 'Of course not, Mrs Challoner. You're needed to chaperone Caroline.'

'I see. Then I'd be happy to come. Thank you.'

Dora smiled at the young woman standing at her brother's side. She was a slight, serious-looking girl, not particularly beautiful although she was certainly pleasant enough to look at.

But, Dora decided, she was too small — even smaller than Dora herself. And too thin; she had no bosom to speak of and no hips worth the name. Her face was pretty enough in a quiet, unremarkable way; her eyes were large, and a rather nice shade of dark blue, but she was just an ordinary, fair-haired girl, no prettier and no plainer than a hundred others one might see in a day's walk through a city anywhere in England. Dora wondered why she had been selected to spend an afternoon on the river with these two handsome boys . . .

'Do you like boating, Mrs Challoner?' Stuart handed Dora

into the boat.

'Yes.' Dora nodded, settled herself down upon a pile of cushions. 'My brother often took me out on the river when we lived in Oxford.

'Ah.' Stuart picked up the pole. 'They punt from the wrong end there. Now, I'll show you how it's meant to be done.' Skilfully, he pushed off from the bank and sent the boat skimming down the river towards the first of the many bridges.

Caroline, seated opposite Dora, trailed her hand in the water, now and then giving Marcus a covert glance. Occasionally the girl's features were reddened by a sudden blush, particularly when Marcus looked at her, or when he addressed a remark to her . . .

Dora felt sorry for her. Poor thing — she hadn't a chance. Dora wondered if Marcus were aware of the emotion he so obviously inspired. Probably not, she decided. Practically every woman he saw looked at him like that.

Later, Marcus took over from Stuart and eventually they arrived at Grantchester. 'Would you like a walk along the bank?' he asked Dora.

'No.' Dora smiled. 'It's too hot for me. I'll sit here and rest. You all go, though.'

'Too hot for me as well.' Stuart took off his jacket and mopped his forehead. 'Mrs Challoner, you won't object to my company for half an hour?'

So Marcus and Caroline strolled off together and were soon out of sight. Dora turned to Stuart. 'Have you known Marcus long?' she asked.

'Oh, yes. We were at school together. Our parents are friends; they live within a mile of each other in London.'

'Is Caroline studying here, too?'

'No, she's doing some sort of secretarial course in town. She's not very intellectual,' he added, grinning. 'She had enough of books in school. Now she sees herself as a career woman, I think.'

'I'm the dunce of *our* family.' Dora smiled, then reddened. 'Not that I meant to imply your sister is one,' she added hastily.

Stuart laughed. 'Mrs Challoner, you're much too kind to imply any such thing. Anyway, it's I who am the dunce of the family. I'm only marking time here until I can go into the army.'

'Will you like that?'

'Oh, rather! I'm looking forward to it. There's going to be a war with Germany some day soon, so I shall really enjoy myself.' He grinned at Dora. 'I fancy myself as a cavalry officer, charging into the breach, you know.'

Dora didn't laugh. 'Everyone says there'll be a war,' she murmured. 'I really can't think why.'

'Can't you?' He picked at a patch of clover and flicked some of the purple flower-heads across the grass. 'Well, don't worry about it. It's certain to be a nice, cosy little war fought far away in eastern Europe. We boys will go off and have fun for a couple of months, then we'll all come home again and show off to crowds of admiring females, and tell them how we settled the Kaiser.'

Dora grimaced. It seemed a terrible prospect to her and she wondered how this child she was sitting with could talk so lightly of something so awful.

Caroline and Marcus reappeared just then, accompanied by a young man and a girl whose pretty, rosy face had obviously been designed for laughter. 'Gil Addams.' Marcus introduced his friend. 'And Jenny Westbrook. Watch what you say to her — her father is Anthony's head of department.'

Dora laughed. 'Do you know my brother?' she asked.

Jenny nodded. 'I'm quite friendly with Mrs Lawrence, too,' she volunteered. 'I take Jonathan out sometimes. He's a dear little boy.'

'*Isn't* he? Such a character.' Dora, as pleased as the most doting mother could have been to hear her little nephew so commended, beamed at Jenny. 'Tell me, Miss Westbrook,' she began, 'how do you —'

'So I'll see Caroline to the station.' Marcus gave Gilbert Addams a meaningful nod. 'I'll be back before midnight. The usual arrangement?'

Gilbert glanced at Dora and saw she was still busily chatting to Jenny. He grinned. 'I'll see you can get in,' he replied. 'Are you going up to town?'

'Mm.' Marcus walked over and touched his aunt's arm.

'Look, Dora,' he said, urgently. 'Caroline's got to catch her train soon, so she and I are going back to Cambridge in a cab. Do you mind if Jenny and Gil go back with you and Stuart?'

'Not at all.' Dora looked narrowly at Marcus and saw he was flushed and his pupils were dilated. 'I think *you* ought to go and lie down,' she said. 'You've had a bit too much sun. Why didn't you wear a hat?'

'I forgot to bring one. But I'll lie down in an hour or so.' Marcus took Caroline by the elbow and began to pull her towards the road. 'I can promise you that, Dora. I'll see you tomorrow.'

'She seems very nice, your aunt.' Snuggled close to Marcus in the cab, Caroline looked up at him. 'Do you think she's guessed?'

'Not a chance. Dora's famous for not seeing what's right in front of her nose.' Marcus took Caroline in his arms and kissed her with some degree of passion. 'Oh, Caro,' he murmured, hugging her to him. 'I *have* missed you. It's been a whole fortnight since I last saw you. Fourteen lonely days and dreary nights.'

'Poor Marcus, have you been suffering?'

'Yes, I jolly well have!' He frowned at her. 'Don't tease, Caro.'

'I'm not teasing. I miss you, as well. But I'm sure that, whatever you've been, you can't have been lonely.'

'It's possible to be lonely in a crowd.' Marcus took Caroline's hands and placed her arms around his neck. 'I'm always lonely when I'm not with you.'

'Minnie's gone away until Sunday. To see her cousin in Sussex.' Caroline kissed her lover. 'You can stay all night if you like.'

'Can I?' Marcus grinned. 'Excellent. For breakfast I have toast, marmalade, black coffee —'

'You'll get whatever is available.' Caroline kissed him again. 'Marcus, have you really missed me?'

'I'll show you. When we get to the flat I'll show you. You won't get very much sleep tonight, I'll make quite sure of that.'

* * *

An adolescent fondness for large quantities of any alcohol

available was a trait shared by both Gilbert Addams and Marcus Harley. A celibate evening was frequently beguiled by the consumption of half a bottle of whisky, not to mention several glasses of some nasty college sherry which, together with the cheap Scotch, made a perfectly noxious mixture.

It was the middle of the week, and Marcus and Gilbert were spending one such evening in the gloomy comfort of Marcus's room. Rain banged against the windows and the dull evening grew darker and more dismal. Gilbert tipped a tumblerful of sherry down his throat and sighed. He looked at Marcus who was sprawled on the bed, his hands behind his head, half asleep. 'What's it like to be you?' he enquired blearily. 'I mean, what's it like to be so bloody beautiful?'

Marcus grinned and reached for his glass. 'It's a bloody liability,' he replied tipsily. 'That's what it's like. Oh, shut up, Gil, why don't you? Or, if you like, tell me what it's like to be so bloody hideous?'

Gilbert Addams threw another log on to the fire and laughed. 'I may be hideous,' he retorted. 'I may be a gargoyle, but Jenny loves me. "Jenny kissed me when we met, jumping from the chair she sat in . . ." What comes next?'

Marcus shrugged. '*I* don't know.'

'You do. Something, something, something, something. Oh, that's it. And, "say I'm getting old, but add, Jenny kissed me". There,' he concluded drunkenly. 'And that's poetry.'

Marcus sniffed. 'You're lucky,' he said. 'Lucky, to have a Jenny.'

'You have a Caroline.' Gilbert nodded wisely. 'And you have a Stephanie, a Delia, a Veronica — all of them mad keen to rip off their dresses and get into bed with you. I don't know what *you* have to moan about.'

'Mm.' Marcus took another gulp of whisky. 'I'd rather Stephanie and co kept their dresses on.'

'Would you? So what is it about little Caroline then?' Gilbert poured himself some more sherry. 'God, this is foul,' he muttered, tossing it back. 'What is it about *her* that makes your trousers too tight and has you palpitating with lust? When we met you in Grantchester that afternoon, I thought you were going to burst.'

'So did I.' Marcus grimaced. 'So did I. Oh, I don't know what it is,' he said. 'Honestly, I really don't know. I suppose I love her,' he admitted, resignedly.

'So what's the problem?'

'Did I say there was a problem?' Marcus sniffed, then hiccupped. 'Listen to me, Addams. You may be a bloody medic, but you're not a psychologist.'

'Does *she* love *you*?' Gilbert Addams leaned forwards. 'Does she re-cip-ro-cate your e-mo-tion?'

'I think she does.' Marcus looked into his glass. 'There's something about her I can't fathom,' he said. 'But she's always in my mind. Whenever she's with me, I'm comfortable — happy. And not otherwise.'

Gilbert Addams giggled. 'She's got you by the balls,' he sniggered. 'Oh, she's run circles round you, hasn't she, the clever little bitch.'

'What the hell d'you mean by that?'

'Was she your first?'

'Well —'

'Yes, I thought as much. "Something you can't fathom" indeed. Ha! Very metaphysical. The fact is, the poor child can't even look at you without wetting herself — and she flatters you speechless.' Gilbert laughed again. 'Believe me, Harley, that's all it is. It's as simple as that.'

Marcus rose to his feet. Unsteadily, he swayed over towards Gilbert. 'If you ever talk about Caroline in that way again,' he began thickly, 'I shall put you in hospital. Do you understand? I shall break both your arms and both your legs, and spoil whatever beauty you do possess.'

'Oh, go and chase yourself.' Standing up, Gilbert touched Marcus very gently on the chest. 'Or, better still, have a little lie down — before you fall down.'

Obediently, Marcus fell backwards on to his bed and passed out.

* * *

Staying with Anthony and Miriam in their little house — too little now that their family had increased to its present proportions — Dora frequently experienced a passing pang of regret that she had not chosen her own marriage partner more carefully. 'I didn't know Ralph at all,' she reflected. 'All I saw was what I wanted to see. The Ralph I married never existed outside my silly dreams.

While she was with Anthony's pretty children, playing with them as she'd once played with baby Marcus, Dora was happy. Three little black-haired, dark-eyed siblings, slim and graceful, all less solid in build than their father; they were a charming trio. She enjoyed taking them for walks, carrying little Katherine in her arms, while Jonathan and Rachel trotted along beside her.

Anthony, as preoccupied with his work and his students as ever his father had been at the same age — for this was the time when he was consolidating some research which he hoped would make his reputation, determined as he was not to be known simply as Stephen Lawrence's boy, competent enough but without the old man's flair — was nevertheless more practical and observant than Stephen ever was.

He noticed Dora's pallor, saw the smudges under her fine brown eyes and he worried about her. 'You're not happy, are you, Dolly?' he asked her one evening when Miriam, tired and heavy and longing to be delivered of her baby, had gone to bed.

'I'm perfectly happy.' Dora had looked at him, heavy-eyed, and the lines around her mouth deepened into a grimace. 'What do you mean?'

'You're *not* perfectly happy. Far from it. You've been miserable off and on for years, but you look terrible these days.'

'Thank you very much indeed, Anthony. You do cheer one up.'

He sat down next to her on the sofa and took her hand in his. 'Won't you tell me what's bothering you, Doll?' he asked. 'What's he doing to you?'

'Nothing. Anthony, don't tease me.'

Anthony laid his arm across his sister's shoulders and pulled her against him. Letting her lean against his chest, he kissed her forehead. 'We've always been good friends, haven't we, Doll?' he asked.

'Yes. But all the same —'

'So won't you tell me what's wrong?'

It was so long since anyone had hugged Dora like that, since she had been cherished and comforted, that she found tears coming into her eyes. There was a pleasant warm smell about Anthony, of recent perspiration mixed with the odours of tobacco and ink. It was like being curled up next to her father, who always smelled just like that. 'There's nothing to tell, really,' she whispered. 'Not really.'

'Oh, yes there is. Don't say anything if you'd rather not. But if you *do* confide in me, I might be able to help — mightn't I?'

'You can't help. But if I tell you — oh, God, Anthony, I must tell *someone* soon, I'll go mad if I don't – you must promise never to tell our parents. Or anyone else. You must promise that.'

'I shan't tell anyone — not even Miriam. Well?'

'He hurt me.' Dora buried her face in Anthony's chest and began to sob. 'He hurt me. Only once — and I think he was sorry when he'd done it. He'd been drinking, you see, and he's never tried to do it again. But he was so cruel to me, and I'm so afraid he'll get drunk again some time, and then —'

'What did he do?'

Dora felt her cheeks grow hot. 'He did what I suppose boys must do to each other at school. Instead of what married couples are supposed to do together, he did — that.'

Anthony's grip on her shoulders tightened. 'Oh, my poor Dora,' he murmured. 'When did this happen?'

'A year or so ago. You see, it's ancient history really. I don't know why I'm still so upset about it; I ought to have got over it by now.'

'He forced you?'

'Of course he forced me!' Dora raised her tear-stained face to Anthony's and stared at him in amazement. 'You don't imagine, do you, that I'd have agreed to such a thing?'

'Well, perhaps some people do. Oh, I'm sorry, Dora — I shouldn't have asked you that.'

'Listen to me, Anthony.' Dora shook his arm. 'I may be naive, I may be stupid and ignorant — God knows the rest of you are always telling me I am — but I know what happened to me. My husband raped me and he did so in a particularly horrible way. He hurt me, don't you understand? He held me down and abused me in the most disgusting fashion.'

'Hush, Dolly, hush. Don't get so upset.' Anthony rocked her to and fro, crooning to her as if she'd been Jonathan or Rachel, cheated of a treat or crying over a cut knee. Dora let him hug her but she wondered if he realized just how upset she was. If that kind of thing was common, if other people did it, if Anthony himself —'

'I'll have to go back,' she sniffed. 'In the end, I'll have to go back to him. He made me promise that I would.'

'I really don't see why you should.' Anthony frowned. 'You could apply for a separation — a divorce, even. He could go to prison for what he did to you.'

'Could he?'

'I'm not absolutely sure, but I think so.'

'Oh, but Anthony, you said a minute ago that you didn't think I had any reasonable grounds for complaint.'

'I never said anything of the sort.'

'You implied it. You said that some people —'

'I never meant to suggest that you were making something out of nothing. Look, dear, it's late. Shall we go up to bed now, and talk about it in the morning? When we're calmer?'

'*You* look perfectly calm to me.'

'Well, I'm not. Do you know what I'd do if I had Challoner here, lying bound and gagged at my feet?'

'No. What?'

'I think that perhaps a red-hot poker might be the ideal thing to use on *him*. Go on upstairs now, Dolly. We'll think again tomorrow.'

Anthony persuaded his sister that she had no obligation to return to her husband, whatever she had promised. A week became a month, then six weeks. Baby David was born. Still Dora did not go home.

Anthony was working peacefully in his study when Ralph arrived at the house in Pearson Street to fetch his wife. Miriam had gone on a visit to some friends, taking David and Rachel with her. Katherine was out with her nanny. Jonathan had gone into Cambridge with his aunt to buy some new shoes.

Anthony heard voices in the hall. He had taken off his

glasses and laid down his pen by the time the housemaid had knocked upon his study door and informed him that there was a Mr Challoner to see him.

Anthony pushed his work aside and stood up. 'Good afternoon, Ralph,' he said, evenly. 'You should have let us know you were coming — we could have prepared a more elaborate welcome for you.'

'Where's Dora?'

'In the town, shopping. Thank you, Nancy. We shan't want any tea, Mr Challoner won't be here long. Close the door after you, please.'

Ralph looked round the study. He picked up a book and let a dozen place markings flutter to the floor. Sitting down, he stretched out his long legs and grinned at Anthony. 'Family well?' he enquired. 'I suppose there's another Jewish brat in the world by now?'

'My wife had a baby son almost a month ago.'

'What d'you call him? Solomon? Isaiah, perhaps?'

'David.'

'David Lawrence. Mmm. Hardly betrays his origins at all.' Ralph yawned affectedly. 'But then, deception's a speciality in your family, isn't it? Deceit and dissimulation are second nature to you?'

'Look Challoner, we won't waste any more of each others' time.' Anthony folded his arms and leaned against his desk. 'Dora's left you,' he said. 'She's had enough of you. She won't be coming back to Hereford, so you might as well go home now.' He bent forward and stared at Ralph. 'Dora's left you,' he repeated, flatly.

'She's what? What the hell d'you mean?'

'You wife has decided not to live with you any more. Isn't that plain enough for you to understand? You great stupid thug, she doesn't choose to be married to you any longer. You are going to have to accept that, so start trying to digest it now.'

Ralph glared at Anthony. 'I don't have to accept anything *you* tell me,' he barked. 'I don't have to listen to anything a purblind little runt like you has to say. Good God, if you weren't so small I'd hit you!'

Anthony lounged against his desk and gazed insolently back

at Ralph. 'I'm somewhat larger than my sister,' he retorted. 'You've had no scruples about hurting her.'

'What the devil d'you mean by that?'

'I mean, you overgrown half-wit, that you've never let the fact that Dora is weaker and much smaller than you prevent you from practising your disgusting perversions on her, have you?' He gave Ralph a look of such distaste that the other man looked away, momentarily embarrassed. 'Oh, just get out of my house, could you?'

'I'll wait for my wife.'

'Then I'd prefer you to wait in the street.'

'Going to throw me out yourself?' Ralph laughed. 'You and that skinny parlourmaid between you?'

Anthony glowered at Ralph, who now rose from his chair and walked across to Anthony's desk. He pushed a pile of papers on to the floor, scattering them everywhere. Then he picked up an inkwell and toyed with it, grinning as Anthony suddenly drew breath.

'Don't look so discomfited, runt,' he said, pleasantly. 'I shan't pour it all over your desk — yet. But really, *someone* ought to teach you some manners. Your behaviour towards visitors is quite appalling. A schoolmaster like you, a scrofulous little bastard who's the result of the embraces between a lecher and a whore, should know his place in society, and should —'

He got no further. Anthony's temper gave way. He lunged at Ralph and punched him hard on the jaw, causing him to fall awkwardly against the fireplace — where he lolled, winded, for a few seconds.

Caught off guard and surprised, Ralph merely stared at his attacker who, if he'd had any sense, would have made his escape without further delay.

But Anthony stood his ground. Ralph, recovering, caught him by the shoulder and pushed him against a wall. He held him with one hand while his other fist smashed into Anthony's face.

Half stunned by the blow, Anthony now staggered around the room, trying to hit his adversary in the stomach.

But he was, of course, no match for Ralph. A good eight inches taller, weighing at least a third as much again, Ralph had no difficulty in picking him up by the collar and holding him against the mantelshelf while he punched Anthony about the face and body, grinning at his victim's helplessness and hitting him just where he pleased.

But, when one of Anthony's flailing fists happened to catch Ralph's jawbone, the bigger man suddenly went berserk. He directed his blows now, hitting Anthony squarely in the face, again and again and again . . .

Having sent Jonathan upstairs to take off his coat, Dora walked into the study, still in her outdoor clothes, and followed by a frightened housemaid who was gibbering something about fetching a constable.

Ralph, bleeding copiously from the mouth, let Anthony go. He glared at his wife. 'He started it,' he muttered, giving Anthony's now prostrate body a vicious kick.

Dora gaped at him, then knelt down to look at Anthony, who seemed to be unconscious. 'What have you done to him?' she cried. 'You've half killed him. Whatever did he do to you?'

Ralph swayed slightly and caught at the corner of Anthony's desk. 'He began it,' he repeated, sullenly. 'You're coming with me, Dora,' he added. 'You're coming back to Hereford — now. Go and get your things. Well, don't stare at me as if you didn't understand English. Move — or I'll kick your precious brother's bloody ribs in.'

Anthony groaned and muttered something — Dora didn't know what.

'Fetch your things.' Ralph grabbed Dora's arm and jerked her to her feet. 'Don't you understand me, you stupid woman?' He pushed Anthony with his foot, rolling him over so that Dora now saw the full extent of the damage to her brother's face. 'You have five minutes,' said Ralph, softly. 'You don't want your Hebrew sister-in-law to become a widow, do you? Not with another half-Jewish brat just come into the world?'

Dora, sickened by the sight of her brother's injuries and only too aware that in his present temper Ralph was quite capable of inflicting even more mutilation, ran out of the room. She found the housemaid and sent her out to fetch a doctor. Going up to Jonathan's room, she took his hand and led him down the stairs to the kitchen, where she left him with the cook.

She returned to the study. 'I'll come now,' she said. 'Could you help me get Anthony into a chair? Please?'

Ralph scowled. But he grabbed Anthony beneath the armpits and hauled him on to a chair. Anthony slumped forward on to his desk, coughing blood on to the carpet. Dora just managed to touch his hand in sympathy as she followed Ralph out of the room.

The blood wiped from his face and his overcoat buttoned to hide his bloodstained jacket, Ralph looked none the worse for his fight. Half an hour later he and Dora were sitting opposite one another, alone in a first class railway compartment.

'Why didn't you come home?' he asked.

'Don't speak to me, you wretch.'

Ralph tried to take Dora's hand. 'Why didn't you come home, Dora?' he repeated. 'You promised me you'd come back. I've missed you.'

Dora snatched her hand from his and folded her arms. 'Don't touch me,' she cried, almost in tears. 'I hate you!'

'Oh, Dora, don't say that. Look, I want you at home with me. Believe me, I'll be kind to you. I won't give you any more reason to dislike me. But I can't do without you. Since my parents died, I've no one but you. And my life isn't worth living unless you're with me.'

'You hurt my brother. You might have killed him.'

'Oh, that was just scrapping; he'll have had worse than that at school. Honestly, Dora, I hardly touched him. And anyway, hasn't your father ever given him a hiding?'

'My father has never hit any of us. Ever. He doesn't believe in beating his children — or anyone smaller and weaker than himself.'

'Doesn't he?' Ralph shrugged. 'My father used to beat me with his riding whip,' he said. 'It didn't do me any lasting harm.'

'I don't want to talk to you, Ralph. Just shut up, will you?'

And the rest of the journey to Hereford was made in total silence.

He was so pleasant, kind, attentive and mild that Dora could almost have believed that he was sorry for the past —

that he had indeed changed. The idea of separation and divorce, of the endless wrangling and bitterness, of the cries of "I told you so", were so appalling that Dora tried hard to convince herself that Ralph had indeed altered for the better.

She tried to be content.

Chapter Fourteen

'DO YOU REALLY THINK THERE'LL be a war?' Dorcas looked up from her copy of *The Times* and regarded Stephen anxiously. 'The leader in here is very pessimistic. But no one in England *wants* a war, do they?'

'Possibly not, so perhaps there won't be one.' Stephen looked back at her over the tops of his spectacles. 'And after all, my dear, what England wants is what counts, isn't it? Perhaps you ought to write to Mr Asquith and tell him that you're definitely against the idea. He might listen to you.'

'Don't, Stephen.' Crossly, Dora shook out the paper on her lap. She closed her eyes and lay back in her chair, enjoying the sunshine which was warm on the terrace that morning. 'All our boys,' she murmured. 'Anthony, James, Marcus — Ralph, even. Oh, it's too awful to contemplate.'

'Then don't think about it. I shan't.'

But, inexorably, England was drawn into a war. The murder of the heir to the Austrian throne, although in far-off Serbia, set off a chain of explosive repercussions which echoed all around the continent, with disastrous effect.

Austria declared war on Serbia. Russia, unable to overlook the threat to her fellow Slavs, mobilized against Austria. And Germany, Austria's ally, mobilized in turn against Russia.

At that stage, everything might have been contained in Eastern Europe; but then France, seeing an opportunity to recover the provinces of Alsace and Lorraine which she had lost to the Germans in the 1870s, decided to snatch back her territories while Germany was otherwise engaged.

The Germans, however, imagining that France could easily be taught a lesson, marched through Belgium and Luxembourg to settle the French once and for all, before turning their attention back to the Eastern Front.

Britain was committed by treaty to preserve Belgian neutrality.

Last minute wrangling and ultimatums from Asquith's Cabinet had no effect upon the government in Berlin. Scornful of Britain's contemptible little army, the only one in the whole of Europe which consisted entirely of volunteers, the Kaiser discounted the threat from England. At midnight on 4 August 1914, German troops were still in Belgium.

Ralph looked at the headline in *The Times*: BRITAIN AT WAR. He had laughed, then flinging the pages into the air, he had let them scatter all over the breakfast table. 'I shall join up,' he informed Dora, grinning. 'I'll go into Hereford today.'

'They won't want you — you're too old.' Dora buttered a slice of toast and pushed a sheet of newsprint away from her plate. 'And what about your leg? You have to be fit to be a soldier.'

But, fit or not, Ralph applied for a commission. He lied about the seriousness of his hunting injury, forced himself to walk normally, although every step was torture to him, and convinced the harrassed army medical officer that he should be passed A1 and made available for active service overseas.

Gazetted a lieutenant in the Warwickshire Regiment, Ralph was sent off to a training camp to learn drill and regimental history, along with dozens of other keen recruits all disgusted to be kept in England when they were anxious to be out there in Flanders, having a crack at the beastly Hun.

Atrocity stories began to appear in the newspapers almost at once; the gutter press was full of tales of the torture and murder of civilians, of the barbarous treatment of Allied prisoners.

But it was not until the autumn of 1914 that news of the true and appalling extent of the British army's casualties reached England. Hardly any of the soldiers, scarcely a trained rifleman of the regular army, appeared to have survived the massacre at Mons and the subsequent rout. There were dreadful stories of whole battalions being wiped out, of brigades practically annihilated. The original British Expeditionary Force had, by Christmas, more or less ceased to exist.

'When are we going?' A group of subalterns crowded round the notice board, craning to see their own names typed on the scrap of flimsy paper pinned to the green baize.

'Next Monday. You as well, Challoner.' An eighteen-year-old straight from the OTC at Harrow grinned at Ralph. And Second Lieutenant Challoner found he was grinning back at this spotty child, almost as excited as the schoolboy.

On 19 May the recruits left for the Continent, none of them ever having dug a trench, handled a grenade or fired a machine gun, but with their understanding of drill as perfect as six months of intensive training could make it, and their spirits as high as it was possible for them to be.

Michael Lawrence and his brother James, who were both happily settled at Ashton Cross and contented enough to be farmers, left it until January 1915 to enlist in the Worcestershire Regiment. Thus they deprived their father of his two most needed sons at the very time when Henry Lawrence was feeling his age beginning to oppress him.

But Katherine now saw her chance and was quick to seize it. She would show her father that she was as intelligent, sensible and capable of organization as any man could be.

'I really do think it will be a waste of pasture to leave the sheep in the lower meadows this spring,' she told her father, as they sat drinking their coffee one evening after dinner — for nowadays, having no wish to sit all by himself for an hour, Henry did not banish his wife and daughters from the dining table immediately after the dishes were cleared. 'They ought to go up on to the hillsides near Cropley, where the grass must be almost as good,' continued Katherine. 'And if the land around Martley is left free, we could buy in some more bullocks.'

'What did you say, Kathy?' Henry Lawrence looked hard at his daughter. 'You were talking of sheep? What do you know about sheep?'

'Enough to be certain that they ought not to be taking up pasture fit for cattle.' She leaned forward and looked back into her father's eyes. 'We'll need to produce as much meat as we can now,' she continued earnestly. 'After all, while this war lasts, the farmers will have to feed the country. And we don't at present, do we?'

'No, we don't. Well, I suppose you're right.' Henry stirred his coffee and reflected. 'I was thinking along those lines myself, of course,' he added. 'We'll have to start growing potatoes, I expect, and put in some other root crops.'

He stood up. 'Well then, Kathy — shall we go and look at the stock books?' he invited. 'Bring your coffee.'

As they walked down the passage to the estate office, Henry looked quizzically at his daughter. 'How d'you think you'd manage at auctions, eh?' he demanded.

'You'd let me *buy*?' This was more than Katherine had dared to hope for.

'I really don't see why you shouldn't. I'd come with you, of course — to begin with.' He put an arm around her shoulders. 'Kathy, my dear, this business might go on for years. I shall need you and your sisters from now on . . .'

* * *

'Here we are, gentlemen. All change. Come on, lads, everyone out now, the holiday excursion's over.'

Thus greeted by a dirty, dishevelled NCO at a French railhead seemingly miles from anywhere, Ralph and his companions gazed about them. They saw a filthy, twilit, shell-holed station and, beyond this, some ruined buildings. 'What *is* this place?' asked a young subaltern, obviously disconcerted by the air of desolation and decay.

'It's the Savoy 'otel.' The NCO grinned. 'Over 'ere's the Palm Court Ballroom and across to your left is the bar. Look, Sir, don't ask me where we are. Somewhere in France — that's all I can tell you, as you know very well.'

Far away to the east, the evening sky was orange, and the men who made up the new draft could hear the crumping of mortars and shells. And now the air of confusion and threat, the dank chilliness and the dismal look of the place, depressed them horribly.

After a night spent in uncomfortable billets in a row of stables in a commandeered farmhouse, the men formed into ranks and began their long march to the Front. The weight of their packs, and the fact that they'd had no breakfast worth the name, oppressed their spirits still further. A column of men marching in the opposite direction shouted to them. 'Where you lot goin'?'

A corporal, who brought up the rear of Ralph's detachment, replied but Ralph did not catch what he said. 'Poor sods,' remarked the NCO to whom the corporal had spoken. 'Poor bloody bastards.' And with this encouraging comment, the column disappeared behind them.

It was clear daylight when the new draft reached the first stopping place on their march, passing through a line of trenches among the batteries. The noise of shellfire was now quite loud enough to make normal conversation very difficult. But the men were, apparently, still a long way from their destination . . .

Ten minutes rest was succeeded by the order to form up again. Stumbling on, exhausted and weighed down by their sixty-six-pound packs, the new draft made its footsore way down an endless mud-walled open tunnel, the main artery to the front line itself.

The racket of bursting shells was now deafening, but only the new recruits seemed to be bothered by it. To the right and left of the zig-zagging communication trench they could see other soldiers sitting, working, talking, dozing — some were even writing letters; it was as if a bombardment wasn't going on at all.

The fact that they were still out of range of much of the ironmongery coming over did not comfort the new men in the least. Every time a rocket went overhead, they flinched and ducked. 'If you duck when you hears the bugger,' remarked their guide, hauling up a man who had fallen into the mud, 'it's too bloody late!'

The officers were now detached from the other ranks and directed to their particular battalion headquarters, and then on yet again to their own Company HQs. This involved more footslogging along wet, slippery trenches and across slimy, broken duckboards to the various dugouts along the seven hundred yards or so of trench frontage held by that battalion.

Ralph was informed that he had been allocated to A Company. His guide led him to a dead-end in a roughly dug trench, pushed aside a sheet of corrugated tin and revealed a small room in which five young officers sat, seemingly doing their best to fill the space with a dense cloud of cigarette smoke. 'Lieutenant Challoner, Sir,' announced the NCO, and disappeared.

The company commander, a regular army officer no more than twenty-five years of age, held out his hand to Ralph. 'Michael Turner,' he said affably. 'Been expecting you all night — what kept you?' He looked closely at Ralph. 'I say, old chap,' he added. 'You look a bit shaky. Shells worry you, did they?'

Ralph opened his mouth to speak, to declare that he had *not* been frightened by the barrage. But his lame leg had, by now, been punished beyond endurance and he found that he could not articulate for pain. He slumped forward and was caught by a tall, well-made lieutenant, who helped him off with his pack and led him to a sort of bed in a corner.

As Ralph lay there, trying not to let the sobs of agony he wanted to express escape him, the others turned back to their game of cards. 'New chap looks a windy blighter,' remarked Captain Turner, under his breath. 'Bit of a slacker, I'd say.'

Slacker! If the man had spat in his face Ralph could not have been more insulted. He clamped his jaws together and glared at Michael Turner's back. Fury now overcame all other emotion and feeling. Slacker! He'd show them. He'd outlive them all.

So Captain Turner was obliged to revise his opinion of his newest platoon commander almost right away. Here was no middle-aged patriot come to do his bit for Blighty and to baulk at the first bit of action. Here, instead, was a born soldier, whose skills in hunting and tracking could be adapted to meet the requirements of trench warfare, whose aggression and courage could be channelled towards the appropriate ends. Ralph had found his occupation at last.

'Damn fine fellow, Challoner,' he remarked to the captain of D Company, who was bemoaning the fact that he'd been lumbered with a nineteen-year-old who did not smoke or drink, and who was trying to convert the rest of his officers to teetotalism. 'Thought he looked a bit of a shirker at first, but he's come on splendidly.'

'Good for him.' The captain of D Company grimaced. 'Do you know, Michael, I'm going to have to get rid of Baker. If he starts lecturing Alex Callan on the evils of drink again I shall have a murder on my hands.'

Ralph's battalion was at that time manning the trenches in the mining area of Northern France, which was a mess of grimy villages, slag-heaps and festering industrial scars, which had not been improved by six months of systematic bombardment. Now this area was a moonscape from a nightmare, pulverized by shells, pocked with craters, defaced by miles and miles of barbed wire entanglements which apparently went on for ever. It seemed that nothing could ever grow there again.

But only five miles behind the front line, the trees grew green in the advancing spring, and the year came on as in England. Men in billets could lie in the grass and hear the birds singing while the war was merely rumbling in the distance.

'Patrol tonight, Ralph?' Captain Turner raised his black eyebrows interrogatively, knowing that his request was a mere formality. Lieutenant Challoner actually seemed to like going out on night patrol, a manoeuvre which involved taking an NCO or two on a frightful journey from the British trenches, through the wire, to slither about for an hour or more in no man's land, listening, watching, doing any damage to German equipment or personnel they could, bringing back any information, and taking prisoners – especially taking prisoners. GHQ's appetite for prisoners was insatiable.

Ralph stubbed out a cigarette and yawned. 'I don't mind going out for a couple of hours, Michael,' he replied.

'Good man. Take Dawson with you tonight. It'll do him good, the blighter's getting very slack lately.'

'Dawson?' Ralph sniffed. 'You're sure?'

'Dawson.'

'Oh, all right.' Ralph stood up and stretched. 'It might buck him up a bit, I suppose.'

Sergeant Alan Dawson hardly relished the idea of being bucked up, especially by Lieutenant Challoner. A regular army man, middled-aged now, with a wife and four children, he was determined to outlast the war. He avoided heroics and danger as much as possible, and although no one could have justifiably called him a coward, he was careful and circumspect. His platoon respected him. Furthermore, he was openly contemptuous of Ralph's flamboyant style, so the two men heartily despised one another.

That night Ralph and Dawson surprised a German patrol engaged in stripping the equipment and cutting the throats of a couple of British wounded. The moon had come out and, lying behind a heap of earth thrown up by a bursting shell, Ralph and Dawson could see the Germans clearly, busily at work only a few yards away from them. The two Englishmen peered over the rim of the crater. Ralph reached for his revolver.

He felt Dawson's restraining hand upon his arm. 'For God's sake, Sir!' he hissed. 'Don't fire, whatever you do. Look, there's half a dozen bloody Huns, and there's just the two of us. You can't help the poor buggers now, can you Sir?'

It was good advice but, unfortunately, the Germans had heard these whispered remarks. Low as it was, Dawson's voice had caught the attention of one of the soldiers, and now the man stared anxiously around, muttering something to his companion. And then the two Germans began to crawl towards the crater in which Ralph and Dawson lay hidden.

Ralph, his eyes glittering now, aimed his revolver and, to Dawson's horror, he fired. He brought one of the Germans to a halt, and the other fell flat on his face in the mud.

It seemed as if the whole German trench opposite answered that one shot. Until then, the night had been relatively quiet. But now machine-gun fire raked the ground where Ralph and Dawson hid. Magnesium flares shot up into the sky, bullets whistled past them like hail. 'Best go home, Sir.' Dawson tugged at Ralph's sleeve. 'Best get back, while we've got the chance.'

'No! I'm going to finish that bastard off and then we're going to deal with his pals. You cover me while I —'

'But Sir! That's suicide. We ought to go back — now.'

'Are you refusing to obey an order, Sergeant?'

'No, Sir.' A flare lit up the sky just then and Dawson saw Ralph's face very clearly. He saw the glint in his pale blue eyes and realized that it would be useless to argue with this madman. He groaned inwardly, found his gun and aimed it at the men a few yards to his left.

'When I say fire, Sergeant, fire. The two on the right are yours.'

Ralph felt later that Dawson had had only himself to blame. Between them, he and Ralph had shot and killed all six Germans, then they had crawled over to the British wounded to make sure that they were indeed beyond help. It had been an excellent night's work.

But, on the way back, Dawson had panicked. He had misjudged the time available to dodge from one shell crater to the next, and a burst of machine-gun fire had riddled his back, killing him outright.

As a matter of courtesy, Ralph had dragged his body back to the Allied lines, but he would just as soon have left him there for the rats to gnaw on. He was no loss, after all. Dawson had been a slacker, a coward; his platoon was better off without him.

That summer Ralph made his reputation. He went on dozens of raids and skirmishes into no man's land and took scores of prisoners. He seemed to be one of those who led a charmed life, for shells exploded harmlessly around him and bullets missed him. If a barrage blew him off his feet, it was never on to the wire, to hang there like a torn doll, dying a slow and hideous death. Careless of his own personal safety, he nevertheless defied death and injury.

'He's in league with the devil hisself.' A corporal watching Ralph return unscathed from a raid in which four of the six men who'd gone out had been killed, spat into the mud. 'He's made some agreement with Old Nick, he must have done.'

'I reckon he *is* Old Nick.' The corporal's mate grimaced. 'He don't need sleep for one thing. Them 'orrible eyes of 'is don't never shut.'

It was true that Ralph seemed to need very little rest. If he had been out most of the night he would still be ready for a pre-dawn raid. His eyes would shine as he led his platoon into a fight.

He terrified dozing sentries: "Wasn't asleep, Sir! Believe me, *wasn't* asleep." And he harrassed men wearily engaged in fresh digging. 'Here comes Mad Harry,' the rankers would mutter, 'Look busy and keen till the bugger's gone on 'is merry way. Then we'll 'ave a fag.'

Captain Turner didn't know how he'd ever managed without Lieutenant Challoner.

* * *

Marcus Harley had spent much of his early childhood in France. But his return to that country was not, as he'd expected it to be, as a trainee shipper bound for the vineyards of Bordeaux. He was now a junior infantry subaltern en route for the smoke-blackened industrial landscape of the Franco-Belgian border.

Gilbert Addams and Marcus Harley had arrived in Boulogne on the same troopship and they found themselves bound for the same sector of the Western Front. Gilbert, in his new uniform of a lieutenant in the RAMC, had been gloomy all through the journey and resisted every effort Marcus made to cheer him up. 'You think it'll be a lark, don't you, Harley?' he demanded, flicking the ash from his Woodbine on to the deck. 'You reckon it might be a bit of fun.'

'No.' Marcus lit a cigarette of his own. 'But there's no point in moaning and groaning now. After all, we *did* volunteer.'

'Huh.' Gilbert Addams grimaced. 'We did, didn't we? Christ knows why. Well, I know why I did. But you! You've come for the ride, haven't you? To take your graces to the grave, and leave the world no copy.'

'What?'

'Never mind.' Gilbert Addams looked across the wharf. 'Look — that chap over there with the lorry, d'you see him?' he asked. 'Well, I've slipped him a few fags and he's going to give us a lift.'

'A lift?' Marcus frowned. 'But we're supposed to stay with our draft —'

'Oh, nuts to that!' Addams picked up his kitbag. 'Are you coming with me?' he demanded. 'Or do you intend to sit on a filthy train for twenty-four hours while it shunts you all over France, then to lug that bloody pack however many damned miles it is to wherever it is we're going?'

'But we don't know —'

'I had a word with a chap on the boat, and I've found out where your lot's stationed.' Gilbert grinned. 'People confide in doctors, didn't you know that?'

'All the same —'

'Harley, *are* you coming, sod you?'

'Oh, all right.' Marcus stubbed out his cigarette. 'All right, I'm coming.'

Marcus and Gilbert Addams arrived at the Belgian border in broad daylight, and there the doctor found another lorry whose driver agreed to give them a lift to the place where, Gilbert had somehow discovered, the rest of their detachment would be — eventually...

Marcus was greeted by his new company commander, and congratulated on his initiative in getting himself to the Front so quickly.

'I'll take you on a tour of the place now,' the captain informed his new lieutenant 'Show you how your own platoon's deployed. It's the usual arrangement,' he added. 'We're in support this week, so we'll be going into the front line on Friday. You'd better tag along too, Addams,' he concluded, as an afterthought.

It soon became clear, however, that Gilbert was in the wrong brigade, and in the wrong area altogether. A telephone message from GHQ demanding to know where a certain Lieutenant Addams RAMC had got to was received by all battalions in that sector, and a matter of hours later the doctor was in yet another lorry, bound for a destination a few miles further down the line. 'Look after yourself, Danny boy,' he said, shaking Marcus by the shoulder. 'No heroics, now. All right?'

As he spoke a shell exploded against a dug-out to their left. Eric Janner, Marcus's company commander, shrugged. 'No one in there,' he remarked. 'Fellows are all out on a digging party. But we'd better shift — it's not very healthy round here.' He brushed the gobbets of earth from his jacket. 'Bloody minnies,' he muttered, striding off down the trench.

On the whole, Marcus found his fellow officers to be a

likeable lot. But as soon as he'd been introduced to Lieutenant Bradlaw he realized that he would be in for trouble, if he were not very careful. The man had held his hand for a moment too long, his handshake had been a little too firm and his smile for the new subaltern had been a little too bright.

Marcus had pulled away and pushed his hair back from his face in a manner which was unintentionally engaging. He glanced around him and noticed a picture of a well-known singer pinned to a beam in the dug-out wall. 'Ah,' he said brightly. 'Whose fiancée?'

Eric Janner thought this was a good joke. 'Fiancée!' he laughed. 'That's Hetty King.'

'Oh, so it is.' Marcus grinned. He took out his wallet and got out a favourite picture of his mother, taken when Anna was about eighteen. '*My* fiancée,' he explained, looking pointedly at George Bradlaw, grateful for the fact that Anna's low-cut evening gown was not particularly Victorian.

The men looked at the photograph. 'I say, she's a stunner!'

'Not half.'

'A very beautiful girl,' agreed George Bradlaw. 'Congratulations.'

When Eric Janner later enquired if he'd like to try a bit of scouting about that evening, Marcus realized that he had to prove himself. 'Yes, I'll go,' he replied.

Night patrols were tedious, frightening and dangerous. To Marcus they seemed more or less pointless. He did, however, undertake his fair share of crawling about in the mud and mess of no man's land.

He led his platoon out on raids and he saw to it that his men brought in the required number of prisoners; they also did their bit towards destroying enemy wire, and lobbed a respectable tonnage of Mills bombs and percussion grenades into German saps.

But the war of attrition was, in that dull, sultry summer of 1915, more or less static. From the long lines of trenches which now stretched from the Belgian coast to the Swiss Alps, the soldiers of both sides threw missiles at each other and made forays into each other's territory. They spent a great deal of time trying to destroy their enemies' wire defences, and almost as much time mending their own.

Sometimes Marcus was frightened, but usually he was bored. Boredom, the like of which he'd never known before, oppressed him and made him lethargic and dull-witted.

'There'll be a big push soon — either in the autumn or early winter,' remarked Captain Janner, over breakfast one morning. 'You'll see some real fun then.'

Marcus gulped his coffee and wiped his mouth on the back of his hand. Real fun, indeed. What would *that* day hold for him? Supervising a digging party? Holding a platoon kit inspection? Or perhaps he could do something really interesting, like delousing his service dress jacket. He yawned.

In August Gilbert Addams was posted medical officer to Marcus's own battalion, and it was thus that Marcus learned the whole brigade would shortly be moving down from Flanders and into France.

'How do *you* know?' demanded Marcus.

Gilbert grinned. 'Some Frog told me,' he replied.

'Frog? What Frog? A soldier?'

'No, a civilian. I treated his ulcer, and he gave me a chicken. And some information.' Gilbert laughed. 'I dare say the Frog heard it all from some Jerry. You poor sods will be the last to know.'

'Oh. Well, then, when are we going?'

'Next week, probably. You don't mean to tell me that you lot up here have heard *nothing*?'

'Well, there've been rumours.'

'No doubt there have. Oh, well, come and have a beer. I've a few bottles of some horrible gassy German muck in my kit, so we might as well drink the stuff.'

Around Béthune there was indeed a great build-up of manpower and weaponry going on. When Marcus's battalion arrived in their new billets, they heard another set of rumours, to the effect that the big push was expected to take place at the beginning of September.

'You've made quite an impression on that Bradlaw chap,' remarked Gilbert, as he and Marcus sat in a muddy hollow one evening smoking some expensive French cigars which Gilbert had, he said, been given. 'He's taken quite a shine to you,' he added, grinning.

Marcus didn't laugh. 'He's a very competent soldier,' he retorted sharply. 'And he's given me no trouble of that kind, so you can just wipe the leer off your horrible face.'

Gilbert shook his head. 'Don't be so touchy, Danny boy,' he said calmly. 'That wasn't exactly what I meant. Marcus, how many actions have you been in so far? Raids, I mean, that kind of thing.'

Marcus considered. 'A dozen,' he replied. 'Maybe more.'

'Night patrols?'

'God knows. Thirty, perhaps.'

'Never been hit?'

'No, I've been lucky —'

'Quite. Have another gasper. I watched you coming back yesterday,' Gilbert continued. 'The Bradlaw fellow was covering you.' The doctor rolled his eyes. 'He was shielding your lovely body with his own. I was quite touched.'

Marcus shrugged. 'If he wishes to do that, why should I complain?' he asked.

'Why indeed?' Gilbert grinned again. 'And when the real fun, as that lunatic Janner insists on calling it, begins — well, you'll be all right, won't you?'

Captain Janner's real fun was, as it happened, to be deferred until the end of September, when the bloody shambles, which would later be dignified by the title of the Battle of Loos, began. Before that, however, Marcus's battalion was informed that it would be involved in an action of its own, to take some enemy trenches which, so the divisional commander had decided, were just that bit too close to the British lines. Spies had discovered that these German trenches were not too strongly held. It ought to be a walkover . . .

The artillery barrage had begun the previous day; high explosive had made a tangled ruin of the enemy's wire, and although the Germans were only too well aware that something ominous was in the offing, they had no way of knowing which of the periodic pauses in the Allied bombardment heralded an actual attack.

At five o'clock on that still, dewy morning Marcus and his platoon were in position in the forward trench, ready to go over with the first wave of men, their objective being a line of broken, twisted trees which shielded the enemy positions for twenty yards or so.

The Germans were sending over the usual collection of shells and grenades, retaliating to the Allied offensive in the prescribed fashion. Everything was going much as expected.

'Stretcher bearers!' A shout from one of the communication trenches, which lay at right angles to the front line trench, cut through the racket of artillery fire. 'Stretcher bearers!'

Gilbert Addams came pushing his way along the duck-boards. 'Who is it?' he yelled, his voice barely audible above the din.

'Lieutenant Bradlaw. Hit in the face. Sniper's bullet.'

'Hang on, I'm coming.'

There was no need for Gilbert Addams to take all the risks he did. Other MOs stayed in their dug-outs and waited for the wounded to be brought to them. But Gilbert Addams could often be seen nipping in and out of the trenches, anxious to be by a wounded man's side as soon as possible.

When that call went up for stretcher bearers, the MO had been busy bandaging a man who had been hit by shrapnel as he waited to go over the top. The doctor had finished his task and, slinging his field kit over his shoulder, he shoved his way along the communication trench towards the sound of the shout.

But all the trenches were now crowded with men and equipment and when he arrived at the front line itself, his progress was seriously impeded. Gilbert Addams had never been a patient man ...

Whatever made the doctor think he was immortal was never established. But, abandoning the effort to push his way through the mêlée, Gilbert took an easier route. To his absolute horror, Marcus saw his friend suddenly leap on to a firestep, clamber out of the shelter of the trench and run across the open ground to where his patient waited.

'Get down, Gil!' Marcus was on his feet now, his own body exposed to whatever German sniper might take a pot shot at him. 'Gil, you stupid bastard! Get *down!*' As the doctor raced past him, Marcus lunged forwards, meaning to grab his ankles and bring him down before a bullet did.

But Marcus missed him. A split second later the German grenade hit Gilbert Addams squarely between the shoulder blades, knocking him back into the trench, flat against the parados. Entangled in Gilbert's backpack, the bomb exploded. And Marcus shut his eyes as a warm, wet mass of blood and body spattered all over him.

The wounded man, who lay only feet from where the doctor had been blown to pieces, blinked as he tried to wipe the blood from his face, moaning as he demanded to know where the sodding MO had got to.

Lieutenant Bradlaw died later that day. Marcus felt doubly bereaved.

* * *

The summer had been damp, and the wheat harvest had been nowhere near as good as hoped.

Dora studied the books and sighed. The estate would make a loss that year, that was obvious.

At first, Dora had been at a loss how to manage the wide acres which her husband had so suddenly and completely abandoned to her sole charge. But with Henry Lawrence's help and encouragement, she had gradually come to grips with the mysteries of the estate books and begun to understand how the hierarchy of tenant farmers, labourers and casual seasonal workers all fitted together.

Dora and Katherine lounged on the terrace of the Grange, enjoying a brief spell of September sun. Raising herself on one elbow, Dora picked at the fringe of the blanket upon which she lay. 'Could you come and stay for a few days?' she asked Katherine. 'Could you come round the estate with me and tell me what I ought to be doing now the harvest's in?'

'I don't think your husband would like it if I interfered here,' Katherine stated. 'I can just imagine his reaction if you were to say, "Oh, darling, I put those fields down to pasture because Katherine said I should." Do admit, Dora, he wouldn't be pleased.'

'He wouldn't know.'

'You wouldn't tell him?'

'Of course not.'

'Oh.' Katherine grinned. 'Well, then — we'll get some calves, shall we? They can overwinter in the stables, and in the spring we'll start —'

'A dairy herd?'

'Maybe.'

'That would be splendid.' Dora frowned. 'I'd have to ask Papa for the money, though,' she added. 'And he might refuse.'

'He won't. Listen, Dora, soon the government is going to have to give some help to the farmers. The Germans are sinking so much of our shipping that the Cabinet will have to encourage English farmers to grow more food. You'll probably be able to get a grant. And then we'll start a *pedigree* herd!'

She giggled. 'You can borrow Prince Albert,' she added. 'He'll get all those heifers in the family way before you can say ninepence.'

'No doubt he will.' Dora laughed. 'Right, then — we'll do that,' she said. 'And, you never know, Ralph might even be pleased. He might even be glad to come home from the war.'

'He's still loving every minute?'

'Seems to be.' Dora shrugged. 'I can't think why, it all sounds absolutely horrible to me.'

Indeed, Ralph Challoner didn't mind if the war went on forever. Lice, rats, the discomforts of trench life, the unceasing whine and drone of shells, the foul smell of dead horses, dead men, of putrefaction of all kinds and degrees, never appeared to worry him. When the Company HQ disintegrated into a clumsy dug-out full of filthy, contaminated water and lacking in any sort of comfort, making Captain Turner swear and curse the Staff who'd left his men in this pit, Ralph's good humour stayed with him.

So the summer months passed by. There'd been no action worthy of the name of battle. But in September, Ralph came back from a fortnight's home leave, knowing that something big was at last being planned — something which would make the tremendous fight at Neuve Chapelle the previous March, when the Allies had actually broken the German line, appear to have been a mere skirmish in comparison.

Ralph arrived back at Cuinchy, where his battalion was now stationed, on 21 September and found a terrific bombardment going on. All the preparations for a really big push were well under way.

All day of the twenty-third Captain Turner had been at Battalion HQ to receive a briefing on the coming battle. He returned to his company on the twenty-fourth, bringing with him a pile of maps which he distributed among his junior officers, giving them their individual orders which they scribbled down on the backs of the battle plans.

'So tomorrow is *it*,' he said, rubbing his face. 'We'll let the buggers have it. What you chaps have all been waiting for, eh?' He looked at Ralph. 'Tonight, though, I thought we could do a little show of our own,' he added. 'For which I'll need two volunteers. Eh, Mr Challoner? And Sergeant Curtis perhaps? You know Ralph, it's just your sort of thing.'

'Is it, Michael?'

'Oh, yes, I think so. Look, here's what I'd like you to do. There's a sniper, or it might be half a dozen bloody snipers for all I know, dug in a hundred yards or so to our right, where those big mine craters are. They've been giving us hell this last fortnight; the bastards must have known you were on leave. I've sent a couple of fellows out to look at them on two or three occasions, but the poor blighters have been shot to bits before they've even got to within sniffing distance. Damned nuisance it is.'

'So you'd like me —'

'Yes. If you could knock that fellow and his mates out of action, it'll be much easier for us all when we go over the top tomorrow.' Michael Turner frowned. 'It's a tall order, I know. Look here, Ralph — cry off if you want to. Chances are you'll get one in the head, and God knows I don't want to lose a good platoon commander. All the same, if you feel you'd like to have a go . . .'

Ralph stood up and stretched. 'We'll go about eleven, shall we?' he asked. 'Take a few grenades with us — that should settle the buggers. Is it all right with you if I have an hour or two's sleep before then?'

'Good fellow.' Michael Turner grinned. 'I'll wake you up myself.'

'Our blue-eyed boy volunteered again?' News of Captain

Turner's little show had percolated down the ranks, giving rise to a few sniggers and confident predictions that clever arse Challoner would get a bullet through his brain this time, for sure.

'I'll be bloody glad to see the back of him,' muttered Leslie Chase, a corporal who had been Alan Dawson's particular mate. 'He takes too many risks. He might not mind being blasted to glory, but I bloody do. I got a wife and two kids at home.'

He accepted a cigarette from the private standing next to him. 'Last time I was out with him, two men got blown to bits on account of Lieutenant Sodding Challoner telling them to investigate a dug-out which he knew was empty. 'Cept for the fucking booby-trap, of course, which the bastard might have thought about if his brain was any bigger than a bloody pea.'

The private nodded in agreement. 'He's got a death wish,' chipped in a lance-corporal, who was also lounging against the parados of the trench. 'Only it's never 'im as cops it. Always one of us poor bleeders.'

'All right, you men, stand to. Stand to!' A good imitation of Ralph's clipped patrician tones came from behind the grumbling rankers, causing them to throw away their cigarettes and to jump up on to the firestep, staying there for a second or two until they realized that it was Jonas Turnbull, the platoon wit, who'd startled them.

The grumblers attacked him, dragged him down the trench and kicked him into a sump-hole. 'Shut up, Turnbull, you stupid bastard!' Leslie Chase was beside himself. 'As if we hadn't enough to be windy about,' he yelled, as he ducked Turnbull in the filthy water.

'Oh, leave him alone, Les. He can't help it.'

'What?' The corporal glared. 'Oh, bugger off then, you stupid sod.' Leslie Chase released Turnbull and turned to the lance-corporal who'd addressed him. 'You on sentry duty tonight?' he asked.

'No.'

'Let's get some kip then. We've got to be up bright and early to wash our faces in the bloody dew tomorrow.'

'Yeah.' The lance-corporal sniggered. 'Come on, Les, cheer

up,' he said. 'With any luck Blue-Eyes will get it right between the ears in an hour or two, so we won't 'ave to worry about 'im any more, which'll make a nice change. We'll only be fighting the Hun tomorrow.'

The platoon sergeant, Alfred Curtis, hawked and spat over the parapet as he fitted a belt of cartridges around his body. He caught Leslie Chase as the corporal slopped down the waterlogged trench back to his sleeping quarters. 'You're going to find yourself on a charge some day soon, my lad,' he observed. 'I heard you and those mates of yours belly-aching. You make me sick, Chase, you really do.'

Held fast in the sergeant's grasp, Leslie Chase wriggled and frowned. 'We was only havin' a bit of a natter,' he whined. 'Let go, can't you — you'll break my sodding arm.'

Sergeant Curtis scowled, but he let the man go. 'You should be bloody proud to be in Lieutenant Challoner's platoon,' he barked. 'They don't make officers like him any more.'

'Thank Christ for that.' Leslie Chase addressed this remark to his boots but the sergeant overheard him.

'So who would you rather have to lead you then?' he demanded. 'A kid straight from the OTC, I suppose — a skinny little blighter still not weaned from his mother's milk? A nineteen-year-old virgin, liable to go into a blue funk if he hears a rocket come over? You fancy bein' able to tell your friends and relations that your platoon commander was shot for cowardice, do you? Like that bugger from C Company last month? Like that sod who deserted his men in no man's land and ran away? Like the bastard who was found cryin' his eyes out in a shell hole? Eh?'

Chase looked abashed. 'I just hope you get back, sergeant,' he muttered. 'It's fucking suicide what you've been asked to do. Think about it.'

'An' if we succeed, Chase, it might mean that you and the rest of those windy buggers back there will come back tomorrow with your balls intact.' The sergeant lit a Woodbine and puffed smoke into Chase's face. 'You think about that, sonny,' he muttered. 'You just think about that.'

At half past eleven that evening Ralph and Alfred Curtis set out, both now strung about with percussion bombs and an assortment of grenades, belts of cartridges strapped around their waists. They crawled towards the German lines, their target, a mine crater, being a mere hundred yards away from the Allied front line.

They got through their own wire, then through a gap in the German wire, which had been blown by a bombardment of high explosive the previous day and which the Germans had not had time to mend, but which they certainly had their eyes on, all the same. Their machine guns were evidently trained on it, for as Ralph and Curtis slithered through the hole, the ground became alive with bullets spurting in the mud all around them.

They hoped they had not been seen. It was possible, after all, that the Germans would keep this gap in their defences under fire all night, just in case any enemy patrols should try to crawl through it.

Both Ralph and Curtis lay still, hardly daring to breathe. A magnesium flare went up right in front of them, threatening to come down and burn a great hole in whichever of them it might land on.

They lay in the mud for half an hour. Eventually Ralph became aware of Sergeant Curtis's hand gripping his ankle. 'You hurt, Sir?' he hissed.

'No, Sergeant. What about you?'

'Got me in the wrist, Sir. Just a graze.'

'We'd better go on now, I think.'

'Sir.'

Inching forwards, sliding, slithering across the foetid slime which stank in their nostrils and soaked their service dress, groping their way past shell-holes from which the skeletons and half-picked corpses of dead men mocked them, they had come within a dozen yards of their target when a burst of enemy fire seemed to rip a gully between them. The air was filled with smoke and there was a terrible stench of lyddite. When his eyes had stopped smarting and he could see again, Ralph looked around for his companion.

Sergeant Curtis had had it. Half his head was missing and his brains were splattered all over Ralph's legs, while his hand reached out pathetically, as if imploring aid. Ralph looked around him, wondering whether Curtis had been killed by the machine gunner who was now raking the British trenches opposite from side to side, or by a sniper, who might have seen Ralph as well.

He crawled on, very slowly now, towards the crater where the sniper and his friends were assumed to be. The darkness was hardly that now, for the sky was bright with flares and the ghastly illumination of explosion after explosion. Ralph assumed that A Company would have given him up long ago, and he grinned to himself. This fireworks display which was going on all around him was for his exclusive benefit. Inch by inch he continued to slither on, now caked with mud and slime from head to foot, but as determined and cheerful as when he'd set out. He slumped into a shell crater about five yards from his target, and listened.

He could hear muffled German conversation. He could hardly believe it. He'd come all this way without, it seemed, being observed. The shooting had all been at random, the result of a suspicion that there was someone crawling towards the German lines, but apparently the enemy had not seen *him.*

He knew he must act quickly now. He was a good overarm bowler, so taking a chance on being seen — for he knew he would not survive this affair — he raised himself on one elbow and reached for a percussion bomb.

As he did so, the sky around him shone as bright as day; a dozen flares went up all at once. A sudden spurt of gunfire nearly deafened him. He threw himself on to his face, thinking he'd been hit but, except for a graze on his face, he was uninjured. His cartridges were, however, now on fire, exploding with sharp pops around his waist. He could feel his clothing shrivelling away, and knew he was burning because he could smell his own roasting flesh . . .

He could not pause to unbuckle the belt and jettison the cartridges — there wasn't time. Any second now the enemy must see him; he was bound to be spotted, a crawling human firework as he was now. He'd be shot at again. Then his bombs would all explode. He'd be killed and the snipers he'd come to deal with would still be there to plague the company tomorrow.

He was as good as dead now, he knew that. He knelt up,

his figure silhouetted against the background of flares. He yanked a handful of grenades from his belt, pulled their pins and hurled them, one after the other, into the mine crater ahead of him.

Nothing happened. Despairing now, he tugged at the percussion bombs and lobbed these overarm, praying that they'd hit something hard enough to make them explode.

It seemed to Ralph that an eternity of silence went by. Whatever had happened, he wondered? Why had they stopped firing at him, and what in hell's name had become of all that ironmongery he'd thrown into the German position?

The explosion just then was ear-shattering. It threw him backwards for fifty yards, back towards the Allied trenches, back against the awful tangled mess of barbed wire and pickets. The night was black now and completely still.

* * *

Ralph opened his eyes and stared balefully at the medical orderly. Gradually, he focused on the man's uniform and, looking around him, he realized that he must be in a field hospital.

'The officer over here's awake,' remarked the orderly to a nurse. He bent over Ralph's bed and straightened the sheets, as carefully and tenderly as a mother might. 'You're all right, Sir,' he whispered, gently. 'Two of your rankers pulled you off the wire. You've copped your Blighty one now, though, no mistake about that. You'll be out of it now.'

'Out of it?' Ralph, becoming more and more alert as the seconds ticked on, stared at the man. He realized that he could not move his left arm and that his legs seemed to be useless. He was strapped and constricted by bandages all around his body. He glared at the orderly who was still fussing round him.

'Comfortable, Sir?' The man smiled. 'The doctor will be here to see you in a minute.'

Ralph still glared. He was evidently so badly wounded that he could not move his limbs. Below the knees, he could not even feel his legs. Suddenly a horrible thought struck him. He grabbed the orderly's hand. 'My legs,' he muttered. 'Have I —'

'Both broken, Sir, but cleanly. They'll heal.' The man turned to the nurse who was now standing by his side, and addressed her in the kind of whisper which medical staff always seem to assume that their patients cannot hear. 'Still badly shocked, poor bloke,' he murmured. 'Sister, was he the one who knocked out all those Jerries? You know, up near the brickstacks?'

'Yes.' The nurse smiled. 'Yes, I do believe he was.'

'They should give him the VC, then. Whether he cops it or pulls through.'

'I expect they will. I heard a rumour to that effect.' The nurse consulted Ralph's chart. 'He's been made up to Captain anyway, the form came in yesterday.'

'Should think so, too.'

'Quite. Look, he's dozed off again. Sleep — that's what he needs.' The nurse looked tenderly at Ralph. 'His wife will be so proud of him,' she whispered. 'So proud — whether he lives or dies, poor man.'

And the nurse moved off down the ward, still talking to the orderly, who turned back once more to give Ralph another look of admiration and compassion.

Chapter Fifteen

CAMBRIDGE WAS COLD AND DISMAL in the damp drizzle of a dreary October afternoon. The streets were practically deserted, for the place was empty of undergraduates, and those inhabitants who remained in the town scurried furtively about their business, as if ashamed to be seen out of uniform.

Jenny Westbrook was waiting for Marcus outside a bookshop. Upon seeing him coming towards her, she ran along the pavement to meet him.

He bent forwards to kiss her. His face level with hers, he looked anxiously at her tired eyes and pale cheeks. 'I'm sorry, Jenny,' he said gently. He took her in his arms and hugged her. 'I'm so sorry. I was fond of him, as well.'

'I know.' Jenny shrugged and tried to move out of his embrace, so he let her go. 'I know you were friends. But, Marcus — *I* loved him.'

She fiddled with the engagement ring which was still on her finger. And then she began to walk, so quickly that Marcus was obliged to run to catch up with her. Eventually, however, she slowed down a little and together they went along Silver Street.

'What will you do now, Jenny?' Marcus took her hand in his. 'Have you made any plans?'

'I intend to go in for nursing.' Jenny sniffed. 'I start my training next week — so you see, I haven't wasted any time sitting around bemoaning my fate.'

'I didn't mean —'

'Oh, I know you didn't. I'm sorry.' Jenny touched her

companion's arm. 'Marcus, could we go and have a drink, d'you suppose? I know it's not very ladylike to go into pubs, but really I —'

'We could go and get drunk.' Marcus laid his arm around her shoulder. 'Come on, Jenny, we'll go and get absolutely smashed. The pubs won't be open for half an hour, though, so we'll go and have something to eat first, shall we?'

'The parents are out.' Jenny looked up at him. 'We could go home, if you like, Marcus. We could finish off the last of Dad's pre-war whisky.'

In the Westbrooks' drawing room Marcus sat on the sofa and Jenny took out a couple of glasses. She fetched the bottle of whisky from its cupboard and poured out two generous measures. 'Here,' she said, handing one to Marcus.

'Thanks, Jenny. I didn't know you drank Scotch.'

'I don't. I've never even tasted it before today.' Jenny took a great gulp of whisky, then coughed and choked. 'Drink up, Marcus,' she added. 'It's half each, you know, and if you don't hurry up you won't get your share.'

She sat down beside him and refilled her glass.

Twenty minutes later, neither she nor Marcus could focus properly. Marcus had had by far the greater share of the whisky, but Jenny was unused to alcohol, and by now the two of them were both completely maudlin.

Jenny began to cry. She leaned against Marcus and wept, burrowing into his chest and butting her head against his collar bone. 'I loved him,' she wailed. 'The stupid oaf, I loved him! Why did he have to do that? Oh, God, *why*? What was the point, what was the bloody point?'

Marcus felt tears come into his own eyes. He kissed Jenny's forehead, then he, too, began to sob. He and Jenny leaned against each other and cried together, weeping into each others' hair.

'I'll never have a husband now.' Jenny pushed her hair off her face and gazed up at Marcus, despair in her eyes. 'I'll never have children. Never have grandchildren.'

'You will.' Marcus took her handkerchief and wiped her face. 'You will get married, Jenny, I'm sure you will.'

'To whom? Tell me, who will there be for me to marry?' She

began to sob again. 'No one,' she cried. 'There won't be anyone left.'

Marcus stayed with Jenny until her parents returned home. When at last they did, he was relieved to find that Dr Westbrook overlooked the fact that his daughter was drunk, and that her companion was almost so. He took his leave, promising to stay in touch.

On the train back to London, he thought about Caroline and wondered if she'd managed to get the flat to herself for a couple of days.

He hoped she had. He needed her — needed her arms around him, needed the feel of her small, warm body curled up next to him. If he could only bury his face in her long soft hair, if he could — just for an hour or two — lie in a warm bed with his dear little mistress in his arms, he knew that the war would go away. That the fear, the cold and the cruelty would recede. That the recurring nightmare of being splashed from head to foot with the blood of the man who'd been his friend would not trouble him; if only Caroline was there.

'Caroline!' Practically falling out of the train, he raced towards her, grabbing her and sweeping her off her feet, kissing her passionately in full view of the crowds of people on the station forecourt.

'You've been drinking,' she observed, beaming at him, as delighted to see him as he was to see her.

'Yes, I have.'

Caroline wrinkled her nose. 'And you've been with some woman. I can smell scent.'

'Jenny Westbrook's.'

'Ah.' Caroline sighed. 'Poor Jenny. Well, come on, Marcus,' she added. 'If we hurry, we'll get a cab. So, how was Cambridge?'

'Cold, wet and miserable, like me. About the flat, Caro —'

'That's all arranged.' Caroline took his hand. 'I'm all alone now,' she told him. 'Minnie's gone off to work in a munitions factory, and I'm having to learn to look after myself. Marcus, I've even taught myself to cook!'

'*Have* you? Goodness!'

'Don't mock.' Caroline frowned at him reproachfully. 'I do

a very decent casserole these days, you know.'

They sat in the cab, close to each other. 'You're still working for that publisher?' asked Marcus, willing the driver to push his way through the other vehicles and take them home as quickly as possible.

'Yes.' Caroline nodded. 'I'm Mr Gregson's secretary now.'

'What do you do with yourself in the evenings nowadays? I mean, is there —'

'I'm an orderly at the local hospital.' Caroline held up her small hands which, once perfectly white and smooth, were now reddened and rough. 'I scrub floors, I set out trays, I clean up the wards and I wash up. Hundreds and thousands of cups, plates and bowls. Oh, Marcus, you can't imagine.'

Marcus grinned. 'What a little heroine.'

'I'm no heroine — I know that well enough.' She shrugged. 'I couldn't even be a nurse. But I try to do my bit for the troops.'

'You'll be working overtime this weekend, then.' He took her in his arms and hugged her, feeling comforted and warmed now that she was with him. He kissed her. 'You can provide comforts for the troops for the next forty-eight hours, non-stop.'

'Troops, plural?'

'Well, troop.'

'Aren't you going home to see your parents?'

'I hadn't intended to.' Marcus frowned. 'Unless, of course, you —'

'I've made no other plans. Oh, dear Marcus, I *have* missed you.'

'Not as much as I've missed you. You couldn't have done.'

* * *

That previous summer Stephen had paid his youngest daughter a long visit, and he had been impressed by her successes and the competent way in which she was managing her husband's estate. Dora had found herself a new land agent and begun to put her uncle's business methods into practice. After years and years of neglect, however, making Ralph's estate a profitable concern was an uphill task, and by the autumn Dora was feeling her age and more.

'How many horses have they left you?' asked Stephen,

closing an estate ledger and leaning back in his chair.

'Not enough.' Dora shrugged and spiked another paper on to a pile she was sorting. 'Well, I don't begrudge them to the army, of course,' she said. 'But I could do with a few more. I don't know how we'll manage when it comes to ploughing.'

'I'll have a word with Henry — see if I can arrange something. You look so tired, dear,' he added. 'Come and spend a few days in Oxford with us, why don't you? Your agent can manage here, and your mother will be very glad to see you. Well, you know that. She can tell you all about her Comforts for the Troops campaign.' And Dora's father allowed himself a faintly ironic smile.

'She's still knitting socks and balaclavas, is she? I hope they have khaki wool now?'

'Oh yes, the purple is all used up. Don't mock, Dora — it all helps to make her feel useful.'

'She's doing other things as well?'

'Oh yes. Rolling bandages, packing dressings. And she helps at the hospital; she has a ward there she says is hers. She keeps her soldiers in flowers, sweets, magazines, she writes letters for them and takes them all sorts of presents.'

Stephen grinned. 'The men gave her a box of handkerchiefs last week and she cried.'

'Oh, poor Mama.' Dora opened another ledger. 'Now, what shall I do about the big field?' she asked. 'Shall I put it down to potatoes? Or to wheat?'

'Potatoes, I think.' Stephen laughed. 'Dora, my dear, I never thought the day would come when you and I would be having a conversation like this. Now, you haven't said if you'll come back with me. But you will, I hope? Just for a week?'

'That would be lovely, Papa. Certainly I'll come.'

* * *

'By the way, Dora, we have a guest for dinner this evening.' Dorcas pulled the curtains back from her daughter's bedroom window and let in a clear shaft of early autumn sunlight. 'An army officer.'

'Oh?' Dora yawned and stretched. 'One of your convalescent patients?'

'No, dear. *My* ward is for men, not officers. The gentleman who's coming tonight is a Captain Atherton.'

'Captain Atherton?' Dora felt the cup of tea she was holding wobble in her hands and was relieved that her mother was still fussing with the window blinds and had not looked round to see that her daughter was now reddening and shaking with apprehension.

'I think that's his name.' Dorcas turned then and smiled at her daughter. 'He was one of your father's students,' she explained. 'Stephen met him in Cornmarket a day or two ago, and since the young man is on leave, your father asked him to visit us. I can't say I remember him — do you?'

'Oh, goodness, Mama — I never took any notice of the students.'

'No, I suppose you didn't.' Dorcas took the teacup from her daughter's hands. 'You look a little flushed, dear,' she added. 'Do you feel quite well today?'

'What? Oh, yes, I'm perfectly well. It's just rather hot in here, that's all. Could you open the window?'

Dora dressed with particular care that evening. She piled her long brown hair on top of her head and arranged some curls around her face, but then took it all down again and pinned it into a neat coil at the nape of her neck. She went through all her clothes twice before she could decide what to wear.

In the end she chose the plainest dress and put on a simple bead necklace. She noticed that her face in the mirror was white. So she touched her cheeks with a little rouge. Just a smudge — not enough, she hoped, for her father to notice, for Stephen made no secret of his dislike of painted female faces.

She dabbed a little scent into the crook of each elbow and gave herself one last glance in the glass. 'You look a hundred,' she told herself. 'And he's probably forgotten that he once thought himself in love with you. He was only a boy then.'

A glass of sherry in his hand, Tim Atherton was standing near the fireplace talking to Stephen. Both men turned round as Dora entered the room. She was glad to see her father's nod of approval as he noted her appearance. She went over to join them.

'Dora, this is Captain Atherton. My daughter, Mrs Challoner.' Stephen smiled from his daughter to his guest. 'I don't believe you've met before.'

'Good evening.' Tim nodded gravely and took Dora's proffered hand. She imagined that she felt a more than casual pressure in his clasp but told herself that she was mistaken.

He looked very different now. All those years had turned a boy into a man, into a thinner, more solemn person than the rather silly, excitable child whose air of nervous insolence towards those older than himself had betrayed his extreme youth and insecurity.

Now he met Dora's gaze candidly, smiled a polite social smile, and — to her enormous relief — Dora felt at ease with him.

The evening passed quietly enough. Tim talked, telling unremarkable stories about his fellow ex-students, but in a facetious manner which suggested to Dora that, notwithstanding his dignified bearing and the air of world weariness which became a seasoned army officer, Tim Atherton was still a teasing show-off with no respect for anyone or anything.

'One wouldn't have thought it of Fred Telford, would one?' he demanded heavily, watching Stephen. 'A congratulatory First — you, Sir, on your feet, applauding him to the echo — and then the fellow became a fishmonger.'

'A what?' Stephen, suspecting that he was being teased, looked quizzically at his guest.

'A fishmonger, Dr Lawrence,' repeated Tim gravely. 'The biggest wholesaler of wet fish in the North of England. Just imagine.' His voice became positively sepulchral. 'All that dead cod.'

Dora giggled. To her surprise, Stephen's mouth twitched and then he laughed. 'Poor Telford,' he said, at last. 'Poor Telford.'

Tim rolled his eyes and groaned. 'Dr Lawrence, the man's gone into munitions now — he's a millionaire. Oh, if only *I'd* had his foresight.'

Dorcas excused herself early, saying that she'd had a tiring day. 'I hope you'll call again before you go back to France,' she said, offering Tim her hand.

As Dorcas took herself off to bed, Stephen lay back on the sofa. He left his daughter to entertain his guest.

'I met you several times at my sister's house,' began Dora, who always felt that it was best to meet potentially embarrassing situations head on.

'Yes, of course. Mrs Harley invited me to one of her parties.' Tim widened his grey eyes; there was a ghost of a grin on his face. 'A very intellectual affair it was, if I remember rightly.'

'Greek particles.' Dora allowed herself to smile. 'Greek particles and champagne.'

'Yes.' Tim glanced across towards Stephen, saw that his chin was resting on his chest and assumed from the regularity of his breathing that he was sound asleep. 'It was very kind of your father to invite me here,' he continued, firmly changing the subject. 'Especially since I wasn't one of his more rewarding pupils.'

Dora laughed. 'I think he liked you nevertheless,' she said. 'Maybe you weren't brilliant, but he doesn't always warm to the clever ones. And he hates a plodding swot.' She looked at Tim. 'Perhaps you showed some vitality.'

'I was cheeky, you mean.'

'I didn't mean that at all.'

'Didn't you? Well, I *was*. He frightened me half to death, so I felt I had to show off in front of the others, and impress *them*. Oh dear God, what a pain I must have been. I hope I'm a little less childish now.'

'I don't remember you were childish at all.'

'Don't you? That's something of a relief. But I was, you know, and you may be glad to hear that I have perhaps grown up a little since we last met. I don't, for example, persist in hankering after things I just can't have.'

There was a silence then. Dora racked her brains for something to say. 'Will you be going back to France soon?' she asked him, to break the oppressive stillness.

'Yes. On Thursday.'

'The day after tomorrow.'

'Mmm.' Tim leaned forward in his seat. 'Mrs Challoner, have you any children?' he asked.

Dora's eyes met his and she felt herself redden. 'No,' she replied. 'Unfortunately, not.'

'You live in Herefordshire, I believe.'

'Yes, that's right. Near Ashton Cross, where my father's family is.'

'My own family has a house near Evesham. I know Hereford well. It's a pleasant little town.'

'Oh, it is. And I'm very happy there.'

'I'm very glad to hear it. Is Lieutenant Challoner in France?'

'Yes, at — oh, I forget the exact place. Somewhere near Béthune, I think.' Dora blushed again. 'I'm not supposed to tell you that, am I?'

'It doesn't matter.'

Dora took a deep breath. She folded her hands on her lap and twisted her wedding ring. 'Mr — I mean, Captain Atherton,' she began.

'Tim, if you like.'

'Tim — you won't mind, will you, if I say that I hope things will go well for you in the war?' Dora looked earnestly at him. 'Oh, there are so many people I care about in France and Flanders just now. I worry about them so much.'

She frowned, not knowing how to go on — wanting to say that she was relieved and pleased that he did not, it seemed, hold her past behaviour against her, but her tongue could not find the words.

'I may take it, then, that you might worry about me?' Tim looked solemnly at Dora. 'That now and then you'll wonder how I am? Dora, is that what you mean?'

Dora nodded. 'Yes. Exactly that. I shall think of you and hope that you are safe.' She raised her voice. 'Papa!' she said, sharply. 'Papa!'

'What?' Stephen stirred, then opened his eyes. He looked from Dora to Tim. 'I'm so sorry,' he murmured. 'Oh, my dear fellow, how very rude of me. I must have closed my eyes for a second and fallen asleep.'

He grimaced, then laughed. 'We old men are all alike, you know,' he added. 'We all sit about, dozing away our twilight years, while you young chaps — Dora my dear, shall we have some coffee?'

'I'll fetch some.' Dora rose to her feet. 'Don't fall asleep again!' She glanced at Tim, who returned her look with the merest hint of his familiar smile. 'Whatever can Captain

Atherton think of you?' she asked.

'Oh, I dare say you managed to entertain our guest well enough. I can't believe you needed my faltering assistance.' Stephen smiled himself then and Dora wondered if he'd heard every word they'd said.

Tim stayed until half past eleven, talking mainly to Stephen now. Dora sat back in her chair, sipped her coffee and looked at them.

Might she have loved Tim? It was much too late for regrets now, but ought she to have married Tim Atherton? No, she decided, she had loved Ralph. Even though he had abused and upset her, hurt her and used her in the unthinking way which, Dora supposed, all men used their wives, she had loved him. How much worse it would have been, to have married a man one did not love, then been obliged to submit . . .

'More coffee, Captain Atherton?' Dora held out her hand for his cup. 'Do have another cup — there's plenty . . .'

'Why did you invite him here?' she asked her father, after Tim had taken his leave and walked off into the night.

'I heard from Anthony that he was in Oxford for a couple of weeks. Then I happened to run into him in Cornmarket, so I asked him to dinner. He's an agreeable fellow, don't you think?'

'Oh, yes, he's very nice.'

'He is. And the evening went very well, didn't it?'

'Mmm.' Dora nodded, and leaned over to kiss Stephen goodnight. 'Are you coming upstairs?' she asked.

'No, I've some work to do.'

'I thought you were tired?'

'Well, I seem to have recovered. My little nap, you know —'

'Ah.' Dora looked at him. 'Goodnight, then.' And she went upstairs.

* * *

'A very pleasant young man, that Captain whatever his name was,' remarked Dorcas, at breakfast the following morning.

'Atherton, my dear. Captain Atherton. You're into your dotage too, I see.' Stephen smiled at his mistress and his daughter.

'I always liked him,' he added thoughtfully. 'He was a

cheeky young rogue, though. Do you know, I once walked into my room in college to find him mimicking me. There he was, in front of half a dozen other grinning idiots — he'd put on my gown and was standing in the middle of the floor, hands behind his back. "Gentlemen," he was saying, "if you'll be so kind as to give me your attention for a moment." He nearly fainted when he saw me standing behind him.'

Stephen shook his head. 'Never did any work, the idle young devil,' he continued. 'Used to spend all his time writing and editing that student rag, do you remember?'

Dorcas nodded. 'Yes, I remember. You were a regular victim, weren't you?'

'Oh, it was all harmless stuff, no real malice in it.' Stephen sighed. 'Atherton won the DSO, you know. The Dean saw the citation in *The Times*. It seems his lot were at Mons, and Atherton took some wounded chap from right under the noses of the Germans. Conspicuous gallantry, the paper said.'

Dora, who had been listening to all this with interest, blushed when she suddenly realized that her father was looking hard at her. She made a great business of buttering a slice of toast and began, then, to chew it thoughtfully.

* * *

Dora arrived back at the Grange on a wet, blustery November day to find a letter from Ralph's commanding officer, telling her that her husband had been wounded, but that he would shortly be invalided home. The letter, from Ralph's colonel, described in great detail the action in which Dora's husband had been injured; it dwelt at length on how brave her own dear man had been, and impressed upon her how proud of him she ought to be.

She gazed blankly at the sheet of paper in her hand. 'Seriously wounded — now, happily, out of danger — displayed the very greatest heroism — complete disregard for his own personal safety — recommended to receive the Victoria Cross — back to England shortly — long convalescence.' These were the phrases which swam out of the scrawl and hit Dora between the eyes, making her head spin.

Suddenly she felt very, very wicked. She realized now that when she'd picked up that envelope she'd torn it open hoping it might contain the worst of news — that it was a message of hope, come to tell her that she was free of him. But instead ...

She sat down. Crumpling the paper in her hand, she burst into tears, and from weakness and excess of contradictory emotions, she cried for half an hour.

The last person she wanted to see at that moment was her Aunt Katherine. Kind, slow-witted Aunt Katherine, who thought that Ralph was a marvellous young man, a fine fellow who was a model husband and a perfect landlord, and who was now a splendid soldier.

But it was, indeed, her Aunt Katherine, who then entered to welcome Dora home and invite her to dinner at Ashton Cross. Finding her niece in tears, she sat down to comfort her.

'He isn't dead, dear child,' she murmured, holding Dora's hand. 'Look, he'll be home soon, the letter says so. My poor Dora, don't cry. He's coming back.'

Coming back. Yes, soon Ralph would be at the Grange again, blighting Dora's life and undoing all the good she'd done on the estate. She would pray for a complete recovery, that he might eventually go back to France, that the War might last that long. 'I'm horrible,' she thought wretchedly. 'Horrible and cruel. That I should pray for such a dreadful thing.' Lying against her aunt's shoulder, she burst into a fresh torrent of weeping.

Ralph was sent back to England at the beginning of December, to a hospital in Oxford. One of the women's colleges had been turned into a convalescent home for officers, and it was there that Ralph found himself for his own long recuperation. Dora went to stay with her parents, meaning to visit him as little as possible.

On her first visit to the hospital, she could not help but observe how much effort had been expended to make it as pleasant as could be. Even at this difficult time of year there were flowers everywhere, and huge bunches of hothouse chrysanthemums filled the air with their dry, melancholy, autumnal fragrance. The sound of gramophone music pervaded the place; all the latest American ragtime records seemed to be reaily available here.

'Mrs Challoner? Oh, I *am* pleased to meet you!' A smiling

nurse beamed at Dora. 'Captain Challoner's so looking forward to seeing you,' she continued. 'He's doing very well now, you know.'

'Where —' began Dora, hesitantly. 'Where is he?'

'In Trafalgar Ward, at the top of the stairs.' The nurse smiled again. 'I'll have a porter show you up.'

Dora nodded her thanks and meekly followed the porter up the winding staircase. She suddenly realized that, unlike all the other visitors now tripping up and down the stairs and along the corridors, she was empty-handed. She had quite forgotten that it was customary to take gifts to the sick.

Another woman passed her just then, her arms laden with flowers and presents. Dora shrugged. She let the human Christmas tree walk on ahead of her, then went into the ward.

'Ah, my own dear wife.' Ralph was out of bed and sitting by a window. Dora saw that he was wearing a rather splendid quilted dressing gown. His legs, which were still in plaster, rested on a footstool. 'How are you, Dora?' he asked.

'I'm well, thank you.' Dora made herself lean over and kiss him. 'I'm glad to hear you're getting better,' she added insincerely.

'Nice of you to say so.' Ralph grinned his wolf's grin. 'And it's good of you to come rushing over here to see me,' he added. 'Are you going back to Hereford tonight?'

'No. I'm spending Christmas with my parents. So I'll visit you every day, for as long as you're here.'

'I see.' Ralph's blue eyes glittered. 'I'm glad to find that you understand your wifely duty,' he said. 'But then, you always were a noble, self-sacrificing little creature, weren't you?' He eyed her mockingly. 'Such an angel. Oh, Dora?'

'Yes?'

'I wasn't, of course, expecting you to stagger in here bowed under the weight of flowers, grapes and hothouse peaches, but do you think that, when you next come in here, you could bring me some books?'

Dora blushed. 'Certainly,' she replied. 'What do you want?'

'Novels, autobiographies, memoirs — anything really.' He reached across to a small table and picked up a scrap of paper. 'Go to Blackwell's or wherever, could you? Get one or two of these. There's a darling.'

Dora looked at the list. 'I'm sure Papa has this one,' she said, frowning. 'And this, and this. He won't mind if you —'

'Get them from Blackwell's.' Ralph looked evenly at Dora. 'I'd rather have my own copies. Even in these straitened times, I would have thought we could run to buying me a few books. And I'd hate to be beholden to Squire Lawrence, after all.'

Dora stood up. 'I'll come to see you tomorrow,' she promised. 'I'll bring some books. Is there anything else you want? Shaving things, soap?'

'I don't think so. Packs of giggling halfwits from the Red Cross come round every day pressing gifts upon us. I already have a couple of genuine badger-bristle shaving brushes, not to mention numerous ghastly handkerchief sachets and half a dozen boxes of writing paper.'

He grinned again. 'I wonder what it is about a wounded soldier?' he asked, looking at Dora. 'I wonder what it can be? I suppose there's a certain glamour about ones like me, whose wounds are nicely hidden away and in respectable places.'

'I'm sure the ladies who visit you mean well.'

'Oh, I'm sure they do.' Ralph laughed. 'Don't you worry about me, Dora — I have everything I need, wine, women and song — I'm in clover.'

The following day Dora carried a great boxful of books into the ward, and on the day after that she visited her husband bearing a huge bunch of hothouse lilies. She smiled and fussed around him, determined not to let him irritate her. For some reason she didn't understand herself, she was intent on playing the part of the devoted wife.

Eventually, it seemed, even Ralph was deceived. He appeared to be genuinely despondent when she left him, asking her to come early the following day, kissing her affectionately as she said goodbye.

She was surprised that he could be so pleasant, was almost touched when he kissed her with such apparent tenderness. 'It's because he's ill,' she told herself, as she walked into the Summertown house one December afternoon. 'Ill and in pain. He's simply too weak to be unpleasant. All this show of affection — it's just a sham.'

She had to believe that. She couldn't permit herself to feel pity for him, otherwise she might begin to love him again.

'We're so sorry to see you go, Captain Challoner.' The pretty nurse blushed at Ralph, then suddenly raised herself on tiptoe and kissed his cheek. 'But of course we're glad you're better. Look after him, Mrs Challoner,' she said to Dora.

She blushed again. 'We *shall* miss him, you know.'

Dora nodded. Attempting a gracious smile, she wished that she could tell the nurse that for all Captain Challoner's wife cared the hospital could keep their model patient for ever.

By June 1916 Ralph was at last fully recovered. His legs, which had both been broken at the shin, had mended cleanly. His burns, although they had left deep, permanent scars, were healed. The only thing which still troubled him was a tendon weakness in his left arm.

He was as anxious to return to France as Dora was for him to leave her. He was wild to be in on the summer offensive, which he knew was planned and would no doubt go ahead, despite the fact that the French had got themselves badly cut up at Verdun and would now be unable to supply their share of the manpower needed for the great Allied campaign.

So Ralph was livid when he was informed that he would be on home service for the next twelve months at least. To his utter disgust he was detailed to report to the notorious Darlaston Military Detention Barracks, near Birmingham — as dreaded a place, in its way, as the trenches themselves.

After the idea had had a chance to mellow, however, Ralph found that he wasn't averse to going to Darlaston. After all, the War Office couldn't keep him in England forever. And in the meantime he'd be of some use to his country, for Ralph Challoner was just the man to deal with a horde of criminals, misfits and villains.

And he was also the kind of chap who could sort out a few of those damned conchies. Captain Challoner VC looked forward to meeting his first conscientious objectors.

Chapter Sixteen

THE DEPUTY COMMANDING OFFICER OF the Darlaston Detention Barracks welcomed Ralph, shaking his hand with the kind of deference due to a holder of the Victoria Cross. He called for refreshments to be brought into his office.

Over the clink of teacups and the rustling of various official papers, the two officers could hear the yells and shouts of NCOs drilling a heterogeneous bunch of men on the parade ground outside. After a few mouthfuls of thick, brown army tea, Ralph put down his cup and looked levelly at the man opposite him. 'What exactly will my duties be?' he asked.

'Ah.' Major Lawley grimaced at his subordinate. 'Duties.'

'Yes.' Ralph had by now decided that the major was a halfwit. A regular army officer, well into middle age, the man had evidently distinguished himself in the South African campaigns, but he had seen no active service for the past twenty years.

The major stroked his shaggy, heavily nicotined moustache and gazed thoughtfully at Ralph. 'Well,' he began, suddenly coming to life. 'As you already know, we have the rubbish of a dozen or more regiments here. Yes, we get all kinds of chaps. All kinds . . .'

'Such as?' prompted Ralph sharply. For the major was evidently about to doze off again.

'Oh — ah — well, let me see. There's your regular deserter, of course. You know, the sort of fellow who habitually goes absent without leave — you'll have come across the breed. "My wife's just had a baby, the cat died." Any lame excuse. We just give them the usual short shrift and back the buggers go, kit bags packed, rubbing their sore backsides. But then there's the occasional really bad egg who has to go up against the wall. Can't be helped sometimes.'

The major's glassy brown eyes stared at Ralph. 'You're not squeamish, I hope?'

'I don't think so.'

'No? Well, of course you're not. Crimson ribbon and all that. But I've known a good few chaps throw up all over the parade ground at the sight of an execution, and they've been sound enough fellows otherwise.' Reflectively, the major took a slurp of cold tea. 'Can't understand it myself.'

'No.' Ralph nodded his agreement. 'And?'

'Oh, yes. Well, there are the usual petty criminals of course. They don't often give us any bother.' He leaned forward and tapped Ralph's cuff with a brown-stained forefinger. 'But these days it's that squad of bloody conscientious objectors who give us more trouble than the rest put together.'

He sighed bitterly. 'They're the ones you'll have to watch, Mr Challoner. I was thinking, perhaps they ought to be your special responsibility. You're a hard man, aren't you? I can see you are. We'll work well together, I'm sure of it.'

Ralph narrowed his eyes and said nothing. He wasn't so certain of that.

The major stood up. 'That's enough chat for now,' he said. 'Come along — I'll show you around.'

Darlaston Military Detention Barracks consisted of a number of wretched wooden huts which were dotted in clusters about a large tarmacadamed compound. In the centre of the compound was the crumbling Georgian mansion which gave the place its name. And all this was surrounded by a high brick wall topped by barbed wire fortifications, which looked thoroughly out of place in a middle-class suburb of Birmingham.

Requisitioned by the Army in 1914, Darlaston House had been the home of some eighteenth-century industrial magnate, and was a pillared and porticoed, once-elegant house in which the officers and men manning the barracks now had their quarters. In consequence, the house now bore all the marks of a group of men living in uncomfortable proximity.

In a state of decomposition when the Army had taken the place over, an air of desolation was all-pervasive now. The house stank of damp and dry rot, of army blankets and rank male sweat, of disinfectant and stale cooking.

But compared with the sheds in which the detainees lived, the house was luxurious. Admittedly damp, it was not waterlogged; spartan, it was not yet a slum.

Those huts, however, were sodden with the rain of the previous year's bad summer, and now they were foul with rottenness. In decaying, they sagged and crumbled and grew fantastic varieties of mould. Black and green fungus spread all across their flimsy ceilings and down their dank walls, dripping noxious mildews upon the men who lived inside these horrid dens.

Having long since warped upon their hinges, the doors and the heavily barred windows now let in the wind and rain. And the stoves inside the huts gave off choking fumes which had the bronchitics and asthmatics coughing all night.

The hospital hut was the dampest of all. Known to the prisoners as the Morgue, it was an ice-cold barn of a place to which one went to die of pneumonia, tuberculosis, or whatever illness the punitive regime at the Darlaston Detention Barracks had exacerbated.

Having displayed the beauties of the camp to his new subordinate, Major Lawley now took Ralph to look at his special responsibility. 'They're a mixed bunch,' he remarked as the two officers crossed a patch of beaten earth next to the parade ground. 'There are the Bible thumpers. There are the idiots. There are the cowards. And there's a certain Mr Herriott.'

'Mr Herriott?'

'Yes.' The major tapped his nose. 'He's one of the clever ones, or thinks he is. You'll have to give him your particular attention. Been here since the beginning of March he has, causing trouble, little bugger. Just been sentenced to another stretch. Excuse me.'

Major Lawley dug his hands into his pockets and eventually found the grubby handkerchief he was looking for. He blew his nose. 'Where was I?' he demanded.

'Mr Herriott.'

'Ah, yes.' The major sniffed. 'Ex-schoolmaster. Socialist, too, I shouldn't wonder. Told the tribunal what they could do with the Military Service Acts and refused point blank to take on any form of alternative service. Blighter said he didn't recognize military authority. Oh, talk of the devil — there he is. Over across the square, on fatigues.'

Ralph looked. He saw a small man in slovenly service dress and full kit, listlessly dragging his meagre body across a strip of tarmac while a barrel-chested drill sergeant bellowed commands at him.

'You've got him into uniform, then,' he observed.

'Yes.' Major Lawley scowled. 'He'll wear the regulation service dress but only to make a point. Fouls it, he does. The man stinks.'

'I see.'

Ralph glanced again towards the recreant. Private Herriott was thin and round-shouldered. He looked cowed and frightened even from a distance. Ralph thought he would soon sort *him* out. And then he would deal with his friends.

Ralph grinned at the major. 'I'll have them all paraded now, Sir,' he said. 'If that's all right with you.'

The older man snickered. 'Keen, eh? Good man. Right — I'll have Sergeant Watson come over right away. Carry on, Mr Challoner. Carry on.'

※ ※ ※

Over the next few months Captain Challoner VC imposed his will on his special responsibility. He bullied the men unmercifully, punished them to the very limits of his authority and made their lives as near to hell on earth as he could. He thoroughly enjoyed his work.

Some reluctant conscripts, convinced perhaps by the eloquence of Ralph's arguments, eventually saw the errors of their ways. They set aside their scruples and, laying aside their blankets as well, they put on their uniforms and became good little soldiers after all. They went off to France and Belgium if not eagerly, then not so very reluctantly. Anything must be better than being locked up with bloody Challoner.

But there was, of course, a hard core of difficult cases. Two

Quakers, brothers — men whom any humane tribunal could have seen were sincere in their convictions, but whose requests for total exemption had been turned down — seemed to acquiesce in their torments.

Obstructing military authority by completely passive resistance, they were permanently on punishment and took whatever Ralph inflicted on them without complaint. Wasting away on their bread and water diet, they became weaker and weaker.

Ralph eventually decided that the pair were madmen. He gave up trying to turn them into soldiers. They provided him instead with excellent entertainment as he edged closer and closer to what he thought must be the limits of their endurance.

Then there was Henry Arnold, Douglas Herriott's special friend. For some reason Private Arnold — an enormous, shambling, apparently brainless ruffian, whose small grey eyes peered piggily at the world from beneath an overhanging ridge of eyebrow — had struck up some kind of friendship with the other persistent defaulter. The two of them were inseparable.

Ralph was unable to understand this mutual attraction. Whatever did a cocky little pest like Herriott see to admire in an oaf like Arnold? Come to that, how had Arnold become a conchie in the first place? He looked a belligerent sort of chap. To Ralph, a pacifist, a conscientious objector and a coward were all the same animal — human dross of the most repulsive kind. And in Henry Arnold, Ralph saw not his own idea of a conchie, but an extremely dangerous type, an unpredictable lunatic, bordering on the subnormal. He promised himself that he would look up Arnold's file and find out what the great lout had in fact said at his hearing.

There was, however, no great taxing of the imagination required to understand the workings of Douglas Herriott's nasty little mind. Ralph had come across his sort before, at school, in the ranks. 'They're always the same kind of fellow,' he explained to Major Lawley one autumn evening, as the two of them sat over a glass each of pre-war malt whisky.

'Eh? How's that?'

'Well, they're always undersized. Weakly. Too clever by half, usually, and always making trouble for the sake of it. And they don't seem to mind getting kicked in the guts now and then.' Ralph took a gulp of whisky. 'Anything to get attention.'

'So what'll you do with the fellow?'

'Ah.' Ralph grinned. 'I've plans for Mr Herriott. He may think he's cock of the walk just now but I haven't even begun.'

But, as it happened, Ralph's plans for Mr Herriott were put into effect rather sooner than he had intended they should be.

'Private Herriott!' Ralph was crossing the parade ground the following morning on his way to Major Lawley's office. Herriott had, he knew, dropped that scrap of paper deliberately. 'Private Herriott! Halt!'

Herriott sauntered on for a few more paces, ignoring Ralph completely. He reached the end of the barrack square and turned to face Ralph. 'Talking to me, were you?' he asked.

Ralph glared at him. 'Stand to attention, damn you!' he barked. 'Hands out of your pockets!' He flicked Herriott's thin shanks with his glove. 'Private Herriott, you address an officer as "Sir".'

'Really?'

'Really, *Sir*!'

'Really, Sir?'

Ralph scowled at Herriott. He felt that he was beginning to lose this particular round and his temper began to rise. 'Look at you,' he spat. 'You're a disgrace to the uniform, you dirty little bastard. Don't you ever clean your buttons? Polish your boots? Where's your self-respect, man? Your pride in yourself?'

Herriott, his shoulders slumping by imperceptible degrees, his hands twitching round to his pockets again, gazed insolently at Ralph. He said nothing.

'Well?'

'Well what?' Herriott looked at Ralph's own brightly polished boots, then peered closely at the captain's own dazzling buttons. 'Oh, I beg your pardon,' he muttered, his mouth curving in amusement. 'Well what, Sir?'

It was going to be a bloody awful day, Ralph could see that. There was a fresh squad of conchies due to arrive that morning. He had a splitting headache, the result of finishing off the whole bottle of that excellent whisky. And there was a terrible shooting pain in his left leg.

To add to all this, the post that day had brought a letter

advising him that he would remain on home service for the foreseeable future, that his health would be re-assessed the following spring. At this rate he'd never get back to France.

He glowered at Herriott. How dare the horrible little sod stand there, staring like that? How much longer would he be obliged to put up with Herriott's particular brand of insolence? Why didn't the runt do something spectacular, then they could have the bugger shot.

But then he looked at Herriott again. No, he wouldn't, would he? He'd never put himself on the offensive; he was too subtle for that. He'd nibble around, slink about, show his ratty little face here and there, infect the other malingerers with his own particularly insidious form of insubordination.

And now Ralph's temper, always threatening to erupt, boiled over. 'Sergeant Lewis!' Ralph had noticed the sergeant marching a string of men across to their quarters. 'Sergeant Lewis. Let those men find their own way back and come over here. Move, man! At the double!'

Lewis came, practically running. 'Sir?'

'This man here — I want him punished. For insubordination.'

'Herriott, Sir?'

'Of course Herriott, man!'

'Well, Sir, what —'

'Let me see.' Ralph frowned, casting about him for some form of appropriate retribution for Herriott's present insolence and innumerable past misdemeanours.

Ralph did, of course, know his regimental history and his Rules for Field Punishment off by heart; he knew what penalties were available. But then, for some reason, the military graveyards of Northern France came into his mind and he looked at Herriott with a sudden and terrifying hatred.

'We'll have a crucifixion, I think,' he said softly. 'An old-fashioned military punishment which it might be a good idea to practise on a few of these insubordinate sods.'

'Crucifixion, Sir?' Puzzled, Sergeant Lewis frowned. 'You mean Field Punishment Number One?'

'No, I don't!' Ralph glared at him. 'I want a cross set up in the centre of the square,' he rapped. 'Wood. Six feet high. See to it — at the double now. As for you, Private Herriott, since you have no respect for the King's uniform, you can take it off.'

Both NCO and private stared at Ralph for a second or two. Then Sergeant Lewis came to his senses and hurried away. Herriott stood still, looking down at his own filthy boots and bedraggled puttees.

'You heard what I said, Private Herriott,' murmured Ralph smoothly. 'Strip!'

Herriott hesitated. He looked again at Ralph and saw a smile on the officer's face which made his spine tingle. He undid the first button on his tunic.

Lewis and another sergeant eventually found two stout beams of wood which they lashed together and set up, cruciform, in the centre of the square. When they had finished knotting the ropes and pegging the cross down, Ralph told them to tie Herriott to it, arms outstretched. 'Not too tightly,' he added pleasantly. 'We don't want to stop his circulation, do we?'

Herriott stayed there, tied to his cross, all day. Platoons of men passed and repassed him, goggling. Curious individual soldiers stared at this shivering, naked man as they marched smartly across the square.

But no one spoke to him. No one would have dared. At nightfall Ralph walked nonchalantly across the parade ground to enquire after his victim's health.

The two men looked at each other. Herriott, tied hand and foot, humiliated in the most horrible fashion, almost purple with cold, hungry, thirsty and now befouled with his own urine, nevertheless stared back at Ralph.

Neither spoke. But, after a minute or two, it was Ralph who dropped his gaze. He'd seen the look on Herriott's face before. On Dora's much prettier face, and on Katherine Lawrence's heavy features, there had occasionally been that same expression, and it was one of total contempt.

Ralph walked briskly away scowling, and was met by Sergeant Lewis crossing the square. 'Permission to untie Herriott, Sir?' he asked, as if the granting of this permission were a mere formality.

Ralph glowered at the man. 'Permission refused, Sergeant,' he growled. 'He's to stay there until 0900 hours tomorrow.'

Sergeant Lewis stared. 'Be a frost tonight, Sir,' he said reasonably. 'And, after all, regulations might allow for tying chaps to limber wheels, but they don't say anything about leaving men outside all night, naked.' He coughed. 'Don't you think, Sir — well, permission to stick a blanket round the bugger?'

'If you wish to find yourself on a charge, Sergeant Lewis, you are going the right way about it.' Now white with anger, Ralph glared so fiercely that the sergeant flinched. 'Release Herriott at nine tomorrow morning,' he muttered. 'Is that clearly understood?'

'Sir.'

As Ralph walked across to the officers' mess, Henry Arnold watched him. Something in the man's dull brain was fermenting busily. He looked at the point between Ralph's shoulder-blades and imagined a dagger there.

Then he turned his attention to the white figure in the centre of the square, still discernible in the fading light. He knew then that he must settle with bloody Challoner. He had no wish to kill Germans, to murder men he did not even know. But he knew Challoner. Only too well . . .

At ten minutes to nine the following morning Sergeant Lewis and another NCO took it upon themselves to release Douglas Herriott. They cut the ropes which had, by now, bitten deeply into his wrists and ankles. Then they lowered him on to the ground, wrapping him in a blanket.

The man was conscious, it seemed, but was past speech and certainly unable to walk. 'Lug 'im back to 'is 'ut, eh?' demanded the NCO.

'Yeah.' Sergeant Lewis grabbed Herriott under the armpits and motioned to the NCO to pick him up under his knees. 'Get a couple of 'is mates to warm the bugger up again.'

Between them Sergeant Lewis and the NCO carried Ralph's victim to his hut and laid him on his bed. 'Get over to the cookhouse,' barked the sergeant, collaring Henry Arnold. 'Get a dixie full of porridge and push it down 'im. Then give 'im some tea.'

He looked round at the other inmates of the hut. 'Any of you gentlemen fancy arguin' the toss with Captain Challoner this morning?' he enquired genially. 'Cos if you *do*, perhaps I ought to warn you that I've been lookin' at the Field Punishment Manual for 1837. A hundred lashes warn't anything particular then, you know. And there's a nice cat o' nine tails hangin' up in the guardroom. Don't think Captain Challoner knows they're there — yet.'

Herriott recovered from his ordeal, the details of which were barracks gossip for days. The behaviour of the prisoners was, for a fortnight or so, exemplary.

Ralph went home on leave for a week, well pleased with his success. But Dora was not impressed. 'Surely,' she said, hearing of her husband's latest attempt to bring his special responsibility to heel, 'surely it's pointless and cruel to keep them in prison month after month, just because the Army hopes they'll change their minds?'

'Why should *you* be so tender of the feelings of a lot of bloody conchies?' Ralph glared at her over his breakfast coffee. 'They *do* change their minds; that's the whole damned point. Why, only last week, two of them —'

'Mr Herriott, Ralph?' Dora grinned wickedly at her husband. 'Will he ever change his?'

'There's a certain sort of person who's always going to be difficult.' Ralph sniffed. 'All supposedly educated working class rabble are insubordinate. And Herriott's an example of the worst kind. He doesn't know his place at all.'

'Ah.'

'Yes.' Ralph rose to his feet. 'You're descended from the lower orders yourself, aren't you, my bastard bride?' he demanded. 'I suppose it's only natural that you'd stick up for the likes of Herriott.'

Dora buttered another piece of toast. 'Mr Herriott seems to have become an obsession with you, Ralph,' she remarked calmly. 'I do rather pity him, you know.'

* * *

During May 1916 the greater part of Marcus Harley's division had been moved down from Flanders, where they'd spent the winter, to Amiens. So far, they'd had it relatively easy. They had been marched up to do their stint in the front line, had suffered the misery of being under bombardment, had taken a number of casualties and then been marched back to billets. Some of them would be glad when July came at last, for this year was to see the Big Push, this would be *it*. The Germans would be dealt with once and for all.

One morning during the first week of that eventful July, Marcus Harley had woken to a still, grey, misty dawn. He yawned and stretched; he heard the mud crack across the chest of his filthy service dress tunic. His feet and legs were wet, for it had rained during the night and he had been sleeping in the open, rolled in his greatcoat and inadequately covered by a waterproof sheet.

In a trench to his left he could hear the sound of breakfast being made, and could distinguish the clatter of dixies above the low grumbling of the officers' servants as they threw together a meal for their masters.

Gradually, all the men around Marcus stirred themselves. They shouted enquiries to those who'd been on sentry-duty during the hours of darkness, they muttered to each other while they waited for the order to stand to. Some were in the mood of elation which precedes an action — some were despondent. All were dirty and unshaven. They had been in this spot for three days, under constant enemy fire, and were, on the whole, wishing themselves back in their billets at Albert.

Marcus rubbed his itching face. How pleasant it would be, he thought, to have a wash, to shave with really hot soapy water using a nice sharp razor. He closed his eyes again. He could now feel the warmth of the morning sun on his stiff body and see the light glowing red through his eyelids.

He propped himself up on one elbow and looked around. The wet earth was steaming and the sky was a beautiful hazy blue. It seemed ridiculous to be going into battle again on what promised to be another hot July day, which would ordinarily be full of the scent of summer flowers, of the hum of bees and a thousand other soft, summer sounds. He could actually hear birds singing in the wood two hundred or so yards away. And, growing in the chalky soil, there were still some scarlet poppies and blue cornflowers, which shook with each new blast of shellfire.

'What time d'you get in, then?' Marcus heard one of his

platoon NCOs call to a mate.

'About three. What about you lot?'

'Around two, I reckon.' The man laughed. 'Did a good night's work, we did. Showed Jerry what-for.'

Marcus wondered how the man could be so full of energy. *He* was exhausted. But the platoon's night patrol had indeed been a success. Marcus and eight others had crept up on an enemy trench, each man holding fast to a string upon which Marcus tugged to give his silent commands.

Spread out in a line, they'd sneaked up on the Germans, then lobbed a few dozen bombs into their trench before the startled Huns had realized what had hit them. Then they were back through their wire and home again before the enemy had had a chance to retaliate.

But now Marcus wanted only to sleep. If only he could sleep. All day, all of the next day, too . . .

With a sickening crump, a shell landed on the roof of a dugout. A second or two later there were curses and exclamations from Marcus's platoon as gobs of earth, metal, wood and mud showered all over them, and the parapet shook. That trench, however, had been empty of men. Perhaps that was a good omen for the day to come.

'Lieutenant Harley. Cup of tea, Sir.'

Marcus shook himself. He sat up properly and took the brimming mug of pale grey liquid from the sergeant's hands. He wondered, briefly, where the water had come from; the bits in it looked like shreds of old corpse, for they had a somewhat meaty appearance and were of a rubbery, gristly texture when they bobbed against his mouth.

What did it matter? He drank the stuff down anyway, grateful for the liquid, for his mouth felt dry and disgusting, as if he had a hangover. He gazed at the mud wall opposite, frowning, for he was now aware of a very painful bruise on his side which had been caused by a blow from a rifle butt a few days since.

'What you thinking about, Mr Harley?' The sergeant from C Company squatted companionably next to Marcus, watching him sip his disgusting tea.

'Nothing, Sergeant.' Marcus turned to look at the man.

'What's going on today?' he asked suddenly. 'Remind me, will you — I can't find my map, and I don't seem able to recall what was said at yesterday's briefing. What's going to happen about the wire?'

'Oh, Jerry's wire's all cut to blazes now, Sir.' The sergeant grinned. 'And your lot's going over at seven, into the wood. We're comin' with you,' he added comfortingly. 'A and C's in the first wave, together, like — it's the usual formation.'

'Is it?' Wearily, Marcus rubbed his eyes. 'So we're going into the wood, are we? A wood's a difficult place to take, you know,' he murmured, as if talking to himself.

The sergeant studied Marcus quizzically. Why was the fellow always so bloody vague about everything? Oh, he was a good young officer, no doubt about that; he looked after his men and went on his fair share of raids and patrols — he was no slacker. But just recently there had been a vacant look in his eyes, and now it was there practically all the time. Perhaps his nerve was going. He was only a kid, after all.

That morning Marcus's battalion was to take part in an action which would attempt to clear the enemy from the southern edges of a little wood, their first objective being the capture of the Germans' front line trenches. The whole battalion would attack over a three hundred yard front, and Marcus, as he had learned from the sergeant, would be taking his platoon over with the two companies in the first wave.

Lighting a cigarette, Marcus inhaled a comforting lungful of smoke. Half an hour after his conversation with Sergeant Callaghan, he led his men up to the parapet to wait for the order to advance.

As they waited for the whistle, the men muttered among themselves, had a last fag, a last bite to eat. Private Russell vomited neatly into the tobacco tin which he kept for the purpose; he always brought back his breakfast before going into action, and Marcus couldn't think why he bothered to have any. The tension grew.

Marcus had to keep shaking himself, to remind himself that all this was real. There was now a marvellous blue haze over the German lines. This was truly a perfect day for lying in the garden at home, reading a nice, new, exciting novel; a day for walking through a deep green spinney with a young and pretty girl; for punting along the Backs . . .

The Allied barrage lifted and Marcus jumped up on the firestep. He was soon out of the trench, closely followed by his men. They formed up in the open and then went charging through the mud and waste of no man's land, making for the fringes of the wood. Struggling uphill now, loaded down with packs which weighed almost half as much as some of them did themselves, the men attempted to bomb the Germans from their fastnesses among the trees.

They failed completely. Relatively safe in a line of coppice, the Germans had held their positions, and when the barrage from the British trenches had lifted they had opened fire with their machine guns. And now they fired volley after volley at the disordered ranks of Marcus's battalion, cutting down every other man.

Ten very long minutes went by. Amid a cloud of dust and smoke Marcus could see that he now had only about half a dozen men still on their feet. Then, something snapped inside him and he decided to give the signal to withdraw, the possibility that this could result in his court martial hardly crossing his mind. For they were still nowhere near the wood, and to stay where they were, or to go on, would be certain suicide.

'Sir! Sir!' An NCO was tugging at Marcus's sleeve. 'Where we goin', Sir? The orders is —'

'Sod the orders.' Marcus glowered at the man. And, even as he spoke, he was thrown flat on his face, knocked into the mud by the corporal who had just addressed him, and whose dead body now lay across his own legs. 'Sod the bloody orders,' he repeated, almost in tears.

A few dozen British casualties had been rescued and were being carried down to the dressing stations as grey clouds came scudding over at about midday. It began to rain, a heavy summer downpour. By early afternoon the men on the battlefield were soaked through, and a coating of fresh mud adorned their already filthy service dress. Marcus's platoon, or what remained of it, squelched and slithered their way across no man's land, ducking and weaving from shell-hole to shell-hole, following their lieutenant like a little herd of dazed sheep.

Eventually they could go no further. Exhausted, half blinded by smoke and half deafened by gunfire, disheartened by their evident failure to achieve anything and well aware that most of the men from their battalion must now be lying dead in the mud, the surviving members of Marcus's platoon now crouched in a large crater. And, by some miracle, the rest of the Company found them there.

Marcus stared at his captain. Had he withdrawn, as well? Was the entire Fourth Army in retreat? Marcus rubbed his eyes with his dirty hands, his mind turning towards a dawn firing squad.

'Ah, Marcus. So there's some of us still alive and kicking.' The captain grinned. He seemed relieved rather than anything else. Obviously it hadn't occurred to him that Marcus and his men had made what could be described, at its most generous, as a tactical withdrawal.

The captain beamed at the lieutenant. 'Another push — that should do it,' he said. 'Then we'll have the sods out of that corner, and we'll be in their forward trenches. Off you go now, old chap, and don't worry about covering fire. C Company will be supporting you.'

'If any of it still exists,' thought Marcus, which he was inclined to doubt. So this was to be his last day on earth, after all.

He set off at the head of his own men and the twenty other poor devils the captain had detailed to go with him. Staggering through the teeming rain towards the broken, twisted trees where the Germans waited, Marcus wondered if his enemies were as tired, fed up and damned well scared as he was.

He heard himself shrieking orders as he stumbled into the wood and took aim at a group of Germans dug in less than twenty yards away. Throwing himself down beside a battered tree stump he aimed his revolver. 'Fire! Fire!' he yelled, blasting away himself now.

Now he was in the thick of it, he didn't have time to think any more. Now, he was just an automaton, shooting round after round into the bodies of mothers' sons, wives' husbands, girls' sweethearts.

Then, as if by magic a German suddenly materialized; there was an enemy soldier a mere ten feet away from him. Marcus fired and the man collapsed flat on his back, shot in the stomach. The soldier screamed, uttered a terrible high pitched shriek of agony and Marcus grinned. The cries of the wounded and dying echoed round the wood and Marcus kept firing, killing, wounding, feeling nothing but the desire to destroy.

The evening was hot and sticky. The smell of putrefaction hung over everything. Nothing much had been achieved by way of an Allied advance.

Marcus's own battalion, however, had eventually succeeded in bombing the enemy from one of their forward trenches, and had taken forty prisoners whom they'd set to work carrying ammunition for their captors.

Although the Germans were still in possession of the wood, they had held on to it at a price, for their losses, Marcus decided, must have been heavy. The battlefield was littered with German dead, and he noticed that a few dozen unfortunate men in German uniform hung suspended on the tangled thickets of barbed wire, blown there to death or horrible injury by the Allied guns.

Even as Marcus watched, a body slipped from high up on the wire and fell heavily, becoming impaled on the wicked spikes of a coil three or four feet below. Nothing could be worse than getting caught on the wire, he thought, hoping the poor devil was dead. Or at least unconscious.

At the end of that ghastly day Marcus had been surprised to find himself still whole. Except for a cut on his shin, he had no mark on him. Half envying those down at the dressing stations who were either going to Blighty or to heaven, he wandered back along a communication trench and flopped wearily into the muddy pit dignified by the name of Company HQ.

'Jolly well done, Mr Harley!' The major from battalion headquarters leaned across the plank which served as a table and shook Marcus by the hand. 'Damn fine show by your lads, jolly good team effort. You showed the Hun what we're made of. Get some more action like that tomorrow and we'll break their line for certain.'

Marcus grimaced. He walked out of the dug-out and found himself a relatively dry shelf of earth. He rolled himself in a bloodstained German greatcoat he'd found and tried to get to sleep. At midnight, it began to rain.

Chapter Seventeen

ANTHONY LAWRENCE LOOKED AT THE brown envelope on the letter tray, picked it up and slit it open. The papers inside were what he'd been expecting all summer. His Majesty's Armed Forces had at last invited him to join them, to put on khaki for King and Country.

Anthony grimaced. Although he accepted that wars were sometimes necessary, that men had to die in order to preserve something more precious than mere individual human existence, he heartily disapproved of this particular war. *This* business was a pointless mass slaughter; the recent awful news of July's disasters on the battlefields of the Somme had proved that beyond a doubt. And why the whole business could not have been settled by negotiation back in 1914 was beyond Anthony's comprehension.

He prepared himself, almost fatalistically, for death — resigned himself to becoming just one more body trampled in an infantry charge. He would be kitted out in uniform, given some rudimentary training, then be sent out to France. Then he, like thousands of others, would be killed while trying to take some useless heap of stones or hole in the ground from a miserable bunch of Saxon conscripts.

He made his will, collected his papers together and put his work in order, sighing over how little he'd achieved.

Despite having enjoyed a brief flirtation with a heterogeneous bunch of Cambridge intellectuals who had in the end come out strongly in denunciation of the war, Anthony didn't see himself as a conscientious objector. Nor was he a pacifist;

he wasn't even opposed to killing, provided it was in self-defence, or in defence of his loved ones. Anthony had no doubts about what he would have done had he caught the putative German raping his wife, mother or sister.

But he had so much work to do. There were books to be written, students to be taught and, he hoped, a reputation to be made. Now he would achieve nothing. 'It's a waste,' he muttered, as he tied up another bundle of notes. 'It's just a bloody, stupid waste.'

More official correspondence followed that first letter. Eventually told to report at the local barracks for a medical inspection, Anthony braced himself for what was to happen, accepting that he would now be sent off to some dismal training camp to be prepared for making the Supreme Sacrifice. He wondered if he'd be going to France or Flanders. Both would be equally horrible.

On the appointed day he took what he thought might well be his last leave of Miriam. Quickly, he kissed his children and without further prolonging his goodbyes, made his way to the barracks.

These turned out to be a dreary collection of wooden huts surrounded by a wire netting fence, a mile or two outside Cambridge. He'd never seen such a depressing place. Admitted by a sentry wielding a bayonet, he was told to go into one of the huts. So he went inside and sat down on a hard chair near the door.

'Oi! You!'

'What?' Anthony looked up and saw a huge, khaki-clad figure looming above him, a man who was almost a caricature recruiting sergeant. 'Are you talking to me?' he asked.

'I *am*.' The enormous Army sergeant glowered down at Anthony. 'If you've come to join up, as I assume you 'ave, or you wouldn't be 'ere, *could* you kindly take your place in the queue and wait until you're called to tell us all about your good self?' The soldier indicated a group of six men standing against a wall in the far corner of the room. 'Over there, *Sir*! *If* you'd be so good.'

God, the man actually spoke like a soldier from a comedy routine. Anthony rose to his feet and did as he was bidden.

'Name?' The sour-faced clerk looked narrowly at Anthony.

'Anthony Lawrence.'

'That your full name?'

'Anthony Stephen Lawrence.'

'Thank *you*.' The clerk inserted Anthony's middle name, scowling as he spoilt the pristine beauty of his form. 'Date of birth?'

'Eleventh of November, 1880.'

Spelling eleventh wrongly, the clerk scribbled that down. 'Occupation?'

'University lecturer.'

'Religion?'

'None.'

The clerk dipped his pen into the ink. 'Church of England,' he wrote.

'I said, none!' Glaring at this officious little NCO, Anthony snatched the pen out of his hand and scored out Church of England. 'NONE' he wrote, in great black capitals, and handed the soldier his pen.

The clerk frowned at his maltreated form and wiped his nose on the back of his hand. 'You want to watch it, mate,' he muttered harshly. 'Mr Smart Alec University Lecturer, you want to watch it; that's all.'

Anthony took his place in the queue of men now waiting to be examined by the Army doctors. Two workmen clad in blue overalls eyed him curiously. 'Why was that bloke carrying on at you?' demanded one.

'Oh, it was just a misunderstanding,' replied Anthony. He shrugged. 'Nothing at all, really.'

Told to go into a cubicle and strip to the waist, Anthony reflected gloomily that this was all part of the systematic dehumanizing process. He had been tagged and docketed, and now he was as good as inside the great machine which was currently occupied in reducing thousands of men like him to mere automata.

He took off his jacket, undid his tie, then pulled off his waistcoat and shirt. He wished it had been winter, then he'd have been coughing and wheezing with his habitual bronchitis and would hardly have represented a desirable specimen of cannon fodder.

As he walked past a window on his way to the doctor's table, he caught sight of himself in the glass. Although he was certainly no Hercules, he was undoubtedly well-made — deep-chested, broad-shouldered, he looked disgustingly fit. The medical orderly bawled out his name, so he slouched, hands in pockets, over to the doctor.

The Army medical officer, a grey-haired, gloomy man whose idea of a pleasant afternoon's occupation was not, evidently, examining a couple of dozen reluctant conscripts, listened to Anthony's chest. He grimaced. 'Turn round,' he said.

Anthony did as he was told.

'Ah.' The army doctor frowned. He leaned against Anthony's back and listened, then he turned to his colleague. 'I say, Arthur,' he muttered. 'Come and tell me what you make of this.'

'Hm?' The other doctor sniffed and looked at Anthony. He leaned against his chest and listened. 'D'you suffer from bronchitis?' he asked.

'Yes.' Anthony shrugged. 'Every winter. It's the damp climate of the Fens, I suppose, and I'm more susceptible to it than most.'

'D'you get breathless easily? Have fainting fits? Palpitations? Ever had pleurisy?'

'No, nothing like that.'

'Oh.' The doctor pursed his lips. 'You can wait over there for a few minutes,' he said. 'Let me deal with these other chaps, then I'll get back to you. Oh, and Mr Lawrence — you'd better sit down.'

Later than afternoon Anthony walked back into the drawing room of the house in Pearson Street. His hands deep in his pockets, he had a peculiar smile on his face — a smile which considerably alarmed his wife, who had certainly not expected to see him again that day.

'Well?' Gently, Miriam pushed David off her lap and rose to her feet, catching her husband by the shoulders. 'What is it, Anthony?' she demanded. 'Why are you here, and why do you look so strange?'

'Can't you guess?'

'They want you to go abroad straight away? You have to leave tonight?'

Anthony wrapped his arms around his wife and hugged her so tightly that he almost crushed her ribs. 'They don't want me to go at all.' He was almost hysterical. 'Oh, Miriam, they don't want me! They don't want me!'

'But why?' Miriam disentangled herself from his almost suffocating embrace and made him sit down. 'What's the matter with you? Are you ill?'

'No — well, yes, sort of.'

'Anthony, explain.'

'I had scarlet fever as a child. I'd forgotten all about it until the doctor asked me.' Anthony rubbed his eyes. 'It was quite a serious attack, you see and it seems that it weakened my kidneys. I have something wrong with my lungs. Oh, and I also have a heart condition; I could have a stroke any day, it appears. And you already know I'm short-sighted.' Anthony grimaced. 'What a splendid specimen of British manhood.'

'Anthony!' Miriam, shocked, took his hand in hers and chafed it, looking anxiously into his face. 'Oh, Anthony.'

'It's all right — it's nothing to worry about.' Anthony looked calmly at his wife. 'I've been like this for twenty-five years or more. I'm not suddenly going to expire. Not like those poor devils going off to France next week,' he added, his face sombre.

'Oh.' Miriam, still concerned, looked at him. 'What will you do now?' she asked.

'I don't know. Stay here for the time being, do a bit more work on that book. The major at the barracks told me I'd be called up for home service eventually; they'll find me something to do in London, he said. Do you know, he actually commiserated with me? Said he could see I was disappointed not to be going off to do my bit, and not to worry, they'd find me something.'

'I see.'

'Do you?' Anthony covered his face with his hands. 'I've got off lightly, haven't I?' he mumbled. 'I ought to be ashamed of myself.'

* * *

Anna Harley scanned the casualty lists every day, her heart thumping as she approached H. Her breathing only returned to normal as she passed that particular column without finding either of her sons' names among those of the dead.

Of the two of them, it was Marcus she worried about more. He was her dearest child, and unlike Robert, who was serving in Palestine, Marcus was still amid the charnel pits of the Western Front. Deep inside herself, Anna knew that Robert would be all right; small, tough, black-haired little troll that he was, he could look after himself. He was a survivor.

But Marcus was different. Marcus, her first born, her beautiful eldest son, might not be so lucky, and it was for him that her tears of anxiety flowed. It was about him she worried day and night.

It appeared that the Somme offensive had failed. The war would not, it seemed, end within the year; but would go on and on, month after wretched month, into 1917. Then Neil, the Harleys' youngest son, would be eighteen and he would go as well. All their children would be overseas then, all likely to suffer death or injury.

'Can you remember what started the war?' Anna asked her husband as the two of them sat side by side on the sofa one evening, in front of a dying fire. 'I'm sure I can't.'

'Belgium. The Belgian crisis.' John kicked a log of wood with his foot, causing a mass of yellow sparks to shoot up the chimney. 'The Germans tramped into Belgium uninvited and then refused to leave.' He paused. 'I can't see that they'll ever go now.'

'Will it go on for ever, then?'

'I don't see why not.'

Anna sighed. It did indeed seem that both sides were now locked in a never-ending stalemate of death and destruction, which had become an end in itself.

* * *

The car bringing the major and a military policeman to the Grange drew up on the gravel sweep at about eleven o'clock on a fine February morning. Dora had seen it arrive and, curious, had gone to open the door to the soldiers herself, causing them some confusion.

They were already somewhat flustered and now they stood hesitantly on the threshold, puffing and clearing their throats, uncertain what to say to this pretty woman who stood so upright and calm, smiling enquiringly at them.

Dora led them into the drawing room and bade them sit down. She sent for some coffee and, as she poured it, she realized that *she* must break the silence. 'Have you come about my husband?' she asked, handing a cup to the major. 'Has there been an accident?'

'My dear Mrs Challoner.' The major's hands began to shake, obliging him to replace his coffee cup on the tray. 'My dear lady, I'm afraid there's been more than a mere accident.' He sniffed and, finding a somewhat crumpled handkerchief in his pocket, he wiped his moustache. 'Captain Verney here will explain.'

Dora glanced through the window and saw that a few snowdrops were in bloom, having pushed their way through a patch of black, frozen earth. She turned to the military policeman. 'Captain Verney?'

The captain gave her a very garbled version of what had happened the day before. He rushed through a brief account of the incident; then he paused to look at Dora, in order to give her time to have hysterics if she wanted to. So many women did, after all.

She merely gazed at him, her brown eyes wide and tearless, her expression perfectly composed. 'Could you give me a little more detail?' she asked.

Captain Verney stared, then he realized — delayed shock, that was what it was. He sighed loudly, relieved — the hysterics would come later, and then the woman's servants could deal with her — put her to bed and all that sort of thing.

'This fellow Arnold,' he began. 'He's a great fat brute, not all there, if you take my meaning. Well, he seems to have taken an unreasonable dislike to Captain Challoner.'

Captain Verney smoothed the creases in his already immaculate trousers and looked up, forcing himself to meet the woman's unblinking stare. 'The fellow — Arnold, I mean — he's a conscientious objector, you see. One of the very worst kind. And he's very thick with another of his sort, a devil by the name of Herriott.'

'Ah, Mr Herriott.' Dora nodded at Captain Verney. 'And?'

'You've heard of Herriott?'

'Yes, my husband did mention him once or twice. Ralph and he did not get on, I believe?'

'Captain Challoner was a fine officer,' replied Captain Verney, firmly. 'He was not required to *get on* with Private Herriott. Well, as I explained just now, Mrs Challoner, this friend of Herriott's, the Arnold chap, he decided that he would attack your husband. And, as I told you, he appears to have — killed him . . .'

'Yes.' Dora nodded. 'You said.'

The military policeman grimaced. God, this was bloody difficult. Why didn't the woman cry? They *all* cried, for Christ's sake! The major himself was by now almost in tears, his great shoulders were humped and his red face was suffused with grief.

Half an hour later the officers left.

'Damn fine woman,' remarked the major, who was still sniffing and periodically blowing his nose hard into his huge khaki handkerchief. 'Splendid example of true British grit.'

'Hard as nails if you ask me,' replied the captain tersely. He tapped the corporal on the shoulder. 'Drive on, Cooper,' he said. 'Drive on.'

Dora sat in the drawing room, going over and over what the captain had said, telling herself that it must be true, and hardly able to contain her delight.

As far as she could make out, it had all stemmed from the fact that Ralph had been determined to make an example of that fellow Herriott. He had put him on fatigues at all hours of the day and night, had bullied him, put him on punishment duties again and again — Dora already knew all that, having had it from Ralph's own lips. To use Captain Verney's expression, Captain Challoner had tried to turn Private Herriott into a soldier.

Herriott had been ill that week with what sounded like influenza; malingering was how Captain Verney described it, but he had allowed that Herriott was not particularly well. Ralph had insisted that, illness notwithstanding, Herriott should continue with his normal duties. He had fainted on the parade ground the previous morning and Ralph had told him to get up.

Herriott, naturally, had not responded, so Ralph had kicked him. 'Stirred him with his foot', in Captain Verney's parlance. Dora could imagine that only too well. She remembered Ralph 'hardly touching' Anthony all those years ago. And then the man Arnold had told Ralph to stop hurting his friend.

Ralph had hit Arnold across the face and yelled at him. He'd lost his temper — even Captain Verney had conceded that. As Ralph and Arnold had faced each other across Herriott's prostrate body, Ralph had slapped Arnold again, striking him repeatedly. And then, from inside his service dress tunic, Arnold had produced the knife.

He had lunged at Ralph — there'd been a brief scuffle — a dozen men had tried to pull Arnold away. But in the mêlée the knife — 'I'm so sorry about this, Mrs Challoner, I'm so very, very sorry' — had found its way under Ralph's ribs and had pierced his heart.

It was impossible to tell if Arnold had actually stabbed Captain Challoner or if, in the scrum, the weapon had simply been manoeuvred into a position where it had done its damage. It could have been guided by one of a dozen hands, maybe by no one at all. Ralph had choked on his own blood and died of heart failure within minutes.

'What will happen to Mr Arnold?' Dora had asked.

'He'll be court-martialled, of course. Shot, I shouldn't wonder. I expect the War Office will let you know.' Captain Verney had coughed, embarrassed by Dora's concern for the murderer. 'No doubt you'll hear, Mrs Challoner — unofficially, of course.'

'Of course.'

And that had been that. So simple, so easy, so neat. Dora could not believe how simple it had been. 'My husband *is* dead?' she'd asked, several times, unable to believe it. Surely Ralph was indestructible?

'I'm afraid so. I'm so very, very —'

And so it had gone on, until Dora, unable to hide her joy any longer, had been obliged to get rid of the men.

She wondered idly if the man who had probably stabbed Ralph would be shot. And if Mr Herriott would survive the tender mercies of Ralph's successor and achieve his ultimate goal of a dishonourable discharge when the war was finally over. If it ever *did* end.

Nursing her happiness like a guilty secret made all the more delicious for being so private, Dora went through the next few months in a serene and peaceful frame of mind which both astonished and impressed her acquaintance.

Only occasionally was her calm disturbed by reflections that Ralph might have done better with another kind of woman — with someone older, less idealistic, less naive.

'If I'd been cleverer, more mature, perhaps I could have changed him,' she thought. 'There *was* good in him; he wasn't all bad.'

Not all bad, no. But sufficiently warped and cruel to negate any virtues he might have had. Looking through the drawing room window one cold March day, Dora found tears standing in her eyes — not for Ralph, but for what he might have been. 'I can't help myself,' she could hear him saying. But had he tried? Had he wanted to change? Somehow, Dora couldn't believe that he had, and so she could never grieve for him.

* * *

'She's the VC's widow.'

'Husband was a fine officer, you know. A hero in France. And he was killed by a conchie.'

'A conchie? One of those who's supposed to be against killing?'

'Yes. Well, it all goes to show.'

Dora provided the district with its main topic of conversation for many months.

The spring that year was early, full of scent and colour; a season of almost supernatural beauty. Dora lay in the new grass and enjoyed the feel of it tickling her face. She got up early and went to watch the fox cubs playing near their vixen in one of the spinneys. No one would ever hunt on that land again, not while Dora was alive. And all the traps for wild animals had been removed from the woods.

Some dog foxes, growing troublesome, had to be shot. But

this did not seem so horrible as hunting them to a bloody and cruel death.

The weather grew very warm. April was beautiful that year. Dora felt that she was waiting for something, but she did not know what it might be.

Chapter Eighteen

'THERE'S A GENTLEMAN TO SEE you, Mrs Challoner. Shall I show him into the drawing room, or will you see him in here?' Dora's young housemaid had put her head timidly round the door of the little study which had been Ralph's gun room, but which was now fitted up as a lady's sitting room. She looked enquiringly at her mistress.

Dora glanced up from the letter she was writing. 'What did you say, Sarah?' she asked.

'A gentleman, Madam. An army gentleman. Very nicely-spoken he is.'

'Oh, I see. Yes, you can show him into the drawing room. Tell him I'll be along in a minute or two.'

Dora stood up and sighed. If it was yet another officious man from the War Office come to bother her with his condolences about Ralph, if it was yet another of his brother officers back from France who had decided to visit the grieving widow, then she didn't want to listen to him.

Dora didn't want to hear any more explanations, and hadn't the patience to listen to any more expressions of sympathy. She was beginning to find the role of brave young war widow, a role successfully being played out by thousands upon thousands of women, something of a strain.

One day soon she'd be able to contain herself no longer. 'I hated him!' she would yell. 'I'm glad he's dead, I hated him! But I'm free of him now, and I won't be constantly reminded of him by all you hypocrites telling me what a wonderful man he was. I hope he's burning in hell for what he did to me!'

But, nevertheless, she composed her face, left the sanctuary of her little sitting room, walked along the corridor, and entered the drawing room, which was full of bright May sunshine.

Standing at the window, his hands clasped behind his back, the tall, fair-haired army captain did not hear her come into the room. 'Won't you sit down, Mr — er —' Dora began, now wondering if he was deaf.

'Thank you, Dora, I will.' Tim Atherton turned round to face her, and then, grinning at her expression of amazement, he flopped into one of the easy chairs by the fireside. 'I'm on leave at the moment,' he explained. 'I'm staying with my family near Worcester, so I thought I'd come over to visit you.'

'Oh, I — I see.' He must surely, she thought, have noticed the astonishment on her face but he chose to ignore it. She sat down opposite him.

'I heard about your husband,' he told her. 'I wanted to tell you how sorry I was.'

'Thank you,' she said coldly.

'I hope you don't mind me coming over unannounced like this?' Tim leaned forward in his chair. 'I very much wanted to see you. I must say, Dora, you look very well. You're coming to terms with it?'

'I think so.' She looked back at him calmly, understood that she was seeing a man who was so familiar with sudden, violent death that he was perhaps unable to take such routine catastrophes seriously any more. 'One must make an effort, after all,' she added, somewhat sententiously.

He nodded very gravely. 'Oh, one must indeed.'

Dora stared. Was he mocking her? She was so recently bereaved, and she might, for all Tim Atherton knew, be giving up whole nights to weeping and despairing of ever being happy again. She decided that her visitor was being very off-hand in his condolences. 'Would you like some tea?' she asked, less than cordially.

'That would be very nice. Thank you.'

Half an hour later, however, Dora had relaxed. She was actually laughing at something Tim had just said. She beamed at him. 'Do tell me what's been happening to you,' she said. 'You didn't give much away when I saw you in Oxford. What did you do after you — after we — I mean, after you left university?'

'I went out to India. I believe I mentioned that I was going to do that?'

'You went out to your tea garden? You became a planter?'

'Well, after a fashion.' Tim laughed. 'I stuck it for a few months. But it was so tedious, you've no idea. Deadly — nothing to do except gaze at acres and acres of hillside and get drunk. I packed it in and moved to Delhi.'

'Where you did . . .?'

'This and that.' He smiled enigmatically. 'I found a few people who could put various things my way. And I met some jolly nice girls and had some fun with them.'

'Did you, indeed.' Dora sipped her tea. 'You haven't ever married, though?'

'No. Over the past few years I've had — well, friends, shall I say. There was one particular friend a year or so ago, but it all came to nothing in the end.'

'I'm sorry to hear that.'

'Oh, don't be. It was all my doing.' Tim grinned again. 'I've decided now that I'm not a marrying man.'

'So you came back to England. Then what?'

'Ah, well — my father had me in his study and presented me with two alternatives, the army or the church. I couldn't see myself dishing out sermons, so I told the old fellow I'd join up. That was back in 1906.'

'Was it the right decision?'

'Oh, yes, I think so. Well, there was bound to be some fun with the Prussians sooner or later, so I thought I'd at least have a bit of excitement.' He grimaced. 'And I have.'

'So you've been in it from the first?'

'I was at Mons with the expeditionary force. I got out unhurt except for a few scratches, but all the other officers in my battalion were killed.' Tim shrugged. 'I keep my head down, you see, and avoid the heroics. That's why I'm still only a captain and not exactly covered with ribbons.'

'Yours sounds a very sensible course of action to me.'

Tim sniffed. 'Don't be patronizing, Dora. I know all about Captain Challoner's VC.'

'And I know all about your DSO.' Dora stood up. 'Come for a walk,' she invited. 'We can go round the gardens; they're very pretty at this time of year.'

The sunny afternoon was pleasantly warm. As they walked along shady paths and through green arbours, Tim rattled on, telling Dora a whole series of outrageous fibs — or at least, she supposed they were fibs — about a particular Society hostess. 'Twins,' he concluded, watching her face. 'One was white as the driven snow, but the other — well, not quite ace of spades, but certainly brownish.'

'No!' Fascinated, Dora gazed up at him. 'And?'

'And the maharajah had been with them at the time, you see, so there were those who were prepared to hint —'

'Goodness!' Dora giggled. 'And what did Sir Julian say?'

'Nothing.' Tim laid his hand upon his heart and assumed an expression of noble acquiescence. 'Nothing at all. Took it like a hero. But poor Lady Walton's never lived it down. She took up bird-watching soon after the babies were born, and these days she actually lives in a hide in the woods wearing nothing but gumboots and her mink. They do say that the land agent —'

'Tim!'

'Sorry.' Tim grinned, then looked at his watch. 'Well, I'd better be off soon,' he added. 'It's a longish drive back and the roads are atrocious. It has been nice to see you, Dora.'

'It's been nice to see you.'

'Has it? Good. Well, I'm glad to find that you're not too cast down. I was afraid you'd be heartbroken and weeping all over the place.'

Dora looked at him and found she could hardly bear to part with him. 'How much longer are you on leave?' she asked.

'Until the end of the week. Why?'

'Would you come over here to dinner tomorrow?'

Tim considered, scuffing the gravel on the path with his shoe. 'Are you sure you want to see me again?' he asked at last.

'Yes, of course I do.' Dora smiled, touched his arm. 'I get so lonely here, all by myself,' she said. 'My father's family over at Ashton Cross are very kind, and I go over there once or twice a week — but the rest of the time I'm quite alone. It would be so nice to have your company. You do cheer one up so.'

'If I come, Dora, could I stay the night?' Tim covered the hand on his sleeve with his own. 'Do you understand me?'

'Oh, yes. Do stay, of course you can, there's plenty of room.' Dora was wondering what she could give him to eat, and had entirely missed the point of his question.

Tim arrived in the middle of the afternoon. Standing behind Dora on the steps, an ungracious expression further souring his mean features, Crawley stared at the visitor. 'Take Captain Atherton's things up to his room,' said Dora. 'Make sure that the bed is well aired and ask Sarah to light a fire.'

Crawley, who had nodded gloomily at Tim, took the case and shuffled off.

'A cheerful individual,' remarked Tim.

'He was devoted to Ralph and he can't bear me.' Dora grinned. 'Poor Crawley, it's all very hard on him.'

Dora was in the highest of spirits. Now she took Tim's arm and led him on a guided tour of the house, showing him everything, boring him with accounts of the Challoner family portraits and heirlooms.

'I don't want to *buy* the place!' he exclaimed, laughing. 'Dora, it's such a great barn of a house — why hasn't it been requisitioned?'

'I don't know. A man from some ministry or other called here and looked it over. He said I'd be hearing from the authorities if the house was needed, but nothing's come of it. We're very remote here — perhaps *too* far from anywhere.'

'Maybe. And you are producing lots of food; no one could say that this estate isn't doing its bit for the war effort.' Tim took his hostess's hand. 'Well, Dora, shall we have a walk before dinner?'

'If you like. Come and see the river.'

Dinner came and went. The servants cleared away and the house was now full of the small, scuffling noises of everything being put to rights for the following morning. Sarah brought in a tray of coffee things and bobbed, blinking nervously. 'Is there anything more you need, Madam?' she asked.

'No.' Dora smiled at her. 'You can go to bed,' she added.

'I'll fetch anything else myself.'

'Good night then, Madam. Sir.' Sarah gave Tim a shy smile and went away.

'You've obviously stolen poor Sarah's heart,' remarked Dora, pouring coffee. 'She never used to smile at Ralph like that. What's your secret?'

Tim did not answer. Instead, he got out of his chair and walked over to the wide sofa where Dora sat. He took the coffee cup out of her hand and sat down beside her. He wrapped his arms around her and kissed her cheek. Then he began to kiss her along her hairline, smoothing the curls back from her forehead while he did so.

'You don't mind this?' he asked after a minute or two — surprised, perhaps, that there had been no token resistance.

'It's rather nice.' Comfortable in his warm embrace, Dora snuggled closer to him and laid her head upon his shoulder. 'You always were nice to lie against,' she added dozily, making herself more comfortable still.

Tim said nothing to that. Leaning over her, he now took Dora's chin in his hand. Raising her face to his, he kissed her firmly on the mouth.

There was no sound but the splutter and crackle of the logs burning in the fireplace. The room grew darker, becoming a warm cavern illuminated only by the firelight. Completely relaxed and more than half asleep as she was, Dora hardly noticed that Tim was unfastening the neckband of her dress and, having done that, was carefully undoing the buttons on her underclothes and kissing her throat. She had had two or three glasses of wine with her dinner and, full and busy as her days always were now, she was very tired. She closed her eyes and actually dozed off.

'Time for bed now, Dora,' said Tim, the sound of his voice startling her out of a pleasant dream.

'Is it?' She yawned. 'Yes, I suppose it must be. Well, goodnight, then. Get up when you please tomorrow.'

'Oh, I shall.' He took her hand, as if to help her up. 'Come along.'

'Come along where?'

'To bed, of course.' Tim kissed her again. 'Where else?'

'What?' She stared at him, suddenly wide awake. 'Whatever do you mean?'

As if a basinful of cold water had just been thrown in her face, Dora sat up straight and jerked her hand away. Jolted out of her comfortable trance, she was now fully conscious again. 'You can't *possibly* be suggesting —' she began.

'Oh, don't be so missish, Dora.' Tim's voice had an edge to it now which Dora had never heard before. He took her wrist and pulled her to her feet. 'I shan't hurt you,' he said evenly. 'But you must come with me now.'

'No!' Panicking, Dora tried to pull away. 'No, Tim, I'm not going to sleep with you. You can't expect —'

'Ah, but I *do* expect.' Tim was perfectly calm, but obviously quite determined. 'You made a fool of me once, Dora,' he continued. 'But you won't do so a second time. Since that day in your sister's house, *no* woman has led me on and got away with it.' He shook her shoulder. 'And you know perfectly well why you invited me here today.'

'But I've *never* led you to expect that I wanted to go to bed with you. Don't be so — so beastly!'

'Beastly, am I?' He laughed and tightened his grip on her upper arm. 'Very well said, Dora. Now you just listen to me. It may be forgiveable to be a flirt at nineteen. But at thirty or more it's just pathetic; in fact, it's absolutely ridiculous.'

He looked around the room. 'Are you coming upstairs?' he asked. 'Or shall I ravish you here, on this extremely comfortable sofa? Now that's an idea, isn't it?' He released her from his grasp, took off his jacket and loosened his tie.

Dora glared at him. 'You'll do no such thing,' she snapped. 'Do you hear me? You've no right whatsoever to talk to me like this. And if you don't go away, at once, I shall call the servants. I'll scream. I'll —'

'The servants! Two old women, a frightened little girl and an old man who, you say, hates you. They'll all have gone to bed hours ago. Upstairs, Dora. Now!'

'No!' Really frightened now, Dora began to edge away from him. 'No,' she repeated. 'Oh, please, Tim — listen to me. You don't understand. You see, I — well, I'm no good at that kind of thing, no good at all. I'd be such a disappointment to you, honestly, it wouldn't be worth your while to do that with me. Don't go on at me. I can't come to bed with you. I won't!'

'Won't you?' Tim shrugged. 'Then I shall just have to carry you upstairs. If you won't undress, I shall take your clothes off for you. If you won't get into bed, I shall lift you up and put you there. And if you won't cooperate when I make love to you, I shall force you. Do you understand that? It's up to you now, Dora. Which way is it to be?'

'He doesn't mean it,' she said to herself as she led the way upstairs. 'He's play-acting; he always liked showing off, and he's obviously overwrought tonight. He's had far too much to drink; he'll pass out in a minute . . .'

She stopped by her bedroom door. 'Not in here, Tim,' she said coldly. 'I know you were joking downstairs but now the game's over.'

'It's not a game, Dora.' He took her by the shoulder and opened the door. Pushing her inside, he closed it firmly behind him. Still holding her fast, he sat down on her bed and pulled Dora down beside him. Carefully, he undid the rest of her buttons and eased her dress down from her shoulders.

His hands were perfectly steady. Obviously, he wasn't drunk, nowhere near it. Despairing now, Dora realized that she couldn't fight him. He was so much bigger and stronger than she was, and she was now as good as paralysed with fear of him.

But then, all at once, a great lassitude overcame her and she couldn't be bothered to struggle any more. 'Let him get on with it,' she thought. 'I don't care. He can't be any more loathsome than Ralph used to be, after all.'

She let him undress her without any further resistance. Obediently she lay back on her pillows, shut her eyes and waited for everything to be over.

He began by gathering her into his arms and kissing her very lightly, just as he had done in the drawing room. Now, he was printing her face with a series of soft, dry kisses, with the merest fleeting impressions. Gradually, he warmed her whole body and gradually Dora became less tense.

'That's better,' he murmured. 'Much better. Darling, don't be afraid of me.'

'I'm not afraid.' She opened her eyes and looked at him. 'I'm not afraid,' she repeated, as if to convince herself. But, indeed, her heart had now stopped thumping, her terror of him subsided and it was replaced by the familiar sensation of contentment which, until half an hour ago, Tim had always brought about in her. And then, almost of their own accord, Dora's arms went round his neck.

He stroked her now and touched her all over — and she found this unexpectedly pleasant. Soon, she was positively enjoying it. To her own great surprise, she wanted him to continue. And then, without thinking what she was doing, she rolled over on her back and closed her eyes while he kissed her neck, her shoulders, her chest, her stomach.

A few minutes went by and then, quite suddenly, there was something new, something never even imagined before. Dora felt a sensation which was like life beginning again, which made her catch her breath sharply and gasp in astonishment.

She opened her eyes and looked down at Tim, at his head which was pillowed comfortably upon her stomach. She took a lock of his fair hair between her fingers and twisted it. 'Tim?'

'Mmm?' Tim shook his hair off his forehead and sat up beside her. 'Lovely Dora,' he murmured, taking her face between his hands and looking at her, his own eyes very dark. 'Lovely, lovely Dora. You taste of honey and roses.'

But then, inevitably, came the part which Dora had always hated. She braced herself, planting her feet firmly on either side of Tim's body, shutting her eyes very tightly, and gritting her teeth.

'Relax a little, Dora,' he said. 'You're much too tense.'

'I'm sorry.' She opened her eyes and looked at him piteously. 'I'm hopeless at this kind of thing,' she murmured in a small, embarrassed voice. 'I tried to tell you so downstairs, but you wouldn't listen —'

'You're absolutely wonderful at this kind of thing.' Tim kissed her face and made her smile in spite of herself. 'You're quite extraordinary. I've never known a woman respond to me as beautifully as you did just then.'

'But that was only because *you* were so clever, because you knew what to do with me —'

'So won't you let me love you now?'

Dora looked at him helplessly. 'I don't — I suppose — well, if you —'

'I'll be very careful. I shan't hurt you. I promise.'

So she let him take her. Dora lay in her marriage bed and welcomed her lover. And he kept his word. There was no pain, no distress, none of the anguish and hurt which Dora had always associated with making love. It seemed, instead, as if sunshine were pouring all over her. She wrapped her arms tightly around Tim's neck and held him close to her. She heard him give a great sigh of pleasure, and then he was kissing her face.

'Dear Dora,' he said. 'My darling Dora, that was marvellous.' But then, as he looked at her, he saw the tears in her eyes. 'Oh, Dora, don't cry,' he said. 'What's the matter? Did I hurt you? I meant to be gentle. I'm sorry if I was rough.'

'You didn't hurt me.' Sniffing, Dora looked back at him. Such a great wave of contradictory emotions swept over her just then that she felt quite overwhelmed. Regret for the past, regret that she herself had been so stupid, ignorant and naive was inextricably mixed with such absolute happiness that she could not even speak. She burst into tears and, covering her face with her hands, she lay sobbing in Tim's arms.

He held her for a minute or two, rocking her, murmuring the kind of endearments he might have used to comfort a distressed infant. Finally, feeling her sobs abating, he pushed her hair back from her forehead and kissed her temples. 'Dora?' he asked. 'Do you feel a little better now?'

'A little.' Still sniffing, Dora leaned against him and hid her face against his shoulder. 'Oh, I'm sorry to be so silly. I'm all right now.'

'Good. Well, I think it's time to snuggle down.' Tim lay down and pulled her close to him. He wrapped the bedclothes around both of them, tucking Dora up as carefully as if she'd been a little child. And soon both of them were fast asleep.

Dora woke in the first half light of a misty spring dawn. She could hear the birds chattering in the eaves outside her window, and she wondered, dozily, why she felt so warm and comfortable, so very, very contented. Then she realized what it was. Turning over, she looked at Tim.

He was still fast asleep, lying on his stomach, his fair hair disordered on the pillow. She smiled and touched his face, expecting him to wake. But he slept on. And then, a sudden curiosity made her push the bedclothes away from his shoulders. She studied him. And the cold air replacing the warm sheets made him stir.

'I thought you said you hadn't been wounded?'

'What?' Waking properly then, he rubbed his eyes and looked at her sleepily. 'What did you say?'

'You told me you hadn't been hurt.'

'Oh. Well, I haven't.'

'But you're *covered* in scars and scratches.' Dora pushed the sheet down still further and stared at his back. 'That's a horrible bruise on your shoulder-blade,' she continued. 'And your arms are a mess, and as for your back — you look as if you've been whipped.'

'Do I? Oh.' Tim was wide awake by now. He raised himself on one elbow. 'My dearest Dora,' he murmured, grinning at her. 'One doesn't scramble in and out of trenches without scraping one's elbows and knees now and then. Cutting one's arm on a bit of tin left in one of Jerry's dugouts doesn't count as a wound. I assure you that I've had iodine put on the grazes. The bruises will heal themselves.'

'Will they?'

'Oh, certainly.' He turned on to his side and showed her his left hand, which had a barely healed gash across the back of it. 'Make it better?' he asked.

She took his hand and kissed it. And he pulled her into his arms.

'You must go to your own room now, Tim.' Dora shrugged on her dressing gown and sat up in bed. 'Mrs Johnson will be up soon, and she brings in my early morning tea at seven.'

'I don't want to go.' Tim caught at a strand of Dora's long hair and began to play with it. 'I don't imagine your housekeeper will bother you this morning,' he added.

'Why?'

'Oh, Dora! Do you suppose the servants heard nothing last night? We must have made enough noise, after all.'

'I suppose we must have.' Ruefully, Dora looked at him. 'Yes, you're perfectly right — they must know you're here with me.' She grimaced. 'And I can imagine them saying, "Can you wonder at it, considering whose daughter she is".'

'What? Why do you say that?'

Dora rubbed her face. 'You remember that party, don't you?' she asked. 'Years and years ago it was — the one at Anna's house, when I was drunk?'

'Oh, yes.' Tim grinned at her. 'I shall never forget it.'

'Well, do you remember what I told you? About my parents, that is?'

'Yes.'

'You didn't believe me, did you?'

'No. Well, not at the time. But about ten years after that I was staying at some old barn of a country house, and I overheard an old bat talking to her crony about Stephen Lawrence's disgusting past.' Tim shrugged. 'So then I knew that what you'd told me was roughly true.'

'Oh.' Dora picked at a loose thread in the sheet. 'I expect you congratulated yourself on your lucky escape?'

'From you, Dora?'

'Yes.'

'Not at all.' Tim took Dora's hand and chafed it. 'Dora, I was in love with you,' he said gravely. 'And I'd have married you whatever or whoever your parents were.'

'Would you?'

'Yes. But you didn't want me, did you?'

'I — I don't think I knew what I wanted.'

'Mm. Dora, you were particularly horrible to me, you know. It took me years and years to get over you. Well, as you know, I never *did* get over you.'

'Tim, I can't believe that.'

'Can't you?' Tim shook his head. 'Do you know what I did when I heard you were married?'

'No. What?'

'I sulked for a month. I picked a fight with the battalion bruiser and got thrashed to within an inch of my life. Then I really disgraced myself by bursting into tears at my first regimental dinner. The colonel-in-chief was there. God!'

'What did you do when you heard I was widowed?'

'Got drunk, and ran down Oxford Street singing "Rule Britannia" at the top of my voice. That was last week.'

Dora grinned. 'I still don't believe you,' she said.

'It's perfectly true.' Tim let go of her hand. 'Well, I suppose I'd better go and disarrange my sheets.'

'Don't go.'

'What about Mrs Whatsername?'

'Damn Mrs Johnson,' Dora declared. 'I expect she's been listening at the keyhole anyway; they all spy on me.' She looked at her lover. 'Can I ask you something?'

'Certainly.'

'Did you mean it last night when you said you'd force me?'

'Force you?' Tim shook his head. 'I'm sure I didn't say that. Dora, I'm a British officer and, I hope, a gentleman. I'd never have thought of such a thing.'

He shrugged. 'Perhaps I'd had a little too much to drink and I was teasing you.'

'I thought that at first. But you hadn't. And you weren't.' She looked into his eyes. 'Were you?'

'Perhaps you needed to be persuaded. Perhaps I persuaded you. I must have suggested something along these lines, then I persuaded you to agree. That's it.'

'Ah.' Dora nodded. 'Tim, when you go back to France, what are you going back to?'

'Same old stalemate, I imagine. Boring. You don't want to know about that.'

But Dora would not be deflected. 'What are you going back *to*?' she repeated.

'I don't know really. It's rumoured that there's going to be another big show soon — Plumer's thing, this one will be. I expect he'll be as useless as Haig when it comes to the point. Oh, God, Dora, I really don't want to discuss the war.'

Dora bit her lower lip. 'I hope you come back, Tim,' she murmured. 'You *must* come back.'

'I shall.' He touched her face and smiled. 'I'll come back — I have to, don't I? And when I do, I am going to drag you, bound and gagged, to the altar of the nearest church.'

'Are you, indeed? I thought you weren't a marrying man?'

'Oh, I've changed my mind about that.' Tim looked at her. 'There was always one person I'd have been only too happy to marry. And you do know, Dora, that no one else will do? You've always known it, haven't you? When you asked if I was married, you knew the answer?'

Dora permitted herself a faint smile. 'I suppose I must have done,' she conceded.

Tim raised his voice to parade ground pitch and announced, very clearly, 'I suppose I'd better get back to my own room now. Don't want to set a bad example to the servants, do we?'

Dora giggled. He grinned at her, then leaned over and kissed her. He found his shirt and trousers and put them on. He made a noisy performance of walking across the floor, rattled the door handle for a moment or two, then went out into an expectedly empty corridor, singing softly to himself that he'd 'rather stay with Dora, with pretty, pretty Dora, and fornicate his bleeding life away' — his own paraphrase of an already much-improved-upon popular song, which would recur to him over and over again in the course of the next few months.

Tim stayed at the Grange until it was time for him to go and catch the train to London. On subsequent mornings he didn't bother to go back to his own bedroom to disarrange his sheets, for the servants would have had to be blind, deaf and stupid not to realize what their mistress and her lover were doing.

One morning an outraged Crawley watched Tim run across the lawn at the back of the house, catch Dora and pull her down into the long grass at the edge of the shrubbery. There he rolled her over and over in his arms, kissing her passionately as he did so.

Mrs Johnson also took advantage of her mistress's current preoccupation to snatch an extra half hour in bed. She imagined, quite rightly, that Mrs Challoner would not notice if she did not receive her early morning tea that week.

Dora had decided that she would sell the house and the land. Or possibly James Lawrence would consider managing it for her when the war was over. She would talk to her uncle about it. But there was no hurry.

Chapter Nineteen

'SO COULDN'T YOU COME HERE? Bring the children, it would be lovely to see them all; and the country air would do them good. Jonathan really ought to learn to ride.'

Dora finished the letter which she had begun to write just before Tim's arrival. She sealed it, walked into the nearest village and posted it. Then she walked back to the Grange across the fields, singing to herself and almost dancing across the damp meadow grass.

It was two days since Tim had gone, but Dora was still full of bubbling euphoria. She skipped across the Long Barrow, startling some dismal browsing sheep and causing their lambs to scamper, bleating, to their mothers. Reaching a meadow full of late cowslips, she lay down among a mass of yellow flowers, burying her face in their wet, cool, scented blossoms. 'He loves me!' she cried, out loud. 'He loves me, he loves me — he's always loved me!' And laughing, she rolled on to her back and stared up at the bright blue sky, hugging herself with delight.

Miriam, encumbered with four children, their nanny and a great mass of unwieldy luggage, nevertheless noticed Dora's feverish state as soon as she stepped off the train.

'You look very pleased with yourself, Dolly,' she remarked, smiling her usual placid smile.

'Oh, I am, I am.' Dora hugged her sister-in-law, then kissed her so effusively that Miriam's hat fell off. 'Miriam, I've *so* much to tell you. Let's get back to the Grange — we can have tea together, and talk and talk.'

Miriam listened calmly as Dora related the events of those

magical five days. 'It all sounds perfectly idyllic,' she agreed indulgently. 'But, Dora, you've been in love before. And your husband was — well, you know why *I* have no cause to remember him with kindness.'

'Tim's as different from Ralph as an angel is from a devil.' Dora lay back in her chair, stretching her arms above her head. 'Tim's a miracle, a present from the gods, a reward for having endured Ralph for so long.'

'Indeed.' Miriam sipped her tea. 'And when the war's over, when this miracle and whatever else he is returns to England, will you marry him?'

'He won't come back.' Dora bit her lip and looked sorrowfully at Miriam. 'He'll be killed, I'm sure of it. No one's allowed to stay as happy as I was when he was here. But, do you know, Miriam, I wouldn't exchange those five days for a whole lifetime of bliss. That week *was* my life. Can you understand what I mean?'

Miriam shook her head. 'If I didn't know you as well as I do, I'd think you were deranged,' she replied. 'Poor Dolly!'

'Don't pity me. I don't need to be pitied. I wouldn't change places with anyone in the world.' Dora stood up and went over to the window. 'Is Anthony coming for the weekend?' she asked. 'Can he get away?'

'He said he'd try to arrange a forty-eight hour pass, so he should arrive late on Friday night. Can your housekeeper see that there's a hot meal for him?'

'She'll do anything for me.' Dora beamed at Miriam. 'Anything at all.'

This was no more than the truth. Mrs Johnson would have walked to the ends of the earth for her mistress. For, the previous week, Dora had dismissed Crawley.

She had not done this without certain misgivings. She had, for example, expected there to be some solidarity among the servants; some muttering and show of displeasure that one of their number should be so summarily told to leave.

But it seemed that the maids were delighted that the valet was going. When Dora had called Mrs Johnson to her study and offered her the post of housekeeper, she had been surprised that the woman had accepted it so readily.

'It's not really my place to say anything, Madam,' she had remarked after accepting the new post and agreeing to the wages offered. 'But Mr Crawley will certainly be better away from here. He's been that odd since the Master died.'

'Odd?' Dora looked at her servant. 'What do you mean?'

'Oh, he mutters to hisself. He walks about the house at night, he drinks the Master's brandy. He frightens little Sarah half to death. Poor man, he's been that sorrowful; he'd be better in a new place where there won't be so many painful memories.'

'Mmm.' Dora nodded. She sent Mrs Johnson back to her duties, then sat down at her desk. She didn't want to start feeling pity for, of all people, Crawley. But she did take out her writing box and fill in a banker's order for an amount which she would normally have considered over-generous as a servant's gratuity — that was, under any other circumstances.

'Thank you, Madam.' Crawley had accepted his last quarter's wages and pocketed the cheque. He looked Dora full in the face. 'You are not dismissing me,' he added suddenly, his weasel's face very spiteful now. 'I am leaving of my own accord. Circumstances — the behaviour of certain people in this house — make it impossible for me to remain here. And also —'

'That's quite enough.' Knowing perfectly well what he meant, Dora reddened. 'Don't say any more,' she interrupted sharply.

She looked pointedly at the cheque, which was sticking out of his breast pocket. 'Mr Crawley, over the years you have tried to hurt me, to injure me, to cause difficulties between my husband and myself. You must surely be satisfied with your many successes. So, let us part as amicably as possible, shall we?'

Crawley nodded. 'I shall leave tomorrow,' he said. 'Mrs Challoner, I wish you — what you deserve.'

Anthony, who arrived that Friday evening wearing a captain's uniform which had never been bloodied, was now employed by the War Office as a cryptanalyst. This was a job which he found increasingly absorbing.

Had he been asked, before the war, he would have replied

that deciphering intercepted German codes would have been his idea of utter tedium. But now he was entranced by the whole business of it, and was happy to sit up through the night with his colleagues in Whitehall, poring over a conundrum, waiting for the whole thing to blossom and make sense — as a large number of the captured messages did in the end.

'It's a beautiful house,' he remarked, looking around him.

'Yes. Parts of it are over seven hundred years old.' Dora led her brother into the drawing room, which was in the most modern part of the house. In this pleasant apartment there were plenty of comfortable easy chairs and also the long, wide sofa where Miriam lay, looking out of the french window towards the twilit water meadows beyond.

Dora watched Anthony kiss his wife, this time without feeling the usual stab of — what? Jealousy? Now beloved herself, knowing that one man valued her above everything and everyone else, she could see another couple embrace without envy. 'Shall we go in to dinner?' she asked.

'Did you wait for me?' Surprised, Anthony looked enquiringly at Dora.

'Of course we did.'

'How very nice of you.' Anthony stood up, held out his arms. 'Then, ladies, may I take you in?'

He sat between them, smiling from one to the other. 'My two dearest objects on earth,' he murmured. 'Both of you and mutton stew. Heaven!'

'He called us objects.' Dora pinched her brother's arm. '*Objects*, Miriam! Did you hear him? The nerve!'

'I was merely quoting, my dear sister. From a book.' Anthony rubbed his arm. 'You know what I mean, do you? A book — a pile of papers bound together, with lots of words printed on the sheets. Have you ever seen one?'

'How do you bear him, Miriam?'

'It's very hard, Dolly. Very hard.'

Anthony grinned at them. 'Any chance of some food, Dora?' he asked, indicating the serving dishes. 'It's all very well for you and Miriam to sit here nattering, but I am *starving* to *death*.'

*　　*　　*

'It's gone on far too long. It's something which ought never to have started in the first place.' Anthony pushed his plate aside and took out a packet of cigarettes. 'Dora, may I smoke in here?'

'If you absolutely must. Weren't you told to give it up?'

'That's not possible at present.' Anthony lit one of the particularly foul-smelling cigarettes which he so enjoyed, sighing with satisfaction as the smoke filled his lungs. 'Yes, it could still be ended by negotiation,' he added.

Dora toyed with a slice of apple. 'I read in a newspaper that there is a factory in Germany where corpses of Allied soldiers are rendered into tallow,' she remarked. 'The Huns make candles out of our soldiers. Anthony, surely such people aren't quite human?'

'Ah, but was the story true?' Anthony looked away from the table and blew out a perfect smoke ring. 'Where did you read it? In the *Daily Mail*? The *Express*?'

'It was in *The Times*.'

'I see. Oh, *well*, then — it must be so.' Anthony tipped his chair back and reached behind him for an ashtray.

Dora frowned at him. Surely a war which had already cost so many lives *must* be worth fighting? That war must surely be just when waged against an inhuman enemy?

Miriam stayed for the rest of June and for the whole of July. Jonathan learned to ride the small black pony brought over from Ashton Cross. And he also struck up a close friendship with one of his female cousins there, much to his sister Rachel's amusement. 'Do you know what *I* saw today?' she asked the family at dinner one evening.

'No.' Dora passed Miriam some vegetables. 'What?'

A warning look from Jonathan was ignored. 'I *saw* —' Rachel glanced round the table, to ensure that everyone's attention was engaged — 'I saw him kissing Eleanor. He was! Don't deny it, Jon — you *were*.'

Jonathan reddened and glared at her. He gave her a look which said, as plainly as words, 'I'll make you sorry you said that.' He fiddled with his napkin and sniffed.

Eleanor, one of Henry Lawrence's grandchildren, was a pretty, well-developed girl of thirteen. She had only undertaken to give her cousin riding lessons, but Jonathan had been in love with her for the past week. He was now experiencing all the torments which his own potentially passionate nature could inflict upon him.

Until he'd seen Eleanor Lawrence, until he'd seen her canter around the paddock on Snowflake, her hair flying out behind her and her blouse blown tight against her figure, he had assumed that all girls were as tiresome as his sisters. But Eleanor had bewitched him.

'Is it true, Jonathan?' Miriam smiled at her son. 'Or did Eleanor kiss *you*? Perhaps that was the way of it, eh?'

Jonathan was not to be teased. Throwing down his now mangled table napkin, he stamped out of the room pursued by the sniggers of his two sisters.

Dora pitied him. Eleanor was already a terrible flirt. With the passage of time she would probably become something of a beauty, and here she was practising her tricks on poor Jonathan. It would be a relief when her parents took her back to Cheltenham.

* * *

The army major, a different one this time, visited Dora during the last week of July. He stood almost to attention as he delivered his prepared speech. 'Naturally,' he began, 'the proceedings of courts martial are not normally made public. But in the circumstances I have been authorized to visit you and — have a chat.'

'A chat?' Dora found this almost funny. 'That's very good of the Army,' she said, trying to keep a straight face. 'Major Nicholson, were you at the hearing?'

'Yes, I was.'

'What can you tell me?'

The soldier coughed and cleared his throat. 'It was a bad business,' he replied. 'A very bad business. That fellow Arnold was defended by one of those smart chaps who think they know all about the workings of the mind.'

Major Nicholson spat out that last word as if it were something disgusting. 'He pleaded that the man Arnold was mentally unbalanced,' he continued. 'That there was no malice aforethought. I won't bother you with all the guff. The upshot was, the court brought in a verdict of manslaughter.'

'Ah, I see.' Dora looked down at her hands. Relief was surging through her that her saviour would not be shot. She wanted to smile, but did not dare — she would have laughed.

The major, looking at the widow, misinterpreted her bowed head, her silence. 'I'm sorry, Mrs Challoner,' he muttered. 'I know this must be very painful for you.' The man's voice was gruff now; he was clearly embarrassed.

Dora looked up and met his eyes. 'I accept the court's findings,' she said calmly. 'If the man was mentally unstable, then of course he can't be held fully responsible.'

'Eh?' Major Nicholson was staggered. 'Well, that's very charitable of you, Mrs Challoner. More than charitable.'

'My husband is dead, Major Nicholson,' said Dora. 'What difference does the verdict make to me?' She rose to her feet. 'Thank you for coming to see me,' she said. 'My housekeeper will show you out.'

For at least a week or more now, Dora had been feeling, if not actually unwell, then certainly different. And so, although it had been lovely to see her sister-in-law and her nephews and nieces, she had been glad when the end of July came and she could take Miriam and the children to the station in Hereford. For she was so tired, and the children were so noisy.

She felt sick all the time now, and she realized she was overdue for a period. She looked at her diary and saw that she had had no bleeding in June either. 'I — I must be pregnant,' she thought, placing her hand over her flat stomach as if expecting it to confirm her suspicions. 'I'm never late, never. And if I missed in June — well!'

She turned back the pages of her diary, checking once again. The last marginal cypher which indicated her monthly indisposition had been entered on 10 May. Today it was 31 July.

The clock struck six as Mrs Johnson came in to tell her that dinner was ready, and did she want a tray in her study or would she eat in the dining room?

'I think I'll have something in here,' replied Dora absently. She looked up. 'Do you know, Mrs Johnson, I've just had the most marvellous news.'

'Really, Mrs Challoner?'

'Yes.' Dora smiled. 'Ask Sarah to bring a tray in about twenty minutes or so, would you?' she asked. 'I have a rather important letter to write.'

* * *

Tim had rejoined his battalion in Flanders in a mood of gloomy introspection which rather worried those who knew him well. 'Had a decent leave?' asked Colin Fryer, the major who was the battalion's second in command and Tim's particular friend.

'It was all right.' Tim tipped back on his chair and stared at the wooden walls of the dug-out where he and Colin were sitting, supposedly working out the duties rota for the coming week, but in fact playing a desultory game of whist. 'Oh, it wasn't bad, I suppose.'

'See Emma, did you?' Colin studied his cards.

'No. She wasn't in town.'

'See any other nice girls, then?' Colin, a married man, was very interested in what he chose to call Tim's philandering, and always cross-examined him in detail whenever he came back from leave. 'Or any not-so-nice girls?'

'I didn't see any girls at all.' Tim stood up and yawned. 'I'm going for a walk,' he muttered. 'Got a bit of a headache.'

'Watch out for Jerry, then. He's sending the big ones over tonight, and you'll have more than a bloody headache if a minnie hits you in the neck.'

'Mmm.' Shrugging, Tim pushed the corrugated iron door aside and stepped outside.

Colin watched him go. Then he picked up a pile of grubby yellowish paper and continued filling in names and duties, wondering, a little anxiously, if Tim Atherton was going to be the next one to crack up.

All around the ruined city of Ypres there was a sense of excitement as the paraphernalia of battle was assembled. Amidst the debris of actions fought there was now all the mess and confusion of those yet to come. Lorries trundled backwards and forwards piling up huge dumps of ammunition, tents stretched in long, long lines across the flat plain, limbers took guns up to the firing lines, columns of men marched into their positions.

At the end of May 1917 the Allies commanded a semicircle

of land to the north, east and south of Ypres. It was from this flat plain of churned-up mud that they were to launch that summer's offensive towards the German lines. First of all, however, it was necessary to capture a ridge of high ground to the south of the semicircle currently commanded by the enemy and from which the Germans could cover the whole of this Ypres salient. It was to be undermined and blown up.

The summer was obviously the time to do it. The weather at the beginning of June was unusually good, and beneath the Messines Ridge tunnelling went on day and night. Each shovelful of earth was dug out by hand; mechanical diggers had proved useless, simply getting stuck in the clay tunnels, where one of them was destined to rust for ever. But the work was eventually completed and enough explosive packed into the tunnels to blow the whole ridge, together with the Germans on it, to glory.

This feat was accomplished at three o'clock on the morning of 7 June. In London Lloyd George felt the shock of this most tremendous of explosions. Wild with delight and elated by success, thousands of Allied troops stormed through the summer darkness, routed their dazed enemies and took hundreds upon hundreds of prisoners.

'Wonderful British Victory.' For once the newspapers told no more than the truth. Thanks was given in churches throughout the land, for the success at Messines proved conclusively that God had at last woken up and was now firmly on the right side.

As far as Tim — and the rest of the British Army — could see, the way was now open to the gates of Berlin. Still euphoric with their success, the soldiers waited for the order to march on the enemy. They waited. And waited . . .

After the Battle of Messines everyone more or less went on holiday. While the War Cabinet in London debated, while the Prime Minister refused Haig the extra men he said he needed, while the Germans regrouped and consolidated their shattered defences, certain that an Allied attack *must* be imminent, the opportunity to bring the war to a conclusion was thrown away.

Skirmishing and shelling, raids and patrols continued. The odd emplacement was taken and re-taken. But nothing dramatic was to happen for the next couple of months. The fine summer weather continued, excellent opportunities for a campaign went unused. The Germans were incredulous. They waited for an attack, but nothing happened. Nothing at all.

Tim was too seasoned a soldier to become agitated by the lack of activity. He certainly appreciated that the longer the Allies delayed, the greater their difficulties would be in the months to come. It was, after all, preferable to fight in dry weather, and if the High Command did not buck its ideas up, the autumn rains would be upon them, making things twice as difficult as they needed to be. Tim had not been in the salient before but men who had, and who knew what it was like in winter, were very gloomy about their prospects.

'I've borrowed a couple of ponies from the riding school. Nice little things they are. Come for a ride, eh?' Colin Fryer pushed Tim's shoulder, manipulating it as if he were trying to galvanize an inanimate object into life. 'Atherton, did you hear what I said?'

Tim rolled over on his bunk and rubbed his eyes. 'I heard you,' he replied. 'Where were you thinking of going?'

'Over towards the old château. There's a café on the way there which still does a decent line in bacon and fried eggs. We could have a bit of lunch and then go on into the countryside for the afternoon.' Colin looked enquiringly at his friend. 'Will you come?'

'All right.' His indifference only too obvious, Tim shrugged. But, all the same, he got up, dressed, shaved and consented to inspect his friend's ponies. An hour later the two of them were riding away from the battle zone, out into the flat fields beyond the range of most of the shells.

The summer sunshine did something to raise Tim's spirits, and after the decent lunch which Colin had promised him, he was almost cheerful.

'So tell me. What the hell's the matter with you these days?' Colin Fryer lay on his back in the sunshine, watching the clouds scud by. 'If I didn't know you better,' he added, 'I'd say you were heading for a breakdown.' He turned over on to his side and looked at Tim's face.

'You think I've a bad attack of wind-up, is that it?' Tim

stared across the flat countryside in which the two officers were lolling, letting their horses rest and crop grass. 'You think I'm ready to be sent down the line?'

'I didn't mean that.'

'Then what did you mean?'

'There's something bothering you. It might help to talk about it.' Colin sat up. 'Is it Emma?' he asked. 'Won't that husband of hers give her a divorce?'

'It's not Emma.'

'Not Emma?'

Tim shook his head.

'Who, then?'

'No one you know,' Tim said gloomily. 'And it won't help to talk about it.'

'Won't it?'

'No.' Tim scowled at Colin. 'But I'm not getting scared, I can assure you of that.' He scrambled to his feet. 'Did we come all this way so that you could ask me if I'm about to crack up?'

Colin shrugged. 'Well —'

'I'm not losing my nerve.' Tim fastened his jacket. 'And now that you know I'm not, I think we'd better be getting back. Don't you?'

Indeed, it wouldn't have helped to talk about it. For Tim was now wishing with all his heart that he'd spent his leave with Emma Hardwick, as he'd planned to do. He should have gone and stayed in her pleasant town house, been made a fuss of and looked after.

That, after all, was what he'd needed. And Emma Hardwick, an unhappily married society beauty who was the most complaisant of mistresses, would have sent him back to Flanders rested, well-nourished and ready for another six months in the front line.

But he hadn't gone to see Emma. He had met Anthony Lawrence in Whitehall, been informed in the course of their conversation that Dora had been widowed, and he had gone haring off to Ashton Cross like a lovesick schoolboy to throw himself at the feet of the object of his devotion.

And then he'd raped her. There was no other word for it. He'd practically dragged her into her own bedroom, torn off her clothes and forced her. He'd frightened and upset the one woman in the world for whom he'd willingly have been tortured to death in order to save her from a passing headache. He'd then lounged around her house for the rest of the week, deluding himself that she wanted him to stay. She couldn't have wanted anything of the sort.

And now, although he knew she must hate him for what he'd done, he'd re-opened a wound in his own heart which he knew would never heal, but which would fester and grow more painful as the years went by.

In Flanders, training went on. In the holiday atmosphere, however, parades and drill were interrupted by football matches, with whole weeks of home leave for thousands of men, with visits to cafés and bars. And then fresh troops from the training camp at Étaples began to pour into the salient.

The fine summer days continued to slip by. But, in the second week of July, concerted attacks on the German lines began at last; and during the final week of that month an almighty barrage of shells poured into their defences. The shelling had never really stopped, it never did — but now it intensified; guns blazed away all day and all night, shaking the earth. The enemy retaliated and casualties mounted; hundreds of wounded and gassed filled the field hospitals.

'I suppose we must be going up to take Passchendaele, Sir?' Tim's servant spat on his master's buttons and polished them vigorously.

'Oh?' Tim looked up from the book he was pretending to read. 'Where d'you hear that?'

'Common talk, Sir. All them Colonials reckon we'll walk it.' Private Hamilton spat again. 'Cocky buggers they are.'

'Mmm.'

'Will we do it, Sir?' Private Hamilton looked towards the east. 'I was here in '15, Sir,' he continued. 'Bloody awful it was. Mud up to your armpits — and you should have seen the poor fucking mules.'

'Well, I didn't.' Tim closed his book, stood up and stretched. 'Watch your language, Hamilton,' he muttered, as an afterthought.

'Sorry, Sir.'

Tim looked towards the east. 'Those slopes look harmless enough to me,' he said. 'We should be able to push through if we get going before the autumn.'

'That's just it, Sir. *If*. An' them buggers at GHQ don't seem to understand that. Begging your pardon, Sir.'

As it happened, the buggers at GHQ would have a great deal to answer for when autumn did come. For British Intelligence, priding itself on its efficiency, had not discovered that the harmless looking slopes which Tim and Private Hamilton could see from their bivouac were, in fact, well camouflaged German fortresses.

The Germans had taken advantage of the inactivity of their enemies, and over the summer they had dug in as if they meant to stay in Flanders for all eternity. Those innocent-looking ridges were now, in fact, a series of virtually impregnable citadels — were scattered with concrete pillboxes not visible from the British positions. They were, in effect, the new enemy front line. The trenches to the west of this were mere machine-gun outposts which the enemy had reckoned on losing when the attack finally came.

Their guns on fixed lines, their troops secure in the comfort of their well-made, well-provisioned positions, the Germans waited. They were confident that any attack, when it came, could be easily repelled.

By the last week of July the fine summer weather had ended and colder conditions had blown in from the Atlantic bringing rain. The countryside around Ypres, stiff, heavy clay, water-logged for most of the year, turned into a morass. There seemed to be nothing but mud. The maps bore no resemblance to the appearance of the landscape as it was now. Woods were no longer woods, fields no longer boasted any vegetation, farms and individual houses were flattened ruins.

Then, at last, the High Command finalized the plans for a massive dawn attack, to take place on 31 July. The fact that Haig had not even seen the terrain over which his troops were to advance was not, apparently, an issue. No one had told the commander-in-chief what the land was like; no one had wanted to depress the great man.

The campaign was designed to widen the salient, to smash

through the German defences and to capture the Channel ports to the north. There were even optimistic hopes of liberating Belgium itself . . .

The barrage from the British guns had by now decimated the enemy's nominal front line. Wire, trenches, dug-outs and gun emplacements were all confounded in one great mass of destruction, blurring the division between the Allies and their adversaries who would now meet each other on that first day in a terrible, grey-brown swamp, over which it was difficult enough to walk and on which it was going to be almost impossible to fight.

At three o'clock on the morning of 31 July the infantry of twelve divisions took up their positions. Tim's battalion had been detailed to advance towards a small ruined hamlet due east of their own lines, and to flush out the six hundred or so Germans who (so intelligence reports had it) were dug in there.

It appeared to be a reasonable objective. This was the type of manoeuvre which Tim's own company had rehearsed dozens of times and completed successfully on many previous occasions. Each of the battalion's four companies had its own particular task to perform: the hamlet would be surrounded, attacked, the bombers would go in, the Germans would be taken prisoner and a new British position established. Simple.

'Mr Goddard?' Tim looked around for the commander of the forward platoon.

The lieutenant nodded. 'Ready, Sir.'

'Mr Allder?'

'Yes, Sir.' Richard Allder's grinning face appeared next to Tim. 'I reckon this'll be a push-over, Sir,' he remarked.

'I hope you're right.' Tim looked round for his other two lieutenants and saw they were ready, so he nodded to the captain of the company on his left.

Both captains then gave the signal to advance. The men scrambled out of their trenches, formed up and these two forward companies set off across the mud.

For a while everything went according to plan. The men moved towards their target in reasonably tight formation — they even took and sent back a few prisoners. But the going, through knee-deep mud, was very heavy and Tim could see that the operation was going to take far longer than originally planned. All four companies were supposed to meet at the hamlet by midday, but looking at his watch, he saw that it was now two o'clock in the afternoon.

Doggedly, Tim's company struggled on through the mud, getting closer and closer to the hamlet, still confident of eventual success. At about half past three, however, a massive, absolutely deafening barrage of enemy fire exploded right in front of them.

It blew the company in two, killing half a dozen men outright and wounding many more. In the resulting confusion a small detachment of the unit, which happened to include Tim, accidentally veered away from their objective. The men began to wander towards where some Germans, in the comfort and security of one of their hidden fortresses, waited for them . . .

Dazed and shocked by the sheer magnitude of the gunfire, the men with Tim now found themselves apparently under attack from north, south and east. But although they hardly knew where they were, although they could not even see their enemy's position and could scarcely begin to establish where their objective was, they had, of course, no choice but to go on. Retreat during a battle was unthinkable — they all knew that.

Tim, who had been partially deafened and half blinded by the bombardment, realized at last that they were at least forty-five degrees off course. He tried to gather together those of his men whom he could see through the smoke and he understood, with some relief, that most of the officers must still be with the main group.

If only they could swing round to the right, they might be able to find the rest of the company, then they would have a better chance of meeting up with their battalion, which ought, by now, to have reached the hamlet.

The day had begun wet and since four o'clock there had been a constant downpour. What few landmarks there had once been were now blurring into a misty twilight, which was illuminated only by fire from the Lewis guns behind them. All through the daylight hours the men's vision had been badly hampered by mist and smoke and now it was hardly possible to see a man a yard away from another. Dusk at four o'clock in July — it didn't seem possible.

They had been struggling through the mud for hours now. Weighed down by packs, the men were up to their thighs in the cloying, awful stuff. Hungry, exhausted, demoralized, they were all wet through and cold, and they well knew there was no hope whatsoever of rescue or respite. They reached the comparative shelter of an empty mine crater, and leaned against the walls of it, too tired to go on.

A private, a mere child of seventeen who had joined up for a dare, was now literally crying with exhaustion. Too chilled and frightened to hide his emotion any more, he sobbed openly, great runnels of tears washing away the dirt on his cheeks. Corporal Turner, recognizing a classic case of wind-up, lit a cigarette and pushed it between the soldier's lips. 'Here,' he muttered. 'Suck that. And stop your bawlin'.'

'Sorry.' Gulping and sobbing, the private tried to inhale. And the corporal, now realizing that he'd given his subordinate his last cigarette, spat and threw the empty packet of Woodbines into the mud.

'Where the fucking hell are we, Sir?' he demanded, looking mournfully at Tim.

'I don't know.' Tim wiped his hand across his eyes and found that he still couldn't focus properly. All he could see was a blurred area of grey mud. 'I honestly don't know. Do any of you?'

'Somewhere in Belgium, Sir.' There was a cackle of demented laughter from the company wit. 'I say, Sir, this beach is a bit dirty, ain't it? Shan't come 'ere for me 'olidays again.'

'Oh, shut up, Walters.' Tim, recognizing the voice of the comedian, glared into the mist. 'One more remark like that out of you, and I'll shoot you myself and tread you into the mud, d'you hear me?' He pushed his helmet back from his forehead. 'We'd better push on,' he said.

The men had just scrambled out of the crater when a fearful whistling sound sheered past Tim's face and Walters lay at his feet, half his face missing and a great bloody mess where his shoulder had been.

Of the men with him — Tim estimated that when he'd been divided from the rest of the company, he'd taken about thirty others — there were perhaps fifteen still alive. He decided that it was pointless to go any further. Their only real chance of survival now was to find a shell-crater and get inside it, to hang on to the sides to stop themselves from drowning, and to wait for the morning. Then, they might be able to rejoin their battalion — if it still existed.

Tim had lost his compass. His map had long since disintegrated into a sodden, unreadable pulp. He peered at his watch. Six o'clock.

He was about to give the order to take cover when the bullet struck him, throwing him forward. Despite the uproar all around him, he actually heard his ribs crack and now he tasted his own blood as it spurted into his mouth, bubbling up from his punctured lung.

As he fell, he knew he was as good as dead, but he just didn't care. Floating on his face in a water-filled shell-hole, he felt extraordinarily at peace with the world.

The bombardment continued all around him, throwing jets of water and mud into the air. Bullets whistled overhead but he hardly heard them. He felt perfectly content, happy enough to die. For death would solve everything.

'Get Mr Atherton out!' Corporal Turner caught his officer's ankle and tugged it hard. 'Come on, you bastards — bloody well pull!' were the last words Tim heard on earth that day.

Chapter Twenty

DORA WAS HAPPY TO BE PREGNANT. After the first two months, she felt extraordinarily well. The sickness of those first few weeks over, she was now eating properly again. She put on weight and her skin took on a fine, glowing translucence.

Her eyes shone, their whites as clear and blue-tinged as a child's. Soon, her dresses would need to be let out, then replaced by garments more suitable for maternity.

She monitored her changing shape in her mirror; each morning she studied the bump in her stomach area, and, observing that it was definitely increasing in size, she hugged herself with delight. She was longing for the baby to be born.

Although Dora waited anxiously for the postman every day, although she willed him to write to her, no letters from Tim ever came. Nevertheless, Dora wrote to him. She posted the letters to the address he'd given her — or rather, to the address she *thought* he'd given her, for when she'd gone to her desk for the scrap of paper on which he'd written his army number and other details, she'd found it missing. She assumed she'd accidentally thrown it away. 'Never mind,' she'd reassured herself. 'There can't be that many T.J. Athertons in Flanders. The letters will find him.'

The news from Belgium was not good. Not even the *Daily Mail* could make much jingoistic capital out of the terrible losses of the autumn campaign. Headlines of 'Massive British Advance' looked somewhat absurd when followed by huge casualty lists. And by the middle of October, it was clear that, although the Allies had continued to advance towards Passchendaele step by painful step, the entire blood-soaked affair was costing far more in life and suffering than any stretch of Flemish mud could possibly be worth.

Anthony declared the whole business to be a total waste of time, men and human effort, and in doing so he seriously upset his elder sister. His implication that her beloved eldest son might die in an entirely pointless action that would not bring the end of the war one minute nearer made Anna lose her temper with him and caused a family rift which took many months to mend.

Both Anna and Anthony, together with various members of their respective families, had come to stay in Oxford for what their parents intended to be a peaceful few days. Stephen had noticed that Anna was very much on edge; and one dinner time he was on the point of telling his son to stop pontificating about the mismanagement of the war when Anna did it for him.

'You think you're so clever, don't you, Anthony?' she had cried. Rising to her feet, her face flushed with anger and her eyes full of tears, Anna banged her fist down on the dining table. '*You* know what ought to be done, don't you?' she shouted. '*You* could have planned the whole operation so much more efficiently than Mr Haig, couldn't you?'

'I never said so, Anna.' Anthony, realizing much too late that he had upset and offended his sister, tried to make amends. 'I'd forgotten that Marcus was in Flanders,' he added, making matters worse.

Dorcas, seeing Anthony's embarrassment, reached for Anna's hand. 'I'm sure Anthony didn't mean —' she began.

'Oh, do be quiet, Mama!' Anna glared at her mother. 'There's no need for you to stick up for him. He's quite capable of defending himself — against me, at any rate.'

'Anna!' Her father's voice cut across Anna's anger, making her turn to look at him. 'Anna, I won't have you speaking to your mother like that. Apologize, will you?' Stephen met his daughter's frown with an ever fiercer one of his own. 'Did you hear me?'

'It's all my fault.' Anthony looked from his father to his sister. 'I'm sorry I've upset Anna.'

'Liar!' Sitting down again, Anna gave her brother a look of utter contempt. 'Oh, you're all the same, you paper soldiers. You sit on your backsides, safe in your warm rooms in Whitehall, and you do nothing but make wise remarks to each other. Oh, you make me sick!'

'I said I was sorry to have annoyed you, and I meant it.' Flushed himself now, Anthony glowered at his sister. 'I'd have gone over to Flanders myself if they'd let me, you know.'

'If they'd let you. Oh, yes, if only they'd let you!' Anna jeered. 'And aren't you glad they wouldn't? Aren't you glad that your rotten lungs, or whatever you say you have, keep you here in good old Blighty?'

'Anna, that's not really —'

'Not really what?' Anna stared at her brother. 'Not really fair? Not really decent? Just remember, Anthony, that fairness and decency no longer come into it — that this war will be won by men like my son, by men who are actually fighting in the trenches, using real weapons and *not* by the likes of you.' She rose to her feet and scowled at Anthony. 'Not by a gaggle of penpushers in khaki who don't deserve the name of soldiers; by men who have more in common with a pack of bloody Girl Guides.'

Anna caught her father's eyes. 'And I shan't apologize!' she added. 'Not to you, not to Mama, and certainly not to *him*.' Bursting into tears, she ran out of the dining room and into her father's study, slamming the door behind her.

'I'd better go and calm her down.' Stephen stood up and walked over towards the door. 'You'll never learn, will you?' he added, giving his son a baleful stare as he went past him.

'I'm sorry, Mama.' Anthony took one of his mother's hands in his and held it tightly. 'I didn't mean —'

'Never mind.' Dorcas shrugged. 'Never mind, dear, your father will talk to her now, he'll cheer her up. Shall we have some coffee? It's awful stuff these days, but since it's made we might as well drink it. Oh, darling!' she added crossly, seeing him fishing in his pocket. 'Put those away. Surely you can do without a cigarette for half an hour?'

In spite of their parents' efforts at diplomacy, it was weeks before Anthony and Anna spoke to each other amicably again.

* * *

Dora's Aunt Katherine, more willing than Anthony to see the war as a righteous struggle of good against evil, of democracy against tyranny, nevertheless wept for her sons, James and Michael, who were both somewhere in that vast, heaving quagmire of the ever-widening Ypres salient. She said her prayers and besought the Almighty to intercede and bring an end to the bloodshed, for it was apparent that this could not be brought about by any human agency.

The heresy that her children might die, might already be dead, merely in order that a field marshal's ludicrously grandiose schemes should come to fruition, was one which kept occurring to her over and over again. Like Anna, she was dreading the delivery of a War Office telegram, closely followed by a letter from the dead soldier's commanding officer, full of empty phrases of commendation.

Dora, on the other hand, hardly thought about the war at all. She was still enveloped in a haze of other-worldly happiness anchored firmly to the past — to five days in May 1917, into which her whole life seemed to have been compressed. She felt that she could happily live on the memory of that week for the rest of her days. And, after all, she had more than memories — she had the baby. She had Tim's child. And if its father was dead, as Dora had now convinced herself he must be, Tim had at least died knowing that she loved him as he'd always deserved to be loved. He must have died aware of that.

Katherine was the first to notice, or at least to comment on, the alteration in Dora's shape. 'You've waited so long for this baby, haven't you, Dora?' she asked, as they both sat upon the mossy steps of the terrace, looking towards the rhododendron walk and enjoying the autumn sunshine.

'A very long time indeed.' Dora folded her hands protectively across her stomach, over her lover's child. She imagined the baby within her, curled in a loose ball, floating safe and secure in the peaceful darkness.

'I'm sure it will take after *you*.' Katherine spoke as if to reassure herself. 'Its only similarity to the brute will be in its surname.'

Dora smiled tolerantly at her cousin. 'There's no need to be so harsh, Katherine,' she said mildly. 'He's dead — he can't annoy you any more. So there's no need, either, to tell me how much you hated him, over and over again.'

'I'm sorry, Dora.' Katherine, now a farmer, a field-girl, a groom and an estate manager all rolled into one, looked at her bruised, blackened fingernails and her ruined hands. 'I shouldn't be so horrible, I know. It's just that — oh, when you married him, I was so unhappy. I cried myself to sleep for a month or more.'

'Did you, Katherine? Why was that?'

'Do you need to ask? I love you, Dolly — I didn't want you to be miserable.'

'Did you love Ralph, too?'

'*Ralph?*' Katherine laughed. 'No, I didn't love Ralph. That's a ridiculous idea. I hated him — it ate into me how much I hated him. I can't explain it. Yet — oh, I can't tell you —'

'There was something, wasn't there?' Dora touched Katherine's arm. 'On my wedding morning, you were going to tell me something and you changed your mind. What were you going to say?'

'Nothing, really.'

'Katherine!' Dora shook her cousin's shoulder. 'I want to know. I've a *right* to know.'

Katherine looked back at her cousin. 'I suppose you have,' she conceded. 'Well, all right then — he killed someone.' She shrugged. 'That's all.'

'He *killed* someone?' Dora stared. 'You mean, he was a murderer?'

'Not exactly.'

'What, then? Explain to me.'

Katherine sighed. 'The Challoners were always very strict preservers of game,' she began. 'Well, you know that. I expect you also know that Ralph used to like going round the woods with one of the keepers, checking the coverts and so on?'

'Yes, of course I know that. It was something of an obsession with him.'

'It was, wasn't it? He used to do it even as quite a young boy. Well, one day, about a year or so before you met him I think it must have been, he and his keeper found a poacher in Cobben's Spinney. It was a child — a boy of about twelve. He'd sprung a gin trap and he was caught fast by the leg.

'Well, it appears that Ralph was delighted to have caught him. Pheasants' eggs had been going missing, and he was sure he'd trapped the thief. Instead of releasing the boy from the trap, Ralph just stood in front of this poor lad, laughing and telling him he was for it now.' Katherine grimaced. 'The brute!

'Anyway, the keeper was all set to release the boy, when Ralph told him to leave him there. He could stay there a bit longer, he said — it would teach him a lesson. And he told the keeper that they'd finish their inspection of the wood and go back for the boy later.

'The keeper protested, but Ralph was determined, as you can imagine.'

Dora, feeling sick now, clutched her cousin's hand. 'But surely,' she began. 'Surely Ralph —'

'They went back for the boy in the evening,' continued Katherine, deadpan. 'He'd bled to death by then, of course.'

'Oh, God!' Dora leaned back against the step behind her. 'Oh, good God! Katherine, are you sure?'

'Yes, I'm sure.' Katherine looked at Dora. 'Of course, it was all hushed up at the time. The keeper was told to keep his mouth shut about what really happened. The official version was that he and Challoner found the child late that afternoon and that he was already dead. As you can imagine, the Challoners were in quite enough trouble for having illegal mantraps in their woods.'

'Yes.' Dora bit her lip. 'So how did the story get out?' she asked.

'A few months later Hardison — that's the keeper — fell out with Andrew Challoner. He came to Ashton Cross and asked for work on the land — said he was tired of being a slave to the Challoners. Dad gave him a job in the stables.

'One night he got drunk and James found him in a hayloft, weeping his heart out. James got him to bed and Hardison told him all about it. And James told me.'

'He could have made it up.' Dora looked at Katherine. 'It could have been a pack of lies he told James. After all, if he'd quarrelled with old Mr Challoner, he might have wanted to make trouble —'

'No.' Katherine shook her head. 'Hardison has no more imagination than a stone. It's true all right.'

'So what did you do?'

'Do?' Katherine shrugged. 'Nothing. What could we do? And in any case, Ralph and I —'

'Yes?' Dora looked into Katherine's beautiful dark eyes. 'You and Ralph?'

'Well, he never wanted *me*. He never made any secret of the fact that he thought I was hideous. But —'

'You wanted him. In spite of disliking him, you wanted him in your bed.'

'No, Dora! Well, yes, I suppose I did.' Katherine sniffed, rubbing her eyes wearily. 'It's disgusting, isn't it? Hankering after a man who was absolutely worthless and who didn't want me anyway.'

'I was just the same.' Dora sighed. 'I deluded myself into believing that he loved me — that I was in love. But I never was. I was infatuated for a year or so — then I came to my senses. Oh, God, Katherine, he was so cruel to me. There was one occasion — well, if I'd had a knife, I'd have killed him.'

'You should have told me,' said Katherine. 'We'd have killed him for you. Out here in the countryside, you know, accidents can happen —'

'I know. That's why I said nothing.'

'Ah.' Katherine pushed her hair out of her eyes, then suddenly she grinned. 'You have the baby, though,' she said. 'We'll see to it that it doesn't take after *him*. And you have the land. Think of it, Dora — you have the *land*! Stephen Lawrence's bastard daughter owns the Challoners' land. I expect old Andrew is revolving in his grave.'

'Mmm.' Dora smiled. She would hug her secret to herself for a little longer. Large now, for her dates, she allowed everyone to assume that her baby was Ralph's child. Her servants, certainly, might suspect otherwise but none of them *knew*. She and Tim had been together for a few days; what did that prove? Nothing. Yet.

So she acquiesced in the role of tragic heroine, carrying her dead husband's child. November would come and go without any confinement taking place. Some simple arithmetic would be done and it would be clear to everyone that the baby could not possibly be Ralph's. But until then, Dora felt that no explanations were necessary.

She turned down her aunt's urgent invitation to go and live at Ashton Cross. 'I want the baby to be born at the Grange,' she said firmly.

Aunt Katherine dabbed her eyes. 'Yes, I suppose you do,' she conceded. 'But if you get lonely, dear, you can always come to us.'

'I know.' Dora, feeling a terrible fraud, smiled at her aunt. 'I'm happy here,' she said, truthfully, lying back on the sofa where she had sat with Tim, resting her head on the cushion which Tim had leaned against.

He might come back. There was always the remote possibility that he was now a prisoner, or that he was lying unconscious in some hospital, and would one day recover and remember her. She had to be waiting for him. He would want to see his child . . .

* * *

Three small battalions, all that remained of Marcus Harley's division, had been sent up the line to Ypres to join in the Big Push of 1917. Before this, however, there had been some respite, for Marcus had passed the first half of that year pleasantly enough. Taken out of active service in February, he had spent a relatively peaceful six months organizing transports, concerning himself with nothing more warlike than the supply of horses to the cavalry lines.

But now he was back in the line himself. Back in the thick of it and well aware that he would not be lucky forever.

He now knew that of all the places in the entire world, Belgium was the most horrible. He thought he had been in hell, but no, that had only been purgatory. The battlefields of the Somme had been a mere preparation for this. And now he was in Flanders, in hell itself.

'You might look a bit more gratified, lad.' His battalion colonel had admonished Marcus, evidently put out that the lieutenant was unmoved by his promotion to acting captain of

D Company.

'I just hope I'll be worthy of your trust in me, Sir.' Marcus attempted a suitably modest smile but failed to produce one.

The colonel dismissed him, shaking his head. They were all the same, these young officers, and he couldn't really blame them. They knew as well as he did that they were being bumped up to higher rank and being made responsible for the lives of a hundred or so men, simply because there was no one else available. Marcus and dozens like him were curtly informed that they were now company commanders, sent off up the line and told to get on with it.

Marcus had been in Flanders since the beginning of August, and by now he could hardly remember any other way of life. On that awful day in September, he and his troops were sitting, as usual, in what they chose to call a trench, waiting for the rations to arrive. They had little hope that they would, for pack mules could hardly be expected to get across the rotten duckboards which traversed that sullen swamp, which now stretched for miles in all directions.

From their positions, Marcus and his men could see nothing but a horrible grey sea of mud, a mire into which anything heavier than a rat floundered and sank. After the wettest August in living memory, this September of 1917 was hardly any drier. The Ypres salient was simply a marsh.

The three million shells which had by now smashed into the mud had completely destroyed the pre-war drainage system. The men knew this and they also knew that it was ludicrous to be trying to make trenches in the mire. So waterlogged was the earth that as soon as a man had shovelled the slurry out of the scrape he'd excavated, the mud and water simply slopped back in again. The deeper he dug, the more the trench filled with water. But still the soldiers struggled to excavate defences.

Marcus had long since decided that hell couldn't possibly be fire. Hell was mud. In particular, it was this awful Belgian mud which sucked men and horses into its apparently bottomless depths, pulling them relentlessly downwards while their limbs were immobilized in its cloying embrace, while their eyes bulged with terror, with the knowledge that they were as good as dead.

Marcus's battalion was due to attack that day. Guns had somehow been dragged across the unstable ground, ammunition had been lugged across the morass. And now the men crouched, waiting for a break in the barrage of artillery fire which was at that moment pulverizing the unstable ground into an even deeper swamp. When it stopped, they would attack.

'We're better off than the poor bloody Jocks, any road,' remarked a sergeant on sentry duty, vainly trying to cheer a private who was tired of being wet through. 'Imagine 'avin a kilt flappin' round yer bum, and yer knees all bare. At least we got a bit of protection.'

Marcus, overhearing that conversation, felt dismayed. Surely, he thought, any country which sends its soldiers into battle in skirts deserves to lose a war. The Highlanders, however, seemed as cheerful as one could expect. Perhaps cold backsides didn't matter if one was used to the condition.

All around the Ypres salient miserable, sodden companies of Allied troops roused themselves to face another foul day to be spent either lurking in their waterlogged ditches or footslogging across the impossible terrain to attack yet another well-defended German position. Following on, or going over with the first wave of an attack, it made no difference. Death or injury was likely, terror certain, pain and misery a matter of course. All along the front line prayers were doubtless now ascending, prayers for a Blighty one. The supplicant probably didn't mind what form his wound took, so long as it got him out of this.

The wretched Allied forces were well aware that their enemies were drier, warmer and far better provisioned than they were themselves. The highlight of any action was undoubtedly the capture of a German dug-out or pillbox. With shouts of triumph, the men would rush into a German fortress and, heedless of the possibility of any booby traps, would loot it for blankets, cigarettes, wood — for anything that might make their own wretched holes more bearable. If the Germans ran away, if they did not need to be bombed out, so much the better. The portable property was then left intact. Killing Germans was, these days, very much a side issue. Staying alive oneself was the main objective now.

'You all right, Sir?' Marcus's company sergeant major edged closer to his commanding officer and passed him a dixie half full of assorted bits of biscuit and evil-smelling canned meat. The strips of sacking which had been used to kindle the cooking fire still adhered, half burned, to the base of the pan and these gave off a scarcely less appetizing smell than the food itself.

'Oh — yes, I'm fine, thank you, Sergeant Dryden.' Marcus accepted his breakfast. He stirred the disgusting biscuit porridge and began to eat. 'Any casualties during the night?' he enquired.

'No. But young Thornley isn't going to last much longer.' Sergeant Dryden rolled his eyes expressively. 'Bad case of wind-up there, and he's beginning to affect the others. We'd better get rid of him, if we can.'

'He's that bad?'

'Oh, yes.' The sergeant wiped his nose on his sleeve. 'Crying in his sleep last night he was, shaking and thrashing about. In tears again this morning. He's no good to us.'

'No, I suppose he's not.' Marcus rubbed his eyes. 'Any sign of the rations yet?'

'They won't get anything up here, Sir.' Sergeant Dryden laughed, making a bitter, harsh sound at the back of his throat. 'They've forgotten about us. The lost battalion, that's what we are. You mark my words, Sir. GHQ's abandoned us.'

The rations failed to arrive, but by raiding the haversacks of a few convenient corpses, the men in Marcus's trench had eventually managed to put together a sort of breakfast, which they munched steadily, sitting in the morning drizzle. They knew that, whatever else happened to them, they would not starve. After all, one had only to put one's hand over the parapet to grab a piece of human torso, to yank the body into the trench and pull off its pack, to ransack it for whatever was inside. Usually it was the same old tinned meat and dry biscuits, but sometimes, if the body were that of a German, there might be chocolate as well.

Marcus put down his breakfast and leaned back against the muddy side of the trench. He wished the tortures of hell on Haig. Had he had the man there, he would cheerfully have murdered him, and then gone light-heartedly to his own subsequent execution. He wondered if Sergeant Dryden was right — if the battalion might never be relieved. They'd been stuck on this ridge now for ten days. Perhaps GHQ would indeed abandon them there, on the assumption that they'd soon be killed anyway, so it was hardly worth marching another hundred-odd men up through the mud to take their place.

'Mr Wilson of C Company's coming over, Sir.'

Marcus looked up at his sergeant, puzzled at the reproach in the man's voice, but then realized that it was doubtless caused by his officer's failure to eat the breakfast provided. The horrible mash of soaked biscuit and canned meat at Marcus's side was now congealing and Marcus felt almost abashed. It was as if his nanny had berated him for leaving his rice pudding. 'Mr Wilson, you said?'

'S'right, Sir.'

'Ah.' If the sergeant had said that a swamp rat was coming over, Marcus could hardly have been less interested. But, all the same, he tried to look rather more alert, more ready to talk through the details of that day's proposed action, as this was what Captain Wilson probably wanted to do.

Wilson appeared at that moment. Having taken a short cut across open ground, he scrambled into the ditch pursued by a hail of sniper's bullets. He squatted on his haunches and lit a cigarette. 'Christ,' he muttered, inhaling. 'That was a near thing. Didn't think the sods would be awake yet.' He glanced around him. 'You look pretty snug here,' he observed.

Marcus frowned at him. Thomas Wilson was so bloody irritating. Pretending that everything was going so well, he always talked as if conditions in general were marvellous and behaved as if victory was just around the corner. 'We couldn't be more comfortable,' he muttered sourly.

His sarcasm escaped Captain Wilson completely. 'Men all right?' he enquired.

'So-so.' Marcus decided not to mention Thornley. Thomas Wilson had no sympathy whatsoever with cases of battle fatigue; he did not recognize the condition of nervous exhaustion, referred to all men who showed any sign of it as slackers, shirkers or — if he were drunk — as downright bleeding cowards. 'What about your mob?'

'We lost Templeton last night. Poor bugger had had it anyway. Bloody great hole in his side.' Lieutenant Templeton thus consigned to oblivion, Wilson grinned. 'Otherwise we're all present and correct.'

'Jolly good show.' Marcus was annoyed to find that he was doing it himself now — adopting that same ghastly tone of facile optimism. In spite of himself he returned Wilson's inane grin and then fished in his greatcoat pocket for his map. 'We're in the second wave today,' he said. 'Is that right?'

'Think so. Unless HQ's changed its mind again. Had any messages?'

'No.' Marcus shrugged. 'Haven't seen a runner for days. And the telephone's no good; it fell into a sump hole and the bloody thing doesn't work any more. So look, are you going over at seven?'

'Seems like it.' Wilson grinned. 'Should be a damned good show. Eh?'

But Marcus had suddenly had enough of this and couldn't agree. Now, he stared at Wilson in disgust. A good show indeed! How on earth could Wilson squat there, tired, filthy, ten days' growth of beard on his pleasant, boyish face, talking as if they were going on a nature ramble? He was so sodding cheerful that Marcus could have strangled him. He looked at his watch. 'Don't you think you ought to be getting back now?' he asked.

'Suppose so.' Wilson grinned again. 'Well, then — see you later, old chap.'

There had been a few desultory plops and thuds as the morning broke, as the first few shells of the fresh daylight bombardment got under way, answering the Allied barrage. The two officers took no heed of this; being under fire was now so routine that neither of them really noticed the shelling. But just then, there was a perceptibly different sound, of a different kind of shell . . .

'Oh, God!' Wilson stared at Marcus. 'Oh, God, Harley, did you hear that?'

Marcus glanced up from his map. 'Hear what?' he asked, suddenly afraid, for Wilson's face was now ashen. 'For Christ's sake, Wilson! What *is* it?'

'Hell, man — it's gas!' Shuddering, Wilson shook his head at Marcus. 'Mustard gas! The buggers are sending over gas shells again and they're going to burst right on top of us.'

Even as Wilson spoke, the first of the shells exploded. Marcus wrapped his arms around his head and, yelling a warning to his men, threw himself flat on the bottom of the trench. More shells burst, releasing their deadly chemicals over the helpless men.

Then, quite suddenly, there was a terrific explosion; a brilliant white flash lit up the gloomy morning. Mud, wooden struts, missiles and debris began to fall on top of the soldiers, burying them alive.

* * *

'God, what a bloody mess!' Grimacing, the Canadian soldier stared at the sight at his feet. He looked pityingly at the prostrate bodies of Marcus and his men, who lay sprawled on the bottom of the trench. Leaning on his spade, he wiped his face with the back of his hand.

'They're all dead,' he muttered, glancing across to where his sergeant stood. 'Poor sods, they're all either burnt or suffocated.' He turned a body over with his foot, and blanched as he saw the face. 'Might as well cover them up again.'

'Hang on.' The sergeant jumped down into the ditch. 'Better make sure they've all had it,' he muttered. He grabbed a body, pulled it aside, then dragged another clear. 'This one, at the bottom,' he said. 'He's still breathing — just. Well, come on, then. Give me a hand. Careful, now.'

So, together, the two Canadians lugged the survivor out of the pit and, placing him on a shelf of relatively dry earth, they studied the man.

'Be kinder to put a bullet into this one,' said the soldier. '*We* can't get him down to an aid post. An' the poor bugger would be happier dead — look at him.'

'Yeah — well. I reckon you're right.' The sergeant drew his revolver and looked around. Then, by some miracle, he noticed a pair of stretcher bearers making their unsteady way across the duckboards which had been laid up to the trench.

'Hey!' He cupped his hands to his mouth and shouted. 'Hey! You two! Over here! Got something for you.'

'Oh, Christ!' One of the two RAMC men, whose stomach was accustomed to the most horrible of sights, grimaced as he looked at the survivor of the gas attack. 'Christ, the poor sod.'

'Must've been incendiaries as well,' observed his companion. 'Can't have been just gas, to have burnt them like this.'

The first man spat on his hands. 'Well, better get him down the line,' he muttered. 'If we can.'

Together, the RAMC men rolled the unconscious man on to a stretcher and then they began the long trek through the slime, back to the dressing station.

Chapter Twenty-One

'KING AND COUNTRY!' KATHERINE LAWRENCE felt her face tighten as she looked at the letter from her brother's commanding officer, in which he expressed his sorrow at the young man's death and offered condolences to his family.

Michael Lawrence had died in the mud of Passchendaele, drowned in a shell crater, his corpse sucked down into a soldier's grave never to be marked by a wooden cross. It did not comfort his family to reflect that he was only one of thousands who went into oblivion thus. Dozens upon dozens of his fellows had gone west in a similar fashion, blown to pieces by shells or struck by bullets and then trodden into a filthy, bloody mess by men trudging or running across their broken bodies. After the war, the grass would grow very green on the Ypres salient.

Katherine pushed the letter back into its envelope and handed it to her father. 'Is James up yet?' she asked. 'He told me he might go out today.'

James, wounded that August in the same campaign, had now been sent back to Ashton Cross. He came home in October, subdued and wretched, grieving for his brother, feeling guilty that he had survived when Michael had died. 'Why him?' he had asked, looking bleakly around the members of his family. 'Why him? He was younger than me.'

It became clear that James would never fully recover from his own injuries, which included shrapnel wounds to his stomach and chest. He was discharged from the army to a reserved occupation, that of farming.

※ ※ ※

'Well, at least he's alive.' John Harley hugged his wife. 'Anna, he's alive, he's not beyond help.'

Sitting together in the cab after their first visit to the hospital, both John and Anna were still numbed with shock. John spoke in a voice unlike his own and realized with dismay that he was still shaking and felt chilled and unreal. 'Don't cry,' he repeated, over and over again. 'Darling, don't cry so. He's alive — he's still alive . . .'

But nevertheless, Anna sobbed. Marcus was indeed alive, but his handsome face was now almost unrecognizable, and great areas of his body had been blistered and burnt by the incendiary bombs and mustard gas. He had been pulled alive out of the trench after the gas attack, but the rest of his company had died there, burnt and helpless, suffocated to death.

Looking at her son, Anna had wondered if perhaps it might have been better for Marcus to have died with them.

In spite of her good intentions to be cheerful for Marcus's sake, and in spite of being forewarned, Dora cried when she first visited him. For she saw a man whose extraordinary beauty had been totally destroyed — a grotesque reflection of his formerly almost perfect self.

'Don't *you* grizzle, Dora,' he'd said. 'It's not that bad. And my marriage prospects are still fairly hopeful, if that's what's bothering you.'

'Marriage?' Sniffing, Dora looked up and tried to meet his eyes.

'Yes. You realize, don't you, that there's now such a shortage of men that some poor desperate woman will be glad to take even me.' He tried to grin to console her. 'In fact,' he added, 'I was propositioned twice last week — once by a very pretty VAD and once by a Red Cross helper. So what do you think of that?'

Instead of laughing, Dora buried her face in her hands and abandoned herself to a fresh outburst of weeping. 'Oh, Marcus, don't joke,' she sobbed. 'You were so beautiful! And now, when I look at your poor face — it's such a pity. Oh, Marcus!'

'Oh, Marcus,' he mimicked her. 'Oh, for Christ's sake,

Dora, I'm one of the lucky ones. I haven't had my lungs ruined and my inside burnt away, I'm not blinded or mad. I shall heal.'

'But all the same —'

'God in heaven!' Marcus stared up at the ceiling. 'Dora, listen to me. I *won't* be treated as a special case. I might be a caricature just now, but I'm not a mental defective who needs to be humoured or wept over.'

'Marcus, I never meant —'

'And the specialist says that the scarring will become less noticeable in time. They're going to try some skin grafting in due course — so soon I shall just look old and interesting. I shan't rate a second glance.' He looked at her steadily now, making her meet his eyes, willing her to believe him as he wanted to believe himself.

Dora, ashamed of herself, dismayed that the person whom she'd come to cheer up had in fact consoled her, dashed away her tears. Leaning over her nephew she hugged him. 'Dear Marcus,' she whispered, her voice still shaky. 'Dear, dear Marcus, at least you're alive. I'm so glad you're alive!'

'So am I. Ah, could you not lean on me, Dora, it's a bit painful.' With his own bandaged hand he patted his aunt's. 'Oh, no, not more bloody waterworks!' he groaned. 'God, I shall be glad to get back to France, away from you and my mother.'

'You're not going *back*?'

'Afraid so. Not until the spring, though, and not to combatant duties. They'll find me something to do behind the lines. Cushy, really. I'll have a comfortable billet in some splendid château, and when I think of all those mademoiselles — well, I can hardly wait!'

To her surprise, Dora found that she was smiling through her tears; suddenly, she felt a great deal better. 'Really, Marcus!' she admonished. 'You're quite awful.'

'I know.' He shrugged. 'I can't help it.'

'Evidently not.' Dora smiled properly this time. 'Now look,' she continued, 'are there any books you need? Magazines? Tell me what to bring you when I come next time.'

'There are just a few things . . .'

Now that Dora felt calmer and was over her first shock, the visit passed off pleasantly. 'I'll come to see you tomorrow,' she promised. 'And I'll bring the stuff you need.'

'Thank you.' Marcus frowned. 'Don't bring my mother, though,' he added. 'She gets so upset; it's bad for her to come. Convince her that her cold's turning to pneumonia or something, eh? And that the fog won't do her chest any good.'

Dora nodded. 'I'll try,' she promised. 'And tell you what — I'll bring the chess set in. You can thrash me.'

'Well, I don't think *you* ought to be gadding about London in your condition,' retorted Anna sniffily, when Dora remarked that the fog was very bad and that Anna's cold would certainly turn to bronchitis if she went out. 'And I'm sure he'll be upset if I don't visit.'

'He loves to see you, of course he does, but he wouldn't want you to make yourself ill.' Dora buttoned her coat and picked up the bagful of things for the invalid. 'I'll give him your love.'

'Yes, make sure you do.' And Anna, in a way somewhat relieved that she need not go to see her son, looked at her sister and realized that Dora understood. 'Give him my love,' she repeated. And picking up a pile of books and papers, she went into her little study and closed the door behind her.

* * *

Since Ralph had died, evidence of chronic mismanagement of the Challoner estate had been gradually coming to light. By November 1917 the solicitors had done their work, the auditors had been over all the books, and the entire estate had been made over, unconditionally, to Captain Challoner's widow. It was obvious that her inheritance was not altogether an unmixed blessing.

'It's worse than we thought.' Stephen looked up from a littered table in the dining room at Ashton Cross, turned over a handful of documents and sighed heavily. 'Much, much worse.'

'Terrible,' agreed Henry Lawrence. 'He's been in debt for years. And now, what with the death duties as well... It seems an intolerable imposition to demand such a tax from the widow of a man who served his country so well, but there it is.'

Dora, newly arrived back from London, looked from one elderly man to the other. 'I hadn't expected Ralph to be solvent,' she said calmly. 'I suppose I shall have to sell?'

'I don't know if it's quite as bad as that. We could mortgage a couple of the tenant farms, perhaps.' Stephen grimaced. 'That place! It's been like pouring money down a drain.'

He looked at his daughter, who was now huge in what he assumed were her final few weeks of pregnancy. 'You'll need a manager, Dora.'

'I have an excellent agent, thanks to my uncle.'

'Yes, yes, I dare say you have. But an agent doesn't have a personal interest. I was thinking of one of Henry's sons. James, perhaps?'

Henry nodded. 'Maybe. The poor chap's hardly fit yet, though. When he's a little stronger — well, we'll see.'

Dora sat down and turned over some sheets in a ledger. 'Will you stay at the Grange for a week or so, Papa?' she asked anxiously.

'Certainly, my dear.' Stephen smiled at her. 'Don't look at me like that,' he added. 'I wasn't about to dash back to Oxford and leave you with all this mess. We shall sort it out between us. Don't worry about it — that's bad for the child.'

James grew stronger. By the middle of November he had begun riding again, and once or twice a week he accompanied his father on his journeys around the estate. He doubted if he'd ever have the stamina to hunt again, but it was something to be alive, able to ride and to look upon the green English countryside. He knew how lucky he was. Then, one dreary afternoon, Dora visited him to offer him the position of manager of the Challoner estate.

It soon became obvious to her that James and Henry had already discussed the matter. But, all the same, James listened patiently, heard his cousin out. 'I can't accept your offer,' he said.

'But why?' Dora stared. 'Why don't you want it, James? I was almost sure, your father thought —'

'Thought what?'

'That you always intended to be a farmer.'

'I did. I do.' James shrugged. 'But all the same, I can't accept your proposal. Or at any rate, not as it stands.'

'Oh,' Dora sniffed. 'Then what *would* you accept?'

'Nothing, as your employee. I'd *buy* the land from you.'

'Buy?'

'Certainly.' James nodded. 'It's very good land. Run down and unproductive at present.... Don't look so annoyed — I know you've done wonders with it since you took control, but you must admit that it's still not producing half it could. It has enormous possibilities, though.'

'Suppose I agreed to sell. Where would you get the money to buy?'

'Ah, well — you'd have to wait for the money. In fact, you'd have to lend *me* some to buy in stock and machinery. But there are government grants available now; you might not have to wait too long to see a return. It would pay you in the end, you know.' He folded his arms. 'Dora, do think about it. You see, I'm not going to be a caretaker like my father. I'm going to farm my *own* land.' He looked at her. 'Well, cousin?'

'Well, James. We'll have to talk to my father and yours about it — discuss it with the old men. But I can tell you now that it's foolish to talk of buying and selling. I'll simply have to give you the place on the understanding that you'll pay me a dividend when you can.' She looked hard at him. 'You'd be terribly lonely up at the Grange, you know. You'd be all by yourself — and you've always been used to such a large family.'

'I'd thought of that. I'd wondered about getting married.'

'Really?' Dora laughed. 'Well, it's long overdue, I must say. I'd thought you were a confirmed old bachelor.'

'Well, that's just where you're wrong.'

'Evidently. Who is she? Someone I know?'

'Geraldine Drew. She's a great friend of Katherine. I've known her for years.'

'I know *her*.' Dora giggled. 'She's a very modern woman, you know. She's fearfully brainy and a staunch WSPU lady; were you aware of that?'

'I need a clever wife.' Now James laughed too. 'And I don't care about her political views. As it happens, I support the campaign for women's suffrage.'

'Do you?' Dora grinned. 'Well, this *is* a day of surprises. Oh, James, I'm very pleased for you. She's very nice, so I do hope she'll have you. When are you going to ask her?'

'I already have. Last May. She accepted like a shot, of course!'

'Oh, of course!' Dora nodded. 'Well — *haven't* you been secretive?'

He looked back at her, his dark eyes amused. 'Perhaps. But then, Dora, so have you. Are you going to confide in me, or leave me to guess what *you've* been up to?'

Dora blushed. 'I don't know what you mean,' she replied lightly. 'Shall we ring for some tea?'

November came and went, and still Dora's baby failed to make its appearance. She decided to remove herself to Oxford for Christmas. Her brother, on leave for a few days, had arrived there a day after she had, meaning to spend a few hours with his parents and sister before he travelled on to Cambridge. Together Anthony and Dora walked across the Parks.

'I may buy a small house here,' remarked Dora. 'I'd like to be near the two of them. To Mama, anyway. Oh, and to Papa. Do you know, Anthony, I've come to know him so much better than I did. When I lived at home, he took no notice of me whatsoever. But these past couple of years —'

'He's only just realized that you've grown up.' Anthony grinned. 'He never said anything to *me* until I was fifteen, when he observed that I'd inherited some of his brains. Before that, I didn't exist. So you couldn't have expected him to pay any attention to you when you were a mere child. He simply doesn't see *children*.'

'That's not so. He always adored Marcus.'

'Oh, *everyone* adores Marcus. Marcus could charm a snake or a crocodile!'

'That's true. Anthony, have you been to see him?'

'Yes, several times. He's getting better, isn't he?'

'I think so.' Dora sighed. 'It's so sad, though.'

'He'll come to terms with it. I honestly don't think it will make much difference to him in the end. I tell you, Dora, the nurses in that hospital — well, when I was visiting, there was this one VAD, and talk about flirting! She was all over him, and I thought it was the soldiers who were supposed to fall in love with their nurses, not the other way about.' Anthony sighed. 'It's Anna who's suffering most.'

'Yes,' Dora nodded. 'Yes, I suppose it is.'

Anthony sat down on a convenient park bench and motioned Dora to sit down beside him. 'Why don't you come back to Cambridge with me for a few days?' he asked. 'Miriam would love to see you, and so would the children.'

'Oh, Anthony, really! I'm about to have a baby. I can't go traipsing all over the country in my condition.'

'You're not going into labour just yet, are you?' Anthony grinned at her. 'I'd guess about February — March at the latest.'

'Whatever do you mean?'

'Oh, come on, Dora! I'd decided long ago that this baby can't be Ralph's child.'

'How do you know?' Dora narrowed her eyes. 'Did Miriam tell you?'

'No. She doesn't betray confidences. I'm just guessing.' Anthony could see that his sister was tired, so he put his arm around her waist and let her rest her head on his shoulder. 'Will you tell me who the father is?' he asked. 'You don't have to, of course.'

Dora shrugged. 'Tim Atherton,' she murmured.

'Tim? Oh, I see.'

'You knew anyway.'

'I didn't *know*. But I knew you'd seen him here a year or two ago. And that you'd known him for ages. And that he always liked you — rather more than liked you.

'So when I happened to meet him in London earlier this year, I told him Ralph was dead. And I said I was sure that you'd be pleased to see him, if he wanted to visit you.'

'Oh, you did, did you?'

'And it seems I was right.'

'Yes, you were.' Dora, unable to decide whether Anthony's blatant interference in her personal life made her angry or otherwise, looked down at her gloved hands. 'Yes, you were quite right.'

'That's a relief. Have you heard from him?'

'No. I think he must have been killed some time last June, otherwise he'd certainly have written to me. I can't talk about it any more, Anthony; I shall start to cry. Can we go home now?'

'When is the baby due, Dora?' Dorcas and her younger daughter were sitting together in the warm drawing room of the Summertown house, Dorcas with her everlasting needlework upon her lap. Naturally, she had been sewing for Dora's baby ever since she had known it was expected.

'You'll be so happy to have Ralph's child,' she continued placidly. 'I think, though, that since you must be overdue now, you ought to consider going to see a doctor. There's a very good man here. And I remember, when I was your age —'

'The baby isn't overdue.' Dora laid her hand on her mother's, staying her needle. 'It's not ready to be born yet. I'm just rather large for my dates. I shan't have the baby until February or March.'

'March? But, Dora my dear, Ralph —'

Dora bit her lip. 'Put your sewing down, Mama,' she said. 'Listen to me.'

* * *

Dora stayed in Oxford over Christmas, glad of her parents' undemanding company. The New Year was ushered in by dull, cold, sullen weather which exactly suited the mood of the nation, for it looked now as if Germany might well win the war. After all, where were the men to come from to defeat the enemy? Soon, boys and middle-aged men would be sent off to France.

There was severe food rationing, which added to the general atmosphere of gloom and misery. The brave and buoyant spirit of 1914 would never be conjured up again.

In January Dora went back to Herefordshire. Geraldine and James had married during the Christmas season and moved into the Grange.

'You're definitely the master here now, James,' she teased, as she looked at the clutter of male belongings littered all over the house. Of an untidy family, James was by far the most slovenly, and Dora's pretty drawing room was now embellished with piles of books, heaps of papers, half-unpacked trunks and even discarded outdoor clothing. Mrs Johnson muttered darkly about another housemaid being needed, and why hadn't Mr Lawrence seen fit to engage a valet?

'Yes, I'm the master. Just you remember it, Dora.' James, who had just come in, stood with his back to the fire. His hands behind his back and his legs braced wide apart, he gazed about his old enemy's domain with an irrepressibly self-satisfied air.

'He looks *so* like a squire now, doesn't he, Geraldine?' Dora smiled archly at James's wife. 'So very patriarchal, somehow.'

'Oh, indeed he does.' Geraldine giggled. 'I'm quite afraid of him. I think, though, that he ought to move away from his hearth . . .'

'So do I.'

'What?' James frowned at the two women, causing them to giggle even more. Geraldine looked at her husband. 'Really, dear, you ought to move,' she said. 'Your lovely new riding boots —'

'— are getting just a little singed,' added Dora. 'James, you'll ignite!'

James, realizing at last that he was about to catch fire, jumped smartly away from the blaze. He grinned ruefully at his cousin and his wife. A rich smell of roasting leather filled the room.

Chapter Twenty-Two

TIM WALKED UP THE GRAVEL sweep and met Dora as she came towards him from the other side of the house, back from half an hour's walk in the feeble January sunshine. He took in every detail of her appearance; he even noticed that she was carrying some hazel wands, slender twigs from which long yellow catkins hung.

And he realized, now, that it had been a mistake to come. She had not smiled when she'd seen him. In fact, she'd looked horrified, almost afraid. He scuffed the gravel with his foot, scowling down at the stones.

Dora, unaware that her expression appeared to be one of mingled terror and disgust, stood still, astonished, staring at him. 'Oh, Tim!' she managed to articulate at last. 'I thought you were dead.'

'Dead? Don't be silly.' Tim grimaced. 'Why ever did you think I was dead?'

Dora frowned and wondered if she were imagining things. Her heart was thumping, banging almost audibly against her ribs. She could hear her own harsh breathing, was aware that her hands were shaking and that perspiration was prickling her back. 'Where have you been, then?' she demanded weakly. 'You never wrote to me — and I've been so worried about you.'

He sniffed. 'You didn't write to *me*.'

'I did! I did write to you. Half a dozen times, a dozen; maybe more than that. I told you all about the —'

'I've had no letters from you.'

'Well, I wrote them.' Anxiously, Dora looked at his sullen

face. 'Where have you come from just now?'

'A hospital in Surrey.'

'Surrey?' Dora stared at him. 'You've come from Surrey? This morning?'

'Well, I was discharged yesterday afternoon. I caught the eleven thirty from Paddington last night. There was a branch line train from Great Malvern in the early hours.'

'Oh, I see.' It now crossed Dora's mind that it was totally absurd to be standing out in the cold discussing the details of his journey, when all she wanted to do was throw herself into Tim's arms and cover his face with kisses; to tell him how impossible it was to express her delight that he'd come back to her. If, indeed, he *had* come back . . .

She fingered her hazel twigs and blinked rapidly, trying desperately to think of something else to say. But the conviction that this *must* be a hallucination, a figment of her disturbed imagination, was still growing.

Indeed, she'd read about things like this — about wives and mothers seeing apparitions of their dead husbands and sons. There was even some woman in Hereford who gave seances, apparently calling up the spirits of the dead. Tim must surely be such a chimera. For surely, if he was real, she'd be hugging him?

'Have you had any breakfast?' she heard herself ask this ghost of her dead lover.

'No. Just some coffee at the station in Worcester.' He took a step towards her, causing her, in spite of herself, to back away from him. 'Dora, I — I know perfectly well that I shouldn't have come here,' he said. 'But I had to see you once more. I'm well aware that I forced you into something that you didn't want. So I needed to apologize.'

He shrugged helplessly. 'I've thought and thought of you,' he added. 'I've been tortured by the memory of how badly I behaved.'

'The memory of how you behaved?' Dora shook her head, completely mystified. 'What on earth do you mean?'

'I didn't think you'd want to see me again.' He sounded close to tears. 'But I couldn't write, or telephone. Not about something like this.' He shook his head. 'I'm sorry, Dora.

Sorry.' He turned away to go.

'Tim!' The sound of her voice made him stop. 'How *could* you think I didn't want to see you?' she cried. 'Oh, Tim, how could you think that?'

He said nothing. And now Dora clasped her hands together, twisted the fingers round each other in a gesture of absolute bewilderment.

'Why have you been in hospital?' she asked. 'Were you ill? Wounded? What happened to you? Are you going back to France?' She wanted to touch him but there was a kind of barrier all around him through which she felt powerless to break. The nightmare intensified and her idle daydreams of an ecstatic reunion were shattered indeed.

'No, I shan't go back to France.' Still Tim spoke in the same dead monotone. 'I'm a regular army soldier, though, so I shall have to stay in the service at least until the war is over. They'll find me something to do.' He looked down at the gravel on the drive. 'Office work in London, I expect.'

He was standing less than a yard away from her, hands hanging loosely at his sides. Then, still not looking at her, he began to fiddle with his cuffs. Dora, by now quite convinced that she was in the grip of some awful dream, some pregnant woman's hysteria — for she'd read about that, too — noticed the embroidered crowns on his epaulettes and gabbled some nonsense about his promotion.

'They had to promote me,' he muttered drearily. 'There wasn't a single major left in my division, and I was the senior captain.' He glanced at her stomach, but looked away again. 'Dora, is there any chance that the child could be mine?'

'It must be! I've worked everything out, it must be yours, there's no possibility at all that it could be anyone else's.' She tried to focus her eyes upon him and willed him to look at her, but he wouldn't. 'Are you angry?' she asked.

'Angry? Of course I'm not angry. Should I be? What about you?'

'I'm delighted. Oh, Tim, I've never been so happy!' Dora's eyes had filled with tears now. 'I lie in bed at night hugging our baby. I'm absolutely delighted that I'm going to have your child, for this will be a love child if any baby ever deserved that name. I just wonder, though — is it dangerous to have one's first baby at thirty-six?'

She felt her self-control dissolving into nothing and knew she was going to burst into tears at any moment. At last, Tim looked up and met her eyes.

'Dora. Oh, my darling Dora, don't cry! Please don't cry!' He almost fell towards her. He caught her in his arms and held her so tightly that she felt her shoulder-blades dig into her back.

He was no hallucination. Holding her fast, he was sobbing into her hair; she could feel tears on her face and knew that they were both Tim's and her own.

They stood together on the gravel drive for five minutes or more, simply hugging each other, unable to say anything, but at last understanding one another perfectly.

Dora could smell a faint odour of medication on Tim's clothes, the unmistakeable scent of hospitals, and she wondered what horrible experience he'd been through to have ended up in an English nursing home.

She examined his face and was relieved to see that, although there were deep lines of stress and anxiety across his forehead and around his eyes, there was no sign of any visible wound.

'Let me go, Tim.' Feeling a little less unreal now, Dora realized that her feet were aching and that her back was demanding that she sit down.

'Let you go? Why?'

'Tim, I'm pregnant! I can't stand still for any length of time. My ankles, you see —'

'Oh, yes, I see.' He relaxed his hold on her very slightly but still kept his arm around her waist. Together they walked slowly into the house, through the hallway and into the warm drawing room.

'I suppose I could have tried to find out what had happened to you,' said Dora, relaxing gratefully upon the sofa. 'But I didn't dare. I told myself that you were dead. I couldn't allow myself to hope, you see. And I decided that when your baby arrived I'd love it for your sake.'

She looked at him solicitously. 'What happened to you?' she asked. 'Why were you in hospital?'

'Oh, I wasn't badly hurt. I had a gunshot wound through

my left lung, which was healing well but then I caught pneumonia and that nearly finished me off. Dora, don't move away from me!'

'I'm not. I just have cramp — let me stretch my legs. That's better.' Dora took his hand in hers. 'Oh, my poor love, you look so different. Ten years older, at least — and you're so thin.'

'You look marvellous.' Tim touched the mound of baby in Dora's lap. 'You're pleased about the child?' he asked. 'Truly? You're not just making the best of a disaster?'

'It's *not* a disaster.' Dora beamed at him. 'Darling, it's a miracle! Oh, I've been so happy, in a quiet kind of way — but now I could sing for joy. Did I stare very much when you first saw me?'

'You looked perfectly appalled — as if you'd seen the devil himself.'

'You looked so solemn. Not at all glad to see me.'

'I thought you'd have come to hate me.'

'Hate you? Why should I hate you?'

'Because of what I did to you. You'd just been widowed and I practically raped you. You can't have forgotten.' Tim shook his head. 'Oh, Dora, I'm so sorry. I never meant it to happen like that.'

'You're not to be sorry. Oh, Tim, you didn't rape me. Nothing like it. You took me to bed and made love to me, and by the end of that evening I was in love with you. Didn't you know that?'

'No, Dora. You never said so.'

'Well, I'm telling you now. You must believe me.' Anxiously, she shook his arm. 'You *do* believe me, don't you?'

'I think I do.' Ruefully, Tim smiled at her. 'Yes, I do believe you. I don't think you'd lie to me.'

'No, I wouldn't.' Dora leaned across the sofa and kissed him. 'I'm the one who ought to be sorry for my behaviour, not you. Now, Tim, will you give me a proper kiss?'

'You will marry me, won't you, Dora?' he asked, five minutes later.

'Of course I will.' She looked up at him and smiled. 'There's nothing I'd like better, you must know that.'

'I've nothing to offer you. No money, no home. Darling, it will be a very bad bargain for you. All your friends will think you're mad if you become my wife.'

'Will they?' Dora looked into Tim's mild grey eyes, so different from Ralph's hard blue ones. 'All the same, I shall marry you. People can think what they please.'

He smiled back at her. 'You're absolutely beautiful, you know,' he said. 'You look lovely, and just now you smell of milk and new bread. And talking of new bread —'

'You haven't had any breakfast! You must be starving.'

'Well, I could eat something — '

'Help me up.'

Tim took Dora's hand and led her into the hallway. Just then, Mrs Johnson came out of the servants' corridor on her way to look for Dora or Geraldine to ask for the day's instructions.

'Can we have some breakfast, please?' Dora beamed at the housekeeper. 'A tray, I think, in my study. Could you send Sarah in with something?'

Mrs Johnson recovered from the surprise of seeing Tim far more quickly than Dora had. She nodded to her mistress and smiled at Captain — no, now he was Major — Atherton. 'I'm glad to see you looking well, Sir,' she ventured boldly.

And, grinning to herself, she went back down the passage to look for Sarah and tell her the good news.

Tim and Dora married in decent obscurity, as soon as the banns allowed. The bride went to church in all-enveloping black, as quietly as a pregnant widow who should have been thoroughly ashamed of herself ought to have done.

Glaring severely at the couple in front of him, at the vastly pregnant woman and the vacant-looking Guards officer who kept his arm around her waist in the *most* unseemly fashion, the rector laid particular emphasis on the fact that matrimony had been ordained by God in order that man might avoid sin.

But, all the same, he left the church feeling as if he'd been addressing a pair of halfwits, and he complained to his wife about it all afternoon.

'Of course, you know who *she* was, don't you?' asked his wife. 'Before she married poor Mr Challoner, that is.'

'No.' The rector sniffed. 'Who was she?'

His wife leaned over and whispered. 'It's true,' she added. 'Mr Challoner's valet told me.'

'Hmm.' The rector grimaced. 'I see.'

His wife picked up her knitting. 'Well, after all, what can one expect?' she continued, as she plained and purled, knitting her righteous indignation into the ribbing of a khaki sock. 'Blood will out. But as for Mr Atherton — well! His family must have been livid. No wonder none of them came. Who were the witnesses?'

'Some of Mrs Challoner's — I mean, Mrs Atherton's — cousins. Miss Lawrence and her brother, and his wife. *They* all looked as if they'd just come in from the fields.'

Tim had to go back to London almost immediately after the wedding and, to Dora's surprise and chagrin, he refused point blank to allow her to go with him. 'I can stay with Anna,' she had cried, distressed.

'I'd really prefer you to stay here.' Tim fastened his case and turned to look at her. 'I know you're safe in the country,' he added. 'I can think of you while I'm away and know exactly where you are. I'll come back as often as I can; it should be possible to get a thirty-six hour pass now and again. Darling, stay with James and Geraldine.'

'Oh, very well. For the time being.' Dora attempted a brave little smile. 'Tim, when the war's over, can we live in Oxford?' she asked. 'I do so love Oxford.'

'Can we think about that later?' Tim patted her shoulder. 'After the baby's born?'

'All right. But I can't stay here indefinitely, you know. And I do want to be with you.'

'Be patient for a while. Wait for the baby. Wait for the war to be over; it can't be long now, whichever way it goes. Germany's ready for a spring offensive, so this year really ought to finish it.'

'The baby will come soon.' Dora frowned at her husband. 'But *I* think the war will go on for ever.'

Dora, now fatter and more ungainly than ever, sat about the housing missing Tim. She had no one to talk to, for James and Geraldine were out all the time, either riding about the estate in the bitter February cold, or locked up with the land agent for hour after hour.

When Tim had returned to Flanders the previous May, Dora convinced herself that she'd never see him again. But now that he had returned, as it were, from the dead, she had such a need of him that she felt it as a physical ache deep inside her, and she often found herself in tears for no obvious reason.

'How do you feel this morning, Dora?' Geraldine drew back her cousin's curtains on a fine sunny day. 'Oh, look,' she exclaimed. 'The first snowdrops out in the shrubbery.'

Dora heaved herself out of bed. 'I wonder if it will be today?' she asked. 'I do wish it would be. I can hardly drag myself about, I feel so bloated.'

'When is Tim's next leave?'

'I don't know exactly. He thought he might be able to manage a forty-eight hour pass for this weekend. Oh, Geraldine, I do wish I could be in London. Why doesn't he want me there?'

'He doesn't want you to be caught in an air raid, that's why. You wouldn't want to be killed by a bomb, would you? Not when you have so much to live for?'

'I suppose not. Oh, Geraldine, I wish you hadn't mentioned air raids. What if Tim's hurt?' Dora's eyes filled with tears again and she gulped.

The baby was born that same day. She took her time coming into the world, but she did not cause her mother any great degree of suffering. After the delivery Dora was strong enough to sit up and demand to see the child.

'Such blue eyes! Neither my husband nor I have blue eyes.' Dora smiled down at the baby, who glared back at her and clenched her little red fists; she was evidently offended to have been expelled from the cosy security in which she'd been cosseted for so long. 'And she's so fair. Her skin's so pale, and I can hardly see her eyebrows.'

'I expect her eyes will change.' The midwife wiped the baby's face and then unfastened the mother's nightdress. 'Now, Mrs Atherton, you are going to feed her yourself, aren't you?'

'Well, of course —'

'Hold her close to you, then. See, *she* knows what to do.

Take her hand, that's right. There!'

'I want to call her Helen,' Dora said firmly.

'Call her what?' Tim was holding his daughter close to his chest, where she dribbled against his khaki shirt, crossly rooting for the nourishment which wasn't there. 'Helen, did you say?'

'Yes.'

Dora looked at him, daring him to object. But he merely nodded, not taking his eyes from his little daughter's face. 'That's fine by me,' he said. 'Helen Atherton. Sounds very English.'

'It does, doesn't it?' Dora leaned back against the cushions on the sofa and sighed contentedly. 'When d'you have to go back?' she asked.

'Not until Tuesday.' Tim rocked the baby and patted her back. 'Oh, Dora, she's so pretty. Aren't you clever?'

'She's much more like you than like me. She has your eyes, and she'll be fair, like you. Do you want to give her back?'

'Is she hungry?'

'Not yet. She yells when she is.'

'Then I'll hold her a while longer.' He wrapped the baby more tightly in her shawl and laid her against his shoulder, then he got up and began to walk about the room. 'You have a rival now, Dora,' he said, grinning at his wife. 'Another woman, younger and altogether more bewitching than you are. You've lost your hold over me!'

'Have I?'

'Oh, yes! I really wanted a daughter, you know.' He stroked the baby's head. '*She* won't be cruel to me,' he murmured. '*She* won't be like her mother was. *She'll* look up to me and think that I'm God Almighty; I shall see to that. I shan't have any nonsense. She's going to know who's in charge.'

'Oh, Tim, don't.'

'Don't what?'

'Say such things.' Dora felt the tears coming again. She was still extraordinarily weepy; the slightest little thing set her off.

'I was only teasing you.' Tim walked back to her and laid the child in her arms. 'I was only joking. Here she is, all yours, to do with as you please.'

'We'll have a boy next time,' said Dora, unfastening her

nightdress. 'Someone for me to love, who'll look up to *me*. And you'll need someone to play cricket with in your old age.'

'Oh, Dora, I *loathe* cricket.' Tim laughed. 'Play up, play the game and all that nonsense — Christ knows I had enough of that at school. I intend to spend my declining years just with you. And now, hadn't we better take you back to bed?'

Helen and her mother did well. Except for the fact that her husband was away from her most of the time, Dora was perfectly happy. Then Tim managed to arrange a week's duty at the barracks in Hereford, and he was able to stay at the Grange for a whole seven days.

'We'll have to go and see the old girl some time.' Tim rolled on to his back and stared up at the bedroom ceiling. 'God, what a pain that'll be. We'll go when Richard isn't there, though. I don't see why you should have to suffer *his* company as well as my mother's.'

'Why don't you want me to meet your brother?'

'Oh, Dora, he's a bore. All he's interested in is his money. And his wife's a fright. He only married her for her twenty thousand, and he's spent his entire married life regretting it.'

Dora laughed. 'Well, if your relations are so awful, why do we have to visit any of them?' she asked.

'Because if we don't, they'll come here. Or at any rate, my mother will. So, when you're feeling stronger, we'll motor over; if I can lay my hands on some petrol, that is. And you can make the old harridan's acquaintance.'

He took Dora in his arms and kissed her. 'How long will it be before I can force myself upon you again?'

'Force yourself upon me?' Dora giggled. 'You can do that any time.'

'Now? Now this minute?'

'If you like.'

'Excellent!' Tim began to unfasten the buttons on Dora's nightdress. 'You're all milky,' he murmured. 'All soft and milky. Lovely.'

As he was about to kiss her, there was a sudden squeal from across the landing. As if she'd been electrocuted Dora sat bolt upright in bed and pushed Tim away.

'I must go and feed her,' she cried, reaching for her dressing gown. She dashed off to the nursery leaving Tim in no doubt about where his wife's current priorities lay.

* * *

They had a pleasant drive from Hereford to Evesham, for their route took them through that part of the green English countryside which is full of fruit orchards and rolling meadowland. Dora was pleasantly surprised to discover that Tim was a good driver; his technique did not include such refinements as swearing, gear crunching and sudden, terrifying bursts of speed which sprayed the car with grit and mud, and which had been a hallmark of Ralph's driving.

'It's a pretty house.' Dora smiled at Tim. 'I always think Cotswold stone is attractive, but this place — well, it's like something out of a fairy tale.'

'It's a decent enough pile, I suppose.' Tim helped Dora out of the car. 'Watch your step now; lots of loose paving stones.'

Dora gazed around at the long, rambling building, at the elaborately gabled roof and the dozens of leaded window panes, all of which sparkled in the spring sunshine. 'Is that a dovecote?' she demanded. 'That little round building over there with the thatched roof?'

'Oh, that stupid thing. Yes, it is.' Tim grimaced and tried to pull his wife towards the door. 'Look, Dora, we haven't come here to make an offer for the place. Could we perhaps go inside and see my mother, and get it all over with?'

'Don't be so miserable, Tim.' Dora took Tim's hand and pinched his fingers. 'She can't be that bad.'

'You wait and see. You just wait and see.'

Letting themselves in through a side door in the stable yard, Dora and Tim walked into a stone-flagged passage, the walls of which were covered with murky oil paintings. There were so many of them that the pale blue paintwork behind them was almost totally obscured.

'Family likenesses,' remarked Dora. 'Oh, Tim — now this man here, he's *you*! Was he your grandfather? An uncle?'

'Oh, God!' Exasperated, Tim grabbed Dora's wrist and practically dragged her along the length of the corridor. Reaching a panelled oak door he flung it open and walked into the room beyond.

'Ah — you've come.' From one of the armchairs near the fireside came a weak, female voice in which there was a very noticeable note of reproach.

'Yes, Mama, I've come. I've brought Dora to meet you.' Tim hauled Dora, whose wrist he still held, into a patch of sunlight, thus bringing her face to face with the woman sitting in a wing chair by the fender.

'Didn't Somers let you in?' Ignoring Dora completely, Lady Atherton looked enquiringly at her son. 'Didn't he hear the bell? That man's becoming so idle — '

'I didn't ring.' Tim scowled at his mother. 'This is *Dora*, Mama. My *wife*.' Sitting down on a sofa opposite his mother, Tim pulled Dora down beside him.

The old woman looked at her new daughter-in-law. Her eyes travelled up and down Dora's body, as if making an inventory, but she said nothing.

Disconcerted, the new bride looked back at her. Her mother-in-law's features were, Dora thought, so like her son's that it was uncanny that the man's should be so good-natured while the woman's positively exuded ill-humour. Lady Atherton's large grey eyes were sharp and spiteful, her well-shaped mouth was set in a line of discontent and her whole deportment radiated disapproval.

'I hope you are well, Lady Atherton,' began Dora hesitantly.

'Do you, indeed.' Tim's mother continued her inspection of Dora's face and figure. 'I knew your father, you know,' she announced at last. 'I must say, it was obvious to me right from the beginning that there was something not quite — well — normal about *him*.' She fixed her eyes steadily upon Dora. 'And how right I was!'

Dora stared. 'Oh, really?'

'Mmm.' Lady Atherton arranged the folds of her silk dress across her knees and continued to gaze at her son's wife. 'Tell me, my dear,' she said, managing to turn the endearment into an insult, 'what does Stephen do these days?'

'Do?' Dora frowned at her. 'My father is a professor of Greek,' she replied. 'At Oxford.'

'Still a teacher.' Lady Atherton nodded. 'Perhaps he needs

the money,' she murmured, as if to herself. 'Such a shame about it all,' she added in the same, barely audible monotone. 'And Miss Marlowe was rich, very rich. Now all that money will go to her daughter.'

Wondering why he said nothing and made no attempt to rescue her from his horrible old mother, Dora turned to look at Tim. She observed, to her dismay, that his eyes were closed. Lying back against the cushions, his arms folded, he appeared to be asleep.

And still his mother talked on. 'Of course, when Sir Michael died, I never even considered remarriage,' she continued relentlessly. 'One simply didn't, not if one were past thirty. Unless, of course, one were a certain type of person.'

'A certain type of person?' faltered Dora.

'Yes.' Lady Atherton smiled, a ghastly, thin-lipped smile which stretched the white skin on her thin face and illuminated her pale eyes. 'How old are you, my dear?' she asked. 'Thirty? You can't be more than thirty-five.'

Dora decided that she had had enough of such ill-bred cheek. She rose to her feet. 'It's been very interesting to meet you, Lady Atherton,' she said. 'I'm sorry our visit must be so short.'

She nudged Tim's foot with her shoe. He opened his eyes. 'We're going now,' she told him, and his grin informed her that he hadn't been asleep at all.

He got up, stretched and yawned. He walked over to his mother and kissed the powdery surface of her cheek. Then, he strode out of the room, leaving Dora to follow him.

'Well?' he demanded, as they drove out of the stable yard.

Dora grimaced. 'I thought we would at least be offered a cup of tea,' she replied. 'And she might have asked after Helen.'

'Poor Dora. Were you expecting grandmotherly gushings and a sackful of presents for our little darling?'

'Well, no. But really!'

'We shan't go there again.' Tim turned the car into the road. 'God knows, I'm not especially welcome at home; they were all glad to get rid of *me*.'

'Why?' Dora looked at him, puzzled. 'What have you done?'

'Oh, it's more what I *haven't* done! I was lazy at school, hopeless at games, and I hated hunting. I didn't give a toss about politics, so my father decided very early on that I had no moral fibre.' Tim grinned. 'Later on I was always getting involved with unsuitable women who had no money.

'Now, my brother is *quite* different. He's a model landlord, he married inherited wealth and *his* morals — and their fibre — are above reproach. My parents already had one perfectly good son, you see, so when I came along I was an expense and an embarrassment.' Tim laughed. 'And I'm still an embarrassment.'

'Are you? *I* don't see that you are.'

'Don't you? Well, darling, the dissolute younger son has crowned his inglorious career by marrying the squire's by-blow. At any rate, that's how the people *my* family know will see it. We'll be the talk of the bridge parties for the next couple of months and then we'll both be consigned to outer darkness.'

Tim looked at his wife. 'I hope you didn't think you were marrying into the upper echelons of the landed gentry and that you might become a real titled lady one day?'

'No, but —'

'Just as well. My brother's very healthy and so are his two sons. Oh, forget about my Mama, Dora. She's just a nasty old woman. *Your* dear little mother is a real lady, and she's worth a million baronets' widows.'

Dora tucked the ends of her hair under her hat. 'What *shall* we do, Tim?' she asked. 'When the war is over?'

'Depends very much on who wins.'

'Supposing the Allies win.'

'What an optimist! Dora, the Germans are bringing all their crack troops over from the Eastern Front. Now that they've dealt with the Russians, they're going to thrash us and the Frogs. This time next month, the Jerries will be strolling through the streets of London.'

'It won't come to that.'

'Won't it? You'll see.' Tim changed gear and accelerated along the main road towards Worcester. 'We could buy a smallish house in Oxford, I suppose,' he said. 'I was left a bit of cash a year or two back, which might just stretch to a cottage or something. You must invest any money you receive from James for Helen, of course.'

He glanced at Dora. 'We're going to be pretty hard up, I'm afraid. I did warn you.'

'Oh, Tim. We're not exactly destitute! I have the money from that tenant farm we sold. And I'm sure James will be a success, so I'll have a steady income soon.'

'I must get a job,' declared Tim. 'I can't allow my wife to keep me.'

'You have a job. You're a soldier.'

'A wounded soldier. I doubt if I'll be passed fit to stay in the army after the war is over.'

'What will you do, then?'

'I'll have a word with John Harley. D'you think he'd help?'

'I'm sure he would. But do you want to become a wine merchant?'

'No. What else can I do, though?'

'I don't know. But we'll look around Oxford, shall we? We'll find a house there just for the three of us, and we'll make ourselves a home.'

* * *

'She was horrible to me, Anthony.' Dora, walking through the shrubbery at the Grange with her brother, frowned. 'She didn't say anything directly insulting, but she made it perfectly clear that I wasn't acceptable.'

'Poor Dolly.' Anthony laughed. 'Oh, people can't resist a little dig or two, can they?'

Dora sniffed. 'Does anyone ever make remarks to you?' she asked.

'About our family?' Dora's brother nodded. 'Oh, yes. There've been one or two occasions when I've wanted to crawl into a corner and cry. Once I hit a man.'

'I can't hit Lady Atherton.'

'But you can avoid her.' Anthony put his arm around his sister's shoulders. 'You're far too sensitive, Dora,' he added. 'You and Anna, you both let it bother you and you shouldn't.'

He looked around him, at the beauty of the spring blossom and the splendour of the maple trees. 'Do you know, Dora, it's so pleasant to be able to visit my sister and her family? And

I'm glad to see you happy at last.'

'At last?'

'Yes. Oh, I was so pleased when bloody Challoner snuffed it. I hated him. Dolly, is it very tactless of me to say that?'

Dora shrugged. 'I hated him myself in the end,' she admitted. She grinned at Anthony. 'Do you remember that time you hit *him*?' she asked. 'You were very brave. He was so much bigger than you were.'

'I lost my temper and went for his knees. God, that was a mistake! He thrashed me; I've never had such a hiding. I couldn't go out for a fortnight and the children screamed at the sight of me.'

Anthony rubbed his cheek thoughtfully. 'My teeth on this side still rattle,' he said.

Chapter Twenty-Three

'WHERE ARE YOU GOING, DEAR?' Hesitantly, Anna touched Marcus's arm, trying not to notice or to mind that he instinctively pulled away from her.

'Out.' Marcus would not look at her. 'For a walk.'

'Shall I come with you?'

'No.' Marcus pulled on his gloves. 'No, I want to be by myself.' And, shaking his mother off, he went out of the house, down the steps and into the street. Soon he was out of the quiet road where he lived and was walking down Highgate Hill.

By the time he reached the station he felt better. It was a relief to be out of the house, away from his mother and her constant solicitude and fussing.

He paid his fare and walked on to the platform to wait for the train. A little girl, hand in hand with her nurse, looked up at him and her small face puckered in fear. Embarrassed, the nanny pulled the child away.

But Marcus was used to being stared at. He'd been gawped at all his life and now the fact that the stares were of pity, horror or even disgust, didn't particularly bother him. He caught the train into central London, then walked the rest of the way.

The weak February sunshine filled the flat, the sitting room of which was already lit up by the darting reflections from the river. Hearing the bell ring, Caroline, who had just arrived home from work, went to the door. She opened it and stared at her visitor, recognition and shock together only too apparent on her face. 'Marcus?' she began hesitantly.

'Yes, I'm afraid it *is* me.' Marcus looked levelly at Caroline, daring her to flinch, to cry, to faint — to express revulsion or horror. 'I haven't come to pester you, though,' he continued. 'I just wanted to see you for a few minutes, that's all.'

'Come in.' Caroline stood aside to let him enter. 'Come in, sit down. I'll make us some coffee.'

'Don't go to any trouble. I shan't stay long.'

'It's no trouble, I was going to have some anyway.'

'In that case —'

'Take your coat off.' Nervously, Caroline hovered around her visitor, unable to decide whether to help him off with his coat or to let him take it off himself. 'Your mother wrote to mine,' she added. 'She told us what had happened to you.'

'Ah.' Marcus gave her his coat and scarf. 'So you were prepared?'

'Yes.' Not for this, though, thought Caroline. I wasn't prepared for this, this total destruction, this awful mutilation. 'Yes,' she repeated, quietly. 'I was prepared.'

'So it's not such a shock. That's maybe just as well.'

She had not seen Marcus for more than six months, not since his last leave, and her memories were of him standing in the sunshine of Regent's Park, laughing and running across the grass — a young, beautiful creature still unmarked by the war.

She had written to him, of course, but in his reply to her first letter, on a postcard obviously dictated to a nurse, he had told her not to come to the hospital, and she had not dared to defy him. He had not written again. 'Marcus, why wouldn't you let me visit you in hospital?' she asked. 'I've been so worried about you, so anxious. And I've —'

'I would have thought it was perfectly obvious why I wouldn't let you visit me.' Marcus took off his gloves, exposing hands which were now a pair of bent, reddened claws. He leaned back in his chair, deliberately letting the harsh light from the window fall upon his face. 'I should have thought it was only natural that I wouldn't wish to see you. Do you mind if I smoke?'

'No, of course not.' Caroline glanced at his hands. 'There are some spills on the mantelpiece, shall I —'

'I can manage, thank you.'

Caroline made herself look at him. His hair had grown again and was now lying around his ears and framing his face; it was far too long to satisfy Army regulations. Then she studied his face.

The right hand side of it was comparatively unmarked. But she saw, with a shudder, that the left side of it around the temple and cheek was hideous. The skin was like pink, smooth rubber, and in healing it had pulled his mouth to one side, making him look as if he were sneering. Perhaps he was.

He knew what she was thinking. 'It's worse on my back,' he said blandly. 'And not much better on my arms.' He inhaled deeply, letting the resulting ash from his cigarette drop down his shirt front and scatter on the floor. 'Mustard gas, you know,' he added casually. 'And a few incendiary bombs thrown in for good measure.'

'Marcus, don't —'

'Don't what?'

'Talk like that.'

'Why? Don't you want to know about it? Everyone else does. Everyone else wants all the gory details . . .'

Caroline went to sit on the arm of his chair. 'Are you still in a lot of pain?' she asked.

Marcus shrugged. 'In quite enough for a sensitive soul like me to put up with.' He laughed mirthlessly. 'Oh, I can take aspirins if it gets too bad.'

'Oh.'

He looked past her, out of the window. 'Not going to cry, are you?' he asked lightly. 'I don't think I can stand another weeping session. My mother, my aunt, my grandmother, even my father —'

'I shan't cry.' Caroline ached to put her arms around him, to hug and comfort him, but she didn't want to offend him by offering pity. She racked her brains for something to say. 'Marcus, I still love you,' she ventured at last.

'Do you?' He stubbed out his cigarette. 'Well, old thing, that's frightfully decent of you. Very noble indeed, I must say.'

Such bitterness brought tears to her eyes. 'Oh, Marcus,' she began. 'You mustn't —'

'I mustn't what?'

'Be so unkind to me. Look, darling —'

She rose from her perch on the arm of his chair and knelt on the floor in front of him. She looked into his face, trying not to mind that his wide grey eyes were now staring at her from a mess of raw flesh, that his eyelids were swollen and without lashes, that his eyebrows were unpleasant tufts of gingerish hairs growing at odd angles.

'My dear, dear Marcus,' she said beseechingly, 'my darling, listen to me. I know that you think your injuries must disgust me; but believe me, once and for all, when I tell you that they don't. I'm not repelled. I'm not appalled by the sight of you, I don't feel sick when I look at your face.

'I hate the men who did this to you. I could weep when I remember what you once were, but how you look now makes no difference to what I feel for you. I love you. I've loved you since I was — oh, fifteen, maybe even before that.' Carefully, she touched his hand. 'Don't you understand?' she whispered.

Marcus blinked. 'That was a splendid speech, Caro,' he muttered. 'Real oratory, complete with all the rhetorical tricks.'

'Oh, stop it. Stop it!' Caroline glared at him. For a few seconds more she knelt there, at a loss, but then she made up her mind. Reaching out to him, she tugged at his sleeve. 'Marcus,' she commanded, 'come to bed.'

'What?' He glowered at her. 'Oh, don't be ridiculous,' he muttered, turning away.

'Come to bed!' Caroline got up and stamped her foot, then she let go of his sleeve and began to unfasten the buttons on her cardigan. 'All right, then, *don't* come to bed,' she cried. She flung the garment across the room. 'We'll do it here, on the hearthrug — it makes no difference to me.' She leaned over him and touched his face. 'Give me a kiss,' she demanded. 'Kiss me, now! I want a real kiss.'

'But Caroline, you can't —'

'A kiss, damn you!' She took his face between her hands and, gently, very gently, pulled it close to hers. 'A kiss, dear Marcus,' she whispered. 'Dear, dear Marcus — please.'

So, hesitantly, he kissed her. Caroline let herself down upon his lap. She wrapped her arms around him and then stroked his hair. A few seconds later she began to unfasten his shirt, bracing herself for what she might see.

'It looks painful.' Very carefully, Caroline ran her hand across his shoulders. 'Poor Marcus, it looks so sore.'

'No tears, now. You promised.'

Caroline nodded. 'I promised,' she agreed. 'Marcus, perhaps we ought to go into the bedroom. It will be more comfortable for you —'

'Will it?' He smiled at her, not bitterly this time. 'I expect you're right,' he agreed. 'But look — are you sure that you want to do this? Really, sweetheart, you don't have to be kind —'

'I *want* to.' Caroline took one of his twisted hands in hers and held it. 'Marcus, more than anything else I want to go to bed with you, to make love to you.' She shrugged, unable to find words which would convince him. 'I love you,' she added simply. 'So naturally —'

'But things are rather different now.'

'They're not.' Caroline's navy-blue eyes looked up into Marcus's grey ones. 'Nothing's changed. Nothing at all.'

Marcus left a couple of hours later, saying he had an appointment at the hospital. Perfectly well aware that this was a downright fib, Caroline nevertheless let him go. He was relieved, she could see that. So relieved that he wanted to cry, or at any rate to be by himself.

She watched him stride off down the road as she had so often done before. Then she went back to bed. She took a pillow in her arms and hugged it. Then she began to weep, letting tears pour out of her as easily as summer rain falls from the sky.

He had another month's leave. She would see him every day, and every day it would be easier. She would take him to bed and love him, she would come to terms with his injuries, she would not even *see* them. 'I'll make him well again,' she vowed, hitting her pillow with her fists. 'I'll make him well again.'

* * *

Anthony Lawrence, at a loose end one morning and wanting company, had invited his nephew into his office in Whitehall. Marcus sat back in one of the leather-padded armchairs and looked around him, grinning. 'You chaps do all right, don't you?' he demanded. 'Next time, I'll definitely go in for this Intelligence lark. It's a really cushy number, isn't it?'

'It's not bad.' Anthony, slightly nettled that Marcus should imagine he had such an easy life, and fully aware that he *had* had a comparatively easy war so far, poured out some coffee.

Marcus took a cup. 'So when are these Yanks arriving?' he asked. 'This year? Next year? Are they coming at all?'

'They'll come. Don't worry, he'll have to send them — he can't go back on his word.' Anthony looked at Marcus.

'Will he?' Marcus looked doubtful. 'Hundreds of thousands of men? Or just a few thousand untrained volunteers who will make no difference at all?'

'It will have to be hundreds of thousands. He's committed himself. And Mr Wilson appears to be an honourable man.' Anthony sighed. 'Oh, God, Marcus, they *must* come, trained or not. Otherwise, it's all up for us.'

'It's that bad, is it?'

'Indeed it is.' Anthony leaned back in the comfortable chair behind the splendid desk in his comfortable office and lit another cigarette. He looked out of his window, staring down at the traffic in Whitehall. 'The Fifth Army's had such a hammering that it's almost useless now. The Germans are within striking distance of Paris, so unless the Americans are here within the month, the Allies have had it.'

'I suppose there's no chance we'll sue for peace?'

'It's unlikely. If we can hold on for just a bit longer, it's possible that the Germans will have to come to terms. The people are starving, you know — they're eating cats and dogs in Berlin, their bread is made out of potato peelings and powdered chalk. It's merely a question of who breaks first.' Anthony stubbed out his cigarette. 'I hope to God it won't be us. How much longer are you on leave?' he asked.

'Until Wednesday.'

'Doing anything special today?'

'This and that. There's someone I want to see.'

'Caroline?'

Marcus frowned. 'How the devil do *you* know about Caroline?' he demanded. 'You Intelligence chaps are supposed to spend your time finding our what Ludendorff's up to, not spying on me.'

Anthony grinned. 'Oh, you know how nosy I am,' he said. 'Anna remarked that you'd had some letters from the daughter of one of her friends, and wasn't it nice of Miss Anderson to write to you. So I —'

'So you put two and two together and made five.'

'Exactly.' Anthony stood up. 'Could I see you for lunch?' he asked. 'I'd like to meet her.'

'Would you?' Marcus shrugged. 'Oh, very well. We're going to that place in Regent Street, the one with the potted palms in the window, do you know where I mean?'

'The Curzon. Yes, I know it.'

'*You* would.' Marcus shook his head. 'I shall tell her that one of my uncles is coming to look her over,' he said. 'That'll scare her silly. She'll think it'll be some old buffer with a chestful of ribbons and a great white moustache.'

'Instead of a pen-pusher only a year or two older than yourself who's never fired a shot in his life. Don't rub it in, Marcus. I'd have gone over and done my bit if they'd let me.'

'I know.' Marcus picked up his hat. 'Look, I'll see you later.'

'Half past twelve?'

'Yes. Not before.'

Caroline was waiting patiently at a table near the window. She looked at the restaurant clock. Ten past twelve. The door opened then and Marcus came through it. She repressed the small shudder which now darted through her, and she smiled at him.

'Hello, sweetheart.' He touched her neatly bobbed fair hair and leaned over her, rested his other hand on her shoulder. 'How are you?'

'Fine.' She held up her face for a kiss, shutting her eyes as his lips brushed her cheek, opening them again to look him full in the face. She had adjusted now. She was looking at Marcus, not at his injuries, and she relaxed.

'I saw your mother this morning,' she said. 'I was walking along Bond Street and I ran into her, wasn't that strange? She told me that her father is coming down from Oxford this evening; he has to go to the American Embassy for some reason.'

'Really?' Marcus frowned. 'That sounds a bit unlikely. Oh, I know — perhaps they're going to use him as the ultimate weapon; they're going to drop my grandfather on the Kaiser.'

'Is he *that* frightening?'

'He's absolutely terrifying.' Marcus giggled. 'I'm surprised, now, that they didn't think of it before; the war would've been over years ago. Now, what are you having? Fricassée of lamb, steak and kidney pie, beef stew? I expect it's all boiled cat really.'

'In that case, I shall have an omelette.' Caroline unfolded her napkin and laid it across her lap. 'I suppose you'll have to go home tonight?'

'Well, I was rather hoping to spend the evening with you.' Marcus looked at her. 'If I did nip home for an hour or two,' he added, 'you could come with me. It's time you got to know the rest of the family better. You can take my word for it that none of the others are quite as fearsome as Mum.'

'I like your mother.'

'Do you? That's splendid. Well, if you and she get on, that'll make things a whole lot easier, won't it?'

'Will it?'

'Yes. In future, I mean —'

'Oh?' Caroline looked narrowly at him. 'Marcus, what exactly *do* you mean?'

'Well, Mum would be the sort of mother-in-law who'd scare any ordinary girl silly. But you're not ordinary, are you?'

'Marcus, are you asking me to marry you?' Caroline leaned back in her chair and smiled at her lover. 'Is that what you're trying to say?'

'Would you consider it?'

'Well —'

'Ah!' Suddenly, Marcus jumped to his feet. 'Caro, my uncle Anthony's just come in. Will you mind if he sits with us?'

Caroline shook her head. 'I'd be delighted to meet him,' she replied.

* * *

'It's the same scent,' said Anna afterwards, when Marcus and Caroline had gone. 'I knew I'd come across it somewhere before; it's been annoying me all through dinner trying to remember where but now I know.'

She shook her head. 'It must be *years* since I first noticed that particular perfume on his clothes and it's been there on and off ever since. To think I never realized. Caroline Anderson, of all people!'

John Harley put down his evening paper and smiled at his wife. 'Why are you so surprised?' he asked.

'I'm not surprised. Well, I am, I suppose. Just a little. It never occurred to me that Mary Anderson's little girl might be special enough to attract Marcus. And when you think of some of the girls he's known, I wouldn't have imagined —'

'— that our son has such a constant heart?'

'No, not exactly.' Anna looked thoughtful. 'Well, yes, perhaps. I mean, Caroline's very sweet, but she's not exactly Venus rising from the waves. And I wonder if he'll be content.'

'I think she'll make him an excellent wife.' John Harley patted his own wife's hand. 'She must know him very well by now. She must be aware of all his faults and failings.'

'Marcus hasn't any faults.'

'Of course he has, dear! Now, Caroline's sensible, intelligent and kind. I think they stand a very good chance of happiness together.'

'Do you, John?'

'Yes, I do.'

'Well, what about all her modern ideas? She has her own flat, you know, and she earns her own living. She's a publisher's secretary these days, and according to Mary Mr Gregson thinks the world of her.'

'So?'

'So will she settle down to domesticity, I wonder?'

'Does she need to? You never did, did you, Miss Lawrence?'

Anna looked sharply at her husband. 'I suppose I didn't,' she conceded. Suddenly she smiled. 'Oh, John, it *is* nice to see him happy again,' she said. 'He's been so wretched these past few months, and he's suffered so much. It's time he was enjoying life again.'

Chapter Twenty-Four

THE YEAR DRIFTED TOWARDS A fine summer. Baby Helen grew bonnier and bonnier, was now as blonde as her father. Her finely grained skin and her light eyes were Tim's own; there was nothing about this little girl to indicate that she was Dora's child.

Dora herself was guiltily happy: happy because she had Tim and Helen, guilty because now and then she remembered that England was still at war with Germany, and that men were still dying in their thousands on the battlefields of Europe. Peace seemed to be as unattainable as ever.

In the Herefordshire countryside, all that carnage seemed far away and completely irrelevant. Dora felt that it could hardly trouble her any more, not when all those whom she loved best were safe from it.

'Two weeks, Tim?' she cried, delighted. He had turned up at the Grange unexpectedly and walked into the hallway carrying a case and with his greatcoat over his arm. 'Two whole weeks?'

'Mmm.' Tim kissed his wife. 'A fortnight's sick leave, to be followed by a thorough medical examination. Do you think I could go and sit down?' he asked. 'I feel like death.'

Looking at him properly now, Dora could see he was ashen and even thinner than when she'd last seen him, three weeks ago. She took his arm and led him into the drawing room. 'What did the doctor say?' she demanded.

'Oh, that I ought to be in bed. That if I didn't watch out I'd have another haemorrhage; my lung would collapse and that would be that.' He smiled weakly. 'Sorry, Dora.'

'Don't be sorry. I'm glad you're home. But you'd better rest all you can while you're here.' She sat down beside him and snuggled up to him. 'I've something to tell you,' she added.

'Oh? What's that?'

'I think I must be pregnant again.'

'You can't be.' Tim shook his head. 'You're still feeding Helen, and it isn't possible to conceive while you're still — what is it — lactating, is that the word?' He ruffled her hair. 'Darling, don't you know the facts of life?'

'Don't be so superior. I'm *sure* I'm pregnant. I feel so sick.'

'Oh.' Tim lay back on the sofa and closed his eyes. 'So when will this one come, then?'

'In April or May.'

'I see.' Tim yawned and in response to a nudge from his wife, opened his eyes again. 'Well, I hope I can manage to hang on that long.'

'Don't say that.' Seriously alarmed, Dora looked anxiously into his face. 'You'll get better, of course you will.'

'Shall I?'

'Yes!' She smiled encouragingly. 'A month in the country, that's all you need. A bit of sunshine, good food, rest — that will set you up again.'

'I need something else, too.'

'What?'

'Come here and I'll show you.' Wrapping his arms around his wife, Tim kissed her. 'The doctor said I ought to be in bed,' he murmured into her hair. 'Why don't you come upstairs and tuck me up?'

'Aren't you tired? You look it.'

'I'm exhausted. Absolutely bloody exhausted.'

'So hadn't you better go to bed by yourself?'

'Come with me, Dora. Come and let me exhaust myself a bit more.' He grinned. 'Then at least I'll die happy.'

* * *

Throughout that summer the Allies moved closer and closer towards victory. Pushing the invading Germans back again, the British and American armies advanced eastwards across France, leaving in their wake a hundred towns and villages which were mere ghost-haunted ruins.

Marcus, now an aide to one of the generals, followed the advancing armies, riding into scenes of such absolute desolation that he found he was becoming almost unbearably depressed. It hurt him to see what men had done to the land, and to each other. And there were so many refugees, so many homeless strays; all were pitiful, and most pathetic of all were the old people and the children, dispossessed and despairing. Yet this was a triumphal progress, or supposed to be . . .

For the umpteenth time Marcus wondered what on earth he would do when the war was finally over. Go into the wine trade, he supposed. In a strange sort of way, however, he actually needed the war. After 1917 he could have been discharged if he'd wanted to be. But he'd been determined to stay in the army, without really understanding why.

'Shall I get you a bath ready, Sir?' Marcus's batman came into the room which his officer had been given for that night, a splendid bedchamber in a château which had miraculously escaped shelling.

'What?' Gingerly, Marcus rubbed his eyes. 'Oh, thank you, Dodds. Yes, you do that.'

'Sir.' The man walked through the bedroom and into the bathroom adjoining. He turned on the taps. 'It all works, Sir,' he announced beaming. 'Real hot water, gallons of it.' He came back into the bedroom. 'Dinner's at eight, Sir. Shall I come and help you dress?'

'No, I'll see to that myself. If you just unpack for me, that'll be sufficient.'

'Right you are, Sir.' The man grinned. 'Jerry's really on the run now, Sir,' he added enthusiastically, unfastening Marcus's kit. 'We've really got the bastards moving now.'

'Mmm.' Marcus found he was unable to share the man's pleasure. It was good news, he supposed, but somehow it didn't seem to matter very much.

By October 1918 it was clear that Germany was on her knees. The Allies rejoiced. A cruel enemy was crushed and humiliated, and now the British were determined to have reparation.

Only that spring, when excited crowds in Berlin had cheered the Kaiser to the echo, and German industrialists — counting their chickens — had carved up France between them, the people in London had cried in the streets for their dead soldiers.

Now these same soldiers' sacrifices would be sanctified. The British wanted revenge, and now that the world was again made safe for democracy, they would have it.

Caroline Anderson married Marcus Harley on a blustery autumn morning in October 1918.

It was, as they all afterwards agreed, the most delightful wedding any of the guests could remember. Everyone was relaxed and happy — and, to crown their happiness, peace was coming any day now, the Armistice would soon be signed.

Anthony, persuaded, no doubt, by Miriam, was prevailed upon to attend a Christian marriage service. He was even observed to mouth the prayers, and it was rumoured that he'd actually sung one of the hymns.

'We don't have to believe,' Miriam had remarked earlier, as she'd buttoned herself into her wedding finery. 'But we ought to have the good manners to go. And we ought to respect other peoples' beliefs, even though they aren't our own.'

'Beliefs?' Anthony, knotting his tie with a vicious jerk, had scowled into the mirror. 'Delusions! Delusions, my dearest. How anyone, after these past four years, could still believe in a God of love is beyond my understanding.'

'Delusions, then.' Miriam put on her hat. 'Have it your own way — they're all deluded. But we love Marcus, don't we?'

'Yes, but —'

'So we go to his wedding; we're flattered that he asks us. We kneel, we stand up and sing as loudly as the rest. We don't embarrass his family. We help to make it a special day for him and Caroline, eh?'

Anthony grimaced but then he smiled. 'You're perfectly right, of course,' he admitted. 'Miriam, you are a wonderful woman! Aren't you sensible? And wasn't I clever to have spotted you before anyone else did, and marry you before you'd had a chance to look around you?' He grabbed her around the waist and kissed her neck.

Miriam laughed, leaned against him for a second or two, then pushed him away. 'We haven't time for any of that,' she said sternly. 'We try to get there on time, as well. So come on!'

Caroline, despite being a modern woman, looked very old-fashioned and pretty in her wedding-dress — so much so that she even impressed her future mother-in-law. For Anna, who was still determined to believe that the extraordinary honour of marrying her eldest son was something for which any woman ought to be everlastingly grateful, murmured to John that she was pleased to see that Caroline had managed to make herself look fairly presentable.

'She looks lovely.' John pinched his wife's arm. 'Quite lovely. And don't you dare to suggest otherwise.'

Anna shrugged. 'It's all very well for you,' she began. 'You —'

'Ah, Mary.' John smiled at Mrs Anderson, who was talking to her son-in-law. 'Anna and I were just saying how charming Caroline looks; weren't we, Anna?'

'May I kiss Caroline?' Anthony moved Marcus aside and did so, without waiting for permission to be granted.

'May I?' Little David Lawrence pushed through a forest of knees and long skirts to peer up hopefully at the pretty lady.

Caroline bent down so that her face was level with his. She offered the little boy her cheek but David took her face between his hands and gave her a fulsome kiss upon the mouth, which made her blush and caused the child to smile with great satisfaction.

'I *do* like ladies,' he confided to his elder sister.

'They seem to like you,' was the acid reply.

※　　※　　※

That November Dora was surprised to receive a letter from her mother telling her that Stephen had been invited to give a series of lectures at a dozen or more colleges and universities throughout the eastern United States and that he intended to go.

As it happened, she and Tim had signed an agreement to rent a house in Oxford for the next six months, so a few days later Dora was in the town supervising removal men and setting her new home to rights. At about four o'clock in the afternoon, she put on her coat and trudged through the November drizzle to see her mother at the Summertown house.

'This American business,' she said, wasting no time. 'It's all very sudden, isn't it? And isn't he a little — well — old? He must be well over seventy. Far too ancient to go gadding off half way across the world, I'd have said.'

Dorcas smiled. 'Take your coat off, dear, and we'll have some tea,' she said. 'You know, Dora, your father is a very fit and active seventy-odd. He's really looking forward to going.'

Her mother led Dora into her little sitting room. 'He was invited years ago, as it happens,' she continued. 'Back in 1912 I think it was, just after David was born. He'd prepared all the stuff, and was due to leave in the September of 1914. Of course, when the war came, everything was cancelled.' She smiled. 'So you see, he's quite determined to go now'.

Dora sipped her tea and let herself thaw out before the fire. 'I think the whole scheme is very ill-advised,' she said. 'And what about you? He never thinks of you. Won't you be lonely?' Suddenly Dora smiled. 'But you can come and stay with us, can't you?' she cried. 'You can have the spare bedroom. It'll be lovely to have you there.'

'Oh, that's very sweet of you, Dora; but I'm going with him.' Dorcas shook her head at Dora's disbelief. 'Don't look so horrified, dear,' she added. 'I *want* to go. I've always wondered what America is like. Do you know, I'm looking forward to it all as much as Stephen is.'

'Are you?' Dora sniffed. 'You don't even like travelling across England,' she said. 'Oh, I know what happened. He talked you into it. He nagged and blustered until you agreed to go.'

'That's not how it was at all.' Still smiling, Dorcas poured more tea. 'Your father isn't like that.'

'Isn't he?' Dora picked up a sandwich and began, morosely, to chew. 'Anyway, it's time he retired.'

'He'll never do that.' Dorcas shook her head. 'Oh, Dora, can you see your father pottering about the garden, wandering aimlessly around the Parks? Can you imagine him sleeping all afternoon and whiling away his mornings with the obituaries in *The Times*?'

'No. But —'

'Neither can I. And look, Dora — it's only for six weeks, we'll be back long before the baby comes. I'll write every day,

I promise you that. Don't worry about us.'

'When are you leaving?'

'December the fourteenth.'

'Do you need any help with your packing?'

'No. It's all done. Now, Dora, don't fret. I'll bring you something nice for the baby. And a present — no, lots of presents — for Helen.'

'Just bring yourselves back safely, that's all I want.' Dora picked up her coat. 'Is Papa in college this afternoon?'

'Yes, I think so.'

'I might call in on my way back through town.'

'You won't grumble at him, will you, dear?'

'No. I shall just tell him what I think.'

Dora arrived back home in a state of intense irritation, annoyed with her father and cross with her mother. She found Tim lying on the floor of the drawing room playing with Helen, surrounded by wooden crates which it had evidently not occurred to him to unpack. When she expounded the elder Lawrences' scheme to him, he merely shrugged.

'Why shouldn't they go?' he asked, offering Helen a wooden spoon to chew. 'Good grief, your parents are old enough to be let out alone.'

'Precisely.' Dora stopped Helen from further investigating a box of matches and sat the child firmly on her father's lap. 'They're too old,' she said angrily. 'What if one of them should become ill?'

'There are doctors in America, I believe.'

'What if either of them should have an accident, then? One of us would have to go all the way to America to rescue them, and *I* couldn't do that.'

Tim lay back in his chair and cuddled Helen to his chest, allowing her to suck his tie. 'Oh, don't be stupid, Dora,' he said wearily. 'I can't imagine your father needing to be rescued from anything.'

'Can't you?'

'No.' Tim got up and carried Helen over to a window, where he pointed out a cat to her and told her she should have one of her own soon. 'Do you think Sarah will have sorted herself out in the kitchen yet?' he demanded. 'I wouldn't mind some tea.'

Dora, heavily pregnant though she was, spent the next few days in a flurry of organization and activity, sorting clothes, arranging furniture and interviewing a dozen or more young women for the post of housemaid. Sarah, the meek little girl from Ashton Cross, had come down to Oxford with the Athertons and was to be their cook but, Dora decided, she could not be expected to do all the housework as well.

Tim, who was recovering from an attack of the particularly virulent strain of influenza which was sweeping across Europe that year, wandered aimlessly around the house, thoroughly bored by all this commotion. He told Dora that as far as he could see there was little difference between one skivvy and another, and why didn't she let Sarah choose a girl she thought she could get on with?

Dora had told him, pretty sharply, to mind his own business which had made him laugh at her.

She had, in fact, been quite pleased that he'd laughed, for since the colder weather had arrived he had become extremely morose and lethargic.

'How are you feeling today?' Dora, who had risen early one frosty December morning and intended to spend that day looking for curtain material, went to sit on the arm of his chair. 'Tim, how are you?'

'I'm all right,' he replied. 'Where's Helen?'

'Out with Nanny.' Dora shook her head. 'She thinks all babies should be thoroughly aired, like laundry. Tim, why don't you come to town with me?'

'Oh, I don't want to go out. I don't feel that well really.'

'Some fresh air might do you good. It's cold but the sun's shining.' Dora smiled encouragingly. 'Put your coat on and come with me.'

'I don't think I shall.' Tim yawned and slid down into his chair. 'I see people I know and they want to stop and talk to me.'

'What's wrong with that?'

'Oh, God, Dora, they're so bloody boring, that's what. All they want to do is tell me what they did in the war. I met Alec Minton in Cornmarket yesterday; he kept me standing in the cold for half an hour while he told me what he did to the sodding Turks in the bloody Dardanelles! Sometimes I think if anyone mentions the war to me just once again I shall hit him.'

'Perhaps Mr Minton needed to talk to you,' hazarded Dora. 'Tim, perhaps he —'

'Oh, bloody flaming hell, Dora! As if I haven't enough horrible memories of my own.' Tim glared at her. 'I don't want his as well.'

'Really, Tim. There's no need to swear at me like that.'

Tim closed his eyes. 'I thought you were going out,' he muttered.

'I am.'

'Can you bring me some cigarettes, then? Sixty of whatever you can get.'

'Tim, you *know* the doctor said —'

'Oh, very well, I'll go and fetch my own.'

Tim heaved himself out of his chair and walked out of the room. Dora heard him coughing as he went upstairs. Shrugging, she buttoned her own coat and went out of the house. 'He's just tired,' she told herself, 'that's all it is.'

As she made her way down the garden path, Tim came out of the house. Hatless, his coat flapping undone, his chest protected from the bitter cold only by the material of a thin summer shirt, he flung one arm around Dora's shoulders and walked on down the path with her.

'Don't you think you ought to have a scarf?' she began.

'Shut up, Dora. You're not my nanny.' He pushed his hair out of his eyes and grinned at her. 'We'll go and buy my gaspers, then we'll go and look for your bloody curtain material. All right?'

Resignedly, Dora nodded. It was something, at least, to see him smile.

Chapter Twenty-Five

STEPHEN AND DORCAS WENT OFF from Southampton in excellent spirits, promising daily letters and reaffirming their intention to be back in England well before Dora's baby would be born.

Dorcas was faithful to her word. She did write every day. Her first few postcards charted their progress through New England, were full of praise for the country and for its generous, hospitable people. Dora began to think that perhaps her parents had been right to go after all. She could imagine the effect that her father would be having on the Americans. He so much enjoyed performing, and she was certain that he must be finding receptive audiences in the New World. 'Your father seems to think very well of our hosts,' Dorcas had written. That meant, presumably, that he was being treated with all the deference he thought he deserved.

'They must be falling over themselves to tell him how wonderful he is,' remarked Dora sardonically, handing Tim the postcard.

'I expect they are.' Tim yawned. 'Of course, he's the kind of Englishman they seem to admire.'

'Yes.' Dora smiled at her husband. 'Yes, I suppose he is. What were you thinking of doing today?' she asked brightly.

'Nothing much.' Tim picked up a newspaper. 'Don't feel up to anything strenuous, I'm afraid.'

Tim made a great and determined effort to rouse himself from his customary lethargy and to enjoy Christmas. Dora was quite touched by his efforts to be sociable, for it was obvious that he was indifferent to the company of anyone but his wife and his daughter.

'Yes, I'll come,' he replied, when asked if he meant to go to such and such a party. He grinned ruefully at Dora. 'I'll come. And I'll try to be the life and soul.' He dressed in evening clothes and went out to dinner with his friends, and although he hardly joined in when a spate of war stories inevitably poured forth along with the port, he kept his temper and did not hit anyone, as he'd threatened to do.

On Christmas Day itself Helen's shrieks of delight and general over-excitedness helped. At nine months old, she was far more interested in the wrappings on her presents than the gifts themselves, and she rolled happily in a sea of coloured paper, ripping and tearing it all with gurgles of evident pleasure.

But, by the end of December, Tim had relapsed. He had used up all his credit of good humour and was badly overdrawn. Looking tired to death and a good ten years older than he was, he slouched about the house, coughing and scowling and smoking cigarette after cigarette.

Dora told herself that when the spring came he would be in better health and would necessarily feel less depressed. 'Shall we go and see Anthony next month?' she asked, trying to interest him in something. 'You know how he cheers you up.'

'We'll go, if you like,' he replied indifferently.

But it was not necessary to go to Cambridge. As it turned out, Anthony and Miriam came to Oxford instead.

On a bleak January day in the third week of the New Year, Anthony telegraphed to tell Dora that he was coming over to see her and that he hoped she could meet him and Miriam at the railway station, for he had a very bad cold.

'What's the matter, I wonder?' Anna, who was spending a few days in Oxford, where she needed to use one of the libraries, turned the telegram over in her hand and frowned at it. 'Why's he coming here?'

'I really can't imagine.' Dora was mystified and also very worried. She was counting the hours to Anthony's arrival.

That evening found Anna, Dora and Tim on the station platform, all wrapped in greatcoats and shivering as they peered down the line waiting for the train to arrive. As soon as Anthony and Miriam stepped from their carriage, his sisters fell upon him.

'What's the matter, Anthony?' Anna, her authority as the eldest still as firm as it had ever been in childhood, shook her brother's arm, expecting a prompt reply.

'What's wrong?' Dora, on his other side, pulled at his cuff. 'Anthony, what is it?'

He said nothing. So Dora shook him harder, her fingers digging in to his arm. 'What *is* it, Anthony?' she repeated, almost angrily now. 'Are you ill? Oh, God, it's your heart, isn't it? You never got over that influenza you had in October, did you? Or is it the children?'

'Don't, Dora.' Anthony shook both his sisters off. 'It's not me at all, and the children are fine. Can we get to your house? Then I'll tell you.'

'Well, Anthony?'

'I don't know all the details. But the telegram from the railway company was perfectly clear. They're both dead.'

He looked at his sisters, gazing calmly at their shocked and stricken faces. 'I'm sorry to have had to be the one to tell you,' he added. 'Especially you, Dora, in your present state.' Anthony shivered and sneezed. 'Could I have some brandy or something, Tim?' he asked. 'I think I'm in for another bout of that bloody influenza.'

Tim, for once more alert than his wife, filled a glass and handed it to his brother-in-law. 'What else do you know, Anthony?' he asked.

'The telegram said that more information would follow. But it's already quite plain. The train was derailed coming off the river bridge. The last two carriages ended up in the water, and seventeen of the people inside them were drowned. Our parents were two of them. Here.' He felt in his pocket, pulled out a sheet of yellow paper and passed it to Tim. 'You can read it. There's no other interpretation, is there?'

Tim took the scrap of paper and read it through. 'No,' he agreed. 'No, there isn't.'

Dora was surprised, afterwards, that she'd taken it all so calmly. She heard herself asking her brother if he was warm enough. She walked through to the kitchen and told Sarah that the family had just had some rather distressing news, so could she quickly make a light meal for five people and bring it into the drawing room? Going upstairs, she sorted out some sheets and fetched extra blankets, then made up a bed in the spare room.

Anthony and Anna, on the other hand, sat silently on either side of the fire. Anthony coughed now and then, kicked a stray log of wood and stared into the flames. Eventually Anna began, noiselessly, to cry.

Miriam took Dora aside. 'Can we stay the night?' she asked. 'Anthony ought really to be in bed but he insisted on coming here straight away. And you know what he's like — nothing I could have said would have made any difference. Perhaps we might stop here for a day or two, do you think?'

'Of course you can. You must.' Dora glanced over towards her brother. 'Miriam, he looks so ill,' she cried. 'Can't you move from Cambridge? Couldn't you persuade him?'

'So where could we go?'

'You could come here. You could live in Oxford now, couldn't you? Now that my father is dead, there's no reason why Anthony can't take his place.' Dora realized the full implication of what she'd just said. 'Oh, Miriam!' she whispered, and began to cry.

But it was only after everyone had gone away that the shock really hit Dora. She felt the baby churning inside her, she shivered uncontrollably, then she lay down on her bed and cried and cried.

'How could they both have been drowned?' she asked Tim, tears pouring down her cheeks. 'Why didn't anyone help them?' For it seemed ludicrous to Dora, a very bad joke on the part of Providence, that her parents should have gone safely across the Atlantic in the winter gales only to be killed in an accident crossing a mere *river*. 'How could it have happened?' she demanded, studying her atlas, tracing the contours with her index finger and appealing to Tim for an answer.

'I don't know, Dora.' He closed the book, wiped Dora's face with her handkerchief and laid her head on his shoulder. 'I don't think it really matters how. It's happened and it's something you'll have to accept.'

'How *can* I accept it? I can't imagine anything more horrible.'

'They were together, Dora. Think how much that means. And think how much the other would have grieved if there'd been a survivor.' He stroked her hair and kissed her. 'They wouldn't have known much about it, I'm certain of that.'

'Is drowning in icy water quick?' Dora looked into her husband's eyes, wanting an assurance that it was.

'I don't know, darling. But I expect it is.' He rocked her in his arms, holding her like a child, hoping that she might fall asleep.

There were no difficulties over Stephen's will. Everything was sorted out with the minimum of delay, for his intentions were clear and unambiguous. His lawyers had done their work well and even the heavy post-war death duties had, by various stratagems, been minimized. It was as if Stephen had not expected to return from America, so precise and recently updated were his directions to his executors.

Dora opened the stiff white envelope and drew out several sheets of closely written paper. She read through all the paragraphs, but had to do so a second or third time before they made very much sense to her. She passed the handful of papers to Tim. 'What do you make of all this?' she asked.

He leaned back in his chair and gave the letter his attention. 'Henry Lawrence inherits the Ashton Cross estate. It's left to him in trust and he can divide it among his own children as he thinks fit. Anthony receives the house in Banbury Road, together with various bonds, dividends, what have you. As for you and Anna, you are to have annuities of — I say, Dora, that's pretty generous!' He handed the papers back to his wife. 'Is that what you were expecting?'

'I hadn't any idea what his intentions were. And in any case, he has a legitimate child who has a better claim on his property than any of *us*.' Dora studied her fingernails. 'This daughter — Judith, I think her name is — she could contest the will and have everything he owned made over to her.'

'But if she doesn't, you'll be quite well off.'

'Shall I?' Dora sniffed. 'Yes, I suppose I shall.'

Tim and Dora bought the house in Oxford which they had rented since the previous autumn and which they had both decided they liked. A modest Victorian town house in a quiet road about a mile from Dora's childhood home, it was in a pleasant situation next to a park and behind it there was a large garden in which Tim and Dora imagined their children playing in later years.

Noticing some snowdrops doing their best to push through a mass of weeds and brambles, Tim had put on old clothes and, on sunny days, he hacked down the thistles and self-sown saplings which formed the main part of the garden's vegetation. Dora let him get on with it; he seemed to find it relaxing to chop down great stands of withered stinging nettles and forests of old and useless raspberry canes. He had, in any case, dismissed her idea of employing a gardener, telling her that they could not afford it.

'Don't be silly,' she'd said, laughing. 'Of course we can afford a gardener — he'd be glad to work for thirty shillings a week.'

'Ah, but I don't have thirty shillings a week to spare.'

'Well, I have.' Dora had hugged his arm. 'Darling, I've plenty of money.'

Crossly, he'd shaken her off. '*You* might be a woman of substantial means,' he'd muttered. 'But I'm not a millionaire. Dora, since I'm your husband, it's my responsibility to provide for you and my children. And I have to live within my means.'

'Oh, Tim, that's stupid.' Dora walked across to the window. 'Of course we can have a gardener,' she said decidedly. 'I shall advertise in the local paper this weekend.'

'You won't, Dora.' Tim glowered at her. 'You'll do nothing of the kind, do you hear me? When you married me, you promised to love, honour and obey me. And that means you'll bloody well do as I tell you.'

'Don't you dare talk to me like that.' Hurt and angry, Dora stared back at him. 'I'm not one of your subalterns.' She folded her arms across her pregnancy and shrugged. 'Oh, dig your rotten garden yourself, then,' she muttered. 'I hope you get lumbago. It'll serve you jolly well right.'

Tim got on with his gardening. He did not develop lumbago,

and he seemed to benefit from the exercise. Helen, who appeared to prefer her father's company to anyone else's, frequently escaped from her nursery and crawled around the garden looking for him, shrieking with delight when she found him busy at some horticultural task, which he readily abandoned to swing her up into the air.

'Really, Major Atherton, I don't know what Mrs Atherton can be thinking of, letting the child grub around in all this dirt.' Helen's nanny retrieved her charge from her father's rather muddy embrace and gave Tim a withering look.

Nanny Truman did not approve of Tim at all. Why a gentleman like him — she had heard that his brother was a baronet, if you please — should take pleasure in digging a vegetable patch was beyond her comprehension. She found it faintly disgusting that her employer should engage in *any* physical toil. And Tim's eccentricity was doubly embarrassing, for people could see him from the street, and what would *they* think?

Sarah came into the kitchen just then, poured out a cup of tea and went to the door. She walked down the garden path and gave the cup to her employer, who took it from her and said something, at which Sarah giggled. Nanny Truman grimaced. He was over-familiar with the servants, too . . .

'He is rather *odd*, don't you think?' asked the nurse as she and Sarah sat down to their lunch later that day.

'Odd?' Sarah looked sharply at Nanny Truman; then she realized what the nurse was getting at. 'He ain't odd,' she snapped. 'Mr Atherton's a real gentleman, one of the very best there is. Don't you dare say he's odd.'

She attacked her meat, slashing it angrily. 'An' a gentleman can hold a spade as well as a navvy, so if he wants to dig his garden for the sake of his health, why shouldn't he?'

'Because it's not proper, that's why.' Delicately the nurse speared a piece of carrot on her fork. 'His fingernails are black these days.'

'Don't matter to me if they're sky blue pink!' Sarah grimaced. 'Hadn't you better get Miss Helen out of the cat's dish?' she demanded. 'Gentleman or not, her father wouldn't be very pleased if he knew her nanny fed his daughter on the moggy's dinner.'

'What?' Glancing round, Nanny Truman saw that her charge was indeed investigating the contents of the cat's saucer and that bits of meat were adhering to her woolly cardigan. She scooped the little girl up and berated her. What a household, she thought, sourly. The kitchen occupied by a cook who was a flagrant Socialist, the master of the house openly encouraging Sarah to be forward. If it wasn't that dear Mrs Atherton — now there was a lady, born and bred — needed her, she'd leave and find herself a respectable situation.

Tim was poring over his plans for a rose garden when Dora looked up from her own book and spoke to him. 'What did you say?' he murmured, ticking off Madame Hardy and Celsiana in the catalogue at his side.

'I said, I do hope Anthony won't sell the Summertown house.' Dora sighed. 'I hope they'll move to Oxford. It would be so nice to have them near us, and the climate here would be so much better for Anthony's health.'

'Well, why don't you write to Miriam and tell her so, then? I think we'll have Gloire de Dijon on the trellis.' He looked up and grinned at Dora. 'Then she can put some pressure on your brother.'

'I don't think she'd do that unless she was sure that was what he wanted.'

'I think I'll order Alba Maxima too. Then, Dora, you must convince Miriam that it's what he *does* want. I'm sure the colleges here would be fighting over him if they knew he was considering a move.' Tim took one of his newly acquired gardening manuals from the bookcase. 'It's all quite simple really.'

In the event, cunning on Dora's part turned out to be unnecessary. Anthony and Miriam would move to the Summertown house the following month, for Miriam had put her foot down and informed her husband that she had no desire to become a widow just yet. 'You know you'd like to live in your old home,' she added persuasively. 'And this house here — well, it's very nice, but it's much too small. So, Anthony, don't you think — to please me —'

Anthony had shaken his head and smiled back at his wife.

'I expect your parents would be glad to have you living near to them, wouldn't they?' he asked.

'Yes, they would.' Miriam nodded. 'Now they're so old, and my mother's health is not so good — well, it's difficult for my father to manage everything. So we move for their sake, don't we? And so that David can have a bigger bedroom? Poor henpecked husband, you give in to your wife's complaining, eh?'

'I do.' Anthony bowed his assent. 'I give in to your demands.'

Tim, who enjoyed Anthony's company, consented to visit the Summertown house with his wife. He joined in family parties with every appearance of good humour. But he remained depressed; some days he was downright sullen. When it was too wet to go out into his garden, he did nothing but stare vacantly out of the window, scowling at the rain.

Dora had given up trying to distract him from his worries — whatever they were. For, when she asked him what was wrong, he merely shrugged. 'Nothing's wrong,' he would reply shortly. And sometimes he would even walk out of the room, as if annoyed that she'd spoken to him.

'What's the matter today?' asked Dora one morning, seeing him frowning as he read through his bank statement.

His scowl as he looked back at her ought to have told her. But still she smiled at him.

He sniffed and tossed the paper across to her. 'That's what's the matter,' he replied. 'I am worth exactly seven hundred pounds, six shillings and fourpence. In the not-too-distant future, it appears, I shall be living off my wife, for I shan't have any money of my own.'

'You won't be living off your wife. You have that annuity from your uncle, you have your army pay, and if you're discharged you'll have a pension.'

'Oh, yes, a pension.' He grimaced. 'I was forgetting about that. It might just keep me in cigarettes. No, Dora, there's only one thing for it — I shall have to go on hoping that I'll get a bit fitter, and then the army might keep me on. My regiment's marked for India, you know.'

He sat down in an armchair and stared out of the window.

'The MO wants to see me next Friday, so if I'm not passed fit —'

'Tim, there must be something else you can do.'

'There isn't.'

'You said you were going to ask John —'

'I have.' He shrugged. 'I saw him a few days ago.'

'Did you? I thought I could smell smuts on your clothes. Well, what did he say?'

'That he'd take me into the business when I'm fit enough — in six months' time maybe. He was just fobbing me off, you see.'

'He wouldn't do that. If he said he'll find you a job, he will. But Tim, do you want to go into the City?'

'No, not really. But it's either that or India. And I can't see you being happy as an army wife out there.' Tim sighed. 'Mrs Major Atherton, terror of the cantonment — that's not you, is it, darling?'

'Not really.' Dora got up and went round to Tim's chair. 'Well, at least you went to see John,' she said, kissing him. 'A few weeks ago you wouldn't have walked into Oxford by yourself, let alone have gone off to London. That proves you're getting better.'

'Does it?'

'Oh, yes!' She smiled at him. 'You must be patient, dear Tim. You must try not to get so cross with yourself.'

'Dora, don't give me a lecture.'

'I'm not going to. But you must remember that you were badly hurt, you were ill all winter and that you can't expect to recover your strength straight away.'

She looked hard at him, then sat down on his lap. 'I know,' she said. 'Couldn't you write?'

'Write? Write what?'

'A novel, a play, poetry — anything.'

'I don't think so, Dora. I don't think I've the stamina to tackle a novel. And as for poetry, I'm no Siegfried Sassoon.'

'Oh, well, it was just an idea.'

'Not a very good one, I'm afraid.' He shifted beneath her weight. 'Could you get up, please, dear?' he asked. 'You're so heavy these days.'

Chapter Twenty-Six

WHEN, A FEW DAYS LATER, Tim received a letter from the War Office informing him that he was to be discharged from the army on medical grounds, he was devastated. He went out of the house with the paper crumpled in his coat pocket, stayed out all day and returned home just before midnight – completely sober, Dora was relieved to see, but so white and upset that she was seriously worried.

He was morose and silent for almost a week. Then he began, in a way, to accept it. 'Poor Dora,' he said one morning, as if noticing her for the first time in days. 'You really haven't been very fortunate in marriage, have you? First you take a sadistic brute who treats you abominably, then you marry an idiot who can't even earn his own living.' He sighed. 'It must be terrible having me loafing around your house all day.'

Dora, fully aware that almost anything she might now say would be wrong, looked evenly back at him. 'I don't mind you being at home,' she said carefully. She handed him the newspaper.

'Oh, I don't want to read that rubbish.' Tim dropped *The Times* on the floor and slid down into his chair. 'Do you spend much time regretting the fact that you married me?' he asked, eyeing her curiously. 'Do you lie awake at night, blaming yourself for your mistakes?'

'Oh, don't be so silly.' Dora shook her head. 'Marrying you wasn't a mistake.'

'It was!' He laughed bitterly. 'And now you're paying for it, literally. Aren't you?'

Suddenly, Dora had had enough of this. She got up and went over to him, leaned across him and pinched his arm, hard. 'Damn you, Tim Atherton!' she cried, beside herself. 'Damn you, you miserable, self-pitying, useless creature. I'm sick of listening to you moaning and complaining all day long.'

She glared at him in exasperation. 'Can't you *do* something for a change?' she demanded. 'Go out for a walk? Or plant your stupid rose-bushes?'

'What?' He scowled at her. 'You'd like me to go away for good, wouldn't you? Well, perhaps I shall. Then you'll be perfectly happy, won't you? When I'm not here to get on your delicate nerves.'

'Oh, it's not that.' In despair, Dora shook her head. 'I don't want you to go away,' she wailed. 'But, honestly, I don't know what to say to you these days. Every time I open my mouth I seem to upset you. But I *don't* want you to leave, and I don't want to quarrel.'

She walked away from him and went to look out of the window at the raw March day and the drizzle pattering against the glass. 'I'm going back to bed,' she announced. 'My back aches dreadfully this morning; it's an effort to sit up.'

'Poor Dora.' Suddenly concerned, Tim got up and walked over to where she stood, wrapped his arms around what he could of her waist and let her lean against him. 'Poor Dora, does it hurt very much?'

'Oh, God!' Dora twisted out of his embrace and glared at him. 'Listen to me!' she cried. 'If you say "poor Dora" just once more, I shall hit you. Do you understand? I shall hit you, hard, and then I shall scream.'

'Sorry.' Tim now looked extremely contrite. 'Shall I come up with you?' he asked. 'If I lie down next to you, I can keep you warm.'

Dora opened her mouth to say no, but then she looked at Tim's face and realized that to refuse him now would be to hurt him more than he deserved, no matter how tiresome he was. 'Yes, all right,' she replied wearily. 'That would be nice.'

They went back into their bedroom, lay down together and fell asleep.

They woke at midday to find the sun shining through the

curtains. In her nursery across the landing Helen could be heard warbling to her nanny, who clucked and admonished by way of reply. 'Could you manage a walk?' asked Tim, rubbing Dora's back absent-mindedly. 'A little stroll, before lunch?'

'I expect so.' Dora sat up. 'Just a short one, though. Half an hour, no more.'

They walked across the Parks towards the river, Tim supporting Dora around her waist. 'Could we sit down for ten minutes?' he asked. 'I'm not going to grumble and moan again, but I should like to talk to you. May I?'

'Of course you may.' Dora sat down gratefully upon one of the benches by the path. She turned up her coat collar and tucked her hands inside her sleeves. 'Talk away,' she invited. 'What is it?'

'I know I was being ridiculous this morning.' Tim managed a rueful smile. 'I must be very tiresome sometimes, and you're right to get annoyed with me. But — '

'There's no need to apologize.' Dora snuggled close to her husband and smiled at him, relieved that he was approachable again. 'I do understand how you feel.'

'Actually, you don't. You can't.' Tim frowned. 'Dora, I want to tell you about something.'

'What?'

'Something which happened during the war. It's not very pleasant, though. Perhaps you'd rather — '

'Oh, for goodness sake, Tim! Just tell me.'

'All right. Stop me if I upset you, won't you?'

'Yes, I'll do that. Well?'

'Well.' He rubbed his eyes. 'Back in 1916 I was in France, stationed near Amiens. We were there for the summer campaign; we were going to crush the Germans, win the war, all that nonsense.'

'Yes, I remember you mentioning that. Marcus was there, too.'

'Was he? Yes, I suppose his lot must have been. Anyway, that August my battalion was at Fricourt. One morning we were told that we had to mount a raid to capture a mine crater from the Jerries; a mob of them had occupied it, you see, and they were sniping our trenches from it. The whole thing was a bit pointless because even if we'd captured the damn thing we couldn't have held it for long. But, the major had told us to try, so we had to get on with it.'

'What happened?'

'We went out that night. We managed to capture the crater just before dawn. We took all the Germans prisoner, and for once we had hardly any casualties of our own. So we left a platoon guarding the place and we went back to our trenches feeling very pleased with ourselves.

'Then my company sergeant major told me that one of my lieutenants was missing. He and a few other chaps had gone out to do a little show on their own, to pinch a machine gun from Jerry or something, I don't remember exactly what. Most of his platoon had come back, but he wasn't accounted for. And as it happened, this particular chap was a very close friend of mine . . .

'Who was he?'

'Harry Nolan. He joined up in 1915. But I'd known him for years; he was on the same staircase as me in college.' Tim looked at his wife. 'You might even remember him — a little dark man, blue eyes, typical Black Irish. Your father was his tutor. Dora, I'm sure you met him once.'

'I don't remember him. But go on.'

'I put his platoon sergeant through it. The fellow was in a terrible state of funk, he mumbled something about the platoon having been ambushed or some other nonsense. They'd been overwhelmed, he said, and Mr Nolan had ordered the men to withdraw. That didn't sound like Harry — he liked taking risks.

'But, anyway, I was concerned about him. I asked the CSM if he'd come out with me to look for Harry. I was sure that he must have been wounded, you see, and was lying somewhere between our lines and the crater.'

'So what did you do?'

'Sergeant Lloyd and I went out together. We crawled across no man's land and found Harry — Lord knows how, but we did.' Tim looked at his wife. 'The next part's very unpleasant, Dora — d'you want me to stop?'

'No. Tell me the rest.'

'He was in a shell-hole with a couple of wounded Jerries. We finished them off — they'd had it anyway. And then we got in beside Harry and told him we'd try to get him back to our lines. He was in no state to be moved, but by now it was nearly light, and we couldn't hang around any longer. It took us half an hour to cover twenty yards, dragging Harry between us.'

'How badly hurt was he?'

'One of his eyes was gone, his cheekbone was shot away, and he had a stomach wound you could have put your fist in. And I hadn't any morphia with me — I cursed myself for that. Well, we were within sight of our own trenches when Harry mumbled that he couldn't go any further and to leave him.

'I said I'd carry him the rest of the way. He was only a little chap, you see. But he wouldn't let me. "I've had it," he said. "You get back, Tim, leave me here." I told him I couldn't do that. "Oh, come on, Sir," said Lloyd. "Mr Nolan's right. You can't carry him — the bloody Jerries will shoot you the minute you stand up."

'And I let them persuade me. I left Harry in the shelter of a ruined brick wall. We gave him a water bottle, some rations — God knows why, the poor devil couldn't have eaten anything — and I went back with the sergeant. I told Harry I'd fetch him in the evening.

'We got his body back just after nightfall. We saw that he'd been biting his hand to stop himself from moaning, so that he wouldn't attract the attention of other rescuers. But a German patrol had found him just before we did and he'd been bayoneted.'

Tim wiped his hand across his eyes. 'He wasn't cold, Dora,' he whispered. 'He wasn't even cold.'

Dora, her spine still tingling with horror, took Tim's hand and chafed it. 'You don't hold yourself responsible for his death, do you?' she asked.

'Of course I do! Haven't you been listening at all?' He snatched his hand away and glared at her. 'I was his commanding officer,' he cried. 'I shouldn't have left him. I ought to have carried him back.'

'Then you'd have been killed, too. What good would that

have done anyone?'

'I failed him.' Tim grimaced, as if in pain. 'I failed him. When he needed me, I deserted him.'

'You didn't. He knew perfectly well he was dying and he wanted you to live. You did as he asked. Do you suppose that it would have helped him in any way to know he was responsible for your death?'

'I was responsible for his. And I can't get it out of my mind. It's driving me insane. Every time I close my eyes I see that bloody shell crater, those two dead Germans, and Harry — '

'How long have you been fretting about this, Tim?'

'I don't really know.' Tim sighed wearily. 'I'd forgotten all about it a day or two after it had happened. But when I was in hospital something made me think about Harry, and it's been tormenting me on and off ever since.'

'Because you survived and your friend didn't.'

'What?' Tim frowned. 'Oh, yes, I know what you mean. Guilt of the survivor and all that stuff. One of the MOs gave us a lecture about it. Oh, Dora, it's not just that. It's the whole stupid business, the thought that we put up with so much agony for so long. That so many men died such awful, useless deaths. You civilians, you've no idea what it was like.'

'I suppose we haven't.'

Tim stared across the park towards the river. 'We hated the civilians, you know,' he said. 'More than the Germans, we hated the people back in England. Do you know, Dora, some of the chaps refused to go home on leave; they said they couldn't stand it. The idea of all those old men in England, the ones who'd started the bloody war, carrying on their safe little lives, dying their comfortable, easy deaths, was just too much to stomach. And then there were all the bloody women, so proud of themselves for visiting the hospitals, for selling flags and knitting.'

'Tim, that's not really fair.'

'Isn't it?' Tim laughed bitterly. 'You've never even sat in a trench, Dora. You've never crouched in a hole in the mud, cold, hungry, filthy, tired to death, while the Germans chuck shells at you, while your men are being blasted to pieces all round you, while some are going mad with pain and others are crying like babies out of sheer bloody terror because they can't escape, because there's nowhere to run to.'

'No.' Dora shrugged. 'We did have it easy,' she conceded. 'You've a right to be sour.' She wondered what on earth she could say to him now.

But then, all at once, she remembered what she'd suggested to him a while back. 'You ought to write, Tim,' she said. 'I really think you should. I don't mean that you should write about the war; write anything you want. But if you create something, as you're making a garden at home, I'm sure it will help you to get well again. Will you try?'

Tim looked at her. 'Well, maybe,' he agreed. 'One day.'

'No!' Dora shook his arm. 'No, not one day. Start tomorrow. You *can* write, Tim, you know you can. I remember reading some of your articles and reviews years and years ago. And my father used to read that magazine you edited. There! You didn't know that, did you?'

'No, I didn't.'

'You wrote something about him once, do you remember? It was very uncomplimentary, but it was also very funny and it made him laugh.'

'Did it?' Tim actually grinned. 'Oh, my God! I didn't refer to him by name, did I?'

'No, but it was perfectly obvious whom you meant. What a cheek you had. You should have been sent down for insolence!' Dora smiled at her husband and shook her head. 'Poor Papa,' she added. 'What had he ever done to you to deserve such treatment? It was a parody of one of his lectures, that's what it was. Anna asked him what he was laughing at and he showed her. She was appalled!'

'So *that's* why she doesn't like me.' Tim stood up and stretched. 'We ought to go home,' he said. 'Lunch will be ready and we don't want to upset little Sarah. Dora, I must find another job. I can't sit around the house all day, scribbling.'

Dora got up and took his arm, and began to walk along with him. 'Now listen to me,' she said, 'you don't need to go out to work just yet. You're not strong enough and the annuity brings in enough for us all to live on very comfortably.'

'I won't live off my wife.'

'Why not?'

'I can't explain. But don't let's start all that again.'

'I thought you loved me?' Dora looked up at him. 'I thought you wanted me to be happy?'

'I do love you. That's why I won't live off you.'

'Oh, Tim, you do talk rubbish.' Dora shrugged. 'Well, you'll start work tomorrow,' she added decidedly. 'I shall stand over you with a whip and make you get on with it. That's partly what's the matter with you; you've had your own way for far too long.'

They turned into St Giles. 'Look, the sun's shining,' she observed. 'You can do some gardening after lunch. Then you'll feel you've achieved something today.'

Tim did as Dora told him. Whatever the quality of his writing may have been, the actual discipline of doing it seemed to relieve his depression. He was happier, employed, than he'd been for months. He worked very methodically, sitting down at the table in the dining room at nine every morning and working steadily until one in the afternoon.

The pile of notes grew. Dora, now as tired and lethargic as her husband was suddenly energetic, encouraged him. 'And you know, Tim, that I need you as much as you need me,' she said, as she lay curled up beside him one evening. 'Isn't that what really matters? Don't pull such a face. I didn't marry you to be provided for. I'd refuse to be a pet who is kept by a man to entertain him in return for my board and lodging.'

'It's I who am the pet, fed and clothed in return for my not exactly sparkling company.' But Tim grinned as he said that, and then he leaned over Dora and kissed her. 'I've finished my notes, by the way,' he added. 'Tomorrow I shall start my first draft. Will you sit by me and hold my pens, as David Copperfield's Dora did? Will you simper and smirk and tell me what a clever chap I am?'

'No, I shan't! I'll find you a penknife and you can sharpen your own pencils. Then I'm having lunch with Miriam. Tim, what's this book going to be about? War experiences?'

Tim shook his head vehemently. 'Oh, God, no!' he replied. 'The war's over, and most people will want to forget it now. Besides, there'll be umpteen thousand of that sort of book coming on to the market soon; up and down the length and breadth of England chaps are scribbling down what they did in the trenches. No, I'm doing something quite different.'

'What?'

'It's private until it's finished.' Tim wrapped his arms around his wife. 'Darling, shall we go to bed?'

'I'm too tired to move. You'll have to carry me.'

Tim laughed. 'I couldn't possibly do that,' he said. 'You're probably as heavy as I am by now.' He traced the outline of her figure through her dress. 'You're spherical,' he added, grinning at her. 'A perfect O!'

'A fat, ugly lump — that's what you mean, isn't it?' Dora bit her lower lip. 'I dare say I'm quite repulsive just now.'

'You're beautiful. Absolutely lovely. Come on, I'll show you how lovely I think you are.' With a theatrical grimace he heaved her on to her feet and picked her up in his arms. 'I think — I could just about stagger — up the stairs,' he gasped. 'Dora, if I have a heart attack, you're to blame.'

Six weeks after he'd begun to write his first draft of whatever it was, Tim had amassed a great pile of manuscript. Dora, now as consumed with curiosity as any Pandora could possibly have been, eyed the folders of foolscap and longed to know what was inside.

Then, one fine spring afternoon, Tim took Helen to the park. Carrying her in his arms, a practice of which Nanny Truman heartily disapproved, and in any case taking the baby out for airings was *her* job, Tim walked off down the road and disappeared. Dora went into the drawing room and took the first folder from the top of the pile.

It was good stuff, she decided. A novel, obviously semi-autobiographical, it was nevertheless completely without introspection or self-pity. In fact, it was almost too cynical and brittle.

But it was *funny*. Tim had captured a mutual acquaintance with dreadful precision, which was only just short of caricature. Dora, reading her husband's description of this unfortunate woman, giggled until the tears came into her eyes.

She decided that she must make a copy of the first two or three chapters and send them to a publisher. Scribbling furiously, she transcribed page after page, hastily stuffing all the papers back into their folder as she heard Tim and his daughter coming in through the door. 'You've been *hours*, dear,' she said glibly, as she took Helen in her arms.

'I know.' Tim, his colour better than Dora had seen it for months, took off his coat. 'We went over to the college gardens to look at the deer. Any chance of some tea?'

Dora took advantage of her husbad's subsequent afternoon absences, and a week later she sent some of Tim's work off to Caroline Harley with instructions to lay it before her employer without delay.

Caroline, by now only too well aware that most ex-army officers could not write to save their lives, vetted the work, but then, as delighted with it as Dora had been, she showed it to Mr Gregson. Only that morning he had decided that if he had to read another set of military reminiscences he would go quietly berserk, so he took the envelope from his secretary with a jaundiced scowl. 'What have we here?' he demanded unenthusiastically. 'Yet more poetry?'

'No.' Caroline handed him a cup of coffee. 'A novel. The first three chapters.'

'The usual subject?'

'Oh, no. It's funny. Read it while you have your coffee.'

So Mr Gregson, who had a high opinion of his secretary's judgement, did so.

'Splendid stuff.' Mr Gregson grinned at his assistant. 'Where d'you find this fellow, Caroline?'

'He's a relation, sort of.' Caroline smiled. 'You liked it?'

'It's just what we need.' Mr Gregson grinned again. 'We'll have him in and make him an offer.' Then the publisher looked at the great pile of unsolicited manuscripts lying on the left-hand side of his desk. 'Have a quick glance through that lot, will you?' he asked.

* * *

Instead of being pleased with Dora and complimenting her upon her initiative, Tim was furious with his wife.

'You did *what*? He glared at the letter Dora held out to him; he read it through, then scowled at her. 'You're an interfering, spying, high-handed meddler,' he said angrily.

'Dora, how dare you behave like that?'

'I'm sorry.' Dora, her euphoria abruptly replaced by sheepishness, got up and laid her hand on her husband's shoulder. 'You will finish it soon though, won't you dear?' she asked meekly. 'Mr Gregson is so anxious to see it.'

'I'll finish it in my own good time — if I finish it at all.' He glowered at her over the newspaper.

'I'm sorry I interfered.' Dora rubbed Tim's shoulders in a way in which she knew he found particularly relaxing. 'But I thought you'd never send it off yourself. I was afraid you'd throw it away.'

'So you decided to do what *you* thought was appropriate. You'll be telling me to eat up my greens next, and forbidding me to go out after dark.' He pushed her hand away. 'Don't maul me like that, it's very irritating.'

'I'm sorry, Tim.'

'Oh, all right.'

'Will you get on with the book?'

'I might.'

'Oh, Tim — '

'I expect I shall. But Dora — '

'Yes?'

'If you *ever* interfere like that again I shall be very cross with you, and — '

'You don't know how to be cross.' Bravado coming to her rescue now, Dora grinned. 'You're the most good-tempered man I've ever met.'

'Am I?' He did not smile back. 'You've never seen me lose my temper,' he muttered, his eyes narrowed. 'But, very occasionally, I do. So be warned!'

'I don't believe your rages would be anything like as terrifying as my father's were.' Dora gave her husband a defiant stare. 'You're nothing like as frightening as Papa.'

He looked back at her then and said nothing further. But there was a steeliness in his grey eyes which made them look as cold as the sea. Dora remembered that, gentle as he always was with her, Tim was after all a professional soldier, a man trained to murder. 'We finished them off,' he'd said of those two wounded Germans at Harry Nolan's side. She shuddered.

But then, suddenly, he smiled at her. He got up from his chair and fetched his notebooks from the sideboard. 'I'd better get on with my work, hadn't I?' he asked equably. 'I can't afford to upset this Gregson fellow now.'

※ ※ ※

Dora felt the first faint pains of incipient labour that fine May evening. At four o'clock the following morning the baby was born, as easily and safely as Helen had been.

'It's a boy, Mrs Atherton. A lovely little boy, quite perfect.' The midwife wiped Dora's face and motioned to her assistant to clean the mother's lower limbs. 'What a lot of water you were carrying,' she added. 'He must have been fairly swimming in it, bless his little heart.'

'Can I see him?' asked Dora. 'Can I hold him, now?'

'Of course you can.' The midwife helped her patient to sit up. 'Just one moment now — let's make you comfortable. Here you are.' She handed Dora a shawled bundle.

The baby was very pale. Whereas Helen had been scarlet in the face, this child was almost ashen. And, unaccustomed to the light, he was frowning; he kept his eyes tightly closed. Dora shielded his face from the lamp and spoke to him. 'Darling?' she asked gently. 'My dear little boy, won't you look at me?'

At the sound of her voice, the child stirred and opened his eyes. Two very *dark* eyes — their irises were almost black — gazed suspiciously into hers. He screwed up his face again; again the frown became apparent, and a furrow appeared between his already well-marked dark eyebrows. His little mouth puckered, but he did not cry. Dora now saw that he was the image of her father. Her brother must have looked just the same when he was a few minutes old.

'Oh, Stephen! Dear little Stephen!' She hugged him close to her and he frowned all the more, but he let her rock him and murmur silly female endearments.

Dora looked up at the midwife. 'Will you go and fetch my husband?' she asked. 'He's still downstairs, I think.'

But Tim had heard the cries of delight from above, and had roused himself from an uneasy sleep on the drawing room sofa. He picked up the book which was lying crushed beneath him and went up to see his wife.

'Come and meet Stephen,' invited Dora. But Tim stood hesitantly in the doorway. He was, it seemed, a little overawed by the paraphernalia, the smells and the very feminine exclusiveness of birth.

'Come in, Mr Atherton.' The midwife, seeing he was embarrassed, smiled encouragingly and ushered him into the room, where he sat down on his wife's bed.

'Look at your son.' Dora gave the baby to his father and smiled at them both. The baby stared critically at Tim, then he glanced again at Dora. He gave a great yawn and, apparently satisfied that both his parents were more or less acceptable, he fell asleep in his father's arms.